Mann in the Crossfire

A Jarvis Mann Detective Novel

By
R Weir

Copyediting by:
YM Zachery and JB Joseph Editing Services

Cover Design by:
Happi Anarky
www.happianarky.com

Thanks to Kim
for helping me keep the dream alive
of being a full-time author

Thanks to all of my beta readers,
who helped make
Mann in the Crossfire
the best it could be.

Chapter 1

I was sitting in a bar in Centennial, eating salty pretzels from a bowl while nursing a Sprite that did little to enhance my tough PI image, though I tried to flex my biceps from time to time to balance the effect. This establishment aspired to be like another well-known chain. The all-female wait staff wore tight yellow t-shirts that showed lots of cleavage, and snug black shorts that left little to the imagination. There wasn't a smaller-than-a-D-cup-filled shirt in sight, much to the glee of the randy male clientele.

The one male working there was behind the bar. His chest could almost fill a D cup himself. He was large, with muscles, upon muscles, mid-thirties Fabio face with shorter brown hair and sideburns, his presence there to fill alcohol orders, but to make sure the male customers didn't go too far. From what I'd seen, too far must have been quite far, as there were lots of hands on waists and butts, that lingered, along with the testosterone stench.

Like a trained detective, I noticed all, observing the back and forth, including those coming and going. I'd been watching for an hour now, day two of my surveillance. Alert to a face I was searching for, while keeping an eye on the bevy of televisions, the NBA prominent on all the screens. The Nuggets were in the midst of another mediocre season, but at least a few screens had a couple of the better teams playing incredible basketball. I admired the ink extensive tattoos the players had, in many cases covering all skin showing, and wondered if I should get one as well. A design with knives and pistols on my bicep to enhance my tough guy image when flexing was required.

I felt a presence next to me as a large man sat on the barstool to my left. He was a couple of inches taller than me though his cowboy boots added another inch or so. His cowboy hat, black jeans and white shirt with gold western stitching filled out his look.

He shook the March snow off his hat and long brown leather coat, before removing and placing them on the open stool next to him. If he'd been wearing spurs, silver star and a six shooter on his hip, I'd have said, 'Howdy Sheriff.' But I left that remark for another time.

"Hello Brandon," I stated with my glass in hand.

"Jarvis," replied Brandon Sparks.

Turning around, I saw two other large men in leather jackets that had followed him in, taking up a table behind us. Both were scanning the room, alert for danger. Bodyguards for the important man, it would seem.

"You're a hard man to track down these days," commented Brandon.

"Had to change my phone number," I explained, my eyes fixed on the coming and goings. "Issues with unfriendly foes and too many calls trying to sell me products I don't need."

"Not your usual hangout."

"Boone's sold out. Now a dinner club. Not the type of place for me to unwind. I've been searching for a new joint to frequent and believe me, this isn't it. Tonight I'm working. How did you find me?"

"Guess."

"Had someone watching me, I would assume."

Brandon nodded while ordering a drink. His usual was Jack Daniels, and he didn't stray from his routine. We had worked a time or two together, where he provided resources that had helped me. I was indebted to him to the point I'd probably have to sell my soul to even things up. Being that his business was construction, his Sparks Builders company had a hand in erecting many of the finest buildings along the Front Range. His side business was criminal activity, though never proven by me or the authorities. The good he'd done likely outweighed the bad. Consequently, there was a friendly rapport between us.

"I probably should have called Sue and given her my new number," I said. Sue was his assistant and right-hand woman who handled much of the day to day business at Sparks. "I've been a little busy. Had to get new business cards made. Apparently using white-out and writing the new number on existing cards isn't professional, at least according to Miss Manners." I continued to scan the entrance, the place busy, confident he'd be arriving shortly.

As if on cue, through the front door walked in the man whose chiseled face I'd studied and couldn't miss. He went straight to a booth where a beautiful thirty-something blonde woman was sitting, a good ten years younger than he was, her grand entrance happening twenty minutes earlier. She stood up to greet him, his arms quickly wrapped around her, a long passionate kiss and groping of her butt, which played out for nearly a minute, before they sat down.

I swallowed down more pretzels with another swig of Sprite, before standing up; sodium and sugar giving me an edge.

"Excuse me for a minute, Brandon," I said, while grabbing the large envelope on the bar.

Slowly walking over, I came up to the booth and spoke the man's name. He was a local celebrity, owner of three car chains, and star of his commercials, claiming he can sell a car to anyone no matter how bad their credit. He was a cocky SOB from what I'd learned about him via surveillance, and a cheating husband. As far as I was concerned, he was a pompous idiot, but I smiled to put him at ease.

"No autographs," he said dismissively. "I'm here with my lady, having a private dinner."

I tried my best not to laugh, while handing him the envelope after confirming who he was. "You've been served. Have a nice evening."

He wasn't the least bit happy, but I didn't care. I strolled back to my seat.

"Isn't that Perry Hester?" asked Brandon with a hint of amusement.

"Yes, it is. Business owner, TV star and all-around ass. Been cheating on his wife." I tutted.

"I thought you weren't doing that type of work anymore."

"Need to pay the bills, no matter how much I dislike it. But she hired my lawyer, Barry, who hired me. Money was good and didn't require anyone shooting at me—so far."

"You may have spoken too soon, as he is coming over here."

Perry lumbered across the floor in his two-hundred-dollar black leather shoes, trying to look tough as he stood behind me. He had the envelope in his hand and slapped me on the back with it a couple of times, to show me he was in control. I turned around on the barstool to face him, sipping the soda, my eyes soaking him in. He was about an inch taller, at 6'1" and probably had twenty pounds on me, though they weren't solid like mine. Trying to convey strength, he did his best to hold in his stomach, but only a girdle could control it. His red hair matched his red face, anger filling his eyes. The man was a shyster, a poor pitch-man and all-around bad actor. There was nothing about him which would intimidate me.

"I'm not accepting this," he declared, dropping the envelope in my lap. "Take it back to that frigid bitch and tell her she's not getting one dime if she wants to divorce me."

I grinned as I put down my glass, grabbed the envelope and placed it back on his chest.

"Perry, we're in a room full of people, witnesses to what a jerk you are. You're here with your girlfriend, ready to run off to a hotel for the night, while your wife is at home raising your two kids, whose names I doubt you remember." I stood up and gave him my tough guy glare. "If it had been a different night, then it might be the redhead who works for you providing you blowjobs when blondie isn't available to quell your needs. It would be best you walk away and lick your wounds, because your wife is going to own one, if not *all* of your car dealerships when her lawyer, Barry, is through with you with the evidence we've acquired."

Perry's face was getting redder. "Who are you?"

"Jarvis Mann, private detective. And the man who's seen what a slime ball you are and has it properly documented for the courts to witness. You might as well save money and get a cheap lawyer, because no one is going to advise you to do anything but settle."

Perry took the envelope and tried to give it back to me. When I refused, he took a swing with his left hand. I saw it coming and ducked it easily, slipping and spinning to the side of him in a blur. He twisted to find me, swinging wildly again, this time with his right hand. Putting up my left arm, I easily blocked it, locking my arm around his, twisting my body, flinging him into the bar railing, causing him to gasp in pain. Grabbing at his ribs, one or two bruised from the force of the impact, he still had fight left in him, though not much.

I stood waiting, not attacking, ready to counter, when he lunged his whole body forward trying to use his full weight against me. I took two steps to the side as he passed me, and drove one punch into his sore ribs, not with full force, but enough to knock the last wind out of him. He dropped to his knees and tried to catch his breath.

"You're outmatched, Perry," I remarked, my arms down as I knew he was finished. "Go back to your table and call it a night."

"I'm going to sue you," he spat once he got his oxygen back. "You assaulted me."

"You attacked first. I just defended myself. I'd say all the witnesses here would vouch for that." Confirmation came from the faces I saw while scanning the scene, many moving to the side to avoid getting caught in the action.

"Sit down, Sir, before I call the cops," announced the bartender to Perry. "This gentleman speaks the truth. You attacked first and you're lucky. From what I saw he took it easy on you. He could have torn you a new one without blinking."

Perry looked around and heard similar reactions from everyone in the room. Beaten, he got up, not looking at me anymore, and took the envelope after I handed it to him again. Without saying another word, he slowly and painfully walked back to his girlfriend, who was waiting to console him.

Relishing in the hope that I had ruined his evening, I returned to my seat, thanking the bartender, who topped off my Sprite and pulled out the mixed nuts he'd stashed away under the counter as an upgrade to the pretzels. A full bowl of cashews would have been better, but I made due and munched down on the few I could find.

"I'd not seen you in action before," observed Brandon. "Not too bad."

"He was way out of his league. I'd have loved to punch him a couple more times, but he wasn't worth the bruised knuckles."

Brandon smirked, "Why don't we go somewhere…more *upscale*? A place where the waitresses aren't shoving their breasts in our faces. I know a classy joint down the street. A place quieter where we can talk."

"What about?" I asked.

He paused to finish his drink, tossing down his credit card, telling the bartender he would cover both our tabs.

"It's Rocky and it's not good news, I'm afraid," he stated with a look of concern in his eyes.

As Brandon signed the receipt, I wondered what had happened to Rocky, fearing the worst.

Chapter 2

The ambiance of the restaurant Brandon suggested was worlds away from where we had been. Nice white tablecloths, napkins made of fabric instead of paper, fancy silverware made of actual silver and not plastic, and a soft atmosphere with music playing in the background that wasn't bursting an eardrum. The wait staff wore tasteful long-sleeved white shirts, and black pants; the only skin showing being the hands and from the neck up. There wasn't a single TV in sight, which in this case was fine, as we needed to talk.

When the menus came, I about gasped at the prices. But Brandon offered to pay, meaning cost wasn't an issue. The filet mignon was high on my choices, a major upgrade from the pretzels and cashews currently filling my stomach.

"Now we can think and talk without distraction," said Brandon.

"This is a definite upgrade. Don't your men get to join us?"

"They wait in the car. At the other place I couldn't vouch for the security. Here there will be no issues."

"Don't think I've seen you with this much protection before. Is everything OK?"

The waitress came by and took our drink orders. I wanted tea, while Brandon ordered his JD, along with a shrimp appetizer.

"It's a dangerous world out there," noted Brandon, after she stepped away. "I have enemies always looking to take a shot at me. Best to play it safe."

"Anyone in particular?" I asked, continuing to scan the menu. Too many delicious choices and not enough room in my stomach.

"Nothing to concern yourself with."

I shrugged my shoulders, my thoughts turning to a man I'd worked with professionally a couple of times and who I'd established a rapport with. When I'd last seen him, he was off on his quest to the west coast for revenge.

"You mentioned bad news about Rocky," I queried, expecting the worst.

Our drinks arrived. It was two for one, doubling Brandon's pleasure. Knowing his tolerance, two wouldn't even raise his heart rate. I often wondered if he'd been breastfed Jack Daniels, as it was the only liquid refreshment I'd seen him consume.

"The news I have, is Rocky is dead," he said bluntly, after drinking down half of one glass. "Killed in Southern California, near San Diego. Appears to have died in a fire on a boat he was living on. Possibly arson from the report via the fire department."

The words confirmed what I had feared.

"Ironic," I replied simply.

"It is. It would appear you know of his history."

I swallowed down my tea, finding the taste strong, adding water to find the proper flavor.

"Not until last year, after we took down Vicente Duarte. I researched and ran across an article about Rocky's family being killed. It mentioned his death, his name then Garrett Owens, shortly after from the injuries. Now we know that wasn't the case."

The shrimp arrived. They were large, cold, hanging from the edge of a bowl, with lots of dipping sauce, and flown in overnight, meaning they were fresh. After a bite you could tell the hype was true, the savory taste matching the claim. At Brandon's request, the waitress left and would get the rest of our order later.

"Lost his wife and young son," declared Brandon, as he swirled his drink glass, the ice making an audible tinging sound. "Horrible thing to happen. He was badly hurt and contacted me, as we had worked together a couple times in the past. He felt he could trust me, and no one knew of our connection. With a little convincing, I helped him fake his death, had him flown to a private location and set up his new life, once he healed up. I know he hired you to help find Vicente. Once he knew where the contract had originated he went back to California to learn more. I'd not heard anything from him until I got word of his death. I'd told him to take it slowly, but he was determined."

I put the menu down, having decided on a choice. "I can understand his anger and wanting revenge."

"As did I. But in the heat of the moment, one can make deadly mistakes, as it appears he did."

I drank more tea, still finding it too strong, adding more water until I was satisfied. I wasn't sure what emotions I was feeling about the news. It could have been a sense of denial, finding it hard to believe a man that strong, could be killed.

"Could it be a ruse again?" I wondered.

"Possibly. Though not with my assistance this time. There was a body and a positive ID. I'm under the assumption it was really him. That is why I'm here. I want you to go to California and investigate. See if you can come up with anything on who is involved."

"I know from what Vicente told him, it was someone he used to work for. Or at least someone in his organization."

Brandon enjoyed a long drink of his JD, staring at the glass lovingly.

"Maximillian Conway," he responded, his eyes back on me.

"Yes, that was the name. Rocky said he worked for him. Didn't tell me what he did exactly but did confirm it wasn't of a completely legal nature."

"Rocky was, and I'm sure it's no surprise to you, an enforcer for Max, as well as providing security."

I nodded. "He mentioned real estate, and that Max was involved in other illegal activities. Though no specifics."

"That is why I'm bringing you in to find out."

The shrimp was gone, and the waitress returned to take our dinner orders. I had the filet mignon well done, with garlic mashed potatoes. Brandon had the same, though wanting his medium rare and a side of steamed broccoli. And two more drinks when the beef arrived, as the first was empty, number two in his hand. The nectar of the gods it would seem.

"What do you know?" I asked.

"Not too much. Max and I weren't in competition. I didn't care about what he did or how he did it. I know Rocky provided protection for him, though these days that isn't shocking. Wealthy people are always a target."

"You mentioned he came to you for help after the first bombing. How did you know each other?"

"He did freelance work for me. I'll spare you the details."

Not surprising he wouldn't tell me, as details were often lacking from him. But I could probably take a wild guess.

"Was this while he was working for Max?"

"No, after. He'd left on good terms. Now that he had a family he was trying to find a better way. The work I had him do was going to be his last…how should I put it…'over the line' work. He was trying to have a quieter, simple life. Raise his child and give his wife a different environment to live in."

My tea glass was empty, and the waitress quickly came, filling it half full per my request. This time I added the right amount of water, the first sip confirming it.

"Max just let him walk away?"

"Not completely. There were conditions, though I never knew what they were. But I understood all was square between the two of them. No bad blood or hard feelings. Which is why I'm not certain Max *is* behind this."

"Couldn't the original car bombing have been done by one of those enemies looking to settle a score?"

Brandon shrugged. "Possibly. Again, your job to find that out."

"Vicente said it could have been someone inside that made it happen. He seemed to not know for certain. I will need to find out the other players in Max's organization."

Our meals arrived on a large brown platter, balanced on one hand by the waitress, before she distributed the plates in front of us. They had us cut our steaks and taste them to make sure they were cooked properly. Mine was perfect, a step up from my usual drive-thru, paper bag meal, as was Brandon's. Though with enough JD in you–Brandon now working on his third glass–even the worst meal would satisfy the palate.

We were quiet while eating, though my mind was thinking over my new case. There were a lot of variables I'd have to consider. Sticking my nose into the matter could mean a similar end to me, as with Rocky. But I did owe him, if not a debt, as a courtesy to get answers and closure for the death of his loved ones.

"I will need a couple of days to wrap up this current case," I said, now stuffed with excellent food. "Then make arrangements to fly out there. Any resources at my disposal?"

"Sorry to say, I have little in the way of contacts out there. It would appear you're on your own."

"Fair enough. Not the first time. I guess this is a freebie for past assistance you've provided me."

"Solve this and our ledger is clean. Maybe even a bonus if you do right by Rocky."

"Costly flying out there—hotel, rental car and food."

"I will cover your expenses. Try not to stay at a five-hundred dollar a night hotel."

“I will stay anywhere cheap that is bed bug free. And I will resist calling room service.”

Brandon smiled, while downing the last of his whiskey. Pulling out his phone, he typed out a text, and tucked it back into his jacket pocket. The check arrived, and he put down plastic without even looking at the total. Nice to be rich and not care about the tab. His security detail was waiting for us at the door when we walked out, the snow falling a bit heavier.

“Are you ever going to tell me what is going on?” I pronounced, as we walked to the parking lot flanked by the two men.

“For now, no,” he replied. “You have enough to worry about in California and with mister TV celebrity. Call if you need anything. You have my number.”

Brandon drove away, with me sensing something dangerous had him spooked. But he was a powerful man, who was right, as I had enough to worry about.

Chapter 3

Sitting in Barry Anders' waiting area, passing the time, I tried not to objectify his personal assistant for I was evolving, albeit slowly. It was clear that looks were the main reason he hired the woman, her stunning beauty, and normally revealing attire, eclipsing her fumbling business expertise. Though she did have skills, according to Barry, even if he'd never spelled them out. Today she was dressed more conservatively in black jeans and a pink blouse. The jeans were a size too small, which showed when she walked in her tall pink heels. They made me cringe, wondering how women could torture their feet in them.

She answered the phone and typed on her computer with her long red nails. I wasn't sure how and with what speed and accuracy she managed with those talons. When I arrived, she smiled and said hello, offering me a bottled water, for she knew my preference, yet we had never carried on a lengthy conversation, short of weather small talk. She mentioned Barry was with a client and would be out shortly. Knowing him, and the chatterbox he was, I knew this could mean from anywhere from fifteen to sixty minutes before he would emerge. I found a chair, and a magazine from this year and sat back, relaxing, resisting the urge to covet and flirt with the assistant. Evolving was difficult, requiring effort, but I'd be a better man for it.

I had known Barry for several years now. He was a top-notch lawyer, a bulldog in the courtroom, and a first-rate ladies' man. He could be a major pain in my ass, but he felt the same about me, and we often verbally spared, which I enjoyed. Both of us threw a lot of work each other's way, though the clients weren't always the best, and payment at times would be late or not at all. It was a strong working relationship, with this latest job guaranteeing tip-top money. A rich, cheating husband always led to a substantial payday.

It did take about thirty minutes before Barry came out with his client, who was an Asian female, dressed in a gray pants suit and flat heels. He made his goodbyes and then told his assistant a few things before waving for me to follow him. He was dressed in black jeans today and a red satin shirt. He was a good-looking man in his middle forties, an inch taller and slimmer than me. His auburn hair was neatly cut and combed down the middle, his skin a nice deep tan, even though it was late winter.

When we reached his office, his expensive oak desk was covered with several folders, a notebook computer and large metal no-spill container, likely full of coffee. He sat in his high-back tan leather chair and rocked back after grabbing one of the folders. I grabbed the client chair, sitting down while finding the seat warm from the rear end of his previous client.

"Got a call from Marilynn Hester today," stated Barry. "Said her cheating, no good husband stopped by wanting in the house."

"What did she tell him?" I asked.

"To 'go fuck himself,' I believe she eloquently put it. He was agitated when security wouldn't let him in."

"Advantage of living in a gated, secured housing complex. Why we told her to have them change out the security codes and her locks at home. Is he going to be trouble?"

"From what you've told me, yes that is a possibility." Barry nodded while flipping through pages in the folder. "I'm sure he thinks he can do whatever he wants. I'm assuming you served him last night?"

"I did. He came at me, acting tough and took a swing. I had to set him straight." I did a shadow jab to demonstrate.

He grimaced. "Oh joy. Did he threaten to sue you?"

"He did. But lots of witnesses saw him being the aggressor and me giving him a chance to walk away. I got several names, including the bartender." I pulled a couple of business cards out of my pocket and tossed them to Barry. "Those are the witnesses. On the back of one of the cards is the name and number for the bartender. Perry doesn't have a leg to stand on if he tries to come after me."

Barry took the cards and stapled them to a blank piece of paper, made a couple of notes and added it to the file.

"Good job. You need to go out to Marilynn's house and make sure all is secure, in case he gets past the guards or is able to sweet talk his way in."

"I can do that today, if she is home." I opened the bottled water and took a drink.

"She'll be there for she doesn't work. You have her number.

Call first and arrange a time."

"I have another job lined up and I need to leave town. Is that going to be an issue?"

Barry tossed the folder onto the stack on his desk. "Shouldn't be. Where are you headed?"

"San Diego. Doing work for Brandon Sparks."

Barry whistled. "Do I need to keep a standing plane reservation to come bail you out? Seems like when dealing with Mister Sparks, trouble for you isn't too far off."

"Probably a good idea. I will do my best to stay out of trouble and not call you in the middle of the night."

"I've known you too long," noted Barry with a snicker. "Trouble *is* your middle name. Even if you're skilled at worming your way out, the day will come when your lucky streak will end."

"Luck, skill—I take what I can get. Can I submit my bill after I check out her house and get paid? I need money to help cover my trip to California."

Barry grabbed the container and took a drink, frowning at the taste, before sitting it down.

"Working for free?"

"Brandon is covering my expenses is all. I owe him for past assistance he has provided. Should clear the ledger. Even mentioned a bonus, if I live through it." I laughed, even though I knew it wasn't out of the realm of possibility.

"I wouldn't be sure about clearing the ledger. Guys like him will use you up and spit you out. Might be a hole you can't dig out of."

Barry's words were close to the truth. I wondered if I could ever repay Brandon enough to be free and clear. But I knew I couldn't worry about it, for without his help I'd likely not be breathing. It was my life long goal not to be maggot food.

"Submit your time and expenses," stated Barry. "We'll do the direct deposit to your account. Hopefully you'll get to spend it before your untimely demise."

"Appreciate the positive vibes. I will be sure to haunt you from the great beyond."

"Don't expect me to argue your case about getting into Heaven. That is one not even I can win."

Laughing, I said my goodbyes, walking out the front without

leering, and got in my car. Once I confirmed Marilynn Hester was home, I headed south to Parker, where she lived, dealing with the horrible traffic that was never ending. The March weather was fair today, the streets wet from the snow the day before, although minor from the norm, since this was typically our heaviest snow month.

When I arrived at the gated community security entrance, I gave the security my ID. After confirming with him that Perry Hester wasn't to be let in under any circumstances, he opened the gate and I headed up a winding hill, past several million-dollar homes until I found the correct one.

The massive mansion sat up on a crest, a sprawling ranch on a multi-acre lot. The grass was nicely trimmed, though brown from the harsh winter. Several bare maple trees lined the slate-paved driveway, leading me to a guest parking area to the side of the three-car garage. I had been in the house a couple of times, the size impressive and overwhelming. I needed to make sure security was working properly with an alarm system covering all doors and windows.

As I walked up the red slate steps to the front door, I rang the bell, the musical chimes loud and festive. A Hispanic woman answered the door, her job to keep the house in order. She smiled and waved me in, knowing who I was and offering to take my suede leather jacket. She led me into the main living area, where I sat on one of two matching silver crushed velvet chairs, that went with two sofas filling out the room. The set was complete with stylish coffee table, end tables and lamps, adding additional soft light to the area. Heating had to be challenging in winter with the vaulted ceilings, and skylight windows, though a gas fireplace helped to provide additional warmth.

From another room I heard the click of heels on the marble flooring and I stood as Marilynn strolled in looking out of breath, holding a full wine glass. She waved for me to sit, before taking the sofa across from me.

"What a day," she declared. "Too much to do, and not enough time to do it in."

"The challenge of being mother."

"Do you have children, Mister Mann?"

"No. My life isn't conducive to having children. And please, call me Jarvis."

"They can be a gift and a curse. My youngest boy is ten and my daughter twelve. Keeping on top of them, getting them to do their homework, keep their rooms cleaned and not letting them watch TV or play games on their phones or tablet all night long. Driving them to their dance recitals, soccer and baseball practices. Now this mess with their father. It all is driving me to drink."

With her words she took a long swallow of the burgundy colored wine, swirling the rest of it while sitting back into the corner of the sofa. She was dressed in white slacks, blue blouse and tall black heels that went with her tall, slender body. Her straight blonde hair ran past her shoulders, her skin dark as if she did regular tanning salon visits. Modest makeup, eyeliner, shadow and lipstick masked her age, which I knew to be forty. There was a slight glimmer in her hazel eyes, suggesting that this wasn't her first glass of wine today. Never good to have a mother driving her children around with a half a bottle of vino in her system.

"Must be hard on the kids," I observed, making conversation.

"Oh my. I try not to tell them too much. I mean their dad is a dick, but I resist saying it straight out."

"What do you tell them?"

"That he has moved out and we won't be together anymore. Not really a surprise, as I'm his second wife. I should have known he was jerk since we screwed around behind the back of his first wife before he left her."

It was a story I'd heard before about failed marriages and relationships. The unfaithful gene seems to be widespread. I had experienced it myself. Resisting temptation when its ugly head popped up had been challenging for me. I wanted to pass judgement but knew I couldn't.

"Damn good thing he didn't have kids with his first wife," uttered Marilynn, a little more wine in her. "Who knows what will happen with his latest whore. Probably knock her up and there will be another unloved child in the world." She finished off her wine and stood up. "Where are my manners. Would you like a drink? I can have Carlotta get you a glass."

"No thank you," I said while standing. "I need to get to work and test all of your windows with the alarm company to make sure they're all working properly."

"Do what you need to do. You have free rein of the house. I'll be in the kitchen."

Her heels clicked on the flooring, her walk steady despite the drinking. It looked like she had lots of practice consuming alcohol. Drowning one's pain wasn't a good thing, but I wasn't here to help her with her personal problems, so I began to work.

I had the security code and called the alarm company to do testing. I got to all the doors and tested several windows, all working properly. Then I made sure all the other windows were wired correctly and checked for any other weak points. Once I'd finished, I flagged down the maid to question her.

"Did Marilynn get all the locks changed?" I asked.

"Yes sir, she did," replied Carlotta. "I reminded her several times, as you suggested, and she finally called and got it done."

"Does she do any hide-a-keys outside?"

"I don't believe so."

"Good. Those are never safe and are easy to find." I pointed towards the front and back of the house. "And are you locking doors after anyone comes in from the outside?"

"I do my best to try to watch the kids," she said while shaking her head. "They're children and often forget, leaving me to check."

"When they leave or at any of their events outside of school, an adult should always be with them. I don't think their father will grab them, but it does happen."

"Yes sir. Mrs. Hester or one of her parents are driving them back and forth or staying with them at all times."

"Good. How is she holding up?"

She paused, not sure if she should say anything.

"It's ok Carlotta. You won't get in trouble."

"She is drinking a lot," replied Carlotta, concern filling her face. "I worry about her driving. She is a little…how should I put it…scattered right now."

"Be sure to watch her. If it's not safe for her to drive, call her parents. And you have Barry's number if he needs to arrange a driver for them. He can call for a car service or a cab. I will be leaving town in a few days, or I'd be available too. Don't let her make things worse by driving her kids drunk."

She nodded. "I won't."

Taking one more walk through, searching for any red flags, I determined all appeared secure in the house.

With my work completed, I stopped to say goodbye to Marilynn. She was in the kitchen, the empty wine bottle sitting on the center island, her glass empty, her head resting on the granite top. I grabbed both, putting the bottle in the recycle bin and the glass in the dishwasher.

"I think you've had enough," I said bluntly. "You need to be strong for your kids. Having a dick for a dad is bad enough, they don't need a drunk mother as well."

She raised her head, staring at me. I'm not sure she understood what I said, but she needed to sleep it off. I called for Carlotta and the two of us helped her to the bedroom, lying her down with her clothes on, then draping a blanket over her as she quickly dosed off. As I left, I made sure Carlotta locked the door behind me, and I drove away, worried the worst was yet to come for this family.

Chapter 4

Ever since the Butcher case last year, my life had been in flux. Sleep had been difficult with thoughts of Simon Lions and Junior invading my dreams. I had told myself I wasn't going to let those crazy bastards get to me, but they did. The father may have been dead and buried, but our exchanges had gnawed at me for months now. The son remained alive, awaiting trial, my testimony a key aspect. Yet even though he was locked away, I could feel his cold, calculating and brutal eyes staring at me from afar. I did my best to ward off those lingering feelings, but I'd not had a lot of success.

After what happened to Melissa at the hands of The Butcher, the damage he did both mentally and physically, I kept close tabs on her, making sure she was doing alright. She had tough days, but with the right help from a therapist, and her family and friends, she'd worked her way through it. She had gone back to work after three months of rehab, and was doing well, enjoying her new life as a full-fledged lawyer.

We tried to have lunch together once a week or so. All was good between us, and we were friends again—I'd even call us close friends. This put something of a strain on my relationship with April. She understood the bond we had created but admitted feeling left out. Not out of jealousy, more that she and I hadn't developed that kind of closeness, an emotion I couldn't argue about and needed to work on. We had talked it through on several occasions, with me expressing my feelings clearly. I did not want to lose her in my life, but I'd always be there for Melissa, no matter what. I did all I could to convince April, but those doubts were affecting us and the amount of time we were spending together.

After sleeping alone that night, I began looking over my options for flights, hotels and car rental. As with everything in California, it was expensive, even on the low end. Finding a reasonable hotel ran close to two hundred per night, with car rentals to match. It was a good thing Brandon was covering expenses, for if this investigation took as long as I expected, it would be a high-cost trip that would put my credit limit to a test.

With everything arranged, I submitted my expenses to Barry,

then headed downtown for a scheduled lunch with Melissa. We would be eating today at Maggiano's Little Italy, the first place we'd ever had a meal together. Much like that first time, I felt excitement and trepidation with seeing her, my attempts to keep the butterflies at bay challenging. The plan was to meet there, and she would walk on over from her work. With the weather being cold, and my not wanting to deal with LoDo parking, I rode the Denver light rail, getting off within a couple of blocks of the restaurant, then walking on over. It was chilly, in the mid-forties with a few spots of snow remaining, but the sun was out, the hope of spring in the air.

Receiving a text, I knew she was seated when I arrived, and found her at a small two-person table by the window. As I walk up to her, she stood, dressed for work, looking as always, beautiful with her joyous smile. We hugged, and I draped my leather coat over the back of the chair, before sitting down, happy to be close to her again, though it was a closeness tampered by the past mistakes I'd made and the danger she'd experienced knowing me.

"How are you doing?" I asked, a greeting used a million times throughout the world.

"Good," she replied. "Though tired. I'm glad it's Friday. Been a long week. How are you?"

I wanted to say, all was right with the world when I saw her, but I resisted, for it wasn't true.

"Thrilled it's Friday, too."

"Are you still working that case for Barry?" Melissa asked. She knew all about it from our past conversations.

"Wrapping up my work. Might require a couple of minor things to do. But mostly done. Though I'm concerned about the mother." I explained what I had witnessed.

She frowned. "Sad that happens. Alcohol is never the answer. Though most don't come to grips with it until it's too late. Have you met her children?"

"No. She says they're twelve and ten, not the best age for two parents to split up. Though I'm not sure what age would be better."

The waitress brought us drinks, as Melissa had gone ahead and ordered me a tea with lemon, while she had a caffeine free diet soda. Placing our orders, we skipped an appetizer—Caesar Salad for her, while I ordered lasagna.

Squeezing lemon into my tea, I found it strong which appeared to be common in most Front Range restaurants I frequented. I added water to it from a carafe provided. I was a lightweight when it came to strongly brewed tea, the taste bitter to my palette.

"How are you doing since going back to work?" I queried.

"Not too bad. Tony has me working a couple of easy cases." Her eyes wouldn't meet mine as she spoke, looking down and then out the window.

"That is great to hear. It would be fun to see you cross-examining someone on the stand."

"It's never as dramatic as you see on TV. These cases may never even make it to trial." Her eyes glanced down again, as if she was hiding important information from me.

"You appear to have something you aren't sure you want to tell me."

She glanced up, surprised I had noticed.

"The detective in me," I noted gently. "I can often tell when people are holding back."

She nodded. "I should have known. You've always been good at reading people."

I shrugged. There had been plenty of times when I hadn't read people properly and it had cost me. But I remained quiet, giving her time to work through what to say.

"I have news, I'm not sure I should tell you. Not sure how you'll react."

It couldn't be good if she was this worried. Several possible scenarios flashed through my head, some minor and others the worse possible news. I didn't like where my mind was headed.

"Maybe now isn't the best time," she said, sensing my angst.

"You have to tell me now or my imagination will run wild." *Too late, it already had!*

Drinking through the straw, she downed half of her soda before talking.

"I'm moving down to Colorado Springs. I had a job offer I felt I needed to accept. It's with the law firm Pendleton Brothers, who I worked for before moving to Bristol & Bristol. It's a great opportunity and allows me to move where I will feel…safer."

"You don't feel safe here in Denver?" I asked with a frown. Though deep down I knew the answer, and it had to do me and the dangerous life I led, which had infiltrated into hers.

"After what happened last year, no I don't," she declared, the worry lining the skin on her face. "Mostly I need to get away. Live where there aren't overwhelming memories. I remain haunted about Jessie getting killed outside my place. The stain's still there as a reminder of where she gasped for air, blood everywhere as she died because of that maniac." Her voice shook.

Jessie was a friend of Melissa. She'd died at the hands of The Front Range Butcher, right before Melissa had been taken. Once he had her, he'd led me to her, darting me and then had begun to torture us, before I eventually freed myself, knocking him out. The whole event had shaken Melissa, requiring lots of help. Apparently part of her therapy was to move away from Denver.

"I see you're disappointed," remarked Melissa.

Normally I was good at hiding my emotions. But with her, that wasn't the case. She could read me as well as I could read her.

"I wouldn't say *disappointed*," I noted, pausing to find the right words. "Sad you'll be moving away. Though it's not far, it's not here in town. I've enjoyed spending time with you lately."

"I have enjoyed it, too. But I need to do this for my sanity. Too much has happened here. I want a normal life again, where death doesn't seem to lurk on every corner."

I wanted to say that she was exaggerating the danger level. But I couldn't argue about what she was feeling. She had been through a lot, mostly because of me and the life I led. *Could it be she was running away from me?* But it was the only job I knew and what I was good at. It was better she was safe than to be near me, with dangers everywhere.

"I understand. I hope we can talk from time to time. What will you be doing?"

"I will be a junior partner, working up to being a full partner if I do well. I enjoyed working there as a clerk. Good firm, though smaller, with a clientele different than Bristol & Bristol. But I'm looking forward to the move."

"How does Tony feel about you leaving?"

"Sad, but he understands. He left it open for me to return, if I decided to one day."

The waitress arrived, setting our food down. It smelled wonderful, but I wasn't as hungry as when I first came in. We sat quietly eating, the silence felt awkward, with only the background noise of the restaurant filling the void. Knowing no matter how I felt about it, she was going to do it. I wasn't a person in her life with the right to impede any decisions she made. Supporting her was the proper thing to do.

"I think you need to do what is best for you," I said, after finishing all the lasagna I could handle.

"Thank you for understanding. I know it's not easy for you. I do appreciate all your support these last few months. I talked with April last week and told her to find out how you'd react. She was right on the button with her prediction. She seems to know you well. Even when you aren't the most forthcoming man in the world."

I should have been surprised, but I wasn't. April knew me better than anyone else did, working tirelessly to get past all my fortified shields.

"I'm working on it. Not easy for me to open up and put it all on the line."

"A little advice, Jarvis," observed Melissa as she reached her hand across the table and placed it on mine. "April is a good woman. Strong and independent. No matter how hard it is for you, open up and let her in. I believe she is worth it and good for your soul."

It was hard to argue her point. I needed April in my life to counter all the bad impulses and keep me on the right track. Without making the effort, I would lose her and possibly never find another to fill her shoes, leaving a big, dark void in my life.

When the check arrived, Melissa picked it up, as a thank you for the help I'd provided. As we walked out, I turned to her and embraced her for a long time, before we separated. I hoped it wasn't the last time I saw her. I was a better person for knowing such a great lady.

Riding the light rail home, I got to my car and drove for a while, before ending up at April's apartment. I had a key, but I didn't want to let myself in. I knew she was home, for she had the morning shift and was off work by early afternoon. I pressed the doorbell and she answered, seeing my long face.

"I'm guessing Melissa told you the news," she said with sadness.

I nodded, walked in and hugged her for a long time, hoping to find the key to opening myself up to her as I'd done with Melissa.

Chapter 5

April and I spent the whole Saturday together, reconnecting, if you want to call it that. I knew I had to walk before I run. We took a long, causal stroll in the park, went to the gym to workout, did a little shopping and had a nice dinner out. It was time well spent chatting and being together, beyond the bedroom passion we shared.

From April I could sense relief that Melissa was leaving, if only further south in the state. It was far enough away that I'd have closure on our relationship. April didn't dislike Melissa, for that fact, she seemed to get along with her. They weren't best buddies but weren't rivals or enemies either. April had no fear of Melissa trying to take me back. She knew that wasn't going to come to pass. But it was my heart that held on, even if it knew it would never happen again between us. Now that she was leaving town, there was finality to our bond.

My flight to California was late in the morning Sunday. I attempted to talk April into flying out with me, but she needed to work. We discussed her taking a few days and joining me later, if she could get away. For now, I didn't know how long I'd be in The Golden State but expected it wouldn't be a short one. Because the flight was early, I headed back to my place to pack, being too busy these last few days to prepare anything. I planned on at least a week's worth of clothing, requiring me to check luggage, along with a basic carry-on.

When I pulled up into my parking spot, I saw my private detective sign had been vandalized. Spray painted over the lettering were two words; '*You're Dead.*' It did not make for a happy start to my day.

Since it was early Sunday, there wasn't anyone around. I stepped out of the car, watching for anyone lurking, my gun at my side—the weapon always near these days what with several people not caring for my freeform personality. Sighing once I knew it was safe, I felt relieved no one was waiting in my stairwell and nobody was hiding behind the corner or the dumpster. I touched the sign, the paint was dry. Though in Colorado, spray paint dries almost instantly thanks to the humidity free environment, which didn't tell me much. They didn't sign their masterpiece, leaving no clues of who might have been the graffiti genius. Since the list of suspects with a motive to kill me wasn't short, I had to hold off worrying about it and get packed.

Once I got all the essentials organized and ready, I called my landlord, Kate. It was early in the morning and her day off. She wasn't all that pleased to hear from me.

"I was sleeping," she said, irritation creeping in her tone. "What's wrong?"

"Someone spray painted my PI sign with a threat. Did you happen to notice anyone around yesterday?"

"Always people around, but no one running around with a spray can doing graffiti. What did it say?"

"You're dead."

"Short and to the point. Any suspects?"

"You know my history; the list is endless."

"What can I do to help?" she asked, while yawning.

"I'm heading for California on a case and I don't expect to be back for a while. Can you not only keep an eye on my place but get someone out to clean up the sign? I'll be sure to pay you back once I return."

"You mean *if* you return!"

"Such a positive person early in the morning." I was yanking on Kate's chain—a talent I excelled at.

"Sorry, I had a late night."

I heard stirring in the background; a male voice asking who Kate was talking to.

"Having a sleepover?" I asked innocently.

"I'm a grown woman with needs. Hell *yes* I had a sleepover. And we didn't sleep much, which is why I need to get off this call. I require a few minutes of rest before super stud next to me wants more of my good stuff."

"Slut!" I said jokingly.

"I am, at least for last night, and damn if it wasn't good. Can I hang up now? I feel a hard stirring behind me and I might have to address how to handle it."

"I could give you graphic pointers, but I suspect you're on top of things. Thanks for watching my place."

She didn't respond, but I heard a moan before the phone went dead, happy she had someone keeping her satisfied. She had been an excellent landlord and a good friend, which was most important since my friends list wasn't an extensive one.

Outside, a car pulled up and I looked out to see that it was April. I grabbed my bags and tossed them in her trunk. Once at the airport, we said our goodbyes at the passenger drop off, with a promise to call when I got settled. The long embrace and passionate kiss sealing our feelings for each other, knowing it may be many days before we were together again.

Off through the lengthy security line, and rapid trip on the crowded underground train, I waited at my gate, which changed for a reason never explained by the airline, before finally loading and beginning to taxi to the runway.

I gripped my seat handles as I always did when taking off, thrilled when achieving altitude, happy to listen to music, before coming down with equal trepidation, landing with a thump in sunny California, at San Diego International Airport.

Once I retrieved my luggage from the oval conveyor, I was off to the rental counter and away in my midsized car for the hotel. Checking in was a breeze, and I dumped my two pieces of luggage in my room. It was nice, with queen-sized bed, flat-screen LCD TV, over-priced mini-bar, small fridge and microwave. The hotel served breakfast each morning, with hot high-protein food choices, to fuel my on-the-go work.

Out the window was a beautiful view of the ocean, the crisp salt-air filling my senses when opening it. The weather was typical for this area in March; sunny, humid and in the sixties, drier air coming with spring. I had packed for the warmer weather, leaving the cold and snow behind.

I had a meeting to attend on Coronado Island, the drive not far and across the Bay Bridge. Peeking over the side while driving, I saw the blue water, its waves crashing the white sandy beaches, the view spectacular, the ocean sound relaxing to the ears. I was headed to meet a police detective familiar with the case, who I'd tracked down after several phone calls to sources I'd established in the past. He lived over on the island and it was his off day. He was going to be jogging along a walkway off the beach and wanted to meet on one of the benches. I had my Denver Bronco cap on, making me easy to spot.

It took a while to find a parking spot on Ocean Blvd, but once out of the car, I enjoyed the white sandy ocean view, strolling the pathway. Not far away was the iconic Hotel del Coronado with its peaked red roof, Victorian architecture, and expensive rooms, well out of my price range. It took a few minutes to find an open bench to sit on, and then I texted him that I was there.

There were joggers, walkers and a few riding bikes sharing the path, though the bikers were casual and not running at breakneck speed like the ones I often encountered in Denver. It was pleasing seeing the throng of people working their bodies to various degrees, enjoying the year-round pleasant weather to stay in shape. San Diego, like Denver was ranked in the top ten of healthiest cities in the US, which was easy to see why.

After about ten minutes of people watching, a man walked up and started stretching his legs, one at a time, on the back of the bench. He was in his thirties, with brown skin, good build and runner's legs showing under his gray tank top and black baggy shorts. His deep brown, short, curly hair glistened, sweat rolling off his forehead, which he wiped with the white sweatbands on his wrist. I gave him a minute to finish stretching, and to catch his breath, certain he was my contact from the description I had. He took a seat once he was done and put out his hand.

"Jarvis, I presume," he said, his shake firm and mostly dry.

"Detective Saiz," I replied.

"Please, call me Manny," he answered. "I like being on a first name basis. Makes it easier to be friendly."

"I'm all for that. Thanks for meeting with me. Quite a beautiful view here."

"Really peaceful over on the island," he noted while pointing. "Not cheap living here, but I don't live a lavish lifestyle."

There were a few people out on the beach. Mostly couples holding hands, walking barefoot, though still dressed for the cooler air. The summer bikinis and bathing suit crowds were still a month away. I had read this was rated one of the most romantic beaches in the world. Difficult not to feel love with the warm sand oozing between your toes.

"I understand you're interested in a murder that happened in town," stated Manny.

"I'm a private investigator hired to look into it," I replied. "I always like to talk with the local cops before poking around. Many get perturbed when I dig into one of their cases."

"No problems from me. The more the merrier. I have a case load now that is busting at the seams. If you want to, you can help me with *all* of them."

I smiled. "One is more than enough. Were you told which case?"

"It was mentioned, but you tell me, then we're both talking about the same thing."

"Person killed in fire on a boat a few weeks back. Might have gone under a couple of different names."

"Boat was registered to a Garrett Owens," answered Manny from memory. "There was other ID inside, but it was in ashes. Boat was torched, covered in an accelerant, leaving no other conclusion but arson. Burned it and the body until there wasn't a whole lot left."

The boat was under Rocky's real name. I wasn't sure if the police had made the link to the car bombing years before.

"The fire department couldn't put it out fast enough?" I asked.

"They didn't get to it until the fire had consumed it completely. It was sitting in a marina at the time."

"Couldn't ID the body then?"

"No. Dental records would have helped, but all the victim's teeth had been removed."

My face scrunched in pain. "Ouch! Forcibly removed?"

"M.E believes this to be the case but can't say for certain. Might have been busted out with an item heavy, like a hammer. It wouldn't have been pleasant for the victim."

Torture no doubt. The question was why.

"Any suspects or motive?" I questioned.

He shook his head. "Nothing yet. No physical evidence to work with. But one odd fact was that Garrett died in a car bomb several years earlier. Unless he can rise from the dead, if it was him that was killed a few weeks ago, then he didn't die from the bombing a few years back."

They *had* made the link to car bomb. I needed to query if they knew more.

"Interesting fact. Any theories?"

A lovely Hispanic woman jogged by, waving at Manny. The

wide grin on his face and joy in his response told me they were close friends.

"He didn't die," declared Manny bluntly, his attention back on me. "Or the body in the boat was someone else. Do you have any information that can help?"

Here is where it often got tricky for me. Do I tell him everything, give him tidbits, or tell him absolutely nothing? I decided on a middle-ground.

"I *may* have a few details. Not sure how they all fit. I know Garrett faked his death before. And I believe he was looking into the death of his wife and child, which led him back to San Diego. He would be one tough SOB to kill. Do you have a basic physical description of the burnt body?"

"Big guy. Probably 6'2" or slightly taller. Good sized mass. Though as hot as the fire was, a lot of moisture gets sucked out, causing the mass to shrink. But you could still tell he was a large male. Free safety or linebacker frame."

Though many people could fit that basic description, it did match up to Rocky, which I wasn't happy to hear. *Could it be he finally had met his match?*

"It's a match, for him. Though not conclusive. A little more would tell me for certain."

Another jogger passed by, this lady black in purple spandex from head to toe, smiling and saying hello to Manny. It would seem he was a popular man with the ladies.

"Nothing else to find. No hair, teeth and no body implants were found. DNA would be nearly impossible because of the state of the burned body. Though the case is open, all we can do is go by the registration and general description and assume it's Garrett. Do you know why he faked his death?"

"Not completely. But someone was after him and I believe he was trying to find out who."

"Any leads you'd like to share?" asked Manny.

This was where I'd leave out certain details. Experience had taught me to hold out until I knew I could trust him, which would take time.

"Nothing concrete. That is why I'm here—to dig. I'm hoping you're cool with it."

Manny laughed. "And if I wasn't, would it stop you?"

I smiled. "Probably not since I have a job to do."

"Just don't step on my toes," Manny said as he stood. "If you need me for any type of assistance or a badge to get you in the door, don't hesitate to call me. They don't call me Handy Manny for nothing."

I stood up and shook his hand. "Thanks. And don't worry, I *will* take you up on that offer. I may need a guide to find my way around the city."

"Great. Now I need to take off and catch that lovely lady who just went by and see if she is up for a meal and an evening with Handsy Manny."

I laughed as he ran off, and walked back to my car, happy for once to have a cop not be the stereotypical pain in the ass. At least for now!

Chapter 6

After yet another horrible night sleeping in a hotel room, which was normal for my first night in a strange environment, and thanks to The Butcher images continuing to roll through my thoughts, I was off and running, after stuffing myself with an average tasting breakfast, which at the very least was hot.

To kill time before a meeting with Rocky's former boss, I decided to drive around to get familiar with the city. I had only been here one other time and that was a quick stay to meet with the parents of Aaron Bailey, the computer software engineer who was murdered on the computer hacking case I broke wide open. That was only for a few hours, meaning I still needed to get the lay of the land, for it was easy to get lost in an unfamiliar city, especially the one the size of San Diego.

Much like Denver, the San Diego metro area is surrounded by several suburbs. I had been to Chula Vista, but there were numerous others, like Lemon Grove, Imperial Beach and Escondido. It was a diverse population of race and income levels, with over three million people occupying the region. With its seventy miles of coastline, San Diego County runs from the southern border of Orange County, all the way to the US-Mexican border. The hotel was near the airport in Mission Hills, which was just north of downtown San Diego, in a hilly region.

I hopped on one of the main interstates, I-5, which ran north-south along the San Diego Bay before connecting to the bypass at the southern end, to I-805, which ran north-south further in the city. Taking I-805 back north, it would split off onto I-15, which continued north. Or I could hop onto I-8 which ran east and west through the heart of the area.

I soon realized what a huge region this was. I'd have to rely on my cell phone GPS to navigate where I was going, as I could never learn the whole area in the abbreviated time I'd be here.

After traversing a large section of the city, I got back to I-5, heading north and hopped off on La Jolla Pkwy. I was on my way to the La Jolla Beach & Tennis Club to meet up with Maximillian Conway. I called his office yesterday and talked with his assistant, who seemed unmoved to provide me time for an appointment.

When I finally used Rocky's real name and told him to pass it on or I'd come down in person and make a scene, he agreed to give Max the name. It was probably an hour later that I'd received a call back giving me a time and location for today to meet with him.

Fighting through traffic was challenging, but I arrived in plenty of time. At the front desk, I gave my name and was given a visitor pass with instructions on where to go. The place was impressive inside, but even more so outside, the club situated near the ocean, a beautiful sandy beach with plenty of places to sit and enjoy the view, though I wouldn't get to experience it firsthand. Instead, I headed towards the tennis courts, where he was playing on the east side of the property.

There were twelve asphalt courts in all, with high fences around the outer edge and see-through windscreens pulled down to protect players from the breeze coming off the ocean. It had netting between the connected courts to keep balls within the proper playing zone. Most of the courts were in use, and I soon found him competing in a doubles match on one of the outer courts.

I walked over, and sat on the lush green grass, stretching my legs, watching the play. The players looked to all be in their fifties or sixties and in excellent shape, the match competitive and intense.

I recognized Max from the picture I'd found on the internet. He was the tallest man on the court, probably 6'3", slender, the muscle tone in his arms and legs any man would wish for, no matter how old. He wore a blue visor over his brown cropped hair that defied his age, with wrap-around sunglasses shielding his eyes. His tennis shorts and shirt were pure white, as if brand new. His tennis shoes squeaking as he moved around the court.

The match went on another fifteen minutes before they concluded, with his team winning. I stood up and walked towards the gate, waiting for him to come out. He excused himself from the group, saying he had business to attend to. He waved for me to follow him back towards the main building, to an area with several tables shaded by large trees. Sitting his gear on one of the chairs, he removed his sunglasses and took a seat. A waiter came over asking if we needed anything. He wanted an Old Fashioned, while I asked for ice water.

"May I see ID?" he said with a baritone voice.

I pulled out my Colorado license and showed it to him. If he was impressed, he didn't say so.

"From Colorado. Long ways from home."

"I go where the action is."

"You mentioned a name I'd not heard in several years." His eyes scanned the area to see who else was around.

"Garrett Owens. I'm here inquiring about him."

"He has been dead a few years now."

"True of his wife and child, but not him."

Max glared at me in surprise. "How do you know this?"

"I worked with him on a few cases. He was alive and breathing, though going by a different name."

The waiter brought the drinks. Max took a good swig and asked for another to be brought. It would seem my news had caught him off guard. Or he liked to consume alcohol after a tough tennis match.

He studied me, looking thoughtful. "I did not know this. You're certain he wasn't killed?"

"Absolutely. I was helping him track down the killer of his wife and child last year. The trail led back to your organization."

I decided not to implicate him directly, since Vicente didn't say it was him, only that it was someone inside his organization. Keeping control of the conversation would give me an edge.

"Are you accusing me of having him killed?" declared Max with anger in his tone, the veins in his neck rising.

"Not at all. I have no evidence that was the case. Only that it was someone inside who hired this man to kill Garrett and his family."

Max took another drink, finishing it off. The waiter brought the second drink, while taking away the empty. He grabbed hold of the glass and swirled the liquid and ice around, trying to ascertain calm.

"There was no issue between me and Garrett. He was an exemplarily man and left on good terms. I was sad when I'd heard he and his family were killed."

I wasn't certain I believed him about the good terms. In the type of business Max ran, allowing a man who knew many of your secrets had its risks, to him and to others.

"He had no issues with anyone inside your organization?" I

asked after sipping water through my straw.

He stopped to think over what to say. “There are always issues in any organization. But to have him killed? I can’t think of anyone who would have a huge disagreement leading them to murder him, his wife and cute little son.”

“The information he got was solid,” I remarked firmly, keeping the pressure on. “I was there when Vicente Duarte told him about it. Does that name mean anything to you?”

There was a hesitation in his response. But I couldn’t tell for certain if the name sounded familiar to him or not.

“I have not heard of him.” His eyes looked right at me when he said it. If he was lying, he was good.

“Could someone in your organization know him?”

“Possibly. I could ask around. If it was someone I’d want to know why.”

“Fair enough. Can you tell me what Garrett did for you?” I asked the question, but I was certain I knew the answer.

“Protection. He was the head of my security detail.”

More direct eye contact. Max wasn’t flinching any.

“His job was to protect you?”

“In a manner of speaking. Protecting the company and its assets to be more precise. He took care of ‘issues’ that needed taking care of.”

A vague answer, though not surprising.

“Care to elaborate?” I asked.

“No. That is all I will say. I believe you can figure out the rest.”

“What *is* your business, Mr. Conway?”

There was no hesitation. “Real estate. I own a great deal of property here in Southern California.”

“And this business requires the type of security a man like Garrett can provide?”

A man stopped by the table to say hello, as he and Max shook hands. After a few pleasantries, he moved on.

“It did, and still does,” Max said once he knew the man was out of earshot. “There are people…organizations…that are always looking to move in on your territory. It must be protected at any costs or you won’t last long.”

“Why do I think there is more going on here other than real estate?”

"You may believe what you want. It is never a good idea to get on my bad side." The tenor in his voice was harsh on the final sentence.

I certainly wasn't in a position to get on his bad side.

"Who handles your protection now?" I asked.

"I have a competent man handling things. No need to give you a name."

"Was he underneath Garrett before he left?"

"He was. Garrett groomed him as his replacement."

Max was nursing his second drink now, taking small sips. My water was as good as water gets. High class clubs like this always have the best refreshments.

"Will you have any issues with me looking into this?" A question I needed to ask, not that he would stop me from working the case.

"Not if you don't impede on my business. The case is several years old, and the police haven't found anything or made any arrests. I'm not certain what you'll find and why you're even looking into it. If Garrett has an issue with me and my business, he should come to me and speak. I always had nothing but the most respect for him."

"He can't—he is dead now," I stated, hoping to throw him off balance.

Max looked stunned. "I thought you said he faked his death."

"He did. But he came out here late last year to dig further after he received the information from Vicente Duarte. He was found dead in a boat. He and the boat were torched a few weeks ago. I'm here to solve that murder *and* the one of his wife and son."

He swallowed down the rest of his drink, not knowing what to say.

"Did he come to talk with you or anyone in your organization?" I asked.

"Hell no. As I told you earlier I thought he was killed several years ago. I hadn't seen him since he left."

I did my best to read his face. It seemed he was telling the truth. Though lying was probably a big part of his business and why he was successful.

"And why did he leave your company?"

"Personal reasons. He wanted a quieter life than the one he had now that he was married with a child."

"After he was declared killed, did you look into his death at all?"

"No, it was a police matter. I left it up to them to find the answers." His tone wasn't convincing. I was cracking through his rigid facade.

"It would seem a powerful man like yourself, with loads of respect for Garrett, would want to find out who killed him."

The veins in his neck were rising again. "He'd been gone for several months. I assumed his past was involved."

"Any suspicions on who might have put out the hit?"

He shook his head. "None whatsoever. And I certainly didn't think it was someone who worked for me."

"Again, I ask, do you have any issues with me digging into these crimes?"

"No!" Max replied aggressively, pausing to gather himself before continuing. "I'd want the person or persons who did this to face charges."

"Good. Not that it matters, as I'm going to do my best to get answers. If it leads back to you and your company, my nose *will* be squarely in your business."

I don't think he liked what I said, red filling his cheeks, as he stood and grabbed his tennis bag.

"I believe our meeting is over."

He started walking away, his cell phone in hand as he began sending a text. I followed him right out the front door, dropping off my visitor badge when I passed the main desk. An expensive black limo pulled up and a bulky man in a dark blue sports coat got out and opened the door. He saw me and stepped to block me, putting his hand on my chest to keep me away from Max.

All I could do was smile, before grabbing his wrist, twisting it behind his back and slamming him into the side of the car. He had a gun, which I removed and tossed into the backseat, the pressure on his arm keeping him motionless, knowing I could dislocate his elbow. Max looked at me, his eyes seething.

"Release him!" he growled angrily.

"I will, but no more touching. Understood?"

Max nodded his head, telling his man to stand down. Releasing his arm, I stepped back, noticing a few people watching.

"Mister Mann, go about your business. I think you'll find Garrett's death will not lead back to me or anyone that works for me."

"Rocky," I said.

"Excuse me?" stated Max in surprise.

"His name after his wife and son died. He changed it, going by his son's middle-name instead. A tribute to remind him he was going to find out who killed them. I'm his proxy, for I'm going to find out for him, and heaven help you and anyone who works for you if the trail leads back your way, as I will rain down a hell storm on those responsible."

I walked away, convinced I'd made a strong statement, feeling cockier than I should have, for the hell storm might be coming after me.

Chapter 7

I had only been in San Diego for little more than a day, and I had already made an enemy. I had lost my cool, which wouldn't endear me to the locals. Complaining to the Chamber of Commerce might be an option, but I doubt they would care and would probably just tell me to go back to Colorado.

Sometimes I just had to show I was a badass to make sure all parties involved knew where I stood. At least I had Manny on my side, though who knows how long that would last. Causing aggravation was a trait I had finely honed through the years. A power that worked in all regions of the country.

Driving back, I stopped at a San Diego fast food institution, Jack in the Box, and grabbed a burger meal with a chocolate shake. It wasn't worth coming a thousand miles to eat, but the food was hot and filling.

While sitting in the car replenishing my stomach, I called April as she was working the evening shift tonight and was at home, though I discovered differently.

"I'm wheeling and dealing," she said, when I asked what she was up to.

"I don't think Victoria Secrets barters."

"Funny," she replied, sarcastically. "I'm trying to get the price down on this bike I want. The guy is a hard ass."

"Did you show him your badge and gun?" I joked.

"I was holding that in reserve. But I may need it, for he won't budge, even though I know there is wiggle room on the price from what I've learned on the web."

"I'd say use your feminine charm, but while I'm away I don't want you to be tempted."

"I tried that. I think the guy is gay. Normally my charm works, but he seems immune."

I laughed. "I would agree, on the gay part. You're challenging to resist. I know I'm not immune. Hold your ground. You don't need to go into debt just to go riding with me."

"I will. He must cave eventually. Maybe it's too early in the season. How is California?"

"Warm and a tad humid. But no snow, which I can't complain

about. I'm already making friends."

April snickered. "When you say that I know you mean the opposite. Hopefully whomever you pissed off isn't packing a big gun or a lot of clout."

"I believe Max has clout, though we will see. One of his big guns put a hand on me, which didn't go well for him. I do have a cop here who appears to be helpful."

"Try not to screw that up."

"Are you saying I have a history of aggravating cops?"

"Yes, you do. Remember, that is how we met."

"And yet you eventually slept with me anyway." I was smiling ear to ear at my humor.

"Don't remind me. I've always had an issue of picking the wrong men. At least I can tolerate you."

She was probably laughing on the inside, but maybe not.

"I love you too. Good luck with the bike. I'm sure you can wear him down."

"It worked on you," she said with a chuckle. "Try to stay out of trouble. I'd love to come to California, but not to bail you out or identify your dead body."

"No guarantees."

Our call ended after the give and take snarky banter I enjoyed. Our relationship continued to strengthen, which was important me. With Melissa leaving, I'd need April more than ever to keep me on the right track, which she was strong enough to do.

Manny had been kind enough to provide the address of the home in Oceanside, where Rocky's family had been killed. The city, as its name suggested, was by the ocean, stretching inland for several miles, and the third largest city in San Diego County. I made the drive, dealing with the afternoon traffic as I did in Denver, moving at much less than the speed limit and attempting not to get agitated by it.

The home was inland in a large stretch of residential structures, all with unique and differing styles, mostly single storied, with a few two storied buildings sprinkled in. Landscaping consisted of palm trees, yucca plants and various bushes, with varying bright colored flowers. Yards were comprised of rock and gravel, with a few with grass, from well-manicured and green, to spotty and poorly maintained. The house was near the end of a dead-end road, with white picket fencing and a modern Victorian styling.

I parked out in front and walked up the concrete driveway. The scorch marks remained from where the vehicle had intensely burned, the outline permanently etched for all to see. A palm tree on the edge of the driveway still showed burn marks. Walking the scene, I envisioned what it would be like. Rocky stepping out, then an explosion ripping the car apart, flames engulfing it, killing everyone inside, while knocking him to the ground, injuring him seriously; the horror of those you loved killed in a matter of seconds. An ending you would never predict.

There was no car in the driveway, leading me to believe no one was home. They wouldn't be able to tell me much, but the neighbors might. I started with the last house on the block and knocked on doors. It wasn't until the second one I got an answer. A graying older woman with big rectangular glasses opened the white door cautiously and asked what I wanted.

I showed her my ID with my thousand-dollar smile, which didn't seem to ease her fear any, ready to slam the door which was barely open. I asked her if she had been here when the car exploded across the street from her.

"Who are you again?" she asked, apparently not able to read my ID.

"Private detective. I'm investigating the car explosion from a few years back. I wonder if you were home and saw anything."

It seemed to ease her mind and piqued her interest as she opened the door all the way. With a better look at her I could see she was only about five-foot tall, dressed in beige slacks and flowery indigo blouse which clung to her thin frame.

"Oh my, yes," she expressed confidently. "It was extremely loud. I thought a plane had crashed. It shook my whole house. I ran outside and saw the flames. It was horrible."

"What did you do after you ran outside?"

"I pulled out my cell phone and called 911. Even from across the street I could feel the heat from the fire. And I could hear screaming, though it didn't last long. That poor lady and her son didn't stand a chance." She was shaking her head in sadness.

"What about the man, did you see him?"

"No, I couldn't. My eyesight isn't the best." She tapped on her glasses. "I guess they found him unconscious on the ground several feet away. He was badly hurt and died later from what I remember."

"Did you know them?"

"Only in passing. Said hello a few times. They had only lived there for a couple of years. I remember seeing him and gasping at how big he was. I thought he was a football player. My husband was a huge fan of the Chargers and knew all the faces of the players and told me he wasn't."

"Did you see anyone around before it happened?" I asked, turning and pointing to the street. "Any cars you didn't recognize?"

She shook her head no. "Nothing out of the ordinary. I take our little schnauzer out each morning for a walk and all appeared normal to me. It was probably twenty minutes after we got back inside when it happened. I think it was around 8:30 or so."

I thanked her and handed her my card to call me if anything else came to mind. I hit a couple of other houses and got mostly the same information. When I got to the house right next door, a man answered.

When I told him what I wanted, he put shoes on and stepped outside. He was dressed in jeans and tank top, brown skin from sun and heritage, with lots of tattoos on his muscular arms and legs. He waved to a couple of metal chairs on his front lawn for me to sit. He was smoking his vapor device that had a hint of herbal substance, which displayed in his glassy eyes. He was feeling friendly and talkative, which was always good for getting information.

"Fuck, I hated what happened to Garrett," he said after a long puff. "He was a great guy and good neighbor. A lot nicer than the assholes that bought the place afterwards."

"You were friends with them?" I asked, trying to stay downwind from his smoke, which came out in a huge billowing stream.

"Hell yes. My wife was friends with Claire and their little boy, Rocky. We would have dinner together a couple times a month. Garrett would come over and sit right here with me in the evening and shoot the shit."

I wanted to ask if he smoked the cannabis vapor as well but resisted.

"What did you talk about?"

"Everything. Sports, politicians, women. Drink a few beers until it was late, and we'd head to bed."

"Did he ever talk about his work?"

"A little, though not much," he said after a long puff. "I know he worked for a hotshot real estate mogul. I don't remember his name. Said he did security, but that was about it. I know he quit the job a few months earlier. Said he was looking for employment better suited for a husband and father. It sounded like his job was a little hairy at times. But he'd never elaborate."

"He wasn't working at the time of the explosion?"

"I don't think so. I do know he was gone for about a week on a trip. Asked me to keep an eye on the house and check on Claire, as she was home alone with their son."

"Do you remember when he left in relation to the time of the explosion?"

He took a long puff again, letting the smoke float into space. It seemed to be keeping the bugs away, which was a plus.

"I'd say about two, maybe three weeks before. I talked with him shortly after he got home, asking how it went. He said it was fine but was a dead end and not the work he was looking for."

"Were you home when their vehicle blew up?"

"Hell, yes I was. I was getting ready for work and was in the living room when it happened. Knocked out several of my windows from the force of the blast. I ran outside and saw the car. I ran towards it, because I heard the screams, but the heat was too intense." He stopped to take another puff, his hand shaking at what he was describing. "I saw Garrett on the ground but couldn't get to him either. You can see the burn marks on the driveway and the tree still. The fence pickets had to be repainted. It was horrible. I couldn't do a damn thing for them. All I could hope for was the end would come quickly." He appeared sad reliving the moment.

"Did you ever see Garrett afterwards?"

"No. He was taken away. They said he was badly hurt. I tried to visit him, but they wouldn't let me see him. Said I wasn't family and that was all they would allow. I heard about his dying a few days later. It sucked, for I'd lost a friend. He was a good guy. I never could understand why anyone would kill him."

"Any reason you could think of why someone would want them

dead?" It was the million-dollar question.

"Hell no. I figured initially it was an issue with their SUV that caused the explosion. I know they had it in the shop a few days earlier, because it wouldn't start. Made me think someone fucked up and wired the vehicle incorrectly. When I heard the rumor it was a car bomb, well I was stunned."

The car repair was an important lead I needed to look into.

"Any ideas on where they had it repaired?"

"No idea. Lots of places around here where they work on your cars. I mean it's California, and there are more cars than room on the road for them. I did ask what the problem was, and Claire told me they'd needed a new battery."

Interesting the car was serviced. I'd have to ask Manny about that one.

"Did you tell the police about this?"

"I sure did. Told them anytime they want, I'd help no matter what. Garrett and Claire were great people. My wife cried for weeks about what happened. Hell, I even shed a tear or two, which ain't like me. I want the bastards caught that did this. String them up by their nuts is what I'd say should happen. To this day, the police haven't gotten shit. Do you think you can catch them?"

"I'm sure gonna try."

"You be sure to call me if you do, because I want have a crack at them."

I smiled. "I'll be sure to drop them on your front lawn, once I've taken a piece out of them myself."

Chapter 8

Visions arrived in my sleep to varying degrees of The Butcher and his gruesome acts, one time waking me up uncertain where I was, ready to fight back.

I laid back down, finally falling asleep, the frightening images not returning. All I could do for now was hope they would fade with time and this new case would allow me to forget, even if only temporarily. I made it through my night in a little better shape, sleeping a few hours, now adjusted to the noises and comfort of the mattress, which was firmer than I liked.

After a long hot shower and breakfast got my energy level ramped up, I had contacted Manny and arranged to meet outside the Oceanside Police Headquarters, to discuss more in detail the bombing. The building was located smack dab in the middle of a retail shopping center, with Dollar Tree, Petco, barbershop, a public library, gas pumps and many others in the Mission Plaza Real Shopping Center. *Get all your shopping done and file a police report all in one venue.* This seemed like an odd location for a police station, but I'm sure those retailers felt safe to have them close by, as only an insane person would commit a crime with them next door.

When I arrived, I texted Manny. He wanted me to wait outside the building, which was fine with me, since the weather was tourist perfect; warm, sunny, cloudless, with hardly any wind.

After about ten minutes, he stepped out, dressed casually in tan slacks and royal blue polo, waving me to follow him. We made it to a gray Chevy Silverado extra cab, and we hopped in, where he tossed me a folder.

"A list of everyone we interviewed in the Owens' neighborhood," he said, while starting his truck. "Most didn't have any information that was helpful. But the one guy next door did mention about their SUV being serviced shortly before the explosion. If you read down, with a little work, we found where it had been repaired at. We went and talked with them and found nothing that put up any red flags that would make us think they were involved."

"How long did they have the car?" I asked while flipping

through the pages in the folder.

"Two days."

"Really. Seems like a long time to replace a battery."

"They said they were backed up and couldn't get to it right away. The detective that talked with them said they had a lot of cars there they were working on. He didn't see any reason to question them." He pointed to the report when I got to it.

"This wasn't your case at the time?" I queried, continuing to thumb through the pages.

"No. I was a newbie, recently promoted. It was handed over to me after he left the force a couple of years ago. The case has been idle since then. I only recently started looking at it because the name on the boat matched the one with the car bomb."

"Any chance we can visit that shop?"

"I thought as much. We'll drive over. It's been several years, meaning the personnel working there could be different."

"All we can do is ask."

Manny steered us there, working his way through the city like an expert, hopping on highway 76 heading west, then jumping on I-5 heading south, before exiting on Oceanside Blvd. A couple of exits and turns and we pulled into a parking lot of rectangular, flat roofed buildings with lots of bay doors running several blocks. Towards the end was a gated area, with lots of vehicles parked, a sign reading Oceans Auto Repair & Service.

Manny parked outside the gate and we walked to the office. A large, heavy-set man sat behind the counter arguing with someone on the phone. He held his finger up to us, telling us to wait.

"Lady, we aren't trying to screw you over," he asserted. "You brought in the car for one thing and we fixed it, then something else went wrong. It happens, but we didn't break it on purpose. The car is twenty years old. Things going wrong with it are normal. If you aren't happy, you can take the car to someone else and they'll tell you the same thing."

He listened for a few more minutes, the tone of the lady on the other end could be heard by all in the room. His patience was nearing a breaking point, and all he could do was shake his head and mouth obscenities.

"I have other customers I need to talk with. I've done all I can do for you. Have a wonderful day." He softly hung up the phone and took a long drink from his coffee cup. “I wish I had liquid stronger than Starbucks in this mug. What can I help you gentlemen with?”

Manny pulled out his detective ID and showed him. He glanced at it before taking another drink of coffee and then wiping his face with his stained sleeve that was rolled up to below his elbow.

“I hope she didn’t call the cops and complain,” he said jokingly.

“We’re here on another matter,” stated Manny. “About an SUV you worked on a few years back. A couple days after you did repair work, it blew up. Owners’ names were Garrett and Claire Owens.”

“Going back in time. What was the date again?”

Manny provided it for him, which he promptly entered into his computer to look up.

“I remember now. Bad battery, causing it not to start. Nothing major and certainly nothing to cause a car to explode.”

“The vehicle was here for a couple of days. Is that unusual?”

“Not really. There are times we get backed up and don’t get to it the first day. That was a while ago. I don’t remember the exact circumstances.”

“Were you the one who talked with the detectives?” Manny leaned in with his elbow on the counter.

“I don’t recall. We had a couple people who covered the desk back then. Now I’m the only one.” He had his arms crossed, his chin resting in his palm, rubbing the day-old growth on his face.

“Are you the owner?”

“Yes. I had a partner, but he passed away a few years ago.”

Manny glanced at me, with a suspicious expression. “Sorry to hear. What happened?”

“Hit by a car crossing the street, if you can believe the irony. Killed instantly. Kaleb was a good guy. Was a shame it happened.”

He genuinely looked sad about the death, as I carefully read his expressions and mannerisms. It would appear from what I could tell, he was telling the truth.

“Did they catch the person who did it?” asked Manny, his line of questioning excellent.

He shook his head. “No. Car was stolen and abandoned. No witnesses to the hit and run, as it was late at night.”

“Can you give me the date it happened?”

He thought about it for a minute, then rattled it off. It was only a few months after Rocky was killed. I made a note of it on my phone.

"Which of your techs worked on the Owens' SUV?" I asked, deciding to jump in.

He looked again at the computer screen. "Eugene Washburn."

"Can we talk with him?"

"Doesn't work here anymore. Kaleb fired him because he stopped coming into work shortly after."

"How long had he worked here?" I inquired.

He had to search for that on his computer as well. "Only about a month. He was an oddball if I recall correctly. Lots of tattoos and shaved waves into the sides of his hair, from the temples on back. The rest of his hair was long and tied into a ponytail. He had an old sixties Camaro he was fixing up. Kaleb let him do the work on it here at the shop in his off hours. The tattoos looked to be gang related to me. But Kaleb said Eugene didn't run with them anymore. I didn't question it, as he rarely was wrong about people we hired. But he definitely missed the mark on this guy."

"Do you have an address?" queried Manny.

"I think it's somewhere here in the system." He started typing away but made a face. "Odd. He isn't in here anymore."

"Are you certain?"

"I'm typing it correctly. It's like someone deleted him from our system."

"Do you have backups you can refer to?"

He made a frown. "Do we look like Pep Boys? I'm lucky this thing fires up every morning. We need to hire a smart-ass tech savvy kid to bring us up to speed. We're still running Windows XP. But we haven't the time or the money, leaving us to limp along with what we have."

We pressed him on a few more things, but we didn't get much else. As we walked out to the Silverado, Manny turned to me.

"What do you think?" he asked.

"I'm thinking something smells fishy and it's not the ocean."

"Agreed. We need to dig into this further."

He drove us back to police headquarters to do research on Kaleb and Eugene.

Chapter 9

We were sitting at Manny's desk in the section where the detectives worked. It was an open area with no dividing walls and probably ten other workstations. Manny's was in the back corner, a plain beige wall with mounted whiteboard behind him and no view of the outside, as there wasn't a window in sight. He was typing away on his computer trying to find Eugene Washburn, hoping he was in the system.

I sat waiting, playing with my visitor badge, looking around. There were several other detectives working, filling out paperwork, typing on their computers, one reading a magazine, another looking at his cell phone. All but one was male, with a female on the phone being animated in her conversation. I enjoyed the action of the room, the work these detectives did under pressure-packed situations. The world of crime constantly in motion, rarely seeming to stop. It was a hard and unappreciated job they did every day. And a job I was thrilled not to have.

There were a couple of Washburns that came up on the search. Having photos of both, it was easy to find the right one, though it was going back before the explosion. His hair was different, and a few less tattoos, but it was him from the description we had. He was a small-time crook mostly, with nothing major on his record. Assault and theft charges that didn't stick. There was an address, it was several years old, but might provide us a lead.

Manny had gotten the last name of the partner who had been killed. Kaleb Leigh had been struck by a car after leaving a bar, walking home alone at around 1 a.m. The bar was about four blocks from his house, with no witnesses to the hit and run. Bleeding with bones broken, a man found him in the street and called 911, but the paramedics arrived too late to save him. The stolen car was found the next day, having been torched to destroy any evidence in a lot of an abandoned warehouse several miles away.

The thought was the person panicked and incinerated the car to cover their tracks. Any link to the car bomb had never been made. The cases never connecting. Now that we knew, Manny and I didn't think it was coincidence.

"There has to be a connection," I proclaimed.

"How do we bridge them together? What we have now certainly isn't enough to tie them to each other."

I thought for a minute, Vicente Duarte coming to mind.

"Can you find any link to Eugene and Vicente Duarte?" I wondered.

Manny didn't know the name.

"Who is he?"

"A possible connection."

"We don't keep family trees in the computer database," Manny relayed with a smirk.

"See if someone bailed him out of jail on his arrests. There should be a record there."

Manny typed with a single finger on each hand, then he clicked and scrolled through several pages with his mouse, before finding what he was searching for.

"It says his mother bailed him out the first time. Angeline Washburn was the name. The second time he stayed in jail for a week before the charges were dropped."

I grinned. "Mom couldn't or wouldn't bail him out the next time. Do we have an address on her?"

"It was the same as he gave."

"How old is he?"

"Twenty-six now. Would have been around twenty when he was arrested."

"Do you think he lives at home?" I asked.

"One way to find out. We can pay them a visit."

We were on our way to the address when Manny asked a question.

"You mentioned Vicente Duarte being a connection. What was the connection?"

I thought about it for a minute, thinking about what to tell him. My history had been to leave out key details from the police. Mostly because they pissed me off and often shut me out, leaving me high and dry, without solving the mystery. An item that didn't look good on my PI resume. But Manny seemed different, so I decided to fess up. Well at least if asked about it, I wouldn't lie.

"Vicente Duarte may have been the man hired to kill Garrett

and his family," I stated.

"Holy shit. That is big news you neglected to tell me." Manny appeared to be agitated.

"Sorry. I'm used to cops not letting me in on the case and freezing me out."

"And how did you come about this information?"

I took a second before responding. "Because this man, Garrett, was alive last year and working with me to find the killers of his wife and son. It led to Vicente, who we questioned, and he learned he was the one hired for the hit. At the time Garrett was known to me as Rocky."

Manny glanced at me, his eyes lighting up. "I've heard that name before."

"It was his son's middle name. He faked his death and assumed that name as his new persona."

"How did you meet him?"

"He was brought in by a contact of mine to help me on a couple of cases. Saved my hide big time the first time, along with a woman I loved, a close friend and his son. He was a client who paid me to help him find Vicente."

"What happened to Vicente?" asked Manny, his eyes forward as he was driving through the heavy traffic.

"Best I not tell you. I will say street justice was served but led Rocky back out here to California to chase down who paid Vicente."

"Which was?"

"He didn't know for certain. But said he thought it was someone inside the organization he used to work for."

Manny glanced back at me. "Maximillian Conway?"

I nodded. "You know that from the file."

"Yes. Background on the victims is a standard part of the investigation. He hadn't worked there for six months. Conway is rumored to have ties to an illegal activity or two. But locals mostly leave him alone. It has been thought he has connections with the police that allows him latitude to carry out his business unscathed."

"Payoffs?" I uttered, knowing it was a dirty word when spoke about the police.

"Nothing I'd ever say out loud at work. He brings a lot of business to the area and makes key contributions to local politicians. These are good things, if he isn't leaving bodies all over the place."

"I talked with him and he insists Rocky and him left on good terms and would do anything to bring his killer to justice."

"You believe him?" inquired Manny.

"He seemed truthful, but I have my suspicions. I've been fooled before. Men who lie for a living often are hard to gauge."

The Silverado pulled up in front of the home. It was a multi-family building; duplex or triplex, it was hard to tell for certain. There was an old, rusted out seventies Lincoln sitting on the street, with two flat tires. The house looked run down, badly in need of paint and patching. The yard was mostly weeds, the bushes in front badly in need of trimming. We found three doors, each with a different letter. The address we had was C, which was around the side. We walked up the brick pathway, we had to dodge weeds growing through the cracks to nearly a foot in height.

When we reached the door, before he knocked, Manny told me to stand to one side, as he didn't trust what might come out or even through the door. He pounded on the faded, peeling wood, and stepped to one side, one hand on the gun in his holster.

The door opened to reveal a fifty-year-old heavy-set woman in a baggy, flowered dress standing in the opening asking what the hell we wanted. If she was a threat, it would only be from the second-hand cigarette smoke which hovered around her like an aura.

"Are you Angeline Washburn?" asked Manny, his hand resting on his gun, the other now holding his badge in plain sight.

"What the hell has he done now?" she wondered in the deep voice of someone who smoked a couple packs a day.

"Nothing yet. We were hoping to talk with Eugene about a car he worked on a few years back."

"He isn't home. Out working on his car. About all he ever does, besides banging the woman of the week he brings by."

Manny put away his badge and removed his hand from his gun.

"Where is he working now?"

"No idea. He doesn't tell me much. Has money, but who knows where it comes from. I should have thrown him out a long time ago. But I'm not working these days. I need him to help cover the rent. Government doesn't pay shit to help someone like me."

“Any idea of when he’ll be home?”

She reached into her pocket and pulled out a cigarette, lighting it up, before taking a long draw, coughing out the smoke in our direction. Apparently her aura needed additional infusion.

“Not a clue. He comes and goes as he pleases. Brings the latest whore of the week home at all hours. They wake me up with their loud fucking. Don’t know why they have to make all that damn noise when doing it. His father and I were never that loud. Hop on and get it over with was all he ever cared about.”

Mom seemed like a real winner, as was the father who was no longer around. It always amazed me how people with no money found the cash for their cigarettes and alcohol. It seems those habits were more important than food or rent.

“Thank you. We’ll check back later.”

Manny and I walked back to the front and climbed in the Silverado.

“Stakeout time,” I said.

“I have to get back to headquarters and work other cases,” replied Manny. “You’re free to watch him. Once you get him what are you going to ask?”

“Probably how he scores his bevy of whores that drives his mother crazy.”

Manny laughed. “And after he enlightens you on his skill with women?”

“What he knows about the car bomb. And if he knows Vicente. I gauge for reactions when I throw out names.”

“And what if his reaction is to try and shoot you?” stated Manny bluntly.

“What I always do, which is to do my best not to let the bullet hit me.”

“Does that always work?”

I put my hand out flat and wiggled it to say not always. And I had the scars to prove it.

Chapter 10

Manny dropped me off at police headquarters and I drove my rental back to the hotel. I had a couple of packages waiting for me that I'd had shipped. They were my guns, ammo and holsters, which was challenging to take on a plane, as security frowned upon weapons on airlines these days.

Taking them back to my room, I opened them to find my Smith & Wesson .38 and Beretta 9mm, with ammo and holsters. I had a room with one of those safes that hotels charge you an arm and leg extra to use, and put the 9mm away with the extra ammunition, and tucked my .38 with belt holster on my back hip, pulling the shirt tail out to cover it as much as I could. One of the reasons why many of my shirts were purchased a size larger. Once in the car I'd lock it away in the glove box. But I needed my guns as insurance in case someone tried to shoot me, which was always a real possibility in my line of work.

I grabbed lunch, this time chicken from the Colonel, and drove back to the house where Eugene lived and waited. I had the windows down while I enjoyed my finger licking good drumstick, smelling the late winter warmth of the bay.

My eyes were watching all in the neighborhood travel by. Many cars were older and in bad shape. Several had the sounds of deep bass coming out of them, shaking the ground as they drove by; a stereo system worth more than the car itself. I had the rental connected via Bluetooth to my cell phone, playing music, enjoying rocks songs via my stakeout playlist, though softly.

Time went slowly, with no sign of him. My food was gone, as was my drink, but the need to pee wasn't. Stepping out, I found a convenience store to use the facilities and get more to drink. When I returned, I parked in a different location hoping no snooping neighbor would report me as suspicious. Though in this area, suspicious would have to be overtly blatant, as some of the activity appeared to be of an illegal nature.

It was coming on 4 p.m. by the time a Camaro came down the street. It was a sixties model, in midnight blue on the front half, primer on most of the back. I heard it before I saw it, the loud exhaust pipes roaring up and down with each shift of gears. It pulled past the house and then did a U-turn before pulling back up, parking as close to the tri-plex as it could behind the Lincoln.

He wasn't alone, a woman was in the passenger seat and even from a distance I could see him leaning over, grabbing and kissing her. The groping continued for several minutes before he stepped out, walking with a noticeable limp around the back and opening the door for her. He struggled to pull her out, before slamming it shut. She seemed drunk, for she staggered when she walked, barely able to handle the stiletto heels she was wearing to go with her tight spandex pants, which left little to the imagination, and tube top that barely held her bouncing chest.

I was out of my car, the gun holster tucked away on the back belt as I rushed towards them. I yelled out his name and he stopped, looking at me. He was good sized, maybe two inches taller than me at 6'2", and heavy at two hundred plus pounds, but not in shape, with a hairy belly that peered out below his undersized shirt. He had the shaved head like I had heard at the repair shop, with lightning bolts cut into both sides, the black hair long on top and down the back. He was in shorts and tank top, tattoos with impressive ink designs covering all skin showing, a masterpiece of artwork on his darken skin. As I approached, he kept walking. I yelled his name again. This time when he looked at me, his anger showed.

"Leave me alone, cop," he yelled. "I don't have time for your shit. I have a lady to please."

The options I had to work with on that statement were endless. But I kept it simple.

"Try to keep it down, you're keeping your mother awake."

"What the fuck did you say!" he uttered, turning now. I had his full attention.

"You're too loud. When having sex be mindful of those in the next room. They don't want to hear your groans and her faking orgasms."

He took a couple steps forward. "Asshole, are you saying I can't satisfy my lady!"

"As wasted as she is, I doubt she'll be awake when you finish. And you might want to keep a hold of her or she might fall down and flop out of her tube top."

He glanced over at her, who seemed barely able to stand, but he didn't seem to care. I had his full attention.

"If you weren't a cop, I'd bust you in the chops for saying that shit."

"What makes you think I'm a cop?"

He looked me up and down, frowning. "I know the type and haircut. You have cop written all over you. I'm figuring Vice."

I should have been offended, but instead I just smiled.

"I need to talk with my stylist. I may need to go for a fresh look. But you're dead wrong, I'm not a cop. Which means you can take a swing if it will help your manhood." I wasn't sure why I was goading him, but it felt good.

"You're baiting me. I'm not going to fall for that. Leave me alone."

"Not until you answer my questions."

He searched around to see what options he had, which weren't many. I was skilled at being a pest. Because he thought I was a cop, he wouldn't try anything physical.

"The sooner you talk with me, the sooner you can lay the wood to your lovely lady."

He thought about it, then grabbed the girl's arm and put her back in the car, since standing wasn't working well for her.

"Puke in my car and you get to clean it up," he yelled to her, before closing the door. "Ok slick, ask away."

"Tell me about your time at Ocean's Auto Repair & Service."

"That was a few years back. How come?"

"Part of a case I'm working on. Person killed in a car bomb."

There was a flash of fear in his eyes, he seemed uncertain of what to say.

"Do you have information you'd care to share?" I said, responding to his reaction.

"No. Why should I. And what does that have to do with me and where I once worked." His eyes were darting around, not looking at me directly.

"You worked on the car. Two days later it blew up. Tricky thing to ignore when trying to figure out what happened."

Lie detector tests measure changes in heart rate, excessive moisture, and nervous reactions to questions. Eugene had all the symptoms. Lying wasn't a skill he excelled at.

"I don't know anything about that. Hell, I only worked there a short time."

"I know. You stopped showing up for work almost to the day when the explosion happened. Why did you stop coming in?"

"I didn't like working there. I wanted to find better employment." His eyes continued to be everywhere *but* looking at me.

"Did you find something better? Maybe paid well enough to complete the task and then walked away?"

"You're nuts, man," he said, though not convincingly. "I think it's time for me to stop talking with you."

He went to the car and opened the door, pulling out his girlfriend, who was half-asleep. As he started walking away, I decided to blurt out a name.

"Vicente Duarte," I said loudly.

His body reaction to the name was a clear giveaway. He stopped dead in his tracks. He knew it, there was no doubt. He looked back at me with an evil stare but didn't speak.

"He is dead, though not before he told us all about what happened. It is only a matter of time."

Eugene kept on walking, but he was affected by all I told him. He didn't seem like the mastermind to the plot, only a player. But he was scared by what I'd said. Scared people often do stupid things without thinking about them. I'd need to keep an eye on him from a distance and see where he ran to. At the very least I probably ruined his night of loud passion.

I walked back to my car and pulled away, driving slowly past the house. He was standing there watching me and we made eye contact. I'd gotten under his skin which was a good thing.

I went around the block and parked on the next street, with clear vision on his car. I'd wait until nightfall to see what he did. When hunger and exhaustion overcame me at around 9 p.m., I left, heading back to the hotel hoping for a good night of sleep, knowing I'd be back early the next day waiting for him to make a move.

Chapter 11

I had called Manny early the next morning, and he was free to join me for the watch, at least for the morning hours. I met him at police headquarters with good old stakeout food of a dozen donuts, with coffee for him and juice for me. We used his Silverado, as Eugene might remember my car, and took up a vantage point on the next block, arriving at 7 a.m. Manny had a nice camera with telephoto lens, along with binoculars to give us a birds-eye view. Eugene's car was sitting there, which was no surprise, as he didn't seem the early riser type.

"Donuts with sprinkles don't fit the cop profile," remarked Manny.

"Yet you're eating one and getting them all over you."

"I don't fit the normal stereotype of the cop."

I was enjoying a devil's food frosted cake donut, which was fresh and warm.

"I've noticed that. What will it do to your image if you have to jump out and sprinkles go flying off your shirt while in foot pursuit?"

"Who gives a damn about image. The sprinkles will give me the sugar boost to run the thief down."

I had to laugh at the thought of a super cop hyped up on multi-colored sugar specks. *Whatever edge you needed to catch the bad guys!*

"You're certain this guy is going to run?" questioned Manny.

"There was no doubt I spooked him. The question is where does he run to and how soon? Hopefully to the person who hired him."

"You think he is that stupid?"

"Didn't seem all that sharp. After talking with his mother, I think it's hereditary. Time will tell us for certain."

Much of our morning was spent talking about sports and politics. Manny was upset at the Chargers leaving for Los Angeles, for his family were season ticket holders. The drive wasn't that far, but it seemed like a stab in the back, leading them not to renew. This led into the conversation at the lack of an NBA team and how the Padres had been bad for an eternity. After debating sports, we turned to politics and the divisive nature of them. We seemed to have similar liberal views, but could agree the entire system was a mess, no matter which side of the political spectrum you were on. New blood was needed to make changes. The question was who that would be, as it certainly wasn't true of the latest regime.

The interaction was enjoyable. The last few stakeouts I'd been on I was either alone or with Rocky and he didn't talk a whole lot. Though he'd spoken more now than in the past, his demeanor was to close his eyes and rest, until needed. I wasn't sure how he did it, but he was always ready to go when the time came. His heart rate could go from sixty to one-twenty in a blink of an eye. I did miss him, to a certain degree, especially his skill set. It was hard to imagine he was dead, and I wasn't sure I believed he was. But if it was true, I planned on finishing the case for him. I owed him a debt I planned to pay off.

The morning wore on and now only three of the dozen donuts remained. Manny walked away needing a bathroom break. I wasn't sure where he went, for he didn't say, but there weren't many businesses nearby, and he wasn't gone long. Doubtful anyone would bother a man taking a wiz with a badge and gun.

It was after nine when Eugene finally came out. His girlfriend wasn't with him, likely sleeping off the night of booze and debauchery. He lumbered to his car with his noticeable limp, carefully climbing in before the engine roared to life and headed down the road. Manny kept a good distance keeping him in sight. I had my Rockies ball cap and sunglasses on in case he could see me in his rearview mirror.

We headed south on I-5 for about forty-five minutes before he veered off onto state highway 52, heading west. Exiting on Regent Road, into the community of North Clairemont, which was part of San Diego. From there we made several turns until we came to a neighborhood that looked a little rough.

Most of the homes were modular type, single story and of basic rectangular or square box design. Many looked in disrepair, with peeling siding and paint. Yards were full of weeds, with an occasional dead tree here and there. The streets were lined with a few older cars and trucks, many in bad shape. This was a poor neighborhood it would seem, an area where crime might be an issue.

Eugene's Camaro pulled to the curb in front of one of the

houses, one of the better kept homes on the block. We drove on past about a block, before doing a U-turn and pulling up to the curb about three houses down. Eugene sat in his car waiting, before two men came outside, both dressed in torn jeans and muscle shirts, with multi-colored do-rags on their heads. Sunglasses covered their faces, their skin dark and littered with tattoos. Each was armed, a large handgun in a shoulder holster under their armpit.

Eugene climbed out, greeting them both with firm handshake and quick embrace.

"Are you carrying?" asked Manny.

I had put on a light jacket, to cover my holster, my Berretta concealed.

"Yes."

"Good. I hope we don't need it. But it appears we're in someone's gang territory. Otherwise they wouldn't be walking freely with their guns showing."

"My experience is we will be challenged for being here, eventually."

"Yes, we will."

Manny got on his radio and called in to let the San Diego North Division know he was in their territory, with the wheres and the whys. After he was done, he gave them the address of the house and one of the cars' license plate numbers. Impressive he'd remembered them, for neither was written down. It didn't take long for them to relay the information which was sent to his phone.

"Look at the name registered to the car out front," stated Manny, handing me his phone.

There were two names listed, one the owner of the home, the other from the registration on the car. The home owner was Miguel Prisco, leader of the gang in the area. The car owner was Luciano Duarte. Either it was a coincidence he had the same last name as Vicente, or he was related. I was willing to bet on the latter. My instinct had been spot-on to follow Washburn. Now to see where this information led me.

"Vicente said his men took care of the hit and he supervised," I acknowledged. "Luciano could be one of his men, being they likely are family."

Manny nodded. "I doubt we can walk up there and get him to admit to it. He might be a perturbed about Vicente getting killed."

"I agree. And the odds aren't with us right now. Though we may not have a choice, it looks like they're walking our way."

Miguel and Luciano walked briskly towards us, muscles swelling, their stride with a confident sway to it, faces clenched in full-on menacing mode for us to see. Eugene trailed behind them, appearing less ominous, but I suspected wouldn't cower to prove himself, though he didn't appear to be armed.

I pulled out my gun and held it low, between my legs. Manny had his out as well, holding it next to his leg with his right hand, his badge in his left, prepared to firmly face them.

"You don't belong here," stated Miguel, as he stopped several feet short of the Silverado, his hand near his gun. "I know everyone on this block and those that don't belong better leave or they will leave in pieces."

Manny's window was down. He held out his left hand, displaying his badge.

"You're a cop," observed Miguel. "Why are you on my turf?"

Manny seemed calm, as if he'd dealt face-to-face with other gang members in the past. Which was a good thing; I wasn't quite sure what to expect.

"We're working," replied Manny. "Running down several leads which brought us here."

"You aren't one of our friendly neighborhood cops, I know them all," proclaimed Miguel.

"We're from Oceanside. Crime was committed there."

"Then you need to go back there. You aren't wanted here and could get yourself killed."

"Sounds like a threat," said Manny with a calm you wouldn't expect.

"More of a warning," answered Miguel. "People who don't belong around here often don't live long. Cops have an even shorter life span, if they aren't on the list of those we allow in."

Eugene walked up to Luciano and whispered in his ear, his expression changing when he heard the words. Luciano did not share what he learned with Miguel. Maybe Miguel wasn't involved with the car bombing. If this was the case it might be something I could use as leverage.

"We will drive on," voiced Manny. "We got what we wanted. You gentlemen have a great day."

He sat the gun on the seat and put the truck in gear, and slowly drove away. I made eye contact with Luciano, who stood staring at us with a look of vile anger on his face, his hand on the butt of his gun ready to act on his violent urges. My heart rate was through the roof, the tension building as I watched through the back window, until we were clear and safe. It took a few minutes for me to calm down, thankful we'd left without a violent confrontation. Once I felt safe, I put my gun back in the holster.

"Did we learn anything?" wondered Manny as I wiped my brow.

I smiled grimly. "Yeah we did. And it's not to drive into that neighborhood without heavy backup!"

We headed back to Oceanside, as I contemplated what to do next, though a stiff drink was first on the list.

Chapter 12

Manny had other cases, so I headed back to the hotel. I could use a drink, but the hotel had no bar. It was either pick up alcohol at a liquor store or find a neighborhood bar. The thought of drinking alone in my room wasn't all that enticing so I asked the front desk about establishments nearby.

When in an unfamiliar city, you must go by the recommendations of those who lived there. I was told that not too far away was a place that boasted over one thousand different whiskeys. The outside didn't look like much, with its faded burgundy painted facing, weather-worn beige awning, and rectangle box shaped building with flat roof, that looked of World War Two design – later confirmed by the sign saying, "Since 1947." But the Aero Club Bar was a neighborhood favorite, a dive in the truest sense of the word.

Once inside, at first glance, the wall of whiskey jumps out at you. An impressive display spanning ten-foot-high and twenty-foot-long, with bottle after bottle of distinct brands of whiskey from all over the world, layered all the way to the ceiling, lit up for all to cherish. Brandon, with his love of Jack Daniels, would be in heaven with all the international malted barley and rye options of which to sample.

Needing nourishment, I had learned they didn't serve food so I'd brought with me a Subway turkey, bacon, cheese on wheat inside. Thankfully I was told they were fine with bringing in your own meal and drinking on an empty stomach wouldn't end well for me.

I found an open padded stool with an unobstructed view of one of the flat screen TV's and ordered a beer. They had twenty options on tap, and I wasn't picky. I told the lovely, long blonde-haired lady with a joyous, welcoming smile to surprise me. It arrived in a cold, tall glass, with the business logo and name plastered on it, and a one-inch head on top.

Sipping down, I found it refreshing after my experience from earlier, a couple bites of the foot-long sub an excellent chaser. I was more relaxed now, though not thrilled of the danger I had encountered. I'd faced it many times before in my career, never once relishing it, but nevertheless understanding it was the career I had chosen. Part of me knew that the day would arrive when the grim reaper of death, in all his glory, would come knocking and I'd have to let him in. Hopefully I'd be old, senile and unaware, going peacefully off to the afterworld in no pain.

After a couple more sips and bites, I took in the rest of the bar. From the ceiling, various model aeronautics, mostly vintage, though a few modern, dangled from wires above the whiskey bottle display. Across the rest of the ceiling were lighted neon signs from various brewers, a few others scattered on the walls above the four u-shaped black vinyl covered booths. Vintage framed black and white photos of airplanes and a few celebrities filled in empty spaces on the wall, especially towards the back, where the two pool tables resided. The mahogany hardwood floors creaked with each step, another sign of the age of the building.

Though it was a small space, they packed a lot in here, and with its charm, it would make a wonderful place to own or work in. Now that my beloved Boone's was gone, this was the type of establishment I was looking for to frequent and unwind but hadn't been able to find. If I couldn't locate one, maybe I needed to find several financial partners and start my own dive. It was fun to dream.

"I don't think I've seen you in here before," noted the female bartender.

"I'm from out of town," I replied.

"Where are you from?"

"Denver."

"I hear it's beautiful there. Rocky Mountain High." She sang it like the John Denver song while wiping down the counter.

"It is. Though it's gorgeous here too. You have mountains and the ocean. Plus, it's warmer."

She grinned. "It is, though at times a little too warm during summer. Why are you in town?"

"Work related." I kept it simple.

"What type of work do you do?"

I hesitated but figured there was no reason not to answer truthfully. "I'm a private detective."

Her chestnut eyes lit up. "Really. Are you here working a case?"

"Yes. Though at the moment I'm relaxing, trying not to think about the case, enjoying my beer and sandwich."

"Sounds exciting compared to what I do every day."

I wanted to say, yes, but more dangerous too, though I resisted. "There are moments of that, but plenty of boring times as well. Not the glamour TV and the movies make it."

"How long are you in town for?"

"Not completely sure. We're making headway, but cases are always fluid. Once you think you have an answer, situations throw you a curve."

"If you need to unwind, this is a good place to sit your butt down."

I nodded. The atmosphere and company was enough to get me back here. "I'm sure I'll be back. Since the hotel I'm at is lacking a bar, a good drink for a hard-boiled PI is a must. That stereotype at least, is accurate."

She laughed and walked away to help another patron who'd entered. It was early afternoon still, the clock showing 3 p.m., leaving the place quiet. I finished my sandwich, and ordered one more beer before paying and leaving, happy to leave the concerns of the case behind, if only for a short while.

I reached my hotel and decided on changing and working out. The hotel had a small gym, with a treadmill, two exercise bikes, free weights and Nautilus machine. I started on the treadmill, with a slow walk before working up to a jog, getting my heartrate up. After twenty minutes I went to the free weights, doing curls and squats, before moving to the Nautilus, doing arm and leg presses, and chest fly pull downs. I had worked up a significant sweat and was headed back to my room for a shower, when my phone rang. It was Brandon calling for an update.

"Any progress?" he asked.

So much for leaving the case behind!

"I've made headway…" I went on to tell him about what I'd learned, including who I'd figured was a relative of Vicente, and someone who knew the man who had worked on the SUV of Rocky's family.

"Sounds like a good lead. What do you plan to do with it?"

"I will be talking with the San Diego Police Street Gang Unit. Manny is working on getting a meeting with someone familiar with this gang. Walking into their territory and asking questions isn't a wise thing to do."

"Understandable. If you need backup, let me know. I'm sure I can come up with a few options that would be adequate."

"Right now, I'm good. This cop, Manny, seems like a tough guy and is quite helpful and accommodating. He didn't even flinch when talking to the leader of the gang, Miguel."

"You haven't pissed him off yet?"

"I'm holding that in reserve. When in foreign territory, always keep the local police on your side."

There was a pause before Brandon continued. "I need another favor. A big one. Since you're in California, when you get time, I need you to check on someone else in Orange County."

"Who would that be?" I wondered, not thrilled with more work to do.

"You aren't going to like it, but it would be huge favor to me and for once I'd owe you."

I was afraid to find out who it was. If it was big enough to finally put me in the black with Brandon, it had to be someone I wouldn't be happy about seeing. It then hit me on who it might be.

"You don't mean…" I stopped as I couldn't say the name, for it was one I'd tried to put in the past and forget.

"Yes. Emily. I need you to make sure she is safe."

I nearly swore into the mouth piece, mouthing the multi-syllable word instead. If I was smart, I'd hang up the phone now and hoped he wouldn't call back. But I knew otherwise.

"I know you aren't happy about this, especially after the last time you two met."

"No shit, Brandon, the woman tried to seduce me and then shot me in the ass. The two of us together is a bad combination." I was angry at the thought of seeing her.

"I know. But she might be in danger, a danger possibly because of my work. And I need to know she is safe. She hasn't returned my calls."

I shook my head, telling myself no, no, no. Trust was an issue when it came to Emily. My trusting her and me trusting myself when around her. But I couldn't say it out loud to Brandon.

"Jarvis, I'd do it myself, but I can't leave right now. Could be leading people to her. I'm asking nicely and don't want to pull out the, you owe me card."

He had that much on me, leaving little choice. It was too bad I wasn't still in the bar, because a good shot of whiskey might be in order.

"Tell me where she is," I uttered, regretting the words as I said them.

Chapter 13

Sleeping didn't come easy for me, the thoughts of what had happened between Emily White and I in the past invaded my dreams all night. It was a change of pace from The Butcher dreams, though hardly better. I hadn't thought much of her recently, though other events often reminded me of the mistake I'd made with getting involved with her. The fact being she was a client and was a little bit bat-shit crazy, though I didn't realize this until it was too late.

Her manipulation of men, one being me, another her ex-husband, had led me to shoot her in the leg. She would return months later, saying she had received help for her problem, only to try and seduce me. When I refused, she shot me in the ass. I never saw her again after that day, which was fine by me. But now I'd have to go searching for her, which didn't leave me with a cheery feeling inside.

On today's agenda though was a meeting with one of the members of the Street Gang Units to learn more about Miguel Prisco and his gang, and what I'd be up against. Manny had arranged the meeting with Gary Zimmer who was part of the Gang Suppression Team. He was going to be in the area and wanted to meet at the Pit Stop Diner, which was in one of the outer buildings of the Mission Plaza Real Shopping Center, where the Oceanside Police Headquarters resided.

Once inside, I found an old-style fifties diner, complete with 1962 New Yorker sedan parked inside, next to two early 1900 gravity feed gas pumps. Time travel nostalgia graced the walls, from pictures of celebrities and cars from the fifties and sixties, to license plates and hubcaps.

I went through the line ordering a burger, fries and chocolate shake. The prices were definitely from modern times and I plopped down the credit card to pay.

Once I had my food, I carried my plastic tray to a table by a window with three chairs. The burger and fries were good, though the sodium content was through the roof. The shake was fabulous—so thick I could hardly drink it through the straw. I got halfway through my food when Manny walked in with Zimmer.

He and Manny were of similar build, with Zimmer in jeans and a t-shirt, hardly looking like a cop, other than the 9mm handgun in a holster on his belt. They went and ordered, while I paid, before we all sat down.

"Gary used to work in Oceanside," said Manny after a couple of bites of his chili-cheese-onion hot dog.

"I came here for lunch regularly," added Gary. "I was feeling nostalgic and thought it would be worth the drive. I get a cheese quesadilla and chicken burrito every time I come here."

That didn't sound like fifties diner food to me, but who was I to quibble?

"Why did you move to the gang unit in San Diego?" I asked, in between munching on my salty fries.

"I needed a new challenge. The gang issue, like most big cities is taxing to deal with. We have a tight lid on it right now, but it's always a volatile powder keg ready to explode."

"Did Manny tell you who we were interested in discussing?"

"Miguel Prisco. I heard you drove into his neighborhood. Lucky Manny was with you waving his badge, or you likely would have taken a brutal beating and then been dumped somewhere to expire. No one enters his zone without permission."

"Jarvis stayed cool under pressure," noted Manny. "He was ready to act if they became aggressive."

Apparently, he hadn't noticed me being uncomfortable at the time. It was good to know he thought I could handle myself in a volatile situation.

"Tell me a little about Miguel?" I inquired.

"Prisco has been running the gang for many years now. Protects anyone within his territory. It's his family. Fathered a few kids with a couple different women but treats them well. His gang runs with about fifteen to twenty other members at any given time, ages running from late teens to early thirties. The numbers change as a few their own and others…well, how should I put it… 'disappear.' Usually after crossing him. He runs a tight ship. Acting on your own, whether it being a crime, or selling drugs or guns, without his approval is a capital offence in his mind. Any type of fracturing within the gang, he deals with quickly."

"You said right now you have a tight lid on things. What have you done to keep it under control?"

Gary finished his burrito, wiping grease from his face. He looked down at the cheese quesadilla and decided to wait.

"We work with the various gangs, trying to keep them out of each other's territory. When two or more gangs collide, it can be chaos. We barter peace agreements between the various rivals and lately those terms are being adhered to. But we're talking about pride driven strong-willed men here, who must prove their worth. Often times doing that means going up against a rival to show they have what it takes to be in the gang. When that happens, the violence can spiral out of control quickly. We step in with force to contain the violence, but that doesn't work without diplomacy, wheeling and dealing."

"Have you ever known of this gang being paid to put out a hit on someone?" I asked.

An expression of surprise filled Gary's face. "Was this hit on another gang member?"

"No. At one time he was a security person for Maximillian Conway."

"Wow. The real estate king of southern California? Nothing we know about would lead me to believe any connection there. Do you have a source?"

"Vicente Duarte," I said, while wiping grease from my face with a napkin. "Have you heard of him?"

Zimmer nodded. "I have. He worked here within Prisco's gang before moving to Denver several years ago, starting his own business. I believe I heard he was killed recently."

"He was. Right before he was killed, he told an associate of mine that he was paid to put out a hit on him and his family. It was a car bombing in Oceanside. The wife and son were killed, but he survived."

"I remember that event. I thought all were killed."

"With help, he faked his death. He'd been quietly investigating it when it led him to Vicente. He forcefully got him to confess."

Manny quietly was taking all of this in while finishing his second hot dog. Gary had held out long enough and dived into his quesadilla which admittedly looked mighty tasty.

"His cousin, Luciano, remains in Prisco's gang," said Gary, after two bites.

"We know," I replied after finishing a couple more of the fries.

"There was a lead that brought us to him. A man who worked on the car shortly before the explosion. Eugene Washburn. Have you heard of him?"

"No. He isn't in the Prisco gang as far as I know."

"After talking with Eugene and letting him know I was investigating, he went into Prisco's neighborhood and talked with Luciano. I'm not completely sure Miguel himself knew about the bombing. We didn't get a chance to ask though as that is when they came up to Manny's car. Though I observed Eugene whisper into Luciano's ear. That is when I got the evil stare from him."

"You think he told Luciano about you being connected to Vicente's death?" wondered Zimmer, his mouth full of food.

"From the look I got, I'd say yes. The question is, would Miguel be in on it? I would imagine the payoff for the hit was quite a bit of cash."

"Prisco has never been in the hitman business that we know of. It is possible they did it on their own. Vicente was often a loose cannon and one who could rival Miguel. They clashed constantly. One of the reasons why he left actually. It was rumored Miguel let him live on the condition he moved far away. Denver was a good place for him to put down roots."

"Why didn't his cousin go with him?" I asked, then took a couple bites of burger—grease, ketchup and mustard getting on my fingers.

"Not certain. Maybe he wasn't as eager to be the man, like Vicente. Could be he stayed behind in hopes of taking over someday. The inner politics of gangs isn't an exact science. Being a fly on the wall listening in would be helpful but doesn't happen. The few who do get out often don't talk about it. They just want to forget and move on."

I had rarely encountered gangs in my private detective dealings, but they didn't sound much different than any other criminal organization. Conflicts between parties within would arise, with challenges to authority bringing changes in the structure, often violently. I needed to find answers, but treading cautiously was warranted around men like these, or I might end up a casualty.

I had finished my burger and fries, more napkins needed to clean my fingers. I continued to savor my shake, debating on getting one to go. Manny and Gary had finished their lunch and were sipping down their drinks. With the amount of sodium, I was certain all our blood pressures had spiked by a few points. The discussion about gangs might have added more to our hypertension.

"Is there any chance of having a meeting with Miguel?" I asked.

Gary looked shocked by the question. "What reason would you want to meet with him?"

"To pointedly ask him about his involvement with the car bombing." *Maybe I wouldn't tread cautiously!*

"His response would likely be less than cordial."

"I can be tactful when asking. If he isn't involved, but one of his underlings is without his knowing about it, what would his reaction be?"

Zimmer nodded, understanding what I was getting at. "Unpleasant, to put it kindly."

"Unkindly towards me or towards Luciano?"

Gary grinned. "Possibly both."

I thought about it for a minute. It was a risk, but one I felt was worth taking to get a step closer to the killers.

"Is it possible? Just him and me, and no one else. I'll even spring for lunch. I'll buy him a burger here if he wants to drive up. I'm sure gang members swoon over nostalgic places like this one."

Gary finished up his drink, while thinking it over. He went to the fountain machine to get more Coke. All the caffeine and sugar weren't going to help his blood pressure either.

"I'm not certain. Let me make a few calls. Probably take time to arrange."

"Understood. It can be anywhere of his choosing. Just him and me, alone talking. His people can be watching, but from a distance. I will be alone and unarmed."

"Ballsy," said Gary.

"Stupid," added Manny.

I had to smile. "Add a hyphen and you have my middle name!"

Chapter 14

After lunch, Manny and I went to the Oceanside Harbor, where Rocky's body had been found. We took separate vehicles, as he needed to leave to work other cases but he'd driven over to get me into the crime scene. The slip where the boat was tethered was in the North Harbor.

When we arrived, he showed his badge and we walked in, taking me to the location where the boat burned, the remains still floating there. What I saw was a burnt shell and not much else. The fiberglass resin structure was scorched and melted in many places. The heat and smoke must have been intense, and certainly fatal, if the person on the boat was alive when it started.

"It was about a thirty-six-foot boat, with sleeping quarters underneath," declared Manny. "He'd been living there for several months, with a live-aboard permit. The badly burned body was found on the bed. Coroner said he'd been beaten, shot and as I mentioned, all the teeth were missing. The damage was too great to do a DNA test."

"How long before the fire department showed up?" I wondered, shaking the gruesome description of Rocky's death from my brain.

"Not long after the first call went in. We have two coastal fire stations, and they're trained for swift water rescue in these cases. What we don't know is how long it was before the fire was noticed and called in. And there was an accelerant used to intensify the fire. They believe it was kerosene. As you see, it torched the boat thoroughly."

"Security and cameras didn't catch anything?" I asked.

"Camera was disabled, and the guard didn't see anything. The thought was the guard fell asleep, missing what might have happened, the fire starting after midnight."

After making sure I had what I needed, Manny took off, warning me to not get on the boat itself, since it wasn't safe. I took a tour down the slip, finding it scorched on the fringes, as were the boats on either side, each showing the residue of smoke that had poured out.

Walking to the edge of the wooden dock, I could see the outline on the boat where a name had been. I couldn't make it out entirely, several of the letters had burnt off. However, I could see an R, E and what appeared to be a G, but nothing else. The toxic smell still lingered, even though several weeks had passed, the crime scene tape keeping curious people away. I did want to get inside to try and see if I can find any more clues, but figured it wasn't worth the risk. Not that there was much inside for me to see as the intensity of the fire would have done a thorough job destroying evidence.

The waves from the water were calm today, the dock moving only slightly. There were boats in every slip running up and down the harbor. About three slots down I saw a man in beige shorts, a white tank top and a Dodgers baseball cap working on a thirty plus foot long boat. I walked down and waved at him. He stopped what he was doing and walked to the edge of the back end, wiping his hands on a towel.

"What can I help you with?" he asked.

He was a slender man, probably in his fifties with tanned skin, wearing wrap-around sunglasses to filter another sunny spring day.

"Hello. I'm a detective investigating the fire on the boat a couple spaces down, and I wondered if you know the man who owned it?"

He flipped the towel over his shoulder and shrugged. "I wouldn't say I knew him. In passing we said hello a couple of times. Big guy with long blonde hair. Like mine in a ponytail, though mine is going gray. Could have played Thor in the movies, he had the looks and the build."

By the description, it certainly sounded like Rocky. "Did you ever notice a scar on his face?"

"Yes. Below the eye. I don't remember which one."

"Did you ever get a name?"

"I introduced myself once. He said he was Garrett, if I recall correctly. Like I said, we weren't buddies or anything." He leaned down and pulled a beer out of a cooler. "Would you like one?"

"I would but I shouldn't, since I'm working." I had willpower at times. "Did you notice anything suspicious right before the fire?"

He popped the top on the beer and took a drink. "Nothing I heard or saw. The boat was gone though for several days before it returned. I believe it was that night it caught on fire."

"Were you here?"

"I was. I live on my boat, just as he did. I was fast asleep, when

I heard the sirens. I looked outside and saw the smoke. It was horrible." He closed his eyes, his body shaking at what he remembered. "I quickly got dressed and jumped out of the boat and headed for the main building until they got it under control. I was worried the dock would catch on fire and then it could have been much worse. The boat was fully consumed before they started dousing it. I heard later they found Garrett inside, dead. Such a dreadful way to go."

"Anything else you can recall? Stuff that seemed odd or different?" I was fishing for any details which might provide more leads.

He took another drink. His bloodshot eyes showed it probably wasn't his first of the day.

"Nothing odd. This is California and our state motto *is* odd. Just a guy living by himself on his boat, enjoying life. Lots of us around."

I pulled out my card and handed it to him. "Call me if you remember anything else."

"Sure." He looked at the card, reading what it said. "A *private* detective. Isn't that cool. Like *Rockford Files*."

Fortunately, I understood the reference, even though it was from another generation. "Sort of, though I have better knees than James Garner."

He smiled. "Were you a friend of Garrett?"

"Not friends so much, but associates. I owe him to find out who killed him."

"Was he a PI too?"

I almost laughed. "No. But he did live an exciting life, like Rockford, though on a boat instead of a trailer on the beach."

"From what I saw it wasn't that exciting, up until the fire that is."

I thanked him and started to walk away, when he called my name and tossed me a beer.

"One for later when you're off duty," he proclaimed.

I nodded, then thought of one more question. "Do you remember the name on his boat?"

He stopped to think, then answered. "If I remember right it was 'Revenge'."

There was little doubt of the meaning. "Did you ever ask him about the name?"

"No it never came up the couple times we talked. Many of the boats' names around here are interesting. Mine is kind of boring, compared to others I see. I thought the moniker was cool and sounded tough. Lot of good it did him."

I said thanks, not asking him what his name was and moved on. The boat name did sound tough, not unlike the man who lived there. Whether the name grew out his family's death, I probably would never find out.

I found two other people to talk with, but they didn't have much to add. I went into the Oceanside Harbor office and asked around with those that worked there, but they wouldn't say anything. They were under orders not to talk about the incident, as they called it. Nothing nefarious it would seem, just a business covering their ass in case someone claims they were at fault. I walked out to my car, debating on dinner choices as I drove away, the day winding down.

There was a nagging feeling that wouldn't go away that someone was following me. I had noticed it for short time when I left the Pit Stop Diner, but then it was gone. It appeared to be a small gray or silver metallic SUV, likely a Ford from the recognizable logo. It was much like lots of other vehicles on the road, leading me not to think much of it earlier. But now I saw it again, having been parked in the same lot as I was, and coincidentally enough, it was now pulling out as I was leaving. Since I-5 wasn't too far away, I decided to jump on and see if they followed to confirm my suspicions.

Several turns and I was on the interstate, which for 4:30 in the afternoon, was surprisingly busy. It took a while to merge on, navigating my way over two lanes, working through the start and stop flow. In a matter of a few minutes my tail was now sitting three cars behind me, though one lane over. I went south for several miles, before moving back over and exiting.

I checked my rear-view mirror. They were still there, a couple cars back. I noticed traffic lights ahead. The light at the exit was green but soon went yellow. Taking the opportunity, I floored it and ran the light, making a sharp left turn and pushed it past another light, before pulling into a parking lot and double parking behind two cars, which blocked me from being seen.

It was a couple minutes later, before the Ford drove past, not spotting me. I waited for about five minutes and got back on the highway, returning to my hotel, the plate number burned into my brain.

While sitting in the parking lot, I called Bill Malone, one of my cop friends in Denver. He'd already left for the day, I cursed, forgetting about the one-hour time difference. I don't think he was thrilled.

"I'm eating dinner," he growled, his normal, gruff demeanor on display.

"Do you miss me?" I said, knowing the answer.

"Not really. You'd be amazed with how much work I get done when you aren't calling me constantly. What do you want?"

"I have a plate I need to get run."

He was agitated. "Like I said, I'm home eating dinner. Rachael is giving me the stink eye for just answering my cell phone."

"Tell Rachael I apologize. Tomorrow will be fine for a name on the plate. They were following me, and I want to know who they are."

"Another in the extensive line of your admirers, I'm sure. Text me the plate and I will get it for you tomorrow, once I get into work."

"You're a doll, Bill. Thanks."

"Sure, sure. Now leave me to my steak"

He hung up the phone sounding angry, though that was normal. Our back and forth with his grumpiness on display was all part of the routine. I knew deep down he cared, even though he wasn't one to show it unless it was for his wife or two kids. Nevertheless, he was a good friend and there when I needed him.

Hungry, I drove to a nearby drive-thru, settling on chicken tenders, fries and tea. Once back in my room, I sat on my bed enjoying the meal with the TV on HBO, playing a movie I'd never heard of and the sound down low.

As I ate, I wondered who it was that had been following me. The vehicle didn't seem of gang-style and was probably too general for someone working for Max. Yet they were the only ones I'd encountered other than the local cops. Part of why I ran the plate through Bill and not Manny. Not that I didn't trust him. It was important to be cautious in unfamiliar territory.

One thing was for certain, *nothing* was for certain in my line of business. And I was willing to bet that whoever was following wasn't watching because they were a fan of my work and wanted an autograph. Try as I might, my fame didn't reach beyond the Colorado Rocky Mountains.

Chapter 15

The next day, I was on my way to Newport Beach, which was about ninety miles north of my hotel. This was the last known location where Emily lived, according to Brandon. Whether she still lived there, he couldn't say. He listed a couple places she frequented, which he'd gotten from her credit card statements that he continued to pay, which was unusual for a woman nearing forty.

The trip was around two hours if traffic didn't get in the way, up I-5 and then onto the Pacific Coast Highway, which, as its name suggested, ran mostly along the Pacific Coast. It was a gorgeous drive when I could stare out the window, watching the water crashing onto the shoreline, which I wasn't able to enjoy often since I needed to keep my eyes on the road with all the motor vehicles taking the trip with me.

Even with the beautiful view, my thought was on Emily and how I'd react upon seeing her. Her twisted appetite for no holds barred sex, and perversion in using her partner against her previous conquests made for a volatile situation. The way she used me and other men had brought a lot of pain for many. Once I'd eventually recognized the horrific mess I'd been in, I'd stopped it, though maybe not completely, or quickly enough.

When she'd returned from a sabbatical where she was supposed to receive therapy for her sexual issues, she explicitly wanted me to take her again, with the plan to shoot me afterwards. When I refused, she shot me anyway, though not fatally, since she had made a deal with Brandon to only injure me. A fact he would hold over me to this day. The bullet wound hurt like hell, and my weakness to be easily seduced became all too real.

I had improved myself immensely since then, but her power over me was strong. I kept telling myself it was only a job and nothing more. My job was to find her; that was it. Any sight of her seductive ways and I planned on walking away. The question was would I be strong enough to do so?

Newport Beach was a little smaller than Oceanside, but much like it in many ways. It was built along the shoreline of the Pacific, and had its own harbor and bay, much of it manmade, though it cut much further inland, with several islands of varying sizes.

The town boasted of mild weather, fishing, swimming, surfing, boating and a range of nearly every aquatic sport you could think of. Traits most of the other towns up and down the southern coast claimed. Paradise is what the chamber of commerce called the town, though I'm sure there were pockets in this expensive city that were far from it.

The information I was given showed Emily lived in the Villa Point condos, just off the Pacific Coast Highway midway into town. As I turned off the roadway, I took a left onto Back Bay Drive, the main road that served as an entrance. There were two security gates, and green, wrought iron fencing to keep out the unwanted. There was a silver box on a post for swiping a key card, or calling to be let in. On the display screen, I could find the name of the owner. Emily was listed, and I punched the call button, but no one answered. I didn't think it would be that easy.

There were two gates, the one on the left the direction I needed to go. By chance, someone was coming out, the gate slowly opening. I took the opportunity and pulled through, waving at the person driving by as if I belonged and drove in. I went down the road until I found her place and pulled into one of the parking spots. The buildings were two stories high, of sandstone walls and Spanish clay terracotta shingles. Her condo was on the first floor, where I found and rang the doorbell.

When no one answered there either, I checked the window, to see if I could see anything, but the curtains were closed. Listening to the walls, I heard no noise inside. Going back to the door, I tried the knob, but it was locked, with a solid looking deadbolt. Picking it was an option, but my tools were in Denver. I decided to try other doors in the complex.

On the second try, I got a woman to answer.

"Can I help you?" she said, answering in shorts and a tank top which she filled out nicely.

"I was supposed to meet one of your neighbors here today," I said with my million-dollar smile. "When I ring her bell, she isn't answering. I was wondering if you knew her? Her name is Emily White and lives in this same building."

Her face revealed a disdain for the name. "Yeah, I know her. Don't know if she is home or not. I don't keep track of her."

"Any ideas of her schedule?" I continued smiling in an attempt to wear her down.

Her tone was short. “Honestly, I could care less about when and if she gets home at all.” She was attractive, with black hair down her back, nice tan and hazel eyes, though her pretty face was distorted by her obvious scorn of Emily.

“Seems like you don’t like her,” I noted with a frown.

“She is quite forward with the men around her. A flirt who is always coming onto anyone with a penis. Hits on my husband all the time. I dislike the bitch immensely.”

It was nice to see another person having distain for Emily and how she acts around men.

“Any clues on where she might be?”

She shrugged. “Like I said, I don’t keep track of her comings and goings. I’m only concerned when she is here and ogling my husband. If I recall, she is a consultant. Probably uses that body of hers to bring in business.”

I smiled. “Thanks for the info. And if it’s any consolation, you’re dead right about what she’s like. Don’t allow your husband to fall into her clutches, for it won’t end well.”

I don’t think I made her feel any better as she slammed the door, and I was left to move onto the second floor, where no one was answering, though once I thought I saw a curtain move. It would seem I’d have two options. Wait here for her to come home, or to try the other locations she frequented that Brandon told me about. I decided to wait for now, hoping she was just out and would return soon.

I pulled out my phone and called back home to check on things. My first call was to April, but got her voicemail, leading me to believe she was probably working. I couldn’t remember her schedule.

My next one was to my landlady, Kate, to see if she had gotten my sign fixed.

“Hello Jarvis,” she said. “Are you still in sunny California?”

“I am. I wanted to see about the sign and if they got it cleaned up.”

“They did, though it wasn’t cheap. I will add it to your rent next month, assuming you can pay.”

I chuckled. “When was the last time I was late paying?”

She groaned. “Been a while. But you never pay early. I’m often left wondering."

"No need to worry. I've been working steady, though this job isn't paying much more than expenses."

"Which reminds me, a slickly dressed man stopped in asking about you. I told him you were out of town working. Looked familiar, though I couldn't place who it was."

"Describe him."

She did, and once she finished, I knew exactly who it was. And knowing his personality, I doubted he stopped to have a friendly conversation.

"Perry Hester. You know him from TV and his commercials for his car dealership. He is the jerk I was following for Barry that had been cheating on his wife. Not father of the year material."

"Yeah, now that you mention it, that *is* who it was. Asked if I heard from you, to have you call him. He left me his number."

"Give it to me. I'll decide if I want to talk with him or not."

I took down the number and filed it away in my phone contacts. I'd wait for now for I wasn't anxious to speak with him.

A little while after I'd said goodbye to Kate, Bill called.

"Sorry it took me a little longer, but I ran that plate. It's a rental. Nothing to tell you other than the rental company's name, 'Budget.'"

I wasn't thrilled, as I was hoping for an owner's name.

"No way to get who is currently leasing it?"

"No way. I don't have that kind of power. The people have a right to some privacy. Maybe you can check with one of your FBI buddies. They don't care about people's privacy at all."

I couldn't argue. I would travel down that road if the tail continued. There had been no sign of them this morning when I left. My assumption was they had picked me up at the Oceanside Police Headquarters and for now, didn't know where I was staying. And my plan was to keep it that way.

Since there was no sign of Emily, I called to talk with Brandon.

"Any chance you can see if Emily has had any charges today on her credit card?"

"Sue would have to find that for you. Give her a call and tell her I said it was OK." Sue was quite efficient, pretty and I was certain, didn't like me at all. But she would do anything for her boss.

After he gave me the number, I called.

"What are you wearing?" I said, liking to tease her.

"Nothing designed to attract your attention," she answered bluntly. "What do you want?"

"I need to know if Emily has charged anything today on her credit card. Brandon said to tell you to look it up for me." I liked pushing her buttons but I knew when to stop.

"Hold on." She sounded aggravated, but that wasn't unusual.

"Looks like she is shopping judging from a couple of clothing stores and we've just had a charge at Nordstrom's. Here is the address."

I quickly jotted down the location on my phone, while putting her on speaker. With the wonder of Google Maps, I'd know where she was. I hoped it wasn't too far away.

"Thank you. How is your lady friend?"

"Hotter than the fourth of July!" she answered.

"Good to hear. Nothing better than passion to keep the heart pumping. I'm glad you're with someone that makes your life complete."

"Thank you. Can I get back to work now or do you want the seedy details of our nights together?"

I laughed. "Maybe another time when I need a little pick-me-up. Thanks again, Sue."

After hanging up, I found Emily was nearby, at Newport Center, which was just on the other side of the Newport Beach Country Club her complex was next to.

I pulled on out and found the shopping and business complex easily enough. Tracking took me straight to where Nordstrom's was, the building huge, at two stories high, the structure taking up several blocks. It would be a challenge to find her in there, but I'd do my best.

Walking in through the main entrance of tall curved glass, I quickly found someone to ask where the women's clothing section was. She pointed me in the right direction and I headed that way, past all the perfume which made my nose itch. Finding the women's section wasn't difficult, because it was huge, with racks upon racks of dresses, slacks, blouses, both for casual and business, covering all styles and colors you could imagine. And at prices which would quickly eat up your credit limit.

I was scanning for faces hoping to see her. It had been a few years, but she couldn't have changed too much, unless she had colored her hair. I looked around, when I saw a flash of a familiar body in the distance, heading for the exit. Being far enough back to lose her, I started running, trying to close the distance.

Then, before I had time to react, she looked over her shoulder and saw me, then ran herself. She was in tennis shoes, and moved well, always one to be in shape. She made it to the exit, as I got caught up in foot-traffic and fell behind, cursing to myself for I was afraid I'd lose her.

After shoving my way through the crowd, a few curse words thrown my way, I finally made it outside. I stood, panting, looking forward, left and right, but not seeing her. There were bushes and palm trees on both sides, with an eating area, complete with tables and umbrellas. There were a couple people there, but they weren't her.

Disappointed that I had been so close, I headed for the parking lot, scanning for any sign of her. As I passed a couple of cars, I heard a noise behind me and suddenly she was there, holding a gun to my head, the barrel pressing into my skull.

"Don't move or I'll shoot you!" she said forcefully. "Tell me why you're following me, or I'll blow your head off!"

She didn't have to tell me twice, I knew she was capable.

Chapter 16

The tension in the air was thick. My heart was pounding, and I was certain I could hear her breathing heavily over my own. There was no way to know if she knew it was me or not. If she did know, maybe she was mad about me being there and wanted to shoot me again. Or she might be acting cautious, knowing someone might be after her because of her stepfather. All I could do right now was remain motionless and talk my way out of the situation.

"Not happy to see me?" I said, staring straight ahead, keeping still.

"No, I'm not happy. Tell me what you want." The gun pressed harder.

"Brandon sent me to check on you, to make sure you were safe."

She sighed impatiently. "Sending one of his lackeys after me. Why can't he take the hint to leave me be?"

"Hardly a lackey. But I think he is in trouble and he believes someone could come after you to get to him. Can we put the gun down and talk about this? Someone is going to call the police and then you'll have to explain why you have a gun pointed at me." I reasoned.

"If you aren't one of his henchmen, who are you?"

I now knew she didn't know who it was. It might not help and could only speed up her desire to shoot. But I had to tell her.

"It's Jarvis, Emily. I'm only here to check on you."

"You've got to be fucking kidding me!" she yelled with venom in her tone.

"Nope. Can you please put down the gun and let me turn around?"

She let out a breath of air, and I could sense her arms lowering, the gun finally leaving the back of my head. I exhaled in relief before I turned around slowly to see her.

She, like always, looked fantastic. Tanner than when I last saw her, maybe a few pounds heavier, but nearly all of it firm. She was in tan capris, with long-sleeved mauve t-shirt, both revealing her hourglass figure. Her hair was just past her shoulder, a little blonder than before, with streaks of brown. Her large round sunglasses concealed her eyes, which I recalled were a deep blue.

She tucked away the snub-nosed .38 into her baggy purse, which was looped over her left shoulder. Her expression wasn't of anger but she certainly didn't seem thrilled to see me either. She looked me up and down, before finally smiling. I felt relieved that she might not shoot me, but apprehensive at the smile. I always had to be cautious with her, never knowing for certain what she might try.

"You look good, Jarvis," she said, her voice calm.

"Thank you. You look as you always did, fabulous. Which I'm saying with an air of caution."

"Why? Because of our past? Oh, you're such a wuss sometimes. Honestly you have nothing to fear from me."

"Says the woman who just had a gun pointed me. I believe the last time that happened you shot me in the ass."

She laughed. "True, but I could have shot you in an area much worse. I'm sure the scar on your butt is cute and only adds to the charm of it."

I needed to be careful. Her flirtatious ways continued to be a weapon in her arsenal.

"Can we go somewhere and talk?" I said, staying out of the discussion about my rear quarters.

"We could get a drink and food to eat. Plenty around here to choose from."

"You live here. Lead the way."

She took off walking, while I followed a step behind. We went around Nordstrom's, past their loading dock, onto a sidewalk until we came to the Cheesecake Factory. She opened the door for me and I walked in. In all my life I'd never had been to one before. I was surprised when we got our booth and looked at the menu, finding it was a full-fledged restaurant. I'd always assumed they only served cheesecake, or mostly dessert. Their choices were quite diverse including alcohol.

A twenty-something waitress arrived decked out in white dress shirt, black tie, slacks and apron. Her smile led me to believe she loved her job, which was surprising working for less than minimum wage and tips. For drinks, Emily wanted a Strawberry Daiquiri, while I decided on a Tropical Smoothie.

"No beer today?" asked Emily.

"I'll pass, it's a long way back." I hid mostly behind the menu, as if it would protect me from her. I needed to remain lucid and alcohol wouldn't help me in that area.

"You drove from Denver?"

"San Diego."

"Are you living in California?" Her eyes flashed, curious of the possibility.

"I'm working on another case, for Brandon. A former associate who was killed recently." I was certain she knew who Rocky was, but I decided not to say the name.

She looked thoughtful. "It would seem Stepdad has issues these days. Keeps leaving me messages warning me to keep alert to possible danger. That is why I have the gun on me."

"I don't believe the former associate who was killed is related to his troubles, whatever they may be."

"He hasn't told you about what is going on?" Emily said, her eyes curious again.

I shook my head. "Not in any detail. Do you know what he is up against?"

"Not a clue. We haven't talked much over the last couple of years. I've been trying to make my own life."

"Yet he pays your credit card bills?"

She frowned. "Ouch, Jarvis. Are you taking a shot? I'm guessing that is how you tracked me down. Sue logged in, saw I was shopping here and told you."

It *was* a shot, one I didn't mind taking. Still I only shrugged, stopping to drink my smoothie which arrived in a big glass and colorful straw. It was cold and fruity, tasty and filling. All you hoped for in that type of drink, though I couldn't live on it.

The waitress smiled, asking if we were ready to order. I decided on a Renee's Special, which was a turkey sandwich and cup of soup. Emily chose the Chinese chicken salad. The waitress grabbed my shield and walked away, leaving me eye to eye, and exposed with Emily.

"Sue was doing as Brandon asked," I noted. "What she is paid for."

"She will do anything for Daddy. When he barks, she jumps."

I frowned. "My experience with her says otherwise. It's her job and she does it to the best of her abilities, but she is a strong lady.

She certainly doesn't take any shit from me."

"Sounds like you have the hots for her," declared Emily after taking a drink of her Daiquiri.

"Can't a man compliment a woman without wanting to sleep with her?"

Emily flashed a wicked grin. "Not been my experience."

"You aren't the best expert at relationships."

"Sure I am. I know exactly what men want, and I use that power over them to get what I want."

I shook my head, though I wasn't surprised to hear her say it. It would appear she was the same old Emily from the past, manipulating men to satisfy her end game. I needed to make sure I didn't lapse into my old habits.

"You haven't changed, have you, Emily?"

"I have, to a degree. I don't go around getting men to fight over me. But when I have a need, I use this body of mine however I can. They all think with their dicks, which have a blazing fast gigabit channel straight to their brains. Men like to rule over women, even to the point of abusing them. But we can get back at them and in the end, rule them."

I shook my head in disgust. "It would seem therapy didn't break down that mistrust you have. Not all men are like that."

She laughed. "You're right, they aren't all like that. Most of the ones that aren't are gay. I can manipulate any straight male out there."

Lunch arrived, and my sandwich was tasty, the soup nice and hot. Too bad the quality of the company wasn't up to the food. Though she may have been right about what she said. It had been true with me, using my weakness against me, though in the end I did the right thing. And now I knew I couldn't be drawn into her world and be toyed with.

"I can tell you don't agree," she said, after taking several bites of her salad. "You were able to resist me the last time we were together, though barely. I could feel you crumbling before it became clear I'd have to shoot you instead of fuck you. Likely because of your pretty girlfriend. How is Melissa?"

"She is great. Though she isn't my girlfriend anymore, but we remain close."

Emily's eyes lit up. "How advanced you've become. Keeping

her as a friend. What happened? Couldn't keep it in your pants?"

I didn't answer, but she could see it on my face.

She snickered. "Yep, as I suspected. Weak to those male urges to stick it in as many places as possible. And you couldn't blame me this time. Hopefully you didn't have to shoot the woman who seduced you."

I was getting tired of the act. I stood up and started to leave.

"Oh come now. Did I hurt your feelings?" she said, grabbing my arm.

Grabbing her hand, I squeezed it enough, so she could feel it, and let go.

"I have better things to do than listen to your shit," I proclaimed. "I came, at Brandon's request, to check on you. Not sure why he would even care what happens to you. It must only have to do with the promise he made your mother before she died. You certainly aren't worth the effort to try and save."

I walked out the door, leaving her to fend with the check, which would be paid in the end by Brandon.

As I got back to the front of Nordstrom, I heard someone running up behind me. It was Emily moving quickly, and boy was she fast in her tennis shoes. I stopped and turned to face her.

"I hope you didn't stiff them on the check," I said.

"No. I left them the credit card and said I'd be right back."

"Why did you chase me down?"

"Because, even with all the crap I gave you, I like you, Jarvis. Believe it or not, you're one tough S.O.B. someone who can stand up to me. That *is* quite attractive."

"Sorry. Not interested."

She pouted. "Are you saying you don't want to come back to my place and make sure it's safe for me?"

"I've already been there, and it looked safe enough."

"You know where I live? Great. Please stop by anytime." She pulled a card out of her purse and handed to me. "There is a special number on there, where you can get a hold of me. If you need to let off a bit of steam, give me a call. I can blow that steam right out of your system."

There was the girl I remembered. That wicked look on her face, the one that most men would drop everything in their lives to get a taste of. I was no longer one of them.

"Not in a million years," I asserted, while tearing up her card and throwing the pieces at her.

I thought I heard a big, mournful sigh, as I walked to my car and drove away, back to San Diego.

Chapter 17

I decided to take a me day and worked out, trying to sweat out the experience of seeing Emily again. My time with her was everything I had expected…worse in fact. It had dredged up old, painful memories that were unpleasant to relive. *Why I'd agreed to check on her, was the big question.* I knew it wouldn't end well and she, as was shown, could handle herself with the gun she was carrying. My being there had revealed the sexual temptress in her, which always slithered out when I was around. I should have said no to Brandon, but instead had paid for it with a restless night of sleep.

To begin the cleansing, I took a long swim in the hotel pool, then drove down to where I'd first met Manny and jogged along the ocean as far as I could. Because there was more oxygen at sea level than at Denver's altitude, I felt like I could run forever.

When I was finally gassed and had run as far as I could in one direction, I turned around and walked back, enjoying the seventy-degree weather. The rest of the day was spent resting in the hotel hot tub, making small talk with a few people who were staying there, then going up to my room and taking a long nap, having flushed from my pores the poison that was Emily White.

Once I was relaxed enough, I started making calls. The first one was to Brandon. My report on finding Emily wasn't going to please him.

"I sure hope her mother wasn't half as crazy as she is," I noted. "This game she likes to play is insane. I'm amazed someone hasn't killed her, or at the very least beat the crap out of her."

"She is a complicated woman," countered Brandon. "As was her mother, whom I loved dearly. Until she found me, she had little structure in her life. I believe Emily will require the same to find the proper balance."

"It will take a saint to put up with her."

"Agreed. But for now, you say she is safe? You mentioned she was carrying a gun."

"Yes. She even pulled it on me. Brought back several bad memories."

Brandon chuckled. "I'm sure it did. I know she is skilled with it and won't hesitate to use the weapon if necessary. If things escalate here, I may ask you to get her and bring her back to Denver."

I wasn't thrilled to hear this. "Are you going to tell me what is going on?"

"Best you don't know. All I will say is that there is a dangerous foe I'm facing. Nothing critical has happened yet, but there is talk in the wind it's coming. I must be ready. And I don't need them to use her against me."

"Not sure why you care about her," I said dryly. "Not sure she is worth saving."

"A promise I made, which I keep. If anything, I'm a man of my word."

There were a lot of things about Brandon I didn't know. But he was correct, his word was solid. When he said he'd be there to help me with my brother's situation, he flew out right away, providing additional support, which he didn't need to do, against a strong criminal eliminate. It was a debt I'd never paid off, though this situation and the one with Rocky would be close to squaring things.

"If you need me to bring her back, let me know," I declared, regretting it the moment the words were spoken. "I will drive down and get her. Though I might have to drag her by the hair to get her to come."

"She might like that," asserted Brandon with a laugh, before hanging up.

Even though I was in a calmer mood, I decided to call Perry Hester. He'd left his number with Kate, asking me to call. It was hard to say what he wanted, but at least I wouldn't have to stand up to his machismo in person. His assistant, likely the redhead he'd been fooling around with, answered. It was a good ten minutes before he came on the line.

"Thanks for calling, Jarvis," he said. "I'm sorry about that stunt I pulled in the bar last week. You were only doing your job. I wanted to talk with you to see what options I have."

"Not sure what you mean, Perry."

"You know…see if we can work out an arrangement to take care of the situation."

"You're going to have to give me more than that."

He sighed into the phone. I was baiting him, knowing what he was getting at, but I wanted to make sure he said it plain as day. I wanted no confusion on what he is offering.

"My lawyer says to offer you money to make this all go away. All in cash with no way to trace it back to me. Money for your lawyer as well, to drop all of this and make the evidence disappear."

"How much are you offering?"

"How does fifty thousand sound?"

I should have laughed. He was worth way more than that, his wife likely coming away with several million in the divorce from his car business.

"You've got to be kidding," I said spitefully.

"Not at all. It's money free and clear. No taxes to pay Uncle Sam, to do with as you please."

"Perry, do you know how much your wife will get in the divorce? It will be a much larger number than that. If you want to make a deal, you need to work with her lawyer and add a whole lot more zeros."

There was complete silence, as if he had muted the phone. I sat and waited. I'm sure he was thinking about sweetening the deal.

"Fifty thousand for each of you. That's my final offer."

Now I was laughing.

"You find my offer funny?" he grumbled, his tone becoming agitated.

"Perry, tell me the name of your lawyer."

"Why?"

"You need to fire him because he is giving you lousy advice. With this little bribe, I will call your wife's lawyer and her price tag will now increase."

"Why you mother fuc…" I hung up the phone on him before I heard the entire rant. I then called my own lawyer, Barry.

"Guess who I just heard from," I stated. "Perry Hester. He offered me a bribe."

"Really. How much?"

"Fifty thousand first, for us to split and then fifty each when I said no. All in cash, tax free."

He gave a hearty laugh. "Does he not realize with the evidence we have we'll make significantly more?"

"Apparently not. Said he was told to extend an offer to make it all go away."

"Where did that come from?"

"He says his lawyer."

Barry snorted. "His lawyer is a shyster. When I heard he hired him, I knew this case would be easy. He doesn't know how to litigate. And now we have a case to squeeze him for more. I could get him disbarred for suggesting that to his client. We're going to clean up, Jarvis."

"We'll see. If he is that desperate let's hope he doesn't do anything stupid."

"Marilynn knows not to talk with him and to stay home as much as possible. If you think I need to have a bodyguard watching her, I can hire someone. A little extra overhead isn't going to affect the profit margin on this one. We will own his dealerships before it's all over."

"I'd have someone on standby just in case. Not sure who to hire, since the best man is in California right now."

"When you see him, tell him to come back home," joked Barry. "And don't tell me you were looking in the mirror when you talked with him."

I smiled. "April would be a good option, if she can get out of work. I'd love to see her drop Perry onto his keister. I'll be calling her shortly. I'll talk with her and see if she is up for the job."

"If she is interested, have her call me. How is California?"

"Warm and sunny. Lots of tanned bodies, many of which are nice to look at. And no one has tried to kill me—yet!"

"My odds are on that changing, since I know you've been stirring the pot like always. Try not to cause an earthquake."

Once done with Barry, I called April. We had been texting back and forth today once her shift had ended. She answered on the second ring and I immediately asked her about her work day.

"Typical day," she answered. "Lots of paperwork and a couple of domestic calls, which are always a joy. And one shoplifter who tried to run away that I had to chase down. He couldn't even get a block before his asthma kicked in, the idiot."

"May have a bodyguard job for you," I proclaimed. "Working for Barry watching the wife of that mini-celebrity, Perry Hester."

"The cheating husband? Why does she need protection?" she

asked with a surprised tone.

"Not sure yet if she does. But the husband tried to buy me off. Figure he's getting desperate and could take it to the next level."

"How much did he offer?"

I told her the amount.

"Oh my. A lot of money to turn down."

"We'll all get more in the end. His business is worth many millions. With this, Barry figures she'll take him for most of it."

"I can probably take time away. Will she be any more fun than the last lady I watched over?"

She was talking about a school professor during The Butcher case. They had been on opposite sides of the political spectrum, which made for less than pleasurable conversation between them.

"Not certain, though she does like to drink, which could be fun under the right circumstances."

"Not while watching over her. But if Barry pays enough, it could get me more money for my bike."

"They aren't coming down on the price?" I queried.

April sighed. "Not yet. But I'm holding out. Time will tell."

"Call Barry and let him know your availability. Pay should be good and easy money, if Perry doesn't make a run at you."

"I'm sure I can handle him."

There was no doubt in my mind she could. She had taken care of a Russian Mobster with no problem and then survived a serious bullet wound from the same man before killing him. Provided Perry didn't hire serious muscle, she'd be fine.

"How are things going in California?" asked April.

"Fine. I had to take a trip up to Orange County and visit a former client…" I told her of my encounter with Emily and all her thoughts and opinions of men.

"She's probably not too far off, with most men," noted April. "But I know you well enough now to know you won't fall for her crap anymore."

I hoped she was right about that, but happy she had confidence in my fidelity. Her trust in me meant a great deal.

"She certainly tried. I walked away, but Brandon says I may need to drag her back to Denver. Not sure I can survive a plane ride with her."

"I can always come out and kick her ass. Maybe that will

straighten her out. If it comes to the point Brandon wants her back, I can always show up and fly her back. I should be mostly safe with her."

I laughed. "One never knows. She uses everyone, if it means she gains what she wants. But if it comes to that, I may take you up on the offer. On one condition?"

"And what would that be?"

"You spend a day with me first. The bed in my hotel room sucks, but it would be a whole lot better with you in it."

"I suppose you'd want me in bed minus clothing," April said with thrill in her voice.

"You can wear a garter belt and stockings, if the mood strikes you."

"It often does, so long as you're only wearing socks."

I laughed and started a round of X-rated dialogue, which April enjoyed—she could be quite explicit—to stoke the fires for a future visit.

Chapter 18

I was sitting in the shade on a green park bench in Gershwin Park, waiting for a meeting with Miguel Prisco. The park had a nice open grassy area, with one tennis court, one basketball court, and a playground with jungle gym, slide and swings, all on a nice soft white sandy surface, likely trucked straight from the beach. The ideal place for children to enjoy themselves, sans the water.

It was just before 9 a.m. Sunday morning. There was no activity yet, which was both good and bad. Good that no one would be around if things go south, but no witnesses either, if they decided to kill me.

I had come unarmed, per the deal Gary Zimmer had made, dressed in jeans and a plain white t-shirt I'd bought at the store, the packaging creases still showing in the material. The meeting had been arranged with certain conditions, which is why I was dressed the way I was.

On edge, heart racing, perspiration testing deodorant, hands lightly tapping the table top, I sat and waited, sensing eyes upon me, from a distance. After about fifteen minutes Miguel walked up from a midnight black SUV, which had pulled up on the street and stood next to the table. One of his men walked up with him.

I stood up, and he searched me. I lifted my shirt, revealing I wasn't wired with any listening devices. After thoroughly checking me, he was satisfied and walked back to the SUV, leaning against it with his arms crossed, scanning the area. Miguel and I both sat down, facing each other. I did my best to remain calm, for it wasn't every day I would meet face to face with such a dangerous man.

"It would appear you're being followed," Miguel noted, his eyes hidden behind expensive sunglasses.

I was impressed he'd noticed, though not surprised, as I figured he would have others in the area watching well before I arrived. My tail had returned, though in a different car. They must have changed up after I'd lost them, thinking they'd been made. I wasn't thrilled they were out there but didn't want to miss out on this meeting, for it could be important in finding Rocky's killer.

"Yes, I'm being followed, though I'm not certain who it is. The car is a rental. I have yet to approach him."

"They're not with you?" questioned Miguel, a tinge of disbelief in his voice.

I needed to gain his trust, wanting to be firm and clear, so there was no confusion.

"Absolutely not. Though the tail may be related to what I wanted to address with you. No other reason I'm aware of why someone would be following me."

"Should I have them taken care of?" voiced Miguel strongly, knowing full well this was his domain to control.

"Thank you for the offer. I will handle them myself, when I'm ready."

"Very well. You had questions you wanted to ask me," stated Miguel, getting to the point.

"First, I wanted to apologize for us coming into your territory unannounced. It was unintentional." He nodded, as if to accept what I said. It was always best to be gracious when dealing with bad men. "I appreciate you taking the time to meet with me."

"I understand you aren't a cop."

"No, I'm a private investigator working for a client."

He nodded. "Please ask your questions and I'll decide if I will answer."

I took a quick glance around. The park remained empty. Playground, tennis and basketball courts were vacant. I suspected Miguel had a hand in this.

"A murder we're investigating led us to the man we were following. Not sure if he is one of yours or not. Eugene Washburn is his name."

"Not one of my men, but someone who aspires to be one of us," replied Miguel with no emotion. "What is his connection to the murder?"

"Worked on the car that killed a wife and three-year-old boy."

"If I remember correctly, Eugene is a mechanic and works on cars for living. He has serviced our vehicles as well. Nothing unusual about him fixing a car."

"He worked on the car and a couple days later it blew up from a car bomb. From that day forward, he didn't come to work at the shop where the service was performed."

Miguel shrugged. "Could be a coincidence. You've not provided significant evidence to me."

Now I needed to tread lightly with how I said things. Accusing a man who had worked within Miguel's ranks could end badly for me, if they had remained allies.

"You know of a man named Vicente Duarte?" I asked.

He leaned back, nodding his head. It was hard to tell his reaction with the sunglasses on, but he seemed unmoved by the name.

"My understanding is, he used to work for you and moved onto Denver to start his own organization."

"That would be correct."

"Would you say his leaving was a mutual decision?"

He thought about it for a minute before answering. "It was in the best interests of all parties that he moved on."

This made me believe the split wasn't amiable, but I figured it was best not to press for more details.

"You heard of his death last year?"

"I did." The tenor in his voice showed no emotion.

"Do you have any feelings on his death?"

"No more than anyone else dying. Why?"

"What if I were to tell you now about his death and the person who killed him?"

"For me it is of no consequence. But there is someone within my organization who wouldn't be pleased to learn this."

It wasn't hard to do the math. "His cousin, Luciano Duarte."

He nodded. Now the tricky part and the one that could solicit a response I might not care for.

"Before Vicente died, he told the party who killed him that he was hired to kill that party, his wife and son."

"Hired by who?"

"Someone inside Maximillian Conway's organization."

His mouth twitched. He knew the name, though if he had any connection to him, I doubt he would say so.

"Where are you headed with all of this?" said Miguel, this time removing his sunglasses, his dark brown eyes in full view. They were intimidating to stare into, a leer of confidence and danger, not a minute trace of fear showing, which might be why he was revealing them.

"It is simple math," I responded, with no fear of my own. "One plus one plus one equals a conclusion. A person in Conway's organization contacts someone, namely Vicente, to do a job. He no longer lives in California, but is always looking for ways to make money, and contacts his cousin, Luciano about a way to make a load of cash. Knowing you wouldn't be happy doing outside work, he doesn't tell you. The two of them work on how to do this. Luciano knows a mechanic with the skills to place explosives in a car. How they get the car into the shop to work on is hard to say. Many ways to tamper with a car to prevent it from starting. It comes in for him to work on, he installs a technical device where it won't explode until the proper moment. Kills the family and they all get paid."

Miguel was listening intently, I seemed to have his attention.

"Kaleb Leigh, who is the co-owner of the auto shop and who hired Eugene, finds out, threatens to talk with the police, or maybe he wants a cut of the money, and is killed in a hit and run to silence him. Late at night, no witnesses, and the stolen car is torched to hide the evidence. Or maybe the owner was in on it at the beginning and got greedy. That part still wasn't clear."

"A theory but sounds like no proof," replied Miguel dryly.

"I confronted Eugene on this—his face told me all I needed to know. The next day he went running to Luciano. The same day we travelled into your territory. When you approached our car, Eugene whispered into Luciano's ear, telling him I was the guy. His look also revealed the truth. I've little doubt they were involved."

There was a pause as Miguel processed what I said, before he slammed his fist onto the table. I was startled, and nearly jumped up, thinking he was mad at me. But I held my ground, hoping his anger was directed at Luciano.

"I'm not here to make trouble for you," I stated. "I'm trying to find a killer for my client. Mostly I'm after the money man who hired them. In the end, he is who I want the most."

For now, I was holding back the info on Rocky surviving the car bomb and his most recent death on the boat. I had a feeling someone else was responsible for it.

"If Luciano is involved, I will find out," asserted Miguel. "I don't tolerate that type of shit. It only brings heat on us we don't need. Were you involved with Vicente's death?"

"I was there when it happened," I declared, not giving more detail. "Someone else killed him."

"Who was that?"

I paused, thinking it over, before deciding it was time. "The man Vicente was hired to kill."

Miguel looked confused by my answer. It was important to be clear, so he didn't think I was making up the events for my own benefit.

"The man wasn't killed. His wife and son were, though he was badly hurt. With assistance he faked his death and had been, over time, tracking down leads that led him to Vicente. I assisted in taking him for questioning."

Miguel leaned forward, staring at me, in an attempt to read if I was telling the truth. I looked him right in the eye, never once blinking. He nodded his head, as if convinced, before speaking.

"It is of no consequence Vicente is dead. I have no ties to him that would make me care one way or another. Luciano is another story. If he knows you're involved, which as you stated is likely, he will come after you."

"Understood. But I'm not easy to take out. Others have tried, and he will likely lose any battle against me."

Miguel looked at me, contemplating my words. "Are you as tough as you sound?"

"Tough enough. How tough is Luciano?"

He gave me a tight smile. "Not as tough as I am, but he is a mean motherfucker when angry. And he has men who are loyal to him. He won't fight fair."

I smiled, though I wasn't certain why. "Good to know. I will be ready. What happens to Luciano if you find out he is involved?"

"If that is the case, most of his toughness will be beaten out of him and you won't have anything to worry about."

I assumed that meant he would be dead, but I didn't ask him to elaborate.

"Will you share any info you learn from him with me?"

He laughed genuinely then. "Are we best pals now, that we share secrets?"

"I'd be forever in your debt." I grinned, though I wasn't sure it would sway him.

"I doubt you have anything that would be of value to me. But I will consider it."

"What about Eugene?"

“He is yours to do as you please. He is nothing as far as I’m concerned, especially if he was involved. He will have no place in my business. I need men who follow the rules…*my* rules.”

“Fair enough.”

Miguel stood up, putting his sunglasses back on. “Are we done here?”

I stood as well, nodding my head. I thought about putting out my hand, but it didn’t seem we had built that type of bond. We walked back towards his SUV, his man holding open the door. I felt small standing next to Miguel, and plain, compared to his skin dark covered in lots of tattoos, a black do-rag holding his long black hair. Even with the markings you could see scars on his exposed skin. Battle wounds from the kind of life he led, which we had in common in some sense.

“Amazing on a Sunday morning there is no one here at the park?” I noted. “Am I to assume you played a part in this?”

He gave me another tight smile. “Yes. We put out the word for people to stay away. No reason to have children around in case there was trouble.”

“Were you expecting trouble?” Not sure why I asked. Maybe I needed confirmation I was dangerous, from another dangerous man.

“Zimmer vouched for you, but I like to be prepared. If there had been, it would have been over quickly. No reason to have prying eyes and ears nearby.”

I believed that to be true, especially since I wasn’t armed. Fortunately our conversation had gone smoothly.

We reached his SUV and he stopped and turned, pointing at the blue sedan down the street.

“Are you certain you don’t want my man here to approach your tail?”

I thought about it for a moment, thinking over what might happen, and smiled, feeling mischievous.

“It would be interesting to see what they do. Why not.”

Miguel waved at his man, who started towards the car. When he got within ten feet, it quickly pulled a U-turn and drove away. I had the new plate number but suspected it was a rental too.

“Whoever was driving didn’t have the balls to face my man,” proclaimed Miguel dryly.

I looked at his protection, his arms bulging, lots of tattoos and a large gun tucked in the front of his pants.

"It would take large ones to face him," I said with a smile.

"Do *you* possess what it takes?" wondered Miguel with serious look.

"Let's hope we don't have to find out," I said while walking back to my car; no truer words I had spoken.

Chapter 19

The tail had been run off, but I suspected he hadn't gone too far. I'd barely headed out of the neighborhood when I saw him again. The tinted windows made it hard to get an unobstructed view, but it was clearly a man driving. I tapped the call button on the Bluetooth system of my car and dialed Manny. He was off today, but I thought I'd check to see if he was available.

"Are you home?" I asked.

"I was just about to go for a jog. What's up?"

I told him what I had in mind and if he was willing to go along with it. He was onboard, and currently out for a run along the bay where we first met. Driving his direction, I took my time to keep from losing the tail.

As I hit the bridge, I called him again, letting him know I was almost there, and we kept the line open, watching for where he parked.

Once I spotted him, I slowed down and double-parked next to his truck. My tail wasn't sure what to do, as there were no openings along the curb, cars filled all the spaces. He drove on past and that is when Manny and I quickly switched, him in my rental and I in his truck. I'd told him the color and plate of the car and he pulled out quickly to follow it. He caught up to it and was now tailing, with me right behind.

The tail let Manny pass and he took off, back across the bridge, over the elevated portion, then taking a quick exit on a looping road, putting us back into San Diego. He travelled under the bridge into a parking lot, mostly full of cars, at the Mercado G Northgate Market. He found a spot, parking the rental, sitting and waiting. The tail pulled past, taking a spot several cars down. I pulled in right behind him, blocking any route he had to pull out. Jumping out of the truck, I had my gun pulled.

"Show your hands," I said, yelling at the car.

Manny was quickly on the passenger side, his gun in hand.

"I'm with the police," Manny yelled. "Step out now with hands where we can see them."

The window was down, and he put his hands out, showing they were empty. I walked to the door and opened it, stepping back, as he came out. He smiled looking at me, though I wasn't sure why. He didn't look familiar and I had no idea who he was, but we would know shortly. On waving him over, he came to the back side of his car, where Manny spun him around and frisked him.

He was carrying a 9mm handgun in a shoulder holster, which Manny removed, sitting it on the trunk, along with a knife, blackjack and collapsible fighting baton. Whoever he was, he came prepared for trouble. When Manny was done, the man turned around, hands in the air, holding onto his smile.

"Nice switcheroo, Detective Saiz," he said with a little too much joy.

"You know who I am?" asked Manny.

"I know both of you. Can I put my hands down?"

"Not until we have a better idea who you are," stated Manny. "You appear to be armed to the teeth."

"It's legal. I have a license for the gun. The other items are backup."

"Backup for what?" I questioned.

"Part of my profession. May I show you my ID?"

Manny and I nodded, and he slowly reached into this back pocket pulling out a business card, handing it to me. On it said, "Shark Tail Detective Agency", with his name of "Edwin Ware". I showed it to Manny, who read it. It would appear someone had hired him to follow me.

"You're a PI?" Manny asked incredulously.

He nodded.

"I need to see your licenses—drivers, gun and PI."

He pulled out his wallet, opening it and handing it to Manny, who then handed it to me. It had his picture, all the details matching. Weight 190, height 5'11", brown eyes and blonde hair, parted in the middle and slicked back. He was wearing a multi-colored flowered silk shirt under a tan jacket, beige slacks and Nike Air Jordan sneakers. Even in the fresh breeze he smelled of cigarettes and cheap cologne. The question was, why was he following me?

"You've been dogging me for days now," I declared, lowering my gun. "Why?"

"Someone hired me to. Why else." Again, his tone was too joyful, and it aggravated me.

"Who hired you?"

"Come on now, Jarvis, you know the routine being a PI yourself. I can't tell you who. Client confidentiality."

He knew my name as well. I wondered what else he knew.

"Tell me more about me."

"I know many things, though I won't bore you with the details."

"I could beat it out of you," I asserted.

"Jarvis, that wouldn't be a good idea," interjected Manny.

"Probably right, but that was my first thought. How about we go talk with your client?"

"Not going to happen, slick."

"What are you trying to find out I'm doing?"

He motioned with his hands. "Can't tell you that either. Now, can I get my stuff and go?"

"Are you planning on continuing to follow me?"

He smirked. "Probably. You know the business. I have to pay the bills and make my clients happy."

I knew in time I could figure out who hired him. For now, I wasn't making any headway, and we were gathering quite a crowd of people wondering what the hell was going on.

"Fine. Keep following me, but I won't guarantee I won't turn the tables and follow you."

"Is that a challenge?"

"It is. And in time I'll figure out who's hired you and I will confront them as well. Understood?"

He smiled again and shrugged. I don't think he was worried much about me. But I knew I had one option to piss him off. I grabbed his keys which were lying with everything else on the back of his car, looking them over.

"Remember this the next time you decide to tail me."

I took the keys and threw them on top of the roof of another building in the same parking lot above a Sally Beauty Supply sign. This took the aggravating smile off his face.

"You motherfucking idiot!" he yelled.

It was my turn to smile. "Try following me now."

Manny and I exchanged keys and drove off, leaving the angry PI behind.

All the while I knew I had to figure out who hired Shark Tail Detective Agency to shadow me and why. More things to do.

Looks like I was going to be in California for a while. At least I'd get a nice tan out of the trip.

Chapter 20

There were several directions I could go in, as the sun rose on this Monday morning. Figuring out who had hired Edwin Ware was one, while looking more closely at Maximillian Conway was another. But I decided to go after Eugene Washburn while I could, as who knew what he would do if he found out about Miguel confronting Luciano, whenever that happens.

I arrived at 7 a.m. figuring he wouldn't be an early riser. I was sitting outside Eugene's triplex, a couple houses down, a breakfast of a hash brown-scramble in a Styrofoam bowl and orange juice resting next to me. I could see his Camaro sitting on the street behind the rusted-out Lincoln.

Wanting to talk with Eugene, I needed a place to do it without being disturbed. His home wasn't an ideal location because of his mother, and wasted girlfriend, if she'd stayed the night. He had to work somewhere unless he was living off his riches from the bombing, though highly unlikely it would last him this long but then it wasn't like he was living like a king. I'd follow him and find the right opportunity to get him alone.

While I waited, I thought about the detective that had been shadowing me. Manny had checked on the agency but didn't find much. There was a filing for a license, but little else. On searching the internet, we'd found a website with one main page, and a location listing in downtown San Diego and phone number. When I called it yesterday. I got a recording, though it *was* Sunday evening. I planned on trying again later today to see if anyone answered.

The car was again a rental, from the same company. It would have taken time for them to come out with a spare set of keys to get him on the move again. But I was pleased I'd found a way to aggravate him. I expected he'd be back hot on my tail in short order, though to my relief there was no sign of him this morning.

It was after nine when Eugene came outside and hopped in his car. The loud roar shook the streets, walls and windows, certainly not pleasing his neighbors. He zoomed past me and I was tight on his tail. I had changed rental cars in case Eugene remembered it from my first visit, going to a compact Ford sedan, white in color, basic and bland.

He was moving quickly but I was able to keep up as he headed west into Oceanside. Once under I-5, he turned right onto the South Coast Highway, going several blocks before turning left and then quickly right, down an alleyway. I went to the next block and turned right, and into an open parking lot where I could see his car. He had stopped, parking next to a small, single structure.

Getting out of my car, I looped back the way I'd come on foot, around a fitness center and gym, until I saw a small structure sitting on the lot between the fitness center and a used car dealership, that had very few cars on the lot and appeared to be closed.

The structure had an aluminum awning you could drive a car under, with long florescent lights hanging, and a small office area in back. It appeared he'd set up a small shop for himself to work at, a home-made sign saying "*Auto Repair Services Available*" but with no name. There was no car parked there now, and no one else was around. I figured what the hell, and walked over to confront him directly.

He was in the back when I approached, my eyes scanning my surroundings and seeing no back exit, as it was up against a chain link fence. I heard a noise and soon he was wheeling out a large red toolbox on casters. He saw me, and was about to talk, when he recognized my face. Then surprise and a sense of fear appeared on his mug. Reaching for his back pocket, he pulled out a folded knife, opening it to reveal a shiny, silver blade. I waved my finger at him and showed him my gun under my beige jacket.

"What do you want?" he said, gripping the knife, his hand shaking.

"We need to talk." I had my hand on the grip of my .38, ready to pull it, if necessary.

"I've got nothing to say." He finished pushing the toolbox to where he wanted, his eyes watching me, the knife now sitting on top.

"I talked with Miguel," I stated. "He will be confronting Luciano about the job you did on killing that family. He isn't happy about him doing work like that behind his back."

He was leaning against the toolbox, having locked the wheels. It looked like a heavy-duty steel unit, with deep fancy easy gliding drawers.

"I have no idea what you're talking about," he replied, with no expression of concern.

"Nice toolbox you have there. I'm guessing it's full of lots of tools. Couldn't have been cheap. How can you afford it? It doesn't seem you make a lot working here."

He smirked. "I do just fine. Built up a decent clientele."

"Did you buy this place, or do you lease it?"

"Building is owned by the used car store, they didn't need it since their sales are poor. I rent it from them."

"What type of work do you do?"

"You name it, I can do it. I know cars like the back of my hand." He crossed his arms, seeming relaxed and even proud of his ability.

"How to make them run properly, and how to make them not run?" I was fishing for answers.

"Sure. I can do anything, even on these modern cars."

"Even tell it not to start, making the owner think it's the battery. Then wire it where it explodes at the proper time, killing everyone in it."

He laughed. "You think you can fool me into answering that?"

I shrugged. "Worth a shot. I didn't think you were all that smart."

"Smart enough to know when to call for help."

Now I was surprised, and a little anxious. I flicked my eyes around but didn't see anyone.

"Who did you call?"

"You'll find out. Thought you were smart following me. But a neighbor saw you and called me this morning. Remembered you from the other day when you confronted me."

He seemed sincere, which wasn't good as danger could be coming my way. I remained calm, grabbing my cell phone, while watching him and called Manny.

"I may need help," I declared, my eyes scanning for oncoming trouble.

"What's up?"

"Looks like I may have walked into a trap with Eugene and Luciano. Can you send reinforcements, and quickly?" I gave him the approximate address.

“On it.”

Putting the phone in my jacket pocket, I started to back away my gun now out, but Eugene quickly grabbed the knife and made a lunge at me. I pulled the trigger and fired, putting a bullet in his toolbox and he stopped, startled and probably a little pissed I’d put a hole in one of his prized possessions.

“Next one goes in you,” I asserted forcefully. “I’m walking away. Don’t follow me.”

I turned around to cut through the alley to get to my car, but a big black SUV pulled up, blocking my path. I aimed the gun, backing away to where Eugene was. I turned to him and yelled at him to put down the knife or I’d shoot him. He did as he was told, and I got behind him, pushing him forward, shielding me from the men approaching, one of whom was Luciano.

“About time you got here,” grumbled Eugene. “He almost got away.”

“No worries we’ve got him now,” stated Luciano with a strong confident tone.

He stood there with a big 9mm in his hands, held down by his right leg. Two other men stood beside him with similar guns pointed in our direction. I moved up closer to Eugene, putting my gun against his back. He flinched, his body tense. I understood how he felt, for I had only five bullets to work with against guns that likely held fifteen or more rounds.

“Come any closer and I’ll shoot Eugene,” I warned. “Allow me to walk away and we all live another day.”

“What are you carrying?” asked Luciano unconcerned. “A small .38, with six rounds at most. I think you would be crazy to try and take us on. Put down the gun and we can go talk about this.”

“Not a chance,” I answered, trying to keep the nerves out of my voice. “I put it down, I lose my advantage.”

“Fine. Then we will take away your advantage.”

Luciano, with hardly any effort, raised his gun and shot Eugene in the leg, causing him to crumple down, hitting the floor and taking away my shield. I raised my gun with both hands, ready to fire, knowing I had no chance against the three men before me.

“Your mistake was thinking I cared about Eugene; I don’t.”

Luciano stepped forward, aiming for his head. Eugene tried to yell, but the bullet in his skull ended any resistance, blood splattering in all directions. I should have fired but was shocked by what I saw, freezing at the gruesome sight. He walked up and grabbed the gun away from me, never once fearing the fact that I might shoot, knowing it would be suicide for me against the firepower I was facing.

"Now," he said with all the confidence in the world. "Let's go for a ride. It's time we talk about what I'm going to do to you for killing my cousin."

Chapter 21

I was tucked away in the back seat, sitting between two men, both large, strong and heavily armed. There was little doubt I was in a tough spot, one I was cursing myself about for being sloppy in my pursuit of Eugene. I thought of punching my way free, and pushing one of the men out the door, but knew I had no shot, for the backdoors could only be opened from the outside, per what they'd told me. I needed to see where they were taking me, my eyes scanning for any opening to pounce on, nothing currently presenting itself. The tense ride took a while, driving us back to their gang territory in North Clairemont.

We stopped in front of a house two streets over from where Manny and I had followed Eugene a few days before. I was pulled out of the SUV aggressively and led to the backyard which was decent size, with lots of green grass and a couple of palm trees. The wood fencing was six-foot-high, with no visible routes out of the yard, other than the one we came in on, which was guarded. Yelling for help was a possibility, but I doubted anyone next door would come to my rescue. For the moment I was completely on my own, with only my wits and strength to defend myself with. My nerves were on edge, as I readied myself for what was coming.

The two men from the backseat were on either side of me, about five feet away. Luciano walked up, holstering his gun. He pulled on a pair of black leather gloves and, before I had time to react, punched me in the face with a solid left hook that shook me, but I didn't go down.

I tried to swing back, but my arm was grabbed from behind by one of the men, which allowed Luciano to punch me twice on my side and then two more times in the stomach.

The man released me and this time I went down hard, gasping for air. It took a few minutes for me to get my breath back. I looked up, trying to see a way out but wasn't finding one. I was in real trouble and slugging my way out would be challenging, since Luciano wasn't fighting fair.

"You're in *my* hood now," bragged Luciano, pacing back and forth. "I'm going to break you down piece by piece, until you *beg* me to kill you."

"I thought this was Miguel's hood," I grunted, mustering up energy to speak.

"It is, for now." He pounded his right fist into his left palm numerous times, the popping sound muffled.

I took several deep breaths, filling my throbbing lungs. "He was pissed when I talked with him about the work you did behind his back. He plans on having a conversation with you about this, no matter if I live or die."

His eyes glittered. "And what do you think he will do to me?"

"From what it sounded like—kill you. Were you and Vicente planning on taking over his organization?"

Luciano stopped pacing, both fists clenched before him. "Vicente and Miguel were rivals. But Miguel got the drop and was going to kill him. I talked Miguel out of it, saying it would be better if Vicente moved onto somewhere else and built his own organization. Vicente was working on a big score in Denver, right before you murdered him. It would have given us the resources to take Miguel down. But you fucked all that up for us."

Luciano came down with his fist, crashing it into the back of my head with immense force, nearly knocking me out. My eyes blurred and it took several minutes for me to focus, taking blood and grass in my mouth. I pushed up with my arms with all the strength I had, getting upright on my knees. My head swayed as he stepped in again to take another shot, but this time I drove my fist into his groin with everything I had.

To my satisfaction, he stepped back and dropped to his knees. It was a superb shot, but didn't do me anything good. I felt a sickening thud in my back as one of the men behind me hit me solid with a hard object. I was certain a rib or two was broken, and I collapsed out flat on the ground.

"You motherfucker!" yelled Luciano, enraged. "It will get worse for you. We're going to break every bone in your body."

It was no idle threat, I was certain of that. But with my current pain, I wasn't sure how much worse I could feel. I rolled over onto my back to see it was an aluminum bat they had used to hit me with. I wasn't sure I could get up, but I did my best to talk.

"You did that job on killing that poor family," I wheezed, projecting as loud as I could through coughs of pain. "Blew them up in their car. How much did they pay you to kill an innocent man, woman and child?"

"What does it matter now?" declared Luciano, grabbing his groin, but with effort now was standing. "You're going to die. It makes little difference in the grand scheme of things."

"I want to make sure I was right about what happened. One last happy memory before the end," I remarked, playing to his ego, stalling to gather my strength.

He kneeled to look me in the eye. He motioned for the bat, which was handed to him. If he took a swing, I'd be ready, though I didn't have much left to put up a defense.

"Yes, I was involved with killing them. A cool fifty thousand. And I didn't care about a white trash family. I'd kill another in a heartbeat, and probably for less money."

"And what about Miguel and his rules?" I said, grimacing in pain, buying myself time.

"Fuck him. He didn't own me or rule me. You won't be alive to see it, but I will shoot him in the back and become the new king."

"Luciano wants to shoot Miguel in the back," I stated plainly so everyone could hear. "Oh my, Luciano, you're an ambitious one, aren't you."

"Ambitious enough to do what I want, which includes killing you." He took the bat and rubbed it up and down my legs, sending chills of fear down my spine. "Where should I start? I'm thinking the shins would be sheer agony for you."

Gazing at the bat, I knew it didn't matter where he hit me with it, the damage would be great. I'd heard enough, putting my hand into my coat pocket, pulling out my phone, which remained connected to the call I'd made to Manny. I held it up to show him, his face uncertain and confused.

"You may have gotten my gun," I coughed again. "But not my phone. I may die, but all of this was recorded by an Oceanside cop and it will go straight to Miguel. Manny, did you get all of it?"

"We did, Jarvis," replied Manny's serious voice through the speaker. "Hang in there—help is on the way."

More anger seethed into Luciano's eyes. He raised the bat up and was about to crush me with it when a voice yelled, "Stop." It was Miguel, with several men, each with guns pointed. I would have stood up and kissed Miguel, if I could stand, his arrival saving me, for the moment.

"Drop the bat, Luciano, or you'll die," he said coldly. "Same for your two men."

Luciano thought about it, but knew he was outgunned, his third man by the backyard entryway lying on the ground. He tossed the bat to the grass and rose to his feet.

"Miguel, *this* man killed Vicente," he pleaded. "He was family. The murdering scum needs to die."

"Actually, it was someone else who killed him," I noted, still lying on the ground. "I just happened to be there."

"You know I don't care one iota about Vicente," asserted Miguel. "He was always looking to best me. I thought you were better than him. Not as greedy. But it seems I was wrong. Doing a job like killing that family only brings unwanted heat on us."

"No it didn't, Miguel. Not once did a cop come around here looking at us. And the weak link, Eugene, is now dead."

"Did you kill Kaleb as well?" I asked.

"The owner of the car shop? We did. He found out and threatened to turn in Eugene. We killed him to cover our tracks. Like I said no heat on us, Miguel."

"You don't think there is heat!" yelled Miguel, stepping into Luciano, nearly nose to nose. "He has a cop on the phone recording everything you said. Now the gang task unit will be here in full force looking for you. Are you planning on killing everyone that comes your way about this, including me?"

Luciano remained silent, sweat forming on his forehead.

"Answer me, you idiot!" yelled Miguel. "Just know I *heard* you and your plans to shoot me in the back. I should kill you right here."

"We can make this work," begged Luciano, realizing he had no way out. "Let me kill this guy and we can handle whatever else comes our way."

Miguel stepped back, thinking about what to do. He looked over at me, sizing up my situation, before speaking to me.

"Remember our discussion about not having the balls to face my man?" announced Miguel.

I nodded, not sure what he had in mind.

"Big ones are needed, and you said you hoped you didn't have to find out if you had what it took," added Miguel. "We're going to find out now."

“What do you mean?” wondered Luciano, perplexed by the statement.

“You and Jarvis here are going to fight, hand to hand. Last one standing walks away.”

“You’ve got to be kidding?” uttered Luciano.

I had to agree, I was hurting badly. I wasn’t certain how much I could fight.

“Hand to hand. No weapons. Just the two of you. You got a clear advantage, as it looks like you’ve beaten much of the fight out of him. It should be easy for you, Luciano. Once you finish him off, then you and I will talk.”

“Sure, Miguel. I can finish him off.” His voice didn’t sound confident.

“What do you say, Jarvis? Do you have what it takes?”

I closed my eyes, trying to summon whatever strength and courage I had left. My face was bruised and bloody, and I was certain I had a broken rib or two. But I had no choice. I must stand up and go toe to toe with Luciano or die. I rolled back onto my stomach and pushed myself up, standing, though wobbly. I spat the blood out of my mouth. I eased off my jacket, which hurt like hell, and tossed it to the ground.

“Let’s do this,” I said trying to muster up some confidence, both my fists raised.

Luciano looked a little lost. He always had a weapon in his hand it would seem. Gun, bat, even someone to hold his victim while he beat them. He didn’t look like a skilled hand to hand fighter, since he wasn’t sure what to do with his fists. I hoped that would work to my advantage.

He raised them up, mimicking me, and came forward, taking a wild swing, missing badly, as I easily stepped sideways, then backwards, using my footwork to keep moving, even though my ribs hurt like hell with each step, making breathing difficult.

Luciano turned around and took another swing. This time I blocked it, but its ricocheting effects screamed down my arm. I jabbed him in the nose, a short stinging blow, causing his nose to bleed. He wiped at it with his sleeve, the distraction leading me to jab him again, this time harder, and with two snapping punches that jolted his head back, leaving him open for a right cross that dropped him to his knees. I backed off, dancing on my toes, keeping my breathing steady, the pain remaining, but subsiding some, adrenaline being a painkiller.

When one of his men came over to try and grab me, I punched the guy square in the face, but left myself open for Luciano to lunge into me, driving me to the ground, him on top of me. The force of hitting the ground knocked the wind out of me, and brought back all my rib pain, times two. I covered up with my arms as he wailed away at me with his fists.

A few of the blows landed on my head and shoulder, nothing crushing, but the accumulated effect was taking a toll. Then finally, through his swings, I found an opening, punching with a left straight up into his neck and chin, rocking him, his teeth crashing together, likely chipping several. He flipped backward off me, and I kicked out, pushing him away until I was able to stand up, though it took a herculean effort.

I looked over at Miguel, who had a gun pointed at the man who had tried to grab me. At least he was there to keep it a fair fight.

There wasn't much left in me. The pain was immense, I had to be bleeding internally from how I felt. I had to end this now, or I'd drop to the ground from passing out.

I yelled for Luciano to stand, which he did. His mouth was bleeding, his legs shaky, arms sagging. Coming forward, I went to the body, punches to the stomach, ribs and kidneys. I was working on pure adrenaline now, as the pain with each swing was intense.

His arms were completely down, and I went for the kill, right, left, and right again, with all I had, and straight back to the ground Luciano went, out cold. I dropped to my knees once I knew he was done, ready to pass out myself. I felt a hand on my shoulder, and I flinched, thinking I needed to fight more, but I didn't have the strength.

It was Miguel, keeping me from falling completely over.

"I guess we found out you *do* possess what it takes," he said, a slight tone of admiration in his voice.

It was the last thing I remembered hearing for a long time.

Chapter 22

I was sitting on a jet heading back to Denver, people looking at me wondering what had happened. I was black and blue on my face and walking like a seventy-year-old man, thanks to two cracked ribs and a bruised kidney. The job wasn't done but I needed to rest and recuperate, and I wasn't going to do it in a hotel room after spending two days in the hospital.

I wanted my own bed and girlfriend there to support me. I'd felt this way several times before, thanks to pain and injury from the job I'd lived, but this one had me seriously wondering if it was all worth it. I knew I'd feel better in time, but for now I hated everything about what I did, this dangerous life I led.

Even in a place I felt most uncomfortable, flying on a commercial airliner, I did my best to close my eyes and sleep. First class was nice and roomy, and I even had a pretty female in the seat next to me, who would have been nice to talk with. But I needed my rest, leaning the seat back, a cheap pillow behind my neck.

Miguel's men had taken me to a location, where Manny was waiting. I was in and out, my eyes open and closed as I was moved about, the pain intense. He'd taken me straight to the nearest hospital ER, where I was treated. Even in my distaste for hospitals, I didn't complain, for I didn't have the strength. X-rays and CAT scans revealed the injuries, two broken ribs and a whole lot of bruising, but no major organs severely damaged. Pain medicine was administered and ice and wraps to deal with the swelling. I was the most cooperative, docile patient I'd ever been.

Since I'd left the call to Manny open on my cell phone, he'd heard most everything, and even recorded it. He'd gotten hold of Zimmer in the San Diego Gang unit, the one who had arranged the meeting between me and Miguel, who then, through his channels, contacted Miguel. After convincing him about the severity of the situation, they tied him into the call where he heard much of what Luciano had said.

Angry, he'd gone looking for him, arriving on the scene in time to save me from the beating with the bat that likely would have been my undoing. Though I would have been happier if he'd have finished off Luciano himself, he at least gave me a fighting chance against him, and a fair one, keeping Luciano's men from holding me.

There was no word on what happened after I left, for I figured Luciano had been dealt with. Maybe someday we'd know for certain, but I wanted to know the money man who was hired to kill Rocky's family. Those most directly involved were all now dead. Eugene shot in the head, Vicente burned alive and Luciano—well if he wasn't dead by now, he probably wished he was.

After landing, when the cabin doors opened, I slowly rose out of my seat, feeling older than I ever had. I had no carry-on; my injuries didn't allow it. I made the slow walk to the train station, thankful I had a place to sit, standing on the fast-moving train would have been difficult.

Once in the arrivals area, I saw April standing to greet me, her face happy to see me, though not happy to see my condition as worry creased her brow. I leaned into her, her gentle hug feeling good and bad at the same time. We got my luggage and made it outside, where Bill was waiting to drive us home.

Doctors said I'd need four to six weeks to fully recover and they weren't kidding. After two weeks I felt only the smallest bit normal again. Spending nearly all those two weeks icing and sleeping, the third beginning rehab, doing light walking, simple workouts, and time in the sauna and hot tub at the gym. Instructions were given to do deep breathing and coughing every hour to exercise the lungs to prevent pneumonia. I lost weight, since the desire to eat wasn't there, but nothing alarming. A little excess fat shed was healthy.

I felt, for the first time in many years, a depression invading me, with little desire or incentive running through my veins. April and Bill did their best to push me to get up and move, but I wasn't feeling it. My motivation to push on and feel whole again reached a low point. A wave of self-doubt consumed me, the beating leading me to wonder for the first time in my life whether I was cut out for this line of work. I didn't like it but couldn't seem to overcome it.

Even after four weeks, the motivation to rehab wasn't there like in the past. I knew there was a job to complete, but I wasn't feeling the urge to go back and finish it.

As I was coming to the end of week four, my body was physically feeling better, though I couldn't shake out of my funk. I was sitting on the sofa trying to read a book April had purchased for me, my place a bit of a mess, which was unusual because I was neat and organized when it came to my living space.

The title "*Don't Sweat the Small Stuff,*" was intriguing, but I was having a tough time concentrating, though the parts of the book I did comprehend made sense. Not letting those little things bother you, and keeping them in perspective, was good advice. But what I'd experienced wasn't small or minor, and it didn't appear to answer the bigger questions about myself I was facing–the lack of confidence in my skills and the fear of my own mortality. Both were gripping me and wouldn't let go.

I was flipping through the pages absentmindedly when my cell phone rang. When I saw the caller ID, my heart rate increased.

"Hello, Jarvis," said Melissa in a hushed tone. "How are you doing?"

The standard given by most people when asked, was "great" or "good" and maybe even "fine." I, though, wasn't sure how to answer, for I wasn't completely certain how I felt, even after four weeks of self-reflection.

"I'm hanging in there," I replied finally, using another common response.

"Really? That isn't what I heard."

"Are you spying on me?" I tried not to sound agitated by the intrusion, though it came out that way. My built-in defense mechanism didn't want to reveal to her I was feeling low.

"Come now, you know better. April called me, concerned about how you've been since coming back from California. She said you were injured badly and seemed to have lost your confidence—your mojo."

There was no denying, though I wasn't sure what to do about it.

"She said you need a kick in the pants to get moving again. That is why I'm calling."

"You plan on coming over and kicking my ass?" I asked.

"No. But I thought I'd have a good shot at doing it over the phone. What is the problem you're having?"

I wasn't sure I knew for certain, or at least could admit to it—out loud. There were creeping doubts invading my psyche, fear coming along for the ride, both teaming up to shake me. My smug and snarky attitude had taken a beating, when normally the two had inflicted it on others. Coming close to dying on a regular basis can shake a man, even someone as tough as I was. It was enjoyable breathing in fresh air without being in pain. I wanted the pain to end.

"I'm not sure. It seems…I've lost my…cockiness to face what I face consistently." I said it out loud, but the words were hard to reveal to her. I'd always been strong around her and I didn't like feeling weak.

"I seem to recall you feeling like this before. After your brother was killed, you didn't want to fight on, but you did."

"And look what happened, I lost you thanks to my mistake with Roni. I seem to step into the shit more than I should and it costs me. Both emotionally and physically." My shoulders sagged, feeling bitterness towards myself about my failings.

"Look, I forgave you about the Roni incident. It was a human mistake, one that broke us up. But in the end, we're better friends now than we were as lovers. And I will forever be in your debt for the effort you made to save me from The Butcher. I want to return the favor by saving you from quitting on yourself. You're too good to give up."

I wanted to say I was tired of the pain and the confrontation. This latest incident, along with my time facing down The Butcher, haunted me. The macho games don't do anyone any good and only lead to bloodshed, torment and death. But I couldn't express the words.

"I hear the conflict in your voice. Believe me, I didn't like what I went through. Strapped down to that table while that maniac cut into my skin, the sheer sadistic glee in his eyes...but you never wavered, didn't give up. Told me we'd make it out and damned if you didn't break free from that chair you were strapped to and take the monster down." She stopped for a few seconds, her voice shaky. "And you were there as I struggled to come back from the horror I experienced. You were a rock I needed, along with those in my family that got me to live on. I won't have any greater love for anyone than I have for you. You can't give up. You help people. You save those that can't help themselves from evil. Please Jarvis, fight on for yourself and those who can't fight for themselves."

They were strong words. Words I needed to hear. A kick in the ass to bring me back to my sense of self-worth. I knew I'd have no greater love for anyone other than her either. She was in my corner, as were others like April and Bill. Deep down, even with all the self-doubt and anguish clouding my head, I'd find my fortitude to carry on and finish this case, like I'd finished all of them before this one. I just needed to get back into the flow of things. Find my rhythm, walk those first steps, track down those important clues, and fire off those first punches.

"I hear you breathing," declared Melissa. "What do you have to say?"

"Thanks for the ass kicking," I replied. "You do it well."

"Are you going to get off the couch and start moving forward?" she wondered.

"I hate all that has happened to you since we met," I admitted honestly, my voice now shaky.

She was quiet for a moment. "I hated it too, but then we'd have never met and we'd both be poorer for it."

I agreed, but knew I needed more. She couldn't provide it, nor could April. I needed something else; another hobby or even business to bring balance in my life. What it was I wasn't completely certain. For now, I'd get up and start the road back to being whole again, or at least not as broken as I felt.

Chapter 23

There were many tortured souls in this world, and I had become one of them. Even so, no matter what it took, I planned to scratch and claw my way out, searching for anything that would motivate me. I thought about the things that made me happy: love, sex, desire and friendship. Though I didn't have many close friends, I had enough to feel rich. Connections I made had come from everywhere.

One of those places had been Boone's, a friendly bar with lots of TVs displaying sports, decent bar food and everyone's favorite, alcohol. But it was a place where I'd met people. New acquaintances, close friends, and others who'd turned into lovers. I'd had a few one-night stands, and one longer term relationship, which happened to be April.

I'd been searching for that new happy place to go after they closed a few months back, replaced by a dinner club which didn't appeal to me at all. I'd tried but couldn't find the right mix. I'd come to think I wouldn't find it, at least one close enough to enjoy.

The Aero Club Bar in San Diego had much of what I wanted. Atmosphere, a unique style and a wall of whiskey—though a wall of imported beer sounded better. I'd stumbled upon it on the west coast, but nothing seemed right near where I lived here in Denver. If I couldn't find it, maybe there was an option to build it myself.

I didn't have the expertise, or the money to make it happen. But I might have the drive to push it to be born, and maybe find those with the brains and capital to make it a reality. All I could do was try, work the streets of the people I knew and see if I could sell them on the idea. Time was on my side, for I wasn't in a rush. But I was excited to see where it led, with The Private Eye Tavern as a possible name. It would give me another purpose beyond the private detective business I'd started many years ago. There was work to do, but I was ready to get back into the game. I just needed a test. And I knew where to start.

April had done a few days here and there doing bodyguard work for Marilynn Hester and her two kids, as a preventive measure in case her husband did something stupid. Though physically I still wasn't a hundred percent, I wanted to face off with him and discuss our last conversation, where he'd tried to bribe me. He was a small fish compared to those I'd faced, but I needed to find the strength and courage to challenge him, a baby step in my recovery.

He wasn't hard to find, since he was always working at his main dealership on Broadway. I drove there with a sense of purpose in my Mustang, and once I arrived, I weaved my way through the maze of high-pressure sales people, going straight to his secretary who sat at her desk outside the office. She was one of his girlfriends, making it easy to push her buttons when I walked up.

"Hello Harmony," I said to her smiling, heavily made-up, face.

"May I help you, sir?" she answered.

She was the redhead in his life, the other a blonde. I knew all of this after a couple of weeks of surveillance.

"I'm here to see about Perry's appointment with his girlfriend, Cherie. She dyed her roots and got a wax job, and is anxious to see him at the hotel tonight and is up for whatever he desires."

"Excuse me?" she answered, her face turning red.

"Oh, I'm sorry. You're his other main squeeze, aren't you? I didn't mean to spill the beans. But I'm sure he'd be thrilled if you serviced him in his office to warm him up for Cherie."

She wasn't sure what to do, but she was certainly shocked and embarrassed.

"Harmony, don't worry about it. I'm sure Perry is practicing safe sex and you won't get any diseases from Cherie."

With her face distorted with anger, she picked up the phone and called into Perry's office, asking him to come out, not saying what was going on. When he stepped through the door and saw me, he didn't seem at all pleased. Harmony stood up and whispered in his ear, likely repeating what I said, then walked away beet red, with a hell fire anger any woman would have after what I'd done. It was kind of low on my part, but I considered it therapy for my wounded soul.

"Oh *darn*, I hope I didn't reveal secrets she didn't need to know," I said with false surprise in my voice. "I'd feel *terribly* bad about spilling the beans."

His eyes said he wanted to take a swing at me, but he didn't. He pulled out his cell phone and made a quick call, asking whomever was on the other end to come to his office immediately. It likely was the dealership security, but I didn't care. I walked past him into his office, pulling out a tape measure.

"Perry, you offered me one hundred thousand over the phone to lose the information about your cheating," I announced, surveying the space. "It wasn't enough. You probably have blown that much on your two girlfriends alone in the last year, while not spending a dime on your own kids, the loser that you are." I walked over to the corner, feeling the texture of the wall. "Your company is worth much more than that, which you know. And her lawyer and I know we have an open and shut case, meaning we'll make plenty on our fees. Taking half of your company is certainly a real possibility and likely on the low end. You and your lawyer better start thinking about working on a settlement that makes sense to your jilted wife and us."

I pulled out the end of the tape measure and started getting dimensions on his office. The corporate color, a mauve or plum style, the color of his walls and many others around the dealership, wasn't appealing to me. This was part of the show I was putting on to aggravate him.

"What the hell are you doing?" he asked.

"Measuring for your wife. This will be her office someday. We're getting an idea of what she can do with it. And this color must go. I'm sure once she is in control the marketing team can come up with better hues that will *pop* when people come in."

He put his hand to his forehead, rubbing it, trying to decide his next move. I doubt the stroking was making him any smarter. While he debated internally, a security guard walked in. He was dressed in blue shirt and black slacks, complete with a belt holding mace, a club and handgun. A rent-a-cop, with dreams of being a real cop long since passed.

"You called, Mister Hester?" he said, his eyes scanning back and forth between the two of us.

Perry hesitated, uncertain what to do, while I continued to measure like an interior designer.

"Oh, come now, Perry," I proclaimed. "Was your plan for this poor guard to come in and escort me out? You can see that isn't going to happen."

The guard reached for his belt, but I shook my head, telling him that was a bad idea. His hand stilled and hovered, wondering what to do. He was probably in his late fifties and certainly was no match for me physically. And I'd never let him get close enough to me to use the mace.

"There is no reason for any type of confrontation," I noted. "Let's talk over options and no one will get hurt."

Perry, after much consideration, gave in, waving for the guard to leave, asking him to close the door. He sat in his chair, his shoulders slumped as if defeated. Putting the tape measure away in my pocket, I took a seat across from him and his nice oak desk. It looked genuine, certainly weighing a ton, many a dollar spent on it. His choices in life weren't the best, but you couldn't argue about his taste in office furniture.

"Are you ready to understand the gravity of your situation?" I stated. "Time to realize you have no option. If this goes to court, you'll be ruined. Deal and maybe you'll still have a small part of the business."

"You don't understand," he remarked, fear on his face. "I already sold out forty percent. I don't have much more to give without losing control."

"Why did you sell off so much?" I replied, not sure if what he said was true. If it was it would likely cut into the pool of assets.

He shook his head, uncertain if he wanted to answer.

"You know we'll find out, one way or another. If this goes to trial and you only own sixty percent, then you likely will lose that majority stake, and maybe the whole company."

"I had other debts I had to pay."

"From what?"

He threw his hands over his eyes, not wanting to look at me.

"Come on, Perry. What was it? Women, booze, drugs, gambling?"

He nodded his head, as if to say all of them.

"Wow, you did it all, didn't you? Anything else?"

He shook his head. It wasn't surprising to hear, from what I'd learned about him during my surveillance. The life of excess has its price, and he had lived it to the fullest.

"Who did you sell out the shares to?"

"I can't tell you. Part of the deal, they remain anonymous."

"When we file against you for your assets, it will have to come out. I'm sorry to say, Perry, but you're screwed, because your wife doesn't give a damn about all these mistakes you made. And you're going to pay, big time."

I got up and walked out of the room. Going there, I was hoping to find what I was missing, but realized I wasn't all that bad off, compared to the man I'd just left behind in shambles.

Chapter 24

When I reached my car, I called Barry to let him know what I had learned. He was on his way to the courthouse and couldn't talk long.

"News to me," he said. "Do you think he was telling the truth?"

"Seemed like it. Though he *is* an actor, or at least is sort of one in his commercials."

Barry snorted. "I've seen them, and he *can't* act. I guess we need to look into this and find out who owns a chunk of his business."

"You might want to check on his girlfriends too."

"That should be your job, mister PI."

"Need to head back to California. But I'd say it's time to get someone on the wife and provide full-time protection. If there is another party involved in his business, they may not want him losing his stake. It is possible they're controlling him, maybe even blackmailing him."

"April has been doing a couple of days here and there but can't long term. How long will you be in California?"

"I wish I knew. But I'm sure we can come up with someone else. I have a couple of ideas and will let April know."

"Sounds good. Try to come back whole this time. It's hell interviewing new PIs to work for me and then training them. And I've got you broken in and potty trained where you're bearable to work with."

"Gee thanks, Barry," I said dryly. "It almost makes me think you'd miss me when I was gone."

He laughed uncontrollably and then hung up, leading me to the opposite conclusion. I decided to stop by the Mission of the Invisible Souls. There were a couple of people there that have the skills and might be interested in doing the bodyguard work.

When I walked in, I could immediately see improvements to the place. New paint, furniture, new equipment in the kitchen was just the start. I made my way to Sam's office; the lady who ran the place, and who seemingly was always there. Sure enough, when I stepped in, she was on the phone, angry at someone about a food delivery not arriving.

“We need that meat ASAP,” she demanded. “I got a lot of hungry people to feed, it’s damn cold for late April, and we have a lot of people here in the shelter depending on us to feed them. We’re down to scraps. You need to get it to us in a hurry, or I’ll find someone else who wants our business.”

She listened for a few more minutes and then hung up, a stern expression overtaking her face. I looked her way and smiled, though I don’t think it helped much.

“Anything I can do to help?” I asked.

She looked frustrated. “Can you go over to these idiots and get me my food?”

“Might be a nice change from those I normally run up against. I can drive over and wave my gun around if you want me to?” I grinned while patting the gun under my coat.

“I wouldn’t be so certain. They’re union, and you know what that means.” She stopped to take a drink from her coffee cup. “I see, by the bruising on your face and the way you walked in, that you ran up against someone tough recently.”

I was moving better though still feeling the effects. Bruising was fading, ribs still hurt, but on a pain scale of four now instead of a solid ten, the rest of my muscles only ached when pushed. Now I only moved like a fifty-year-old.

“Should have seen me after it happened. I’m miles from where I was then. But yes, it was several California gang members. I’m lucky to be alive.”

“I’m glad you made it out breathing. I’d have missed you. What can I help you with today?”

I smiled and sat in one of the visitor chairs. “I may need to hire someone for work guarding a woman and her kids, from her cheating husband. You would be perfect, but I can’t imagine you taking time away from here.”

“You’re right, I’d be perfect. Love to kick that asshole husband in the balls. But alas, I’d be hard pressed to leave here. Who were you looking for?”

“I was thinking Parker and possibly T, if you’ve seen him lately.”

“Parker is here today. T did stop in recently, bringing by numerous donations. Not sure where he is living, but it sounded like it was close by.”

"Could you spare Parker for a day or two here and there? I must go to back to California to finish up this case. He'd be working with April on rotating shifts, since she can't commit fulltime."

Sam nodded. "I'm sure we can find a schedule that is suitable. Is there a possibility of danger?"

"Minor. The husband isn't as tough as he thinks. They're safe in their home, as the community is well-secured as is the house. It's when they go outside. Trips to school, sporting events, shopping and all that. He'd be there mostly as a deterrent."

She nodded. "Let me call him. He is up on the second floor helping with the remodel up there."

While waiting, Sam and I talked the whole time about everything going on at the mission. Improvements were being made, and the help they were providing was essential for the local homeless community. Sam had committed her life to it, after one time being homeless herself, following a stint in the military. Her goal was to help whomever she could, like those who had helped her when on the streets.

When Parker showed up ten minutes later, I hardly recognized him, for it had been a while since I'd seen him. He'd put on weight, though nothing out of the ordinary, since his time on the streets had made him quite slender, which was no surprise with the minimal amount of meals he would get on a daily basis. We were about the same height, his weight maybe ten pounds less than me, age close to mine, maybe a year or two older. The age lines on his face leading you to think otherwise, all from his rough time on the streets.

We were similar in many ways, though he'd had a tough time when returning from overseas from fighting in the first Iraq Gulf War where he was wounded. This led him to struggle working, and eventually ending up homeless. He once hired me on a case where other homeless people were being taken away by shady men, one of whom had stabbed him. He recovered and now worked at the shelter. I knew he was tough and could handle himself. It was a matter of whether he would be interested in the opportunity.

"Good to see you, Jarvis," he said when he walked in, shaking my hand before pulling me in for a hug.

"You look great, Parker. Sam says you're invaluable around here."

"Couldn't ask for a better boss."

"I agree." I looked back at Sam, winking at her which made her smile. "I was wondering if you had a minute to talk. I have a possible job, I thought you'd might be interested in. A chance to make decent money, not that Sam doesn't pay you well."

Sam smiled. "I'll leave you two. I must see about what we're going to do for food if my vendor doesn't show. Take all the time you need."

Parker took her chair, running his hand through his hair, which was swept back, ebony in color with a few streaks of gray showing.

"What type of job?" wondered Parker.

"Providing protection for a woman and her two children." I sat back down, the pain better than it was a few weeks ago, though I still winced.

"Protection from whom?"

"Soon to be ex-husband."

Parker rested his elbows on the table. "Has he threatened her?"

"Nothing overt. We're mostly being cautious, as he is a jerk. Came at me when I served him the papers. He didn't get very far."

"Not related to the bruises on your face?" Parker noted.

"No. Those came from a gang member in California. This guy is nothing compared to them. You'd mostly be with them when they need to go out. Kids to school, shopping, when the wife needs to get her hair done…you'd be working with April on shifts. She can't cover every day because of her job with Denver PD. And I need to get back to California on this other case."

"Hopefully not dealing with gangs this time?"

"I should be through with them. Now onto others though they might not be much easier to deal with."

"Are you sure you don't need my help there instead?" asked Parker, looking concerned.

I smiled. "Not at the moment, but I'll keep it in mind. What do you say?"

"What will it pay?"

I told him.

"Not bad," he mused. "I don't have a car right now. Is that a problem?"

"You can use mine while I'm out of town. If I come back, we

can always arrange for a rental. And you would drive them in their car when taking them places."

"You trust me with your Mustang? I'm honored." Parker was grinning from ear to ear.

"You're a good man. I know it will be in excellent hands."

"If Sam is fine with it, I can help out. Tell me when."

I stood up. "I'll let you know before I leave. April and you can work it out."

He stood as well. We shook hands and walked out together.

"Are you in contact with T these days?" I asked.

"Sure, I see him regularly. Why?"

"Do you think he'd be interested? You could alternate shifts, that way you aren't away from here too much. If he is willing?"

"I'll ask him. He is doing well these days, but it's hard to say no to cash money."

"Call me once you know," I said while handing him my card. "He is a good man, too. I know you both will take care of things the right way."

"And if the husband makes an aggressive move?" asked Parker.

"Whatever is necessary. That means more money for our client and possibly a bonus for you."

"Does this guy have money?"

I told him who it was. Even though he didn't watch much TV, he still knew the name.

"Wow! A media star. Might be fun to knock this guy down a peg or two."

I smiled. "I sure as hell enjoyed it."

Chapter 25

We were lying in bed, enjoying a respite from our carnal activities that had ended in satisfaction for both April and me. Lying on her stomach, her naked body was curled up in the blue flannel sheets of her bed, showing enough skin to enjoy. I was next to her, on my back, reflecting on the closeness of the moment. The shared gratification of two people entwined to achieve pleasure on many levels, and for April, if I read it properly, multiple levels. The sexual energy we produced was unparalleled. When the clothes came off, the sparks would fly.

"From your attention to detail, I'd say you missed me," observed April, still catching her breath.

"It has been close to five weeks," I replied. "A lot of pent up urges needed releasing, now that my body can maneuver properly with only little pain."

She smiled. "Though not ideal, considering what happened to you, but maybe we keep the carnal activities more spread out, to build those urges?"

I shook my head while staring at her from my back. "I'd prefer more regular passion. Better for your health the experts say. Besides, the cost of batteries for you can be expensive."

April laughed, her head turned towards me, eyes trained. "Oh, you think that is what goes on in here when you're away."

"I'm a trained detective. I've seen the toys in your drawer."

"Since I've met you, their usage has dropped significantly. I prefer the experience of the real thing, and yours feels supreme."

I smiled. It was always good to know you measured up in a woman's expectations.

"Barry said you talked with him. Said you couldn't cover non-stop."

"They aren't thrilled me taking too much time off at the Denver PD. I can get my two days a week, with one or two extras here and there, but no more. Someone else will have to assist in shuttling the lady and her kids around."

"Do you remember Parker and T?" I asked. She nodded. "Parker is on board with helping and he is going to see if T can assist. They both have military training. If anything goes wrong, I told Parker to call the police immediately and not try to do too much."

"Sounds good. How are they both doing?"

"Great, from what I hear. Especially compared to their life on the streets. They have the proper assistance to keep them on the right track and both are employed."

"I'm off the next two days. We can set up a meeting with Marilynn Hester. We can all meet and work out details. After that, I'm back at work for four days and then off three more. I'm sure we can work out a schedule. Are you sticking around or heading back to California?"

"I will head back once you're back to work. I'll go with you all and we can piece together the schedule. If there are any holes, Sam might be able to cover for couple hours here and there, though not for full days as she is too involved at The Mission."

"If you're heading back, I'm guessing you're feeling better about yourself?" April asked hopefully.

"I am. Melissa called and talked with me. Said you called asking for her help." I paused, a warm emotion hitting me that she had taken this step to help me. "That must have been hard for you."

April rolled onto her side. "Not at all. I want what is best for you and I know you two have a special connection. Not quite like ours, but I know you value her opinions. Bill and I tried, with little success. We agreed she might have an avenue to you we didn't, with all you've been through together."

April was right. Melissa did have a connection to me that I would hear. I heard Bill and April too, but not quite the say way. We'd all been through a lot of battles.

"The accumulated encouragement from *all* of you helped. I'm ready to get back in the game. In reality, I knew I'd get back, in time. I'm hoping to avoid the physical toll as much as I can. Knowing in my line of work I can't dodge it completely."

"I'd be happy if you can dodge it as well. It is no fun watching you go through the pain you do." She ran her hand across my chest and stomach. "This map of scars you have isn't always fun to see, even if I enjoy seeing you naked."

I pointed to her stomach area where she'd been shot. "You have them too. They heal, but with each one the pain often lingers."

April sprung out of bed, the sheets flying off her, with no fear of how she looked naked. A view I always enjoyed.

"I'm hungry and I'm going to get nourishment. I need calories, as I know you well enough that round two can't be far off. I can see stirring down below as you ogle my naked body. Do you want something?"

I laughed, saying I was good for now. I admired her as she walked out of the room, her naked body shimmering in the room light. I was thrilled to be sharing these moments with her. I pulled the sheets onto me as my body cooled off, winter holding its grip on the area even though it had been spring for several weeks now.

I closed my eyes thinking over what appeared to be nothing at all. I felt content with having a blank brain at this moment, not worrying about anything other than the desire for the woman who would be returning to my bed soon.

On the nightstand was my cellphone, which started chirping, telling me I had an incoming call. The area code 619 was one from the San Diego area, though the rest of the number I didn't recognize. I decided to answer in case it was important.

"Do you know who this is?" said the deep voice, which, even across the cellular compressed network, I knew was Miguel.

"I do," I replied carefully, feeling shocked at the call. "Though I won't mention the name."

"Yes, that is best. Never know who might be listening in these days."

"Ears everywhere." I agreed. "What can I help you with?"

"It is what I can help you with. That party from our last encounter gave me a name I wanted to share with you. I will only say it once."

Wow, another shock. It would appear to be my lucky day.

"I'm listening."

"Stetson Poole."

It was a name that I didn't know.

"Any idea who he works for?"

"No. Even if I did, I wouldn't share. You're a resourceful man who can find him on your own."

"Fair enough. Thank you."

"No need for thanks. But keep in mind, if you ever come into our territory again, it will not go well for you." His tone was calm and firm. There was no doubt he spoke the truth.

"Understood."

The line went dead, and I immediately entered the name into my phone. Like he said, I was resourceful and would find out who this person was and who he worked for. But that would have to wait, as April returned, plopping on the bed next to me, with a bowl of ice cream. She ate while lying again on her stomach, her backside exposed for me to enjoy.

"Who was that?" she asked, enjoying a healthy spoonful.

"Miguel Prisco. Leader of the street gang I encountered."

She looked concerned. "What did he want?"

"Besides warning me to stay out of his territory, he gave me a name. A name of who may be the money man in the bombing of Rocky's family. One I'll need to track down once I return to California."

"Interesting. Why would he do that?"

"I'm not certain. I guess we bonded after my battle with his man, Luciano. Might have made an impression."

April swallowed another spoonful. "Yet he threatened you about coming into his territory."

"I'm not part of his gang, that is a given. He was helpful nonetheless, which might make the beating I took worthwhile."

April swallowed a couple more spoonful's and then was licking the spoon, which got my attention, stirring my desire. I rolled over on my side next to her, admiring her butt. I ran my hand up and down the curves. Hers was good sized, but firm, one you could grip well when she was in control on top.

I started kissing her butt cheeks, moving up slowly along her back, to her shoulder blades, and then the neck. I was lying on top of her now, nibbling her ear, feeling her body respond to mine.

"Your facial hair tickles," she said, commenting on the goatee I'd decided to grow.

"I thought you said it made me look sexy," I whispered in her ear in between nibbles.

"Oh it does," she replied in a low moan. "Especially when it brushes up against my thighs."

"I'll be working my way there shortly."

"I knew I'd need nourishment, big boy," she uttered, while finishing the last of her ice cream. "I was certain a little playful licking would set you off."

It certainly did, as I started back down again, slowly reaching her rear end with my mouth, rolling her over until the moans reached the right fevered pitch we both longed for, the exploration lasting longer and building higher than our first time that day.

Chapter 26

We got everything lined up and taken care of for watching over Marilynn Hester and her kids. The rotation looked like it would work out fine, and we got a chance to stress to her that she needed to watch her drinking. Though she agreed to better control her intake, only time would tell. I knew April could handle Marilynn, hopefully getting her to understand staying safe meant staying sober in case danger came knocking and requiring quick reactions.

I flew out to California knowing all would be good for them. I wish I'd felt that confident in what I was chasing down on the west coast.

I got there on a Tuesday, this time booking a different hotel to be on the safe side, this one sitting a little further north of the airport, closer to Oceanside, in Del Mar Heights. Manny had helped by holding onto my guns for me, which I retrieved after checking in. He'd done research while I was away but made little progress on the case.

Upon meeting at the Oceanside police headquarters, I was currently sitting at his desk listening to what he'd learned, which wasn't much, though not for lack of trying.

"Not much on this PI," he said. "Shark Tail Detective Agency is registered, and they have an office in San Diego, but little else. I never got them to answer the phone."

"I had the same issue when I called," I replied. "Did you ever go to their office?"

"No time. I had two murder cases drop into my lap, from another Detective who quit suddenly. I'm buried now more than ever and pulling double shifts and only an occasional day off right now until they promote someone, which will take time."

"I will drop by today and see if anyone is around. What about that name I got from Miguel?"

"Stetson Poole? Nothing came up under that name. I checked all of California and got a big fat zero. No one with that name anywhere. I didn't have a chance to check any further."

"I've got a couple of contacts in the FBI. If they will take my call. Maybe they have information on the name. What about the Eugene Washburn murder?"

Manny got up to get coffee, adding two spoonsful of sugar before he liked the taste. Caffeine was a cop's best friend when working the hours he was working.

"They have your statement about Luciano killing Eugene and have an APB out for his arrest, but there is no sign of him anywhere. I imagine a body might turn up someday. But I'm sure he is dead. Miguel would never let him live after breaking his code. It's not a high priority according to Zimmer. Internal struggles like that one happens all the time and rarely are pursued. Gangs handle their own justice." Manny stopped to take a whiff of his coffee, the steam caressing his nostrils. "How are you doing? You were pretty messed up physically when you left to go home."

"Better, though not totally healed yet. I must keep people from punching me in the ribs a while longer. I remain tender in spots."

"You're looking better. When they dropped you off, I was wondering if you were dead. Miguel's men wouldn't say much, but they at least let me take you to the ER. Did Miguel tell you anything else other than the name?"

"Only not to come back to their neighborhood again, or else. It didn't need to be said, because I have no intention of returning."

"Let me know if you need anything. I'll try to help, but like I said I'm working way too much right now. And my lady friends are bitching at me because I can't spend time with them and they need…"

"Handsy Manny," I said before he could.

"Am I repeating myself?" Manny said with a smile.

"At least one other time. But that is okay. I'm glad you have a nickname. Maybe you need to get t-shirts made and trademark it."

"Anything to augment a cop's pay—legally, works for me. What is with the new growth on your face? Are you planning on going undercover?"

Manny was commenting on my growing facial hair of mustache and goatee, though neatly trimmed and short. I was looking for a change and this is what I chose.

"Wanted to try a different look," I replied. "I've had beards before but wanted to go this route. My girlfriend thought it made me look tough and sexy."

"I can't or will comment on the sexy aspect. But it does change your look. I almost didn't recognize you when you walked in."

"Then that might be good," I declared with smile. "No one will see me sneaking up on them, which would be a nice change of pace."

I left the station, climbing into my rental, this time a black Honda CRV, which was a small sized SUV, but big enough for me. I had the address of the Shark Tail Detective Agency, located in downtown San Diego, or referred to as Centre City by the locals. It was a lengthy drive but was mostly a straight shot on I-5.

The office was only a few blocks from Petco Stadium where the Padres played. As I made my way through traffic, I found the urban corridor with its large modern skyscrapers and newer retail and business buildings like most big cities, to its older structures that had been around many decades, squeezed in between. Street work and construction had to be navigated around, but thankfully my phone GPS was up to the task, though finding parking was challenging, and required burning gas before a spot opened that wasn't too far a walk to reach the building.

Once I figured out I needed a phone app to pay for my parking slot at the meter, I got it taken care of, burning another fifteen minutes of my life.

The streets in the area were either numbers, which went north-south, or letters going east-west. The office was located on Fourth Avenue, between J and K Street, in a building with leased space for living or working. I took the stairs, eventually finding the front door to the detective office on the second floor. There was a sign, but the door was locked. No business hours were posted, which seemed unusual for a business looking for clients.

I ran into a UPS driver who was delivering packages in the building. It was his regular route and told me if there were packages, they were always left with the building leasing office on the first floor if no one was there.

I made my way to a couple of other offices on the floor and no one had ever seen anyone in the suite, not that they paid attention. Still you would think they would have run into each other once in a while if it was a typical nine-to-five establishment. After striking out there, I went to the leasing office on the street level, where a nice older lady was working.

"I'm trying to find Edwin Ware," I inquired. "He works at the

Shark Tail Detective Agency which has an office on the second floor."

"Yes, they're a tenant," she replied, motioning me to sit. "Unless there is a complaint, I generally don't check on them, meaning I can't tell you much."

I smiled and sat down across from her. "How long have they been in the building?"

"Maybe ten months now. They paid their rent for one year all up front. I've never heard a word from them since."

More oddities about the agency. "Do you remember them moving in?"

"Happens on the weekend, when I'm not here. They're given a key and they go from there." She had a shiny cherry wood pen, she was nervously spinning between three fingers.

"Do you remember who looked at the space to start with?"

She stopped to think. "Been a while. If I recall it was a woman. Now that I think of it, she looked at the space for about five minutes with only a couple of questions, before agreeing to lease it."

"What were the questions?"

"Mostly about how quickly they could occupy the space. And how long the lease was for. She didn't want to commit to more than a year."

"Then their lease is coming due soon?"

She nodded. "Yes. I've tried to call them but haven't heard back. My assumption is they aren't renewing."

"Any chance you can let me in and look around?" I gave her my trustworthy smile.

Her pen spinning stopped. "No, I can't do that."

"What if I said I was a prospective client that might be interested in that office?"

She frowned, leaning back in her office chair after tossing the pen on desk. "From what you said earlier, I doubt that is true. And even if you were, I'd still need to get their permission first."

"What if a cop asked about getting in?"

"Not without a warrant or just cause. If you said there was a dead body in there, I'd consider it."

I thanked her and walked out, getting her business card, my mind going over what I'd learned. The evidence revealed to me

Shark Tail Detective Agency wasn't taking or returning calls, the year lease ending without renewing and no one ever seeing anyone in the space.

Once back in my car, my senses grew concerned about them. I planned to sit on this location for a few days and see if anyone showed up. If all else failed, I might have to do an entry on my own, for I had brought my lock picking tools this time, and I was curious what I'd find on the other side of that door.

Chapter 27

I sat on the PI office for three days, spending a fortune on parking with no sign of them. All calls to their business number went unanswered. The more I thought about it, the more it didn't make sense. Edwin Ware was following me in a rental car. *Why was that?* You would think he'd have his own vehicle. And any business like this one needed to at least take calls to get clients, or it would never survive. *But why have an office, if you didn't use it?* The only reason that came to mind was to keep up appearances that is was a bona fide company.

Manny had checked out the business, its licensing and it all looked legal. But Ware's driver's license was odd, for it had the address of the business, despite no sign anyone actually lived there. The postal carrier for the building had said he did leave mail in their building mailbox, and rarely was there any mail at all. None of it made sense, leading me to believe that none of it was real. I needed to get inside and see what was in the office.

It was Friday afternoon, and things were quieting down. The Padres were on the road, meaning no huge influx of people would be coming to a game at the nearby stadium. I had scouted out the key lock on the door, buying one just like it to practice on.

Eventually after a bit of practice, I'd honed my skills, being able to pick the lock in about two minutes. The problem was to keep from being seen. Because it was late in the day on a Friday, I was hoping most of the other offices on the floor would close early.

I walked into the building at around 4:30 and cruised the hallway looking for anyone remaining. A couple people left about ten minutes later and after that it seemed quiet enough. Making it to the door, with a good hunch I had enough time, I went to work.

There was just one deadbolt I had to defeat, the doorknob not being locked. Practice had helped, but I wasn't under the gun of possibly being seen then, the pressure of being discovered drawing out the time it took. It was close to three minutes until I finally had some success and I was in. I stepped through the door and was disappointed to not find much.

The space was divided down the middle by a kitchen area and cabinets, behind it a full bathroom with tub and shower. Behind that, another room. The walls were white, the floors shiny oak hardwood, with a couple of rectangular windows, their blinds closed to keep out the light and prying eyes. What the place was lacking was furniture. There was a small table, two chairs and one filing cabinet. But nothing else in the whole space to give any indication of regular use.

The filing cabinet was empty when I opened it. The top of the desk clean, other than a wired phone, a notepad, two pens and a stapler. The drawers were empty, other than another notepad, a box of extra staples, and paperclips. I picked up the phone and there was a dial tone. Calling my cell phone showed me the number as the one on the business card.

I looked around once more, finding nothing. No food in the cabinets or the fridge, which wasn't even plugged in. The bathroom had toilet paper and hand soap but nothing else.

Searching high and low, I didn't see anything until I came back to the front area and saw it hanging high on the ceiling near the door, with a good angle on the room. It was a camera.

Moving closer, I could see the wires going into the ceiling, giving me the impression it was working. If someone was watching, they knew I was there, which could mean someone could be coming my way. I took a few quick snapshots of the space on my phone and got out of there.

Sure enough, as I made it to the lower level, a large SUV pulled up, double-parking on the street. Two men got out, the driver remaining. They started running and I backed up, ducking into the lower level bathroom, which I'd used several times on my three-day stakeout.

After they passed, I headed towards the building manager's office, to find she was there, though about to leave. She remembered me and smiled.

"Back again, I see," she commented. "I'm about to leave for the day and I'm late for dinner with my husband. What can I help you with?"

My mind raced on what to do. Being gracious and kind might buy me time with her, even though she was in a hurry.

"I'm sorry. I was hoping to get a brochure of your properties and find out about any other available space. I have a confession. Like the Shark Tail Detective Agency, I'm a private detective as well. And I'm looking to move my business into this area, with the option to live in the space. Is that possible?"

She smiled, though you knew she was a little aggravated about someone showing up right at closing time. But business is business.

"Yes, all the lofts are live work spaces. They're set up with basic kitchens, with fridge, stove, sink and cabinets. And a full bathroom. From there, you can build out as you please with a few restrictions."

She handed me a pamphlet, and I found a chair to sit in, providing the proper viewing angle out on the street where I could see the SUV. It sat there, vehicles honking at it, with the driver waving at them to go around him. With a view of the license plate, I borrowed a pen and quickly jotted down the number on the pamphlet. She noticed me eyeing the vehicle.

"Don't you love these people with no consideration for others," she stated bitterly. "At least drive around the block a couple of times, for god's sake."

I nodded, as if to agree. "Anything else you can tell me about these spaces?"

"I'm sorry, but it really is getting late and I need to leave or my husband will be pissed. Can't you come back next week, and we can go over this?"

The other two came outside and were standing on the sidewalk, looking around. I turned my back preventing them from seeing me. After a discussion, they split up, each going in different directions. Apparently they had a good enough description that they hoped they could spot me. A long view of me on their monitoring system certainly helped them out.

"Are you hiding from those men?" she queried, her voice with a nervous timbre.

I pulled out my wallet to show her my ID. "Yes I am. Like I mentioned, I'm a PI and those guys are after me, though I'm not sure why. And I don't think they're the good guys."

She looked at me, pondering what to do. I tried to give her my honest expression gaze, but I suspected the new facial hair might say otherwise.

"What can I do to help?" she asked, her voice now relaxed.

"A back way out of here would be great," I declared, thrilled she was willing to help.

"Come with me." She led me out a backdoor, to a hallway. "Where are you parked?" she inquired.

"I'm out on Fourth Street, where they're parked, though a couple cars up from them. But they don't know what I'm driving."

"See over there," she noted, pointing to the left. "Follow this hallway, out that door. From there take a right and it will take you out onto Fifth Street. From there you should be able to work your way to where you need to be. Plenty of restaurants around here for you to enjoy a meal. I'm sure they will get tired of searching for you and leave. Downtown on a Friday night is full of people."

I pulled out my wallet and handed her two twenties. "Dinner is on me."

She waved her hand at me. "Not necessary."

"I insist. And thank you for being trusting of me."

She grabbed the money and grinned ear to ear. "A skill I have. I've always been able to look at someone and tell immediately whether I can trust them or not."

"Maybe *you* should have been a cop!" I stated with a grin.

"I think I'll stick with what I'm doing now. Boring is more my speed."

I smiled and thanked her, taking her directions. Soon I was out on Fifth Avenue, once I knew it was clear. She had been right, there were restaurants, bars and a few retail shops on both sides. Even though there wasn't a game, there was still a fair amount of foot traffic, the 'Friday night burn off that week of stress and spend your paycheck' crowd on the move.

This section was known as the Gaslamp Quarter, with Victorian architecture across sixteen blocks, an urban playground mostly appealing to the millennials crowd, though I saw plenty of age range in the foot traffic. It should be easy to get lost among the throng of bodies.

I came to a sign that said Gaslamp Strip Club, though the name was misleading. It was a steakhouse and bar, where you can grill your own steak, and not a place where women took off their clothes. Good thing hunger was on my mind, and not nudity.

I strolled inside, taking a seat at the end of the bar, affording me a view outside since it was near the entrance. I ordered a beer from the tap and cheddar bacon fries, while keeping one eye on those coming in. It wasn't overly loud inside; the place only half-full. Pulling out my cell phone, I called Manny.

"I have another plate for you to check on for me," I said. "SUV, with three guys looking for me. I need to see if the registration leads me anywhere."

I gave him the plate, but no details on why they were hunting for me. A cold glass arrived, and I took a long sip as I was thirsty. There was no sign of the two men. Hopefully, they would give up and move on.

"Plate doesn't go anywhere," said Manny. "I type it in and it brings up that it's a government car, but no details. Like where it's out of or with which government agency. Doesn't even give me a make or model."

"Which means it's being used by someone the feds don't want anyone to know about," I mused.

"It would seem so. Only someone inside can give you those answers. Why are they chasing you?"

"Best you don't know. But I did learn the PI office isn't much of an office. No one appears to actually work there."

"How did you find that out?"

I laughed. "Again, best I don't tell you. But right after I learned this, is when the SUV and the three men showed up. I've been dodging them ever since."

"What is your next move?"

"I have a couple of contacts in the FBI. Maybe they can help me. I'll do my best to avoid these people till I'm certain who they are."

"Good luck."

The cheddar bacon fries arrived and were quite good, though I skipped the jalapeno dipping sauce. I didn't need the heartburn from food, I'd had enough of it from avoiding these men.

Since the car was government issue, I needed to find out what agency I was dodging. I found the phone number and called Dezmond Price, who worked at the FBI office in Denver.

Unfortunately, I got his voicemail. Hard to believe our civil servant not working late on a Friday night, but I'd adapt. I then tried another, though Agent Catalina Alegre and I were not always on the best of terms. She answered on the third ring.

"No hot date tonight?" I proclaimed after she answered.

"Who is this?"

"Jarvis Mann, the PI of your dreams."

"More like nightmare. What do you want?" She didn't sound thrilled to hear from me.

"I thought I'd call to say hi and see if you missed me."

"Hardly. You're lucky I answered. I'm only here because of a fraud case I'm working on."

"Still trying to make points with your bosses. Too bad they can't look past you being a female and see what a good agent you are."

"And don't forget, Hispanic. You're correct on that count though, but I suspect you're buttering me up to get information."

"I was sincere in my compliments, but yes it serves me, as I do need to see if you can run down a license plate number for me."

"Don't you have Denver PD friends to handle your trivial tasks?" Her voice was sounding grumpy, which was normal when I talked with her.

"I do, but the plate comes back as a government one, with no info beyond that. I thought maybe you could see who it belongs to, since you're on the inside."

She sighed. "For what reason?"

"The men in it are likely trying to find me to do bodily harm."

She snorted. "What have you gotten yourself into now, that requires people to have the urge to pound on you?"

"Case I'm working on in California. A car bombing and a boat fire, both killing members of a family. One who was an acquaintance of mine."

There was silence on the other end. She was certainly thinking over what to do, but I waited, swallowing several fries before she answered.

"I shouldn't do this," she uttered. "And even if I looked it up, I might not get anymore that what the cops pulled up, because contrary to what you believe, I'm not all that inside when it comes to the inner workings of our government. But I'll see what the computer says."

After I gave her the plate, I heard typing and then more dead air. My fries were almost gone but had been delicious. I was contemplating seconds. Fried foods were the key to faster healing I told myself.

"Like I said, not much more than what you already had. Black SUV, a couple years old, being used out of Southern California. No name on who or what agency is using the vehicle."

"Sounds like you do have a little more than what the cops got. Any thoughts on who the vehicle belongs to?"

"Only this, if it's not in the system then it's being used for covert stuff they don't want the public or lowly agents like myself to know about."

"Then it could be FBI?"

"Yes. Or CIA, NSA or DEA. And a bevy of other secret acronyms the general public don't know about."

"I thought the CIA couldn't work inside the US?"

She laughed. "A fairy tale. Those doing covert work, off the grid, are basically making their own rules."

"Great. That really makes my day. Anything else you want to add to increase my heartburn?"

"Only one thing and I hope you take me seriously. I'd be careful, Jarvis. This could be intense shit you've stepped into. Don't get into it blindly and without backup. If you thought The Butcher was bad, these guys can be a hundred times worse. They will go to extremes to guard their secrets."

Her words didn't help my heartburn any, but I said thanks, finishing off my fries and beer.

The number of people outside was increasing, leading me to venture out. Once I paid the tab, I hit the street going north on Fifth and then west on K Street, my eyes on a swivel watching for anything that looked wrong.

Once on the corner of Fourth and K Street I looked down to see if the SUV remained double-parked. It was dark now, though the streets were lit well. They were gone, no sign of them or the SUV. As I started walking, I saw paper on the windshield of my rental car, under the driver's side wiper. Reaching the passenger side, I checked to see if the doors remained locked and verified no one was inside, but all appeared good. Pulling the sheet of paper out, hoping for a random flyer marketing merchandise, I opened it to find that wasn't the case. Instead it was a note which I read out loud.

"*Leave the case alone or you'll be dead,*" I uttered.

They had found my car and made a statement to me loud and

clear. Something big was going on and I had no idea what it was.

Chapter 28

My eyes were in the rearview mirror all the way back to the hotel. There was no sign of them following me. If they found my car, they could have found out where I was staying.

I watched for any suspicious people in the hotel lobby and on my ride up the elevator, but nobody looked dangerous. Then I checked my room carefully upon entering but found no sign anyone had been inside other than the cleaning crew. But from now on, I'd be watching my backside for tails, sufficiently paranoid someone in the government was watching me. The only question was, why? And did it have anything to do with Rocky's murder? An answer to which I planned on tracking down.

The next morning, I awoke, my gun on the nightstand, ready to use if someone tried to break in. I slept poorly, with any sound out of place awakening me, with all windows closed, the strong locks and swinging bar in place.

After a long shower, soaking my sore body, remains of bruising still lingering on my torso, I went down for breakfast, deciding on a heavy protein option of eggs, bacon, toast and milk, to assist in healing my bones.

It was filling, expensive and added to my room tab. This hotel had a restaurant and bar, which was convenient, as I wouldn't need to go far if I didn't want to. I went back to my room to plot out where I was in the case and the options that remained. Walking away was certainly on the table.

Everything started with Vicente Duarte who, under duress, confirmed what Rocky had learned through whatever sources he had, that Vicente had been hired to kill him and his family. Vicente then added that the person who hired him was from inside Maximillian Conway's organization, which is who Rocky used to work for. This led him to California, where a few months later he was killed in a boat fire, where he'd been living.

Then, along came Brandon, hiring me to investigate Rocky's murder, leading me to come to California where I found the mechanic Eugene Washburn who worked on the car before it exploded, and learnt of his connections to Luciano Duarte, Vicente's cousin, and a gang member. After much pain, I have now learned the name of the person who contacted and paid them for the killing, Stetson Poole. A person who didn't exist so far as I could tell.

Adding to this was a PI, Edwin Ware, who had been following me. Though little information about him existed, and his office didn't appear to be an actual place of business, only a location. After breaking into his office, three men showed up, whom I evaded, but leaving me a message to drop the case or be killed.

The car they were driving was government owned, with a secret registration no one could get access to, meaning it was likely driven by someone in one of the alphabet government organizations. And normally those type of people don't threaten to kill you, which led me to a conclusion that what they were doing was likely not on the up and up.

Even with the bevy of information I had, there wasn't anything solid to go on. If I were to continue this case, there was one name I needed to try and track down. Whoever Stetson Poole was, might be the key. But dying wasn't an option I cared to face. And as Catalina said, I likely needed backup.

With all of this, I called Brandon to see what he thought, leaving a message with Sue, since he wasn't answering. An hour later he called back.

"Have you recovered sufficiently to be back on the case?" asked Brandon. He knew of my injuries and time needed to recover, since I'd told him.

"I'm back in sunny California," I replied. "But I'm uncertain where to go now. I may have hit a wall, one I'm not sure I can break through."

"Give me the details."

I told him everything, down to the last threat left on my car. There was a long pause, as he digested what I said. Doing a video call would have been interesting to read on his face to give me a clue of what he was thinking.

"What is your next move?" he inquired.

"Honestly, I have no idea. If this is government related, I'm not sure I want to dig much deeper. And certainly not without help. This is where I could use Rocky, but that isn't an option."

"No other resources for you to use? What about your cop friend, April? She seemed tough in a fight."

"She is, but her getting away from her police duties for any period of time would be impossible for her. Any spare time is being spent on another case I was working on in Denver, protecting a woman and her two kids. I don't have any other resources out here, other than the Oceanside cop and he is neck deep in cases working nearly non-stop. Even with backup, I'm uncertain what more I can do. It's not in my nature to walk away, but this could be a quagmire not worth pursuing."

"I have no other resources I can spare right now. What about your Russian friends?"

"They're hardly friends. And even if they could help, it wouldn't be free."

"Anyone you hire is an expense, and I will cover it. Rocky was a good man and we owe it to him to at least see this through. He died for a reason. At the very least to find out why."

Walking away was my best option, but yes, I did feel I owed him to try and get a little more info on what was going on.

"What else can you tell me about Rocky?" I asked. "Were you aware of him doing any work for the government?"

"No. But sometimes you work for them when you don't know you work for them. People in this business aren't always on the up and up, playing both sides of the fence."

A trait Brandon shared as well, though I kept the thought to myself.

"What about yourself, Brandon?" I said. "Any contacts within any of the government agencies you can leverage?"

There was a pause. Again, seeing his face would have been telling.

"Nothing I'd like to use at this time. I'm not sure it would provide the answers you were searching for."

"How about the name Stetson Poole? Do you know it?"

There was another pause before he answered. "Doesn't ring a bell. You have connections to track it down."

"I've used them, and he doesn't show up anywhere. Any chance you can use your resources and see if you can come up with useful data. I really need information to work with to keep pursuing this, Brandon. Without it, I'm not certain there is much more I can do."

Once more a long pause.

"I will see what I can find. But if I were you, I'd check in again with Max. If this person was inside, he may know them."

That was my next move, if I had one. If the name was an alias, and he didn't know who it was, then it would likely lead me nowhere. But I was planning on digging deeper in Max's business in hopes of soliciting a response, which might provide me answers on his involvement.

"Yes, that was one option I was considering. May need to wait for Monday before I can get anywhere. Not sure their offices are open on the weekend."

"If his business is beyond real estate, I'm sure someone is around. Besides, Max is a huge health nut. Works out, plays tennis and golfs a lot from what I heard. I'm sure you can find him, even on a weekend. Sue will call you if the Poole name turns up in our search."

After he hung up the phone, a nagging thought coursed through my head. Brandon had previously said he didn't know Max, yet he now mentioned the part about him being a huge health nut. It would appear Brandon had been holding back information about this job and what he knew, a trait my clients often exhibited. This lack of honesty didn't make me feel any better about the job at hand, but maybe he could get a connection to the name that might lead me somewhere, if he was willing to share. Of course, he might already know the answer, but didn't want to reveal it to me. Holding back never makes my job any easier.

As for contacting my Russian connection, Aleksi, I'd hold that in reserve for now. Using him or one of his men might not be a good idea but would be better than trying to do this alone. They certainly were tough enough to do the work. Although controlling them might be an issue.

For now, I planned on relaxing, mulling over next moves. The pool was open, and it was a warm April spring day. A swim sounded refreshing, allowing the flushing of all these worries from my head.

As I reached the pool, I dropped a towel on one of the loungers, and went to test the water. It felt warm, the sun pushing the temperature to near eighty today.

There was a woman doing laps from end to end, showing great form. I found myself watching her, an immediate attraction gripping me, impressed as she glided effortlessly through the water. I sat on the edge, putting both feet in the warm liquid, eyeing her movements, her and I being the only ones there. After ten times back and forth, she stopped, getting to the ladder and walking out.

She was probably 5'10" with nice hips, small chest and good tan. Her hair was long, bleached out to a lighter brown that was nearly blonde. She toweled off, sitting down on the lounger across from me, adding sunscreen to her legs and arms, then putting on sunglasses before lying on her back. If she knew I was watching her, she didn't let on.

She held my attention as I slipped into the water, feeling the need to match her swim effort, trying to show off my ability, an effort of male bravado, even though I was limited and sore from my injuries. I shook off an image of wanting to get to know her, knowing that side of Jarvis needed to remain in the past. Though imagining what might be continued to linger in my thoughts.

Finishing up, I stepped out of the water and dried myself off, figuring I needed to get out of the sun, though it felt good after the initial chill. I was still drying off when the lady on the lounger got up, gathering her stuff to leave. She took the long way around the pool, coming up and passing right in front of me as I got a close-up view of her; long legs, solid body, and nearly perfect skin making her even more striking.

Even as I smiled, she didn't acknowledge I was there as she strolled inches away, the smell of sunscreen filling my nose. But there was little doubt she took the long way for a reason, and it was to get my attention, which worked.

Clearing my head and the temptation to follow her, I grabbed my towel and hotel key card, and made it back to my room to call April, to direct my inflated desire on her.

Chapter 29

After a restful night, thanks to my long and sweaty phone conversation with April, my Sunday morning clear thinking gave me ideas of where to go next. With a little research, I learned Maximillian Conway had a multi-million-dollar home in La Jolla. It was located on the edge of the ocean, not too far from the La Jolla Beach & Tennis club where I had met him last month. He was an athletic person who I didn't imagine would be going to church each Sunday.

With the nice weather, it would be tennis or possibly golf. I had remembered a couple first names of the men he'd played tennis with, listening as they talked smack on the court, and would use that to my advantage. I called into his office and someone answered, as expected. His business was one that was open seven days a week, as Brandon said.

"Hello," I said, sounding a little panicked. "This is Larry and I'm a friend of Max's. I feel silly for calling, but I lost my cell phone and don't have his phone number handy. We were supposed to meet for tennis or golf today, but I can't for the life of me remember what time or which one. I'd hate to make them wait for me. We get used to having all our information handy on our phones and I'm lost without it. Can you help me?"

It was a five-star performance. I spoke as if I was out of breath in a deeper tone, uncertain what to do. She likely wouldn't give me his phone number, but I could hopefully get an answer on where he'd be today.

"I'll see what I can do," she responded. "You said your name was Larry?"

"Yes it is. That would be outstanding. Anything you can do to help would be great." I was laying it on thick, using as much honey as I could.

"I can't give out his phone number, but I can call and see what I can come up with. Please hold."

I sat and waited for several minutes, listening to horrible canned music, with ads for his real estate agency, bragging about skills to find your dream home. I'd never heard a company undersell themselves. They were always the best at what they do and could walk on water. Maybe I needed to do the same to market my business. *The best PI you could ever hire!* A supreme tagline to add to my business cards.

"Hello Sir," she said coming on the line. "I was able to get a hold of Mr. Conway's wife and she said he was golfing today at the La Jolla Country Club. Tee time was at 10:15. Does that help you?"

I was feeling proud of myself; the five-star performance had worked.

"Oh my, yes. You are wonderful. I'll be sure to tell Max how helpful you were. Our whole life is on these blasted phones these days and we're lost without them."

She laughed. "I understand what you mean. If I lost mine, I'd be a mess."

"Thank you. Next time I'm at his office I will have to find you and buy you lunch. Have a wonderful day."

"You do the same."

If Larry ever showed up when she was there, he would be in for a surprise when she expected lunch. Always good to have a little mystery in your life. Maybe I'd send her an anonymous gift card in the mail as a thank you.

I had the information about Max I wanted. I wasn't sure I could walk right in and go out on the course. If not, rounds of golf normally take about three hours or more. I could always get him on the way out. But I'd see about bumping into him before his tee time.

Figuring he would arrive early, I got there by 9 a.m. Bringing up the country club website, I learned there was a bag drop station at the entrance of the rear parking lot. I camped out there watching for him, for he wouldn't be too hard to spot as I remembered him clearly from our previous meeting.

At about 9:40 he showed up, leaving his bag per the rules. I ran him down as he headed for the main entrance to check in. He wasn't happy to see me.

"What do you want?" he declared with a tinge of anger in his voice.

"I've learned several details about Garrett I need to talk with you about."

"Do you not realize I'm about to go play golf. Now isn't the time."

"You're a hard man to track down. Tell me a time and we can talk. But it needs to be soon."

He waved me off and walked away.

"What do you know about someone named Stetson Poole?" I yelled to him before he entered the front door.

This got his attention. He immediately stopped, turning around and came to me, coming within inches of my face.

"What did you say?" he whispered with concern filling his expression.

"Do you have someone named Stetson Poole who works for you?" I replied, keeping my voice low as well.

"Shit," he muttered. "Not now and not here."

I had struck a nerve. There was no doubt he knew the name.

"Then where and when. And it needs to be soon."

He thought about it for a minute. "We can talk after golf today at 3 p.m. at Rocky Point. There is a park there where we can chat privately."

"Where is Rocky Point?"

"You're a smart guy and can find it yourself. Don't be late."

I nodded and let him get to his match. He was right; I could find it using the mapping app of my phone. It was on the southern boundary of Ellen Browning Scripps Park, which sat on the edge of the ocean in La Jolla. It was on the fringe of downtown La Jolla, with places to walk, shop and eat. I decided I could kill the rest of my time there, while getting a relaxing stroll in. Parking was a challenge, but I found an opening close enough that I could walk to the shops and make Rocky Point without any issues.

After being followed weeks earlier, I continued to watch for a tail, but I wasn't seeing one today, which was a relief. One less thing to worry about.

I found several places to stop and look, including the Contemporary Fine Arts Gallery, which had many captivating paintings and sculptures from internationally acclaimed artists displayed. A few of the works I found engrossing, while others made no sense at all to me, no matter how long I glared at them. The atmosphere was calming, and a pleasant change from the crazy world I was living in. Maybe I should purchase artwork for my home-office. Though looking at the prices, nothing here would fit my budget.

After more window browsing, eating lunch, and more browsing, I made my way down to Rocky Point. It was a beautiful park, with green grass, a few trees, playground, picnic tables, walking path, and an unobstructed view of the Pacific Ocean, the sounds of the waves on the water brushing up against the rocky shoreline below.

I found an open bench to sit on, applying additional sunscreen to my arms and face. I remained comfortable in my tan cargo pants, Colorado Avalanche t-shirt, and light gray zip up that hid my shoulder holster, which I'd put on before coming to the park.

It was starting to cool off, but had to be in the lower seventies, where back in Denver it probably was around freezing, with snow, which was common in early spring.

About five minutes after three, Max showed up and sat next to me.

"Sorry I'm late," he said. "It's a bitch finding a parking spot down here on a Sunday."

"No worries. I'm glad you made the time. How was your round of golf today?" I figured a little small talk would help ease him into the conversation.

"I shot an eighty-five, which is about average for me."

"Not bad."

"I try to be good at everything I do."

There was little doubt of that. He was wealthy beyond anything I'd ever reach, short of winning the lottery. A million dollar plus home, a real estate business worth much more than that and probably an illegal business that put it to shame. He drove an expensive European car, while dressing in clothes that weren't off the rack. And I doubt he sat in the drive-thru at McDonalds with the common folk, waiting for his extra value meal.

"You mentioned a name earlier," he said.

"It seemed to rattle you."

He appeared more relaxed now, having time on the golf course to think over what he'd heard and compose himself.

"I wouldn't say 'rattle,' more like 'surprised.' It was a name I'd not heard in many years."

"Someone who worked for you?"

"Maybe. But I need to give you more background. This way you understand what all could be involved."

"I'm listening."

He stopped, turning to look at me. "I need to make sure you aren't recording what I'm saying."

I took off my zip up and showed him as much skin as I could. Then I handed him my phone after powering it down.

"Nothing on me to record anything you say. And my phone, as you can see, is off."

"You're carrying a weapon."

"Only for protection. I've been in a few scrapes lately and someone has threatened to kill me. You have nothing to worry about from me."

He nodded. "What I'm telling you is between us. If you tell anyone else, I'll deny saying any of it. Do you understand?"

I nodded, happy to learn what I could, if he spoke the truth.

"I'm only saying this out of respect for Garrett. He was a good man, as I told you last month. He did much to help me through the years and even saved my hide a time or two."

"I've worked with him and would agree. I have a lot of respect for him."

"This goes back quite a few years. As you know I'm a real estate mogul out here. Mostly in San Diego, but I've stretched up into the Los Angeles area. What you don't know, or least I believe you don't know, is I ran other businesses that were less than on the up and up."

I wasn't surprised by the statement. "I figured as much, though didn't know any specifics."

He gave me a grim smile. "Telling this puts me at risk. But again, I owe Garrett. This business dealt with drugs and illegal arms sales. These deals were brokered with a group, which I'd say were government folks working with the…" He stopped looking around and then whispered, "CIA. Sort of their own Iran-Contra affair, if you're familiar with that event which happened while Reagan was president."

I was familiar with it, though only from what I'd heard on the news or read online. Arms had been sold illegally to Iran, the money used to fund the Contras to fight the government in Nicaragua. It was one of those government operations of 'arming one of our enemies, to secretly fight another,' a tactic I never understood when it came to the whole of politics. It was all done in the background and illegal per laws passed by Congress. The deal was exposed, investigated and charges filed. Though from what I recalled most everyone was pardoned and spent little time, if any, in jail.

"This was an operation sanctioned by the government?" I queried.

He shook his head. "No, I don't believe it was. From what I know it's totally rogue, run by a group working on their own, for their own agenda."

"Which was?" I asked, though I was certain of the answer.

"What else, the almighty dollar, or at least that is what I suspect. I'm not privy to all the inter-workings."

"Flooding the streets with guns and drugs, all in the name of money," I declared, shaking my head in disgust. I wasn't certain why I was surprised; it was all too common. "Why were you a part of this? Don't you have enough money!"

"Not making excuses, but for a man like me, with business and family obligations, there is never enough money. And the housing market and economy here was depressed for several years. I needed to find new business ventures and this opportunity presented itself as a goldmine. I got involved and in too deep before realizing *everything* that was going on. It was just merchandise at first. Then I learned how much of it was hitting the streets and grew concerned."

I wanted to call him on it, about his not understanding what was going on and yell "bullshit" but I resisted.

"You got cold feet and wanted out?" I stated bluntly.

"Yes. And for personal reasons as well. One of my sons got hooked on the poison that was on the streets at the time." He paused for a minute, seeming to get emotional, looking down at his feet. "We did all we could to try and get him off of it, but in the end he couldn't shake it. He eventually overdosed, committing suicide according to the note he left behind." He paused again, running his index finger in the sand at his feet. "From there on I wanted no part of the whole deal."

I wasn't sure what to think. Whether to believe him or not. He was convincing but I continued to probe for answers. "How did they feel when you wanted out?"

"They weren't happy," Max smirked. "Sent nasty people to try and change my mind. That is when Garrett jumped in and made sure they left me alone, in a manner of speaking."

"Should I read that to mean he eliminated them?"

Max looked up at me but didn't respond, the positive answer showing on his face.

"They then backed off?"

"For the time being, they let me out and found others to distribute their goods. Their network was extensive."

I wondered if that was Vicente and Luciano. Vicente had a big arms and drug deal in the works before he was killed. It made sense the two cousins had become a distributor.

"You said 'for the time being,' does that mean you're back in?"

Again no response, only a frown on his face.

"Man, you're a piece of work," I said, reading between the lines.

"I had little choice." His reply sounded like a defeated man.

Sure he had a choice, he just wasn't strong or brave enough to stand up to them.

"Were they responsible for the killing of Garrett and his family?"

Max looked away, uncertain how to reply. "I don't know. Possibly. They weren't too pleased with my leaving and Garrett's defense of me. Could have been a message. One I heard loud and clear. I no longer had Garrett to protect me."

If they'd pulled him back into the business, then yes it would seem they could have been the ones behind it. Or everything he was telling me was a ruse to throw me off.

"And your current head of security wasn't tough enough to protect you?"

"Not from them…" He stopped again, choosing his words carefully. "Let's say he has a stake in keeping me working for them."

"He works for them as well?"

Max tapped his index finger to his nose.

"What does all of this have to do with the name I gave you?" I asked, changing back to why I was there in the first place.

Max, turned back to me, looking me right in the eye.

"Stetson Poole was an alias a powerful person was using inside the organization running the guns and drug business. Garrett mentioned it to me and said be wary if the name came up."

I was surprised he had been forthcoming with this information. Was he protecting himself or was there an ulterior motive I wasn't seeing?

"Did he ever indicate who it was?"

"No he didn't. Either he didn't know or really didn't want to know since he wanted out."

I was told the hit order came from within Max's company and was orchestrated by Stetson Poole. I had no idea if it was true or not, but somehow, I needed to find out.

"Sounds like you have a mess on your hands," I stated bluntly and firmly.

"No shit, Sherlock," replied Max, looking sullen.

I shook my head, thinking I could use Sherlock Holmes and Doctor Watson's prognosticative skills right about now, because the further I dug into this, the more confused I was.

Chapter 30

Receiving information from Max got me thinking about where to head next. I asked him if he'd ever heard of Shark Tail Detective Agency, and he said no, but he wouldn't be surprised if they had a dummy office setup to chase people off. I also learnt the name used for the company running the drugs and guns, though it could have changed since he wasn't trusted and in the loop, as in the past. But it gave me a place to start.

Max had been quite forthcoming with information. I wasn't sure what to think of him and what he was telling me. I normally could judge whether someone was lying, or at the most not revealing the whole truth. He on the other hand I couldn't get a read on. There was a slight twinge in the back of my neck, warning me to be careful with the leads he'd so easily given me. He professed to being indebted to the man he knew as Garrett. But those could have just been words spoken that didn't mean anything, even though it appeared he was sincere.

At this time, I'd be cautious knowing it could be all leading me into a trap. Or it could have been him hoping to drag me into his mess to bail him out as Garrett had done in the past. Either way I had no intention of taking another beating after I'd finally reached the point where I could move around without extreme agony.

Much on the internet is forever, and searching, even for old expired information, can often times yield results. Since I'd brought a tablet with me, I worked off it in my hotel room hunting for the name given me. As was often the case with these types of companies, the name implied import/export. This one for toys, which seemed sick to me.

Happy Child Imports showed up, though down the page as sixth in the listing since it wasn't often searched for. It showed a location in Torrance, which was up the coast.

When Monday morning rolled around I decided to take a drive up along the Pacific Ocean and see if there were any remnants of them left.

It was a two hour drive up north, about forty miles further from Newport Beach where I had met Emily. I took the same route along the coast and then once to Newport, it was I-405 into Torrance, the Monday morning traffic increasing the drive time. Torrance sits in Los Angeles County, its western edge reaching the ocean, and was famous for being the US headquarters of Honda Motor Company, meaning my CRV would fit right in.

It was another warm day, with talks of the temps breaking eighty again. The drive along the ocean was cooler, but once in the city you could feel the sun's heat scorching through the tinted glass. The location of Happy Child Imports was further in town, in a string of buildings combining office space and warehouse storage on Fujita Street.

When I arrived, the building was there but occupied by an athletic goods business I'd never heard of before. After parking on the street badly in need of paving, I walked in the front door and was greeted by an Asian woman in dark slacks and pink blouse covered with a brown apron.

"Good morning, sir," she announced joyfully. "How can I help you?"

"This doesn't appear to be the Happy Child Imports," I noted, with a tone of disappointment in my voice.

"Oh wow," she declared, her face flush with surprise. "I've not heard that name in years. They were here before us. Probably three or four years ago."

"You remember them?" I asked.

"I do. I'm the owner of this store, along with my husband. We looked at the space before they moved out."

"Anything you remember about it?"

She thought about it for a minute. "Strange people. Very secretive. Would only let us look at certain areas in the warehouse. All their trucks were closed, and it prevented us from seeing inside. Computers were turned off as well. We had to agree not to move in until sixty days after they vacated. I didn't ask why but didn't care. We got the space cheap on a sublease for the first two years."

"Did you find anything when you moved in? Anything left behind?"

She shook her head. "Not a damn thing. This place was cleaned from head to toe, with a sanitized smell left behind. No dirt, no scraps of paper, no pallets left outside. Not even toilet paper left in the bathrooms. And all the computer and phone wiring were removed. Ripped out even. We had to rewire the whole space again. Probably why they wanted us to wait sixty days before moving in. They didn't want any evidence they were ever here."

There was little doubt the operation was covering their tracks.

"Did you find that odd?"

"Sure. A toy company not wanting anything left behind. It was obvious there was more here. But my husband and I didn't care. It was a great deal for us and prime location with all the space we needed. I mean it was practically free the first two years compared to what we pay now."

"How about payment. Did you mail off your check to them?"

"Not directly. They had a banker we were to send them to."

"Do you remember the name of the banker?" I asked. I was hoping for a clue.

She stopped to think about what she was saying, realizing she was talking to a complete stranger and telling him info she shouldn't have.

"You're a slick one. Getting me to talk. Who the hell are you and why do you want to know?"

There were two options, honesty or to lie. I didn't think I'd be exposing them to any trouble. I decided on the truth, though not all the details. I pulled out my ID and showed her.

"A private detective," she said after looking it over. "Jarvis Mann seems like an odd name for an American."

"My parents had a relative from England they admired and named me after. Would it help if I used terms like 'bloke' and 'mate' with an English accent?" I joked.

She smiled. "Maybe. Many think I should be speaking with a Japanese accent. But I've lived here all my life. My grandparents were even interned at one of the American Japanese camps during World War Two. Only because of their heritage and fear. They could have spoken perfect English and it wouldn't have mattered."

"A shameful moment in time for our country. Hopefully we learned from it."

"From what I'm seeing these days, it wouldn't appear so. Nevertheless, what does the PI who isn't from England, looking to find out about the former tenants?"

"They may be involved in a murder of a man and his family. A complicated investigative process has led me to them. I'm hoping to find where they moved to. My thinking is they're still in business at a new location and likely under a different name."

She thought about it for a moment, before excusing herself. I grabbed from their counter a flyer of the goods they sold. Most anything you could think of they had here, from athletic equipment to clothing, and supposedly at wholesale prices. Flipping through and seeing what they offered it appeared it was true. I might have get a little shopping in, for one can never have enough exercise gear.

She returned about ten minutes later, with an Asian man, who she said was her husband. She whispered in his ear and he nodded. He came to the counter wearing a similar brown apron to his wife's and put out his hand, which I shook. He was of the same height as his wife, about 5'7", both slender, probably in their fifties, though I might have thought younger if it wasn't for their gray hair, for their skin showed no wrinkles. I could only wish to look this good when I reached their age.

"I'm Miki Yoshino," he said. It was the name on the business. *Yoshino Sporting Goods*. "This is my wife, Tamika. I understand you are Jarvis, a private detective."

"Yes, I'm Jarvis. It is a pleasure to meet you."

"May I see your ID again?"

I handed the laminate card to him to process. He read the ID slowly to himself—every line of listed information, before handing it back.

"Thank you. I see you're from Colorado. Why are you here in California working a case?"

"It is where the evidence led me. I've been down in San Diego mostly. The family who was killed were living in Oceanside."

His eyes glared at me, as if trying to read me. "And you believe if you're given the banker's name, it will help you find the killer of this poor family?"

"It will provide another piece to the case. Hopefully one that gets me closer." I left out my thoughts yesterday with Max and how I was more confused with each new shred of evidence I found.

"Who was killed and how?"

"A husband, wife and three-year-old son. Killed in a car bomb."

He shook his head, turning to his wife, who nodded. “Such horror in the world. The name of the banker was Carlton Gilpin. We made a copy of his address to give you. But please don’t tell him you got it from us.”

Tamika handed me the piece of paper. The address was in the L.A. area from what I could tell.

“Thank you so much. They will never know where it came from.”

“Is there anything else we can help you with?” wondered Tamika.

I opened the flyer to a page I had dog-eared and pointed to several items of clothing.

“Do you have these in my size?”

They both smiled and took me in the back to happily find what I was searching for.

Chapter 31

With a name and address, I finally had data to work with. They included the leasing company that handled the building, giving me another place I could investigate. Though Miki called Carlton Gilpin a banker, he was in reality a CPA. His address was in Anaheim—a bunch more miles to put on my rental.

By the time I was done, I will have seen most of southern California. Thankfully there was an abundance of interstates and freeways to travel on. Though congested, this trip wasn't bad for mid-day.

His office was in the Bank of the West building, the entrance to the other suites where he resided on the backside.

I walked in and took the elevator to the second floor. When I arrived, the door was locked with a sign saying they'd be back at 1:30. This gave me nearly an hour to kill.

Going outside, I scanned for food nearby. Within walking distance was Tom's Place Restaurant. It was a basic diner with large menu, where you ordered at the counter, then picked up your food on a plastic tray when it was done. I ordered a burger, with fries and soda. The food was ready in about ten minutes, and I found an open booth, to sit and eat.

While enjoying my burger, I thought over the connection the CPA would have to Happy Child Imports. My brother had been a CPA as well, with a hidden ledger of money being laundered for a vicious mob boss. Carlton could be doing the same, taking money and then laundering through other accounts for businesses. Proving this would be challenging, and something I couldn't do on my own, even if I could find evidence. I didn't have the expertise. I needed a tactic to shake the man.

I went over options mentally while slowly eating my meal. The fries were salted, even though I'd asked for them not to be. I should have returned them but decided not to make a fuss. Walking up to the counter and showing them my gun would have gotten me fresh salt-free fries but would have been a horrible decision. In this day and age where guns seemed to be everywhere and used to strike out in anger, even for the pettiest of reasons, we all needed to curb that anger and better regulate our rage in other ways.

I finished up as it neared 1:30, and Carlton was just unlocking the door when I returned. Smiling and saying a quick hello, we stepped into his suite. It wasn't large—small waiting area and a back office, where he could talk with clients in private. He said he'd be right back, needing to check messages. I took a chair, finding a financial magazine that wouldn't hold my attention long.

About twenty minutes later, he called out for me to step in, which I did. He didn't offer up his hand, his attention still on his iPhone. Finding a chair, I sat down and waited for him to initiate the conversation, which finally happened after he was done flicking items off the screen with his finger.

"What can I help you with?" he said, iPhone lingering in his hand.

"I need tax help and financial planning," I proclaimed.

"What do you have in place at this time?"

"Not much. Savings, IRA and my business, though I'm not sure it's worth much. I'm a Private Detective."

His eyes lit up. "Really. You work here in the L.A. area?"

I nodded convincingly, which was a lie.

"What is your name?"

"Edwin Ware."

His face infused with surprise, mouth slightly open, the iPhone in his hand dropping as his arm went limp. There was little doubt he knew the name.

"Did you say…Edwin Ware?" His hesitation in saying the name was lengthy.

I smiled. "Yes. Why do you ask?"

"Nothing special." He said, quickly backpedaling. "Thought I might have recognized it. What is the name of your business?"

"Shark Tail Detective Agency." I pulled out the card I'd gotten from Edwin when we shook him down and handed it to Carlton.

He looked at it for a minute, before handing it back as if it was diseased.

"This says your office is in San Diego."

"It is. But you asked if I worked in the area. I cover the entire region of Southern California. Wherever the work takes me."

He wasn't sure what to do. He knew the name and probably thought he'd never hear it again. His tanned forehead showed a few beads of sweat, even though the room was cool from the air conditioning. His lower lip might have shown perspiration too, if it weren't for the bushy mustache. It seemed I had stunned him to silence.

"Can you help me?" I declared. "I have a lot of money coming my way I need to, how should I put it…*shelter* the funds. Need to make sure the government doesn't take too big a chunk to waste in their debt-ridden coffers."

"How much money are we talking about?" he replied, his interest piqued as he finally set his phone down. Greed, for the moment, had replaced his concern.

"Large sum," I said smiling, both hands extended, my fingers rubbing my thumbs. "Maybe six figures or more. If the deal goes down correctly you can add a couple of zeros to the sum. Happy Child Imports is handling the transaction."

He really looked confused now. "I thought you'd dropped that name and were using the other designation."

"Bringing it back." I was sounding confident, knowing he was confirming important leads for me. "No need to worry anymore since all the parties have been eliminated. We have two places to roll in what merchandise we need. More money for all to split."

He was in full on panic mode now, wiping his forehead with his arm, the sleeves on this white business shirt rolled up. "I don't know. It's dangerous to bring in more. It will catch the eyes of the feds. It might be best to filter the new funds through someone else who can handle it."

"That is why we have a sharp man like you to take care of it. You're the best in keeping those nosy government hounds out of our money matters. No matter what import designation we use."

Standing up, he started pacing, all 160 pounds and 5'8" of him. His black shiny hairline was receding, and with my words, more thinning lay ahead. He reached for his cell phone on the table, which he unlocked and started searching for a number. He was about to make a call when I stopped him.

"Put the phone down," I said forcefully, my gun pointed at him, the irony of my thoughts earlier in the diner eluding me. "Time for you to come clean."

Genuine fear showed on his face. I waved my Berretta to get him to sit down, while I grabbed the phone. Looking at the screen I saw a name, Worldwide Toys Inc. I quickly texted the contact to my phone and then deleted the text from his phone, before sitting it on the table before me. I always hated when people couldn't put their phones down while having a conversation.

"Who the hell are you?" he remarked nervously.

"No need for you to know. Just realize I'm onto you and your scheme. I will have the government in your life looking over every inch of it. Time to tell me what you know."

"They will kill me!"

"Yes, they will. But since you're an accessary to the murders of three people, including a three-year-old boy, I really don't care."

His sweating increased. "What are you talking about? I'm not involved in any murder."

"Says the money man laundering guns and drug money for the CIA. I don't think your word means much."

He was shaking his head. "I didn't know what the money was from, just had to clean it through several accounts throughout the world and then transfer it back to wherever they needed it. Normally it was in cash."

"And you charge them a fee for your CPA services."

He nodded.

"Maybe even skim a little, since it's hard for them to notice."

He didn't answer, but you could see the truth on his face.

"Where is this new Worldwide Toys located?"

"I don't know. It's all done electronically. Rarely have I had someone visit me and I've never been to their location. That was true of the other company as well. The less I knew the better."

"A visitor like Edwin Ware?"

"A man showed up once before, using that name. But they said it was an alias and the name could have several faces."

"What about Stetson Poole?"

"I haven't heard that name." His eyes looked right at me, leading me to believe he was telling the truth.

I looked around his office, then stood up, going to his filing cabinets.

"You won't find anything. I don't keep paper copies on hand. Like I said all electronic. Easier to delete if necessary."

"And what will you do after I leave here?" I asked, waving my gun in his direction.

He put up his hands in fear. "Nothing…I swear. It will be like you were never here. Please…just leave me alone."

"Best that you adhere to that thought. If you tell them I was here and what you told me, I'd imagine they will kill you without a second thought and find themselves a new CPA. It might put a crimp in their business for a while, but I'm sure there are plenty around here they can find to wash their dirty money. They may even have a second one on payroll to handle parts of their riches already. The drugs and guns business are a massive one."

"I will, I will. Just please leave me out of this." He begged desperately.

I looked him square in the eye, giving him my 'or else' look and walked out. He had been scared to death. I had little to fear from him, though men like him can flip on a dime in the right situation. It was good I hadn't told him who I really was. Just a nameless stranger who came to scare him, which, it seemed, I'd done a good job of.

Chapter 32

I needed to back off and absorb what I'd learned, heading back to my hotel. The long drive took more than two hours in the rush hour traffic. I was mentally drained, a simple dinner in the hotel restaurant and a return to my room were in order. I hoped for a competitive basketball or baseball option to get lost in.

I found a table and ordered a beer, looking over the menu. It wasn't long before a person stood across the table from me and I glanced up.

To my surprise it was the woman from the pool I had been admiring, her scent flowery, her chestnut eyes inviting. She had walked into the dining area and I had completely missed her.

"May I join you?" she asked in a rich, sultry tone.

I looked up and down, taking full stock of her. Her aqua bikini was covered by an ankle length plum spaghetti strap swim cover-up. Her sunglasses were on top of her hair, her mane wet from the pool. A large baggy flowered purse slung over her shoulder, flip-flops on her feet. Her skin was tanned and perfect—no need for make-up to hide any blemishes, teeth a sparkle of ivory white, a smile no man could resist.

"Be my guest," I replied, placing the menu down, captivated by her presence. "What do I owe the pleasure of your company?"

"I hate to eat alone. I hope you don't mind?"

I didn't care to eat alone either, but I'd done it many times in my life with no thought or concern about being by myself. There were times when being isolated in my thoughts with no one around was fulfilling. In this case it was difficult to resist a beautiful creature joining me.

The waiter came over and she ordered a glass of red wine.

"My name is Jarvis," I said, while putting out my hand.

Reaching out, she cupped my palm, her skin soft. "I'm Kit. It's my pleasure to meet you."

Her hand lingered for a long time in mine, the skin to skin connection invigorating, before I pulled away.

"The pleasure is all mine. Are you in town working?" I inquired.

"Yes. I came in yesterday."

"How long are you in town for?"

Her eyes were fixed on mine. "Depends on many factors. For now, at least a couple more days unless there is a better reason to stay longer."

The words implied a lot. A flirtatious moment with a lovely woman. One I'd experienced a few times in my life. If I wasn't such a cool guy, I probably would have been embarrassed. But I'd gotten good at this game through the years.

"Time will tell then. What type of work do you do?"

"Freelance," she said, adding nothing else. "What about you?"

"I'm in town on business as well. Best I not get into the details. Secretive stuff and all that." I believe I winked at her, though it was involuntary.

She gave me a wry grin. "A spy, it would seem. Am I having dinner with Bond…James Bond?"

I held up my beer and shook my head. "This glass isn't 'a shaken not stirred Martini' I'm drinking," I explained with a smile.

She laughed. "Jason Bourne then."

"I don't think I look like Matt Damon. I'm more a Bradley Cooper type, when the light hits me right." I rubbed at the hair on my face.

She rested her chin on her cupped hands, sizing me up. "Yes, I could see that. Maybe he will play you in the movie about your life."

I leaned forward, matching her glare, with my own. "I'm ready to sell the rights if someone will write the story. Though Hollywood has a tendency of screwing up the plot."

The waiter returned with her wine, which she tasted, and approved. He asked us if we wanted an appetizer, which we agreed upon. Chicken wings with barbeque sauce was ordered, along with another beer.

"Daring, you walking over to join me," I noted.

"Not really. I saw you looking at me at the pool yesterday."

"Really! I thought I was extremely coy in my admiration. How did you feel about that?"

She flipped her hair back. "Flattering, I grabbed your attention."

"I'm certainly not the first man to get lost in gazing at you."

"No. But not all of them look like Bradley Cooper. Most are creeps, with unibrows, body odor and not much upstairs."

I shrugged. “How can you be certain I’m not a creep?”

“Instinct. And you smell nice.”

“Back atcha,” I replied, taking another whiff of her scent, a hint of jasmine and cedar, I surmised.

She sipped on her wine, her left hand curling her hair behind her ear, as it kept flipping into her eyes when she looked down. It was a cute habit, even a nervous one, though she didn’t seem to be nervous. Leaning back in her chair, she crossed her legs, the split in the cover-up revealing her long, smooth, tanned limb, clearly for me to see.

The waiter dropped off the wings, his eyes finding her leg as well, though he recovered in time to take our dinner order. Kit ordered the Caesar salad, while I decided on the herb rubbed pork chop.

“I can’t believe you noticed me watching you,” I said after enjoying a chicken wing. “I thought I was being quite stealthy with my leering. You must have great vision.”

“I see a lot going on around me,” replied Kit after another sip of wine, eyes peering over the glass. “A skill I have honed through the years. As a woman you need to be aware of your surroundings. Plenty of creeps looking to take advantage of you. One or two have tried to spike my drinks. They quickly learned that wasn’t a smart idea when they were caught. Hopefully they learned their lesson.”

“You have no fear of me doing any such thing. I’m a perfect gentleman.”

“A shame. You wouldn’t need to spike anything to get what *you* want. Sometimes a woman desires a man being more…primal.”

I smiled, sensing without a doubt where this was headed, temptation rearing its ugly head at my core, as I savored a couple more chicken wings. She did the same, licking the sauce off her fingers, slowly. The seduction was in full swing, there was little doubt, and I wondered if others around us noticed what was happening. She felt no shame in showing her desire in public.

“I enjoyed your little show, when you walked the long way around the pool, passing slowly in front of me, never once looking my way. Impressive display on your part.”

“It seemed fitting, to see how you reacted. It’s nice to know you were impressed.”

“I’m trained as well. Though my girlfriend might not like you sitting here flirting with me."

Her finger circled the top of her glass playfully. "Where is she?"

I brought up April to see how Kit would react. I could have said she was up in my room sleeping, but I decided what was the harm in seeing what the sensual lady across from me was offering.

"Far away at the moment."

"Good. It would seem we're free to carry this on after dinner, if you desire too."

I grinned like I had struck gold. "Difficult to resist you and your charm. Maybe I should eat lightly."

"Perhaps. Or maybe have them bring the dinner up later and we can leave now."

I thought it over, thinking *why the hell not.*

"Your room or mine?" I asked.

"Mine," she said, while standing up, the cover-up drifting down her leg.

The waiter returned, and we told him our plans and to deliver the food to her room in about an hour. We walked side by side to the elevator, and climbed in, the car empty. As the doors closed, she turned into me and started kissing me. I wrapped my arms around her, kissing back with a fire, our tongues intertwined. I pushed her up against the wall, her hands on my butt, squeezing my cheeks, as I pressed my body into her.

With the sound of the ding, we stopped, her leading the way to her room, where she opened the door with the keycard. She tossed her purse in a chair and turned to me as the door closed. I grabbed her again, kissing her sweet lips, this time my hand running up the inside of her thigh, to her crotch and down the other, as one of her legs curled around mine.

Happy with what I found on her thighs, I moved her towards the bed, tossing her onto it, her mouth open, her eyes with that primal look. I smiled, pulling off my zip-up since it was warm and then, reaching behind my back, I pulled out my gun.

"I maybe a horny male, but I'm not a stupid one," I stated firmly. "What the hell do you want, lady?"

She looked shocked, searching for what to say. It took her a minute to come up with an answer.

"What the hell is this, a robbery?"

"I was about to ask you the same thing."

I checked the rest of the room. The closet and bathroom were clear. I checked her luggage and found a gun, extra ammo, a knife and collapsible baton, all among her clothing. Next to them was a notebook computer and a cell phone. With my eye on her and my gun aimed, I went to her purse and found another gun and a second cell phone. In her wallet her driver's license read, Kit Hinton, the picture matching her face. All her credits cards had the same name. I didn't find anything else that identified what she was doing. What I did find was a pill bottle. It was Chloral Hydrate, a sedative. It could be she had insomnia, or it was meant for me.

"Were you planning on drugging me?" I said, while showing her the pills.

She didn't say anything, just continued to lay there.

"Lady, I've had a tough couple of months and I don't have time for games. Who are you working for? Is it the CIA, NSA, FBI or maybe you work with Maximillian Conway?"

She sat up on the bed. "I don't work for any of them. As I said, I'm freelance."

"Freelance people are normally hired by someone."

"No one hired me. I was trying to learn what you had learned."

"By drugging me?"

"You would have slept well with a happy face. I planned on fucking you first."

I frowned. "My loss. Good thing for me I don't seduce easily these days."

"That is counter to what I had learned. I was told you were easily swayed by a lovely face."

"Who told you that?"

She crossed her arms and didn't answer.

"I can call a cop here in Oceanside and have you busted for the guns you have, not to mention your plan to drug me. You better speak up or I start dialing."

"You know none of that will stick. My guns were legally purchased and everything else is your word against mine."

"You've got to be involved in this case I'm working. Now either tell me or spend the night in jail."

She shook her head. "I can't."

"Why not?"

"Because he'll get mad at me. This was supposed to be a simple recon where I learn what you had learned and then I get away clean without you knowing."

I stepped back, leaning against the wall, my gun now at my side. I didn't feel threatened by her anymore. She could have been working for the other side involved in my case, but for whatever reason I now didn't believe so. The question was, who was she working for?

"I've got all night. Hell, dinner will be arriving soon. Believe it or not my plan after eating was to crawl into bed, relax and watch the ball game. I can do that here and lock you in the bathroom until you're ready to talk."

She was trapped with little options, cursing to herself she stood.

"Fine, I will tell you. But believe me he is going to be mad."

"Who is going to be mad, Kit?"

"Garrett, or as you know him, Rocky."

I blinked at her, shocked.

I'll be damned. He was still alive.

Chapter 33

It was an odd feeling. I was surprised, yet I wasn't surprised. Rocky had somehow once again beaten the odds and was still alive. He'd done it before, which was why I wasn't shocked. Once again overcoming and cheating death was remarkable. Though as I'd learn, just barely and not without taking a fair amount of beating himself.

"He was badly hurt," said Kit, sitting on the bed again. "He is recovering, and now much better than he was. They tortured him on his boat, shocking him, using a knife, cutting into him and even putting a bullet through the fleshy part of his leg. Two guys working for someone. Garrett got loose, killing one of the men and dumping him overboard. The other he subdued, and tried to get him to talk, but he wouldn't say much, no matter what Garrett did to him. He knew he was hurt badly and couldn't continue for too long. He killed him, brought the boat back to the marina late at night, left the dead man on it and set it on fire, before escaping into the darkness. Like before, he needed to disappear and play dead to remove the heat on him."

I holstered my gun and sat in a chair across from Kit. I noticed her sultry tone was gone. No longer needed as part of her ploy to lure me.

"He called you then?"

"Yes. I picked him up. He was in bad shape. I knew a doctor who would be willing to treat him. A good man that I trusted. Garrett got the care he needed and is recovering."

"How do you know each other?"

She looked down, a glimmer of tears in her eyes. "Claire was my sister."

"His wife, Claire?" I proclaimed in shock.

"Yes, the one killed in the car bomb, along with my nephew, Rocky."

"I'm sorry. I know how it feels to lose a sibling."

She wiped the tears from her cheeks. "It still hurts, even after the years have passed. She and I were close. And to murder that sweet little boy was unthinkable. I've been trying for some time to let it go, but I can't. I want the killers found and given a taste of their own medicine."

I understood the pain, which I, to this day, felt about Flynn. And the thirst for vengeance, which I had tasted, though it didn't ease the loss.

"Looking at the hardware you have, I assume you've had training to use these tools."

She nodded. "I have. I did private security work like Garrett did. Like I said, freelance. That is how we met and how he met my sister. It was love at first sight between the two of them."

"And she was why he wanted to quit the business."

The tears continued to flow. "Yes. He'd done enough bad things in his life—horrible even. She was his salvation."

There was a knock on the door. I checked the peephole, and it was the restaurant delivering the meal. After I had signed off on it, I carried the tray into the room, sitting it on the small table.

"Time to eat and then we need to talk more," I stated.

She came over and took a seat, while I opened the Styrofoam containers. The food was good, though my pork chop was lukewarm, but tender to cut. We sat quietly as we ate.

Once finished, I tossed all the containers into the small trash basket and sat back down. I remained silent for a minute thinking over what we had covered. But before I told her much else, I needed to verify her identity.

"Not that I don't trust you," I declared. "But I need confirmation from Garrett, of who you are."

"I had a feeling you would be asking me that. Though I'm not real thrilled about letting him know you made me."

"Explain to him that I'm just that good at what I do. He will enjoy hearing that."

She smiled weakly, her tear-stained cheeks cleaned up from a trip to the bathroom. "If you say so."

Getting up she went to her suitcase and pulled out the other phone. The first thing she did was send a text message. It simply said *"He made me. You need to call."* It took ten minutes before the phone rang. There were tense words on the other side before she told him what I said to tell him. I didn't hear any laughter, but she handed me the basic flip phone.

"Always the comedian," he said, his voice weaker than I remember ever hearing it, but there was no doubt it was him.

"Didn't make you laugh. Maybe because it's the truth."

"I'm not in a laughing mood these days. She is on the up and up. Tell her what you can. I'm certain you've been your usual pest and learned a great deal."

I didn't laugh but felt honored by his praise. "I'd like to meet up, when you feel up to it."

"Soon," he said, before hanging up.

I handed her back the phone. Not a lot to say, though he was always a man of few words.

"Satisfied?" wondered Kit.

I answered yes and then went over all I had discovered, starting at when I first came out to San Diego, up until what I had learned today, leaving out no details. Kit listened to every word, not taking physical notes, likely because she didn't want to be found with them. I wasn't sure her skill level, but if she was helping Garrett, she had to be talented and would remember every word I said.

"That will be helpful and will add to what he learned before they came after him."

"Did he know the two men?"

"No. But he does have pictures of them."

"I have contacts I can trust in the FBI. If you send them, I can pass them on and see if they're in the system."

"I will relay that to him and see what he says."

"Why didn't he just come to me or the man who hired me to find him? We could have helped."

"Have you worked with him much?" she asked.

"I have on a few occasions."

"I assume you've come to know him. He isn't one to ask for help, being fiercely independent. And he needed time to recover. If there was any pursuit of the killers of his family, he needed to be in on it."

"When did you pick up I was in town working on the case?"

"Last week. I noticed you watching the office of Shark Tail Detective Agency. I sent a picture to Garrett and he told me who you were. I then followed you to the hotel and we decided I'd get a room there. I got into your room one day while you were gone. I found your computer, but it was locked out. I noticed it has a fingerprint reader for logging in. That is when we talked about how to get access to it. He said you were a bit of a lady's man and easily tempted."

I shrugged my shoulders. "Your plan was to seduce and drug me, then use my finger to get into my computer and see what you found?"

She nodded. "Yes. Your phone too. I noticed it had a fingerprint reader. I could go through your call logs and emails, seeing what I could find. I'm a computer nerd, with a fair amount of tech background. I do computer hacker espionage on the side as part of my freelance work."

She would come in handy with her tech smarts. I could have used her on the Aaron Baily case.

"And then the plan was to have sex with me?" I asserted with a grin.

"Sometimes in this job you have to do unpleasant things to get the work done."

"Gee, thanks."

"If it's any consultation, you wouldn't have been the worst guy I'd fucked to learn his secrets. I might have even gotten a little pleasure out of it in the process. I've always had the hots for Bradley Cooper, especially when he has the facial hair."

I had to smile. "And what was your plan if I didn't succumb to your seductive ways?"

"I had the pills, which I could have slipped in your beer, if all else failed. Honestly, I thought I had you up until you pulled out your gun after tossing me on the bed. I planned on slipping off my cover-up and peeling off my bikini. Too bad you didn't wait a couple minutes longer and you might have gotten to see me naked and changed your mind."

I laughed. "You weren't easy to resist, but my girlfriend is a cop. I don't need her coming after me with a loaded gun just for a cheap night of pleasure."

"A shame, but perfectly understandable. What do we do now?"

I thought it over. Progress was being made, but there was much to learn. Those we were going up against, if they were who I thought they were, would be challenging. We would need to tread lightly or the possibly of being crushed by them would be significant.

"I'd say you go back to Rocky, Garrett, as you still call him. See if he is good with sending me those pictures. I have a few more things to check on. But I won't do much else until he is ready to see me. This is tricky shit we're getting into, and we may need additional resources and backup, before taking them head-on."

"I will check out in the morning to see him. And I will send those pictures if he agrees."

"Oh, and Kit? Watch for tails. I've been followed on a few occasions. You don't want to lead them to him."

"No worries. I'm quite stealthy when I need to be. Even you didn't spot me when I was following you. Only when I wanted you to see me, is when you did."

I laughed, for she was right. And boy was she an eyeful when I finally did.

Chapter 34

I was cursing myself for missing the fact that Kit had been following me. And she had gotten into my room without me knowing it. She was good, but I needed to catch things like that. Maybe someone else had followed me that I had missed, and was nearby. Working off this knowledge, I needed to change hotels again. Fortunately, I wasn't lacking for options.

Since most of my investigation was taking me north, I found a hotel in Carlsbad, again near the beach, with all the amenities I'd ever need. Gym, pool, free breakfast and even a putting green, not that I played golf. I packed up and moved to the new location, driving around several times, always with an eye in the rearview mirror. No one followed me, for this I was certain.

I checked in and found my room comfortable; sofa, full sized refrigerator, large King bed, with a bright colored bedspread that required sunglasses to protect the retinas. The mounted LED TV was average sized, though displayed all the right channels for my enjoyment. My plan was to be careful enough, allowing me to stay in this room for a longer period of time. I was growing weary of moving.

Once I was checked in, I went shopping. First was to find a burner phone, a cheap device to communicate with Kit and Rocky. She had given me the number of her phone, but insisted that I not use my regular cell phone, because it was always possible that whatever government agency who was involved could be listening in. A burner phone made this harder to do.

Once I found a cheap flip phone, I got it activated and tested it, sending her a text, which was challenging with only a numeric keypad. Messages had to be short, simple and not specific. She answered me back with a "K", so we were connected.

After that since I had a fridge, I decided I needed to add basic food items. Stopping by a local grocery store I picked up beer, ham, cheese, bread, hamburger, juice, bottled water and snacks. A few products to enjoy when sitting in the hotel room and to take with me when working. Plus, I purchased clear tape and thin white string. Both would be used to mark the door when I left, to let me know if someone had been in the room.

After returning and storing away all my purchases, I made a call to Brandon, but only got voicemail. Normally he calls back quickly. After an hour I called his assistant, Sue.

"I've been trying to get a hold of Brandon," I said, slightly agitated. "Do you know where he is?"

"Not a clue. He has not been in the office this week and most of last week."

I grew concerned something had happened. *Could it be whatever he was running from had finally caught up to him?*

"It isn't like Brandon not to check in."

"No, it isn't."

I heard her talking to someone else. I waited until she was through.

"Did you ever find any information on Stetson Poole?"

"I have no idea what you're talking about."

"It was a name I gave Brandon. He said he'd have you check on it and call me back."

"He did no such thing."

We may have butted heads a few times, but I knew Sue was good at her job. If Brandon had asked her, she wouldn't have forgotten, which meant Brandon never gave her the directive."

"Not like him to forget things."

She sighed, as if concerned. "I know. He hasn't been himself lately."

"Come on, Sue, do you know what the hell is going on?"

There was a pause, as she spoke to someone. I then heard her walking and a door closing.

"Honestly, no I don't, Jarvis. I've never seen him this cautious. He has someone guarding me all the time, living in my house. Do you know how difficult it is to carry on a relationship with my lady with an armed man sleeping on your couch?"

I smiled, not that she could tell.

"I'm sure Brandon wouldn't have him there if it wasn't serious."

"It's creepy. He gawks at us, like he wants to catch us in the act for his viewing pleasure."

I grinned even more. I was glad she couldn't see me. "A male fantasy, watching two women."

"Not *my* fantasy. I don't care to exhibit my desire with *anyone* other than her." Her tone came across as genuine spite.

"Do you have any options to find out what is going on? Any type of answers would be helpful."

"Not really. I can snoop around and see if there are any odd emails or letters, as I do have access to his office and his email account. I do my best to stay out of his business. I know what he does at times isn't always completely legal, but I love working for him. He is a great boss and the pay is fabulous."

"Since he forgot, can you see if you can find anything on a Stetson Poole for me?" I requested. "Might have been an alias someone was using. They could be working for one of the well-known government agencies."

"Oh joy," she said with a moan of displeasure. "But since you asked nicely, I will see if there is anything on the name from our contacts."

"If you learn anything worth sharing let me know. But keep it low key. It's best not to trust anyone right now."

"It's that serious?" Sue queried.

"Yes, it is." I paused to let it sink in. "And do your best to keep your clothes on around the gawker. His job is to protect you both. He doesn't need the distraction of two beautiful women enjoying each other."

"I'll try. But this lady has needs to attend to. And my sweetie knows all the right trigger points to satisfy them."

I smiled before hanging up, trying my best not to imagine Sue and her beautiful girlfriend. I pulled out my tablet and began doing additional web research. The hotel Wi-Fi wasn't robust, which was normal, but I made do.

Bringing up the browser I typed in *"Worldwide Toys Inc"*. Unlike their previous business name, the one page on the web didn't list an address, only a phone number. The area code was 661, which I learned was in Santa Clarita, the northern most city in Los Angeles County, sitting in a valley with elevated mountain ranges on all sides.

I tried calling the number but only got a voicemail, asking to leave a message with details of what type of toys I was looking for, and they would return your call. I assumed there was coding one would need to leave, for the call to be returned. If I said I wanted to talk with someone about guns, drugs or a toy not specific to the code, they wouldn't call me back.

With no address, I started searching for warehouse districts in Santa Clarita and there were several. Area codes no longer guaranteed the location, since they floated around these days when tied to a cell phone. All I could really do was drive up there and see if I could stumble across them.

It was a long trip, nearly three hours. I planned to make an early start after a fair night of sleep. Before leaving in the morning, I put a clear piece of tape on the door. If it was opened it would peel loose on one section and would unlikely be seen. As a secondary measure I placed a piece of string on the top of the door before closing it, while putting the Do Not Disturb sign on the doorknob. The odds of anyone catching both was slim. If someone got into my room I should know it.

I started early enough, in hopes I could miss the traffic but failed. Cars were always on the road in California. I thought the Denver traffic was bad, but it paled in comparison. All I could do was get in line with all the other vehicles, arriving when the flow allowed me, the windows up, the air setting on re-circulation to keep the smog and heat at bay.

By the time I got to the first section of warehouses, the temperature was already closing in on seventy, the forecast of cloudless skies spot on.

The long row of rectangular white buildings and pitched roofs ran along Railroad Avenue. The areas around the buildings were cluttered, with one section for storing RV's and another with many transport trucks, storage trailers, mobile office trailers and plain old junk. I found a parking spot on the road that divided the structures and began walking, going from building to building, reading business names. The area was huge and took a while to cover. It was mostly body shops, auto repair places and building supply warehouses. No sign of Worldwide Toys.

Sweat was running off my head as the heat built. There was a warm wind, and I swallowed down water, hoping to keep cool. Once back in the car, I turned the air conditioning on high and enjoyed a ham sandwich I'd made.

The next area of warehouses was even larger, this one I'd have to drive around for there was too much area to walk. It was off I-5, where I exited on Newhall Ranch Road, until I got to Rye Canyon

Road. Most of the area was laid out on a grid, making it a matter of driving up and then back down again.

I got about halfway through the maze of structures when I found it, a plain white sign in black print displaying—*Worldwide Toys*. The building sitting in a secured area, with fencing and guards checking any vehicles coming and going. There was no easy way to get inside. For now, I sat and watched from a distance.

Soon a large semi-truck with a thirty-foot trailer pulled in, driving around to one of the bay doors. It was too far for me to see much, but I caught glimpses of a forklift pulling what appeared to be pallets of strapped wooden containers and running them inside. It took maybe twenty-five minutes to finish unloading. Soon another trailer showed up and it was unloaded. I saw two smaller trucks, UPS delivery sized, at the other bays that were getting loaded with boxes. What I wouldn't give to be a fly on the wall to see what was going on.

Getting inside with the security I saw, would be challenging. On top of the fencing were cameras with light posts to cover the area. I saw a couple of men walking the grounds who appeared to be guards, likely packing guns under their jackets. There was little doubt this was the place. And this type of security to protect toys seemed like overkill. No one would kill to protect a bunch of stuffed animals. I pinned the location on my mapping app to refer to it later.

Two of the smaller delivery trucks were preparing to leave. As they pulled out, I decided to follow them. They headed west and after many hops onto several roads, where twice I nearly lost them, they got onto Antelope Valley Freeway, driving deeper into the mountains, the air getting cooler. Soon the trucks exited onto Agua Dulce Canyon Road, now heading north, where we entered the small town of Agua Dulce, from the sign I saw.

At this point I had little idea where I was, doing my best to track my route. My phone GPS was online, but I didn't have much time to look at it while driving, preferring not to get in a wreck on the way. Once in town there was a few more stops and starts, allowing me to glace down. I quickly saw there was a small airfield in the area and sure enough that was where the trucks headed. Once there they met two single prop cargo planes and began loading the boxes on them.

I took a picture, at least as best as my phone zoom could, of the planes, neither of which had any major markings on them other than the number, which I couldn't make out from this distance. Once loaded, the trucks headed back and the planes, one by one, soon taxied and took off to a destination unknown.

I'd learned a great deal today. Where the warehouse was, and how the merchandise was sent on its way. Tomorrow, I'd return and see where the big semis went to get their loads, likely from ships on one of the local harbors that ran along the coast. Albeit slow, it was progress, which I was happy for.

Turning around, I drove back towards the big city, my stomach urging me to watch for signs along the way to pick up dinner.

Chapter 35

The next morning I left my hotel room, once again leaving the tape and string on the door, both of which were in place when I got home last evening. I decided to make the same trip to Santa Clarita, but in a different vehicle, not wanting to risk being spotted. I had called Manny to tell him what I had learned. He had a day off, coming after working non-stop the last week and said he'd like to tag along.

We used his truck, while I offered to pay for mileage, but he said lunch would be good enough. He knew the location after I told him where we were heading, having gone to Six Flags Magic Mountain that was nearby. It seemed he had a thing for amusement parks, including many trips to Disneyland.

"They're wonderful places to take dates," he gloated. "Get them on those rides and they're clinging onto you for dear life. When the day is over they're extremely worked up, thrilled to jump your bones to take the edge off."

It was nice to have someone to chat with on these long drives. I learned he had several women he spent time with, none of them serious. His life as a cop didn't afford him the luxury to settle down, and with his good looks and charm, there was no shortage of ladies for him to bed. I could have felt jealous, for it was a life I'd once led, but now had hopefully left behind. I was happy having April in my life, keeping me grounded and physically satisfied.

When we arrived, Manny found a decent spot to park, bringing out his binoculars and SLR camera with zoom lens, allowing us a better view without appearing suspicious. Their routine was the same. A couple of large semis showed up, and were unloaded, smaller trucks loaded with whatever they were hauling. Both large semis left together, and we followed the last one as they worked back towards the coast, hopping onto highway 126.

We got the plate numbers and Manny called into his dispatch to have them ran. They belonged to a leasing company. I looked up their name and while we were driving, made the call.

"Hello, I need to talk with a manager immediately," I said with my best angry voice.

"What is this in relation to?" replied the female on the other end.

"Someone driving one of your leased trucks just hit my car and drove away. I need to find out immediately who was behind the wheel."

"I'm sorry. Please hold and I will get someone to help you."

I looked at Manny who was laughing. Nothing better than an angry person on the phone to get someone to give up information.

"May I help you?" said the rugged male voice who now was on the line.

"I need to know who is driving one of your leased trucks, as they just ran into my car and drove away."

"I'm sorry, sir, for the trouble. But I can't give out that information."

I ramped up my anger. "Really! Maybe I should have my lawyer call you and threaten to sue your ass. Now either give me a name on who leased those trucks, or we will take legal action, especially since one of my kids was injured. You don't want to mess around with a pissed off father!"

I could hear the man breathing, nervous and unsure what to do.

"Not saying anything isn't helping. The dollar amount my lawyer is going to slap your company with goes up the longer I wait for an answer."

"Give me the plate number and I'll verify it is one of our trucks."

Giving him the info, I heard the tapping on the keyboard. He asked for a description of the truck, which I gave him.

"Yes, that is one of our trucks. Leased to Worldwide Toys Inc."

"Is there a person's name who signed the contract?"

"Yes. An Edwin Ware."

"Thank you for the information. I will refrain from suing you and will go after them, unless they don't have proper insurance."

"They were properly insured, I can confirm that. Is there anything else I can help you with?"

"That is all for now. My lawyer will be in contact if we need further help."

I hit the call end button and was smiling.

"Nice job," noted Manny with admiration.

"Angry and threatening works well with many people. They really will tell you anything to get you off the phone. The name on the contract was Edwin Ware."

"The detective we cornered?" Manny sounded intrigued.

"Yes. Though I'm dead sure he isn't a real detective and it's not his real name. Maybe security for this group."

"They have an office," Manny pointed out.

"Likely a front to make them look legitimate. Certainly enough to fool people. Fooled me until I started digging deeper."

"You mentioned there wasn't anything in their office, which makes me think you stepped outside the law to learn this."

I shrugged. "As I said before, best you don't know. Being a PI, I'm not constrained by certain rules to follow, like a cop. But I will say there was only one desk, a few office supplies, a filing cabinet, phone and nothing else. And there was a surveillance camera watching for intruders."

"Which is why they were after you and left the note on your windshield?"

"Exactly. There is a lot going on here. A whole lot of pieces and moving parts. The question is, can I put it all together into facts we can use?"

"The real question is—can you live through this or will you end up like your friend?"

I nodded, knowing Rocky had survived, which I continued to keep from Manny. Rocky had paid a price, a price I was hell bent on avoiding for I didn't like spending time in the hospital and in pain. We had both cheated death in the past, but one of these days our luck was bound to run out.

I kept my eye on the road, to make sure we didn't lose the semis, which nearly happened three times when we caught a red light, but were able to make up enough ground. Manny did a great job of maneuvering through traffic, years of practice homing his skills on the Southern California streets. He appeared fearless behind the wheel, an emotion I wish I had being a passenger, for a couple of times I was certain we were about to get into a wreck.

It was a cooler day and even a slight rain was falling. Manny commented on how unusual that was, for the rainy season had ended. But it was a pleasant change of pace after sweating through my shirt yesterday. Though the humidity was higher, I might think otherwise before the day was over. I'd been wearing a light zip-up on all my treks to cover my gun. Today, since I was with a cop, I didn't need to hide it as much, allowing me to shed the covering. I focused on tracking our route, and soon we were headed south through the city of Oxnard.

"I'd say we're headed towards Port Hueneme," observed Manny. "I figured it would be there or Port of Long Beach. They wouldn't want to be transporting that cargo all over the state."

On my phone, I pulled up the website. It was a huge port claiming to be less congested and with higher productivity than other ports on the coast. It was the leading port for autos, fresh produce and general cargo. A perfect place to run illegal goods disguised as toys. Even with customs' random system of inspections, which only checked a percent or two of containers, it was easy to get items to slip through. And with any big business, easy to pay people to look the other way when necessary.

As the two trucks approached the port entry post, Manny backed off, waiting for them to get cleared to enter. Once they were through, he pulled up, talking with security and showing his badge. "Hello. I'm a local police officer doing a follow-up on a couple leads on a case I'm working."

The guard wasn't sure what to do and made a call. After a couple of minutes, he let us drive in.

"Having a badge can get you into most places," Manny noted.

"Glad to have you aboard today. Odds were against me to talk my way inside. Threatening to sue him wouldn't have worked." I pointed out my open window. "I saw them turn right. We should be able to find them, though it's a busy place."

It wasn't long before we saw the two trucks. One had backed up to a container, and after it was unlocked, a large crane lifted the empty shell from the flatbed trailer and stacked it on top of several other containers. The crane moved, then grabbed another container from a huge stack and carefully placed it on the trailer, where the drivers locked it for safe travel. After signing for the shipment, the driver and co-pilot moved, and the second semi backed in, the same exchange of containers taking place. It wasn't long before they were getting ready to head out, likely back to their warehouse to unload.

"What next?" asked Manny.

"Be nice to see what is inside one of those metal boxes," I replied.

"I doubt they will open one up, just because of your curiosity."

"I wonder if they're even guarded after the truck leaves. We might be able to break into one."

Manny grimaced. "I don't like hearing you say that. What if we get caught?"

"You have a badge to flash around."

"True. But that won't save us from a B&E charge or even a bullet to the head. What are you thinking?"

"If someone questions us, you flash it and say we're looking for someone. Part of a murder investigation."

"What would that have to do with us looking inside one of those metal boxes?" queried Manny.

"We say we got a tip and we're looking into it. Word is they're stowing away to get out of the country. What are they going to do, arrest us?"

"No, but they could shoot us or lock us away for a long trip back across the Pacific with our imaginary murder suspect, which wouldn't be pleasant."

The possibility had crossed my mind as I'd been thinking over how to approach them.

"It is up to us to prevent that from happening," I replied. "They're moving out now. We can give it time and see if they leave people around to watch things. If you're nervous about me breaking in, you can close your eyes and claim you didn't see it."

Manny didn't seem all that thrilled with my idea. It wouldn't be the first time a cop cringed at one of my plans.

"I don't think that is going to fly, but we can go over and see what we find."

Two men continued to hang around. Both Manny and I spotted that each of them was armed, carrying a large handgun, which wasn't surprising for the cargo we expected was inside. One wandered the perimeter, keeping an eye out for any trouble, the other standing in front, smoking a cigarette, and carrying a walkie-talkie. Each were large in both height and weight, and wearing jeans, shirt, jacket and ball cap. They could have been massively tough teamsters, but I doubted it.

Many of the containers were stacked on top of each other, lined up one after another for loading onto a trailer designed to haul them, the crane used to maneuver them around. In this area, they were stacked four high, four deep and four across, with space enough to walk in between. It didn't look as if the men were leaving. We gave it thirty minutes, when finally, the two got together and started walking towards one of the office structures nearby. Maybe it was lunch time as it was nearly noon. Maybe they were union workers off to take their mandated break.

We waited a little longer, before stepping out, the rain continuing to fall, though lightly, my ball cap providing protection, my zip-up back on to shield me from the rain and to hide my gun.

I kept scanning for anyone else wandering the area as we walked right up to one of the big stacks in line from where they pulled the two containers to load. We had no idea whose containers belonged to Worldwide Toys. They had a complicated symbol-filled labelling system on the doors, which was Greek to us. And they were padlocked to keep people out of them. I pulled out my phone and took pictures of several of the codes. I'm sure I could find someone to tell us what it meant.

"Looks like we aren't getting inside," noted Manny.

I looked at the locks and they weren't anything special. A typical combination lock you could get anywhere, with a key slot on the back. I had my lock pick tools with me and with several minutes of free time, I could get in. But standing out in the open was risky. I looked around and realized that high above on the light poles there were cameras covering the area. Security could be watching, and certainly there would be recordings.

"I could pick this lock, but we'd be seen," I said, pointing upward. "Damn, I really wanted to see what is inside."

"Maybe we can ask these nice gentlemen," said Manny curtly. The two men were returning.

"Can we help you two?" said the first man who was the smoker, one of his hands in his coat for easy access to his gun.

Manny pulled out his badge. "Looking for a killer. Wondering if you've seen anyone suspicious running around."

He looked at the badge and pulled his hand out of his coat. Thankfully it was empty.

"Only you two," he said, looking at his partner who agreed.

"Got a tip he might be down here. Could be trying to stow away in one of these containers. Any chance we can look inside."

"Not without a warrant. This is private property." He pointed his finger at us, the cigarette ash flying in the breeze.

"Are you the owner of all of these?" inquired Manny.

"No. But I'm guarding them." His tone was sounding hostile.

"Really, what's inside?" I asked.

"Toys," he replied firmly before taking a long draw on his cancer stick.

"Interesting, needing two men with 9mm handguns guarding toys," I stated dryly. "Must be precious cargo. Maybe guns inside."

Both looked surprised by what I said. "What did you say?"

"You know, *guns*. Like pop and water type guns. You know, *toy* guns. What did you think I meant?"

By their expressions, I'd caught them off guard. They knew the contents and it wasn't only toys.

"We have no idea what type of toys are in there. We're here to make sure they make it to their next destination. If they don't, it's our ass!" He dropped the cigarette and crushed it with his steel toed boot.

"Must be valuable kilos in the cargo," I declared. I misspoke on purpose.

This time the other guy stepped forward. "I think you should both leave. Go snoop around elsewhere, before I call management and report you. I don't care if you're cops."

Manny didn't look intimidated. "Call whomever you want, but understand we're watching, and we'll catch the killer one way or another."

We both started walking away, with an eye behind us in case they decided to shoot us. Climbing into his truck, Manny started the engine.

"There are *definitely* more than toys inside," he proclaimed. "The question is what we can do to prove it enough to get a warrant?"

"We need to see what is inside."

"Not easy to do and not an idea I can help you with. I think you're on your own on that front. What about your FBI ties?"

"Shaky at best, if they will help. All I have right now wouldn't be enough."

"What next?"

I looked at him. "Not completely certain, but whatever it is, you don't want to know about it. I'm going to need to break a few rules."

Breaking the rules was never an issue with me when it came to the greater good. It was how to do it without getting killed. That was the challenge, which I contemplated as we drove away.

Chapter 36

As we headed back to town my phone rang. Caller ID didn't identify the number, but I decided to answer. It was Emily White.

"Jarvis, help, I'm in trouble," she begged, out of breath.

I had no desire to help her. Mostly because of our past and the fact that believing anything she said was difficult.

"Emily, if you're in trouble call the police."

"Please, Jarvis. I think this is related to Brandon's issues. He called me again this morning saying he thought someone was coming my way today and to be on the lookout."

Odd he'd not called me. "I'm not in a position to help you. You should call the police."

"There is an Asian man and woman I spotted. They are armed, I can see the bulge. I'm scared, Jarvis."

Though her fear sounded genuine, I'd heard this before from her. All those years ago about someone trying to rape her, and it had been just a trap to pull me in. It was hard to believe anything she said, yet I wondered.

"Where are you?"

"Newport Center, where you found me last month."

"Get somewhere crowded, with lots of people. A bar would be good if there is one nearby. I will call you back."

"What is going on?" wondered Manny.

"Not certain. But can we head towards Newport Beach?"

"Yes, it's on the way."

"I need to make a couple of calls first and I'll let you know for certain."

First, I tried calling Brandon, but only got voicemail and he still hadn't returned my call from a few days ago. I then tried Sue and no answer from her either. Which was odd, because she always answered her phone unless she was in mid-lust with her girlfriend. It was possible Emily wasn't lying. I called her back.

"Did you find somewhere busy?" I inquired.

"I'm at the Back Bay Tavern in the Whole Foods Market. I'm sitting at the bar right now. Those two followed me in and are at a table, watching me."

"Stay there. We aren't too far away. Maybe twenty minutes."

I hung up, wondering what was going on. If she was really in danger, I'd need to handle it. I told Manny where we needed to go.

"Again, what is going on?" he asked, while navigating the traffic like a pro.

"A woman I know says she is being followed by an Asian male and female. I received a warning before I came out here she might be in danger. The person who warned me isn't answering his phone and supposedly called her earlier, saying someone might be coming to get her today."

"You said *supposedly*."

I nodded. "She has had an issue in the past of lying about things like this to manipulate men."

"Were you one of those men?"

"Yes," I said with no pride in my voice.

"Then it could be her trying to lure you in?"

"Possibly. But since I can't get a hold of two people who also were in danger, I'm going to give her the benefit of the doubt. Not that she deserves it."

"Is this related to the murder case you've been tracking down?"

Actually, I wasn't completely certain if they were related, since Brandon had refused to tell me anything.

"I have no idea. I've been given little information from my client. He is the one who hired me to find out who killed Garrett, meaning it's possible. I appreciate you driving me there."

"No problem. Do I need to stick around, since you don't have a car?"

I thought about it for minute. Having his help would be good, but if she was playing a game, I didn't want to get him involved. I didn't need to spoil the good karma we had established.

"I'd say drop me off. If she is in danger, we can use her car. If not, then I'll take a cab ride back to my hotel."

He nodded, stepping on the gas, getting us there in good time, though I couldn't convince him to put on the lights and siren.

Stepping out, I walked through Whole Foods reaching the Back Bay Tavern, surveying the room. There were a couple of Asians in the place, but the two at a table by the door were the best possibility. I walked over to the bar and took a seat a couple of places down from Emily. I shook my head, letting her know not to acknowledge me. I sent her a text message saying to sit still for now and if the two she was worried about were the ones by the door. She answered me back, saying, "Yes".

The bartender asked what I was having. I ended up deciding on a beer, whatever was on tap. He brought me a cold mug and I took a sip, my mind racing on what to do. I glanced over again, gauging who I was up against. The man looked to be about my size, with short black hair on the side, longer in back in a ponytail. The woman was a little smaller, though not by much, her black hair longer, touching her shoulder, clips above the ear keeping it out of her eyes.

They didn't seem nervous, patiently waiting for Emily to leave, each sipping on drinks. The two of them weren't conversing, their eyes watching the room, most likely their attention on Emily. There were two ways into the bar, one via an exit to an outdoor eating zone, the other through the Whole Foods Market. But the exit to the outdoor eating area was blocked by pillars, walls and plexiglass, with no easy, unobstructed route to the street.

This was the exit they were guarding. Making a run for it through the store would be better, but not ideal since there was a fair amount of foot traffic. Neither of the options were good, but they likely wouldn't shoot us with this many people around, if that was their intention.

Sitting there, I couldn't believe I was getting myself dragged back into Emily's freaky realm thanks to Brandon's troubles. I thought I was finally free of her drama. Though it did appear in this case she really was in danger, for this appeared too elaborate even for her to cook up. In the back of my mind I knew it wouldn't end well for me. Why I should care was the real question.

I had a soft spot when it came to helping people, even those I had grown to loathe. Against my better judgement, I was going to help her. I typed into my phone what I wanted her to do and to tell me when she was ready. I was sitting at the second to last chair by the entrance into Whole Foods, my vision trained and prepared to act. The text came through that she was ready.

After paying, she got up from her stool and walked past me into the store. I observed the two people leave their chairs, heading to walk by my direction. I tossed down cash to pay for the beer.

As they neared, I blindly slipped off my chair and stumbled into them, most of my weight hitting the man, who fell into the woman.

"Oh my lord, I'm so sorry," I said melodramatically while grabbing the man's jacket. "I hope I didn't hurt you. Totally my fault, I didn't see you coming."

Neither were pleased, the man looking into my eyes with a glare as I smoothed out his jacket, feeling the gun under his left arm. He spoke to the woman in a different language, either Chinese or Japanese, as she ran off, with him now grabbing hold of me.

"Get your hands off me," he said in a thick accent. "Or I will hurt you."

I pulled my hands off him, holding them in the air, as if to show I was leaving him alone, and then, with full force, jumped into him, pushing him straight back into the brick entryway, snapping the back of his head against the unforgiving surface. He slumped down to the ground, stunned.

"I said I was sorry. Gee, people have no manners these days." I was speaking to the people at the table next to us as they stared, surprised by what they saw, my wicked grin and sarcasm meant to put them at ease. "No worries, folks, he'll be out of it for a few minutes. I'm sure when he comes to, he'll think better of being rude the next time."

Reaching down, I discreetly pulled out his gun with two fingers and dumped it in the first trash container I saw, and then chased after the woman. Emily was supposed to head straight to her car in a hurry, and then wait to hear from me. If she saw either of them, she was supposed to drive away and go to the nearest police station and not wait around.

Running through the store, I made it to the exit, darting around several shoppers with carts and bags, trying not to knock them and the aisle-blocking food displays over, before finally making it to the outside sidewalk.

The Asian woman was standing looking around, searching but not finding Emily, whose car was parked in the lot across from the store. Hearing the pounding of my tennis shoes, she turned to face me, reaching into her coat pocket for her gun. I did the same, showing her I was armed, and she stopped, leaving it in the holster.

"You should head back and check on your boyfriend," I announced smugly. "I think he has a terrible headache and could use your help."

I wasn't sure if she understood me or not. But she smiled,

raising her fists and charged me, jabbing right, left and then right again. I had my arms up and blocked the punches, but then she spun her body with a roundhouse kick.

I was ready, and grabbed her by the ankle in the air, with both my hands, then spun myself, using her momentum, to fling her off balance into a large wooden display of flowers for sale. She crashed with a thud, lying there stunned, covered with daisies, carnations, broken glass and water.

"My apologies," I asserted to the female employee monitoring the display who appeared shocked. "You might want to go inside and call the police."

She looked down at the Asian woman, who was trying to gather herself, and darted inside. I had no plans to wait around and I moved to the curb, my eyes searching, hoping to find Emily. I heard a honk and a red BMW pulled up next to me. I jumped into the passenger seat, and we took off, my eyes looking back, seeing the woman trying to get to her feet. Emily took a quick right, then straight and then left onto San Joaquin Hills Road. From what I could tell, they weren't following us.

"What now?" wondered Emily.

"We get you out of town."

"Where to?"

"Denver, where hopefully we can get you with someone who can protect you."

She looked over at me, making me nervous, she wasn't doing a good job of staying in the lane, the car fading to the right, nearly hitting the curb.

"Watch the road. We don't need to get in an accident!" I yelled.

"I need to go home," she stated firmly.

I shook my head. "Not a wise idea. They likely know where you live and could come looking for you there."

"I have a cat. I can't just leave her there all alone. I need to get her set up with food and water or she'll die."

"A cat?" I said, surprised.

"Yes, a cat. What is wrong with that?" She gave me a long look of anger and I once again pointed for her to watch the road.

"You don't seem like a cat lover. Like I can't see you with a kid either. You don't seem the motherly type." As soon as I said it, I regretted the words I used.

"Oh, fuck you, Jarvis. You don't know shit about me. Maybe I've changed over these last few years."

I should have felt sorry for what I said, but I didn't, our past history preventing those emotions.

"Can't you get someone to watch the cat for you?"

"No. The one thing that hasn't changed are the friends I have. I can get the guy next door to check on her from time to time. But he only does it because I flirt with him."

This was probably the husband of the neighbor I had talked with, who didn't like Emily for her teasing, feminine ways.

"Alright, but we need to be quick about it. Do you have your gun with you?"

"Yes."

I grabbed her purse and pulled it out, checking to verify it was loaded, then I sat it on the seat.

"Keep it handy and in hand. And don't hesitate to use it. Aim center mass and squeeze the trigger like you were trained by Brandon. But you need to be in and out quickly. I will watch the outside."

"Can I pack a small bag? I need a change or two of clothes and my lady stuff."

I sighed. "No more than ten minutes and we're gone. Understood?"

"Yes sir."

She spoke with a smile, as if she was enjoying parts of this, which I found hard to fathom. She was a difficult person to read, seeming to get joy, even deep personal pleasure, out of things a normal person would bitch and moan about. At least I wouldn't have to worry about her complaining too much.

We reached her condo, and she quickly ran inside, while I waited outside, one hand on my gun under my jacket. The rain had stopped, but it was quite humid, reminding me of my home town of Des Moines, one aspect of the land of corn's environment I didn't miss. I'd worked up a sweat, even though it was cooler this evening, the breeze coming straight off the ocean.

My eyes scanned, watching for danger. They would have to get past the security gate, which wasn't guarded or difficult to get through if they caught it opening as someone was coming or going, which is how I had gotten in my first time here. And even if they didn't make it in, they could very well be waiting outside for us to come out, since there was only one way to leave.

I had to assume they knew where she lived and what she drove, while I had no idea what they were driving. And this time, they weren't likely to take me lightly and wouldn't hesitate to use their guns to stop us.

After waiting for a while with no sign of Emily, I checked the time, it had been more than ten minutes and we needed to go. I went to the front door and walked in, calling out her. Her cat came up and started rubbing up against my leg, meowing, her black and white fur finding my pant leg comforting.

I'd never been big into cats, preferring dogs, but this feline was healthy at fifteen pounds. The notion of Emily being a cat lover seemed foreign to me. It didn't seem she loved anyone but herself. Who knows, maybe she *had* changed, if ever so slightly. I reached down to pet it, and it rubbed up against my hand, purring. It didn't seem to care someone was after us, which was probably best for her.

"Emily, let's get going," I yelled again. "We need to get on the road before those two catch up to us."

Finally and to my relief, she stepped out with bag in hand. She had changed clothes, dressed now in an old pair of faded blue jeans and black t-shirt with the band *Coldplay* on it. She grabbed her sunglasses, though it was dark and a visor cap with a horse on the front. With keys in hand, she waved at me to lead the way.

"Hang back so I can make sure we're clear to make it to the car," I said. "If I say anything other than you are good, then wait inside and make sure you have your gun handy."

She smiled and patted her purse, which she held in hand, while slinging the luggage over her shoulder. I opened the door slowly, sticking my head out and taking a peek in all directions. Stepping through, I had my gun at my side and began walking towards the car, not noticing anything suspicious until from out in front of it stepped the woman, her gun pointed.

I went to aim, when I heard a noise as the man appeared out of nowhere from behind me with a gun at my back. He must have had a back-up piece or had fished it out of the trash can. I lowered my arm and he grabbed the gun away, and then hit me hard on the back, knocking me to my knees. It rang my bell, but I shook it off.

“I guess we’re even now,” I divulged dryly, trying to ignore the throbbing ache. My hand wanted to rub my back, but I held off, thinking he would consider it aggressive.

“Even doesn’t matter,” he said, his English not clear. “Where is girl?”

I held off answering, until he pushed the gun barrel to my head.

“Inside.” I did my best to sound scared.

“Call her.”

“I doubt she will hear me since the door is mostly closed,” I replied, feigning desperation in my voice. We were far enough away that he would believe me.

He pulled me up off the ground by my right arm, pulling it up tight against my back and pushed me towards the doorway. He then waved for his female friend, speaking in their native language, as she moved towards the door. She was probably a foot away, her gun at the ready, while we were to one side.

“*Call her*,” he said again, keeping the pressure on my arm.

“Emily, it’s time to go,” I yelled.

There was a short pause before she answered. “Are you sure?” she asked.

“Yes,” I replied, waiting to see what happens. Hopefully she had listened.

“This bag is too heavy. Can you help me carry it?” She wheedled.

“I will be right there.” I started to move, but he stopped me, his grip tightening.

“No walk inside.” He waved for the woman to go instead.

She wasn’t stupid, and took her time, pushing open the door and peering inside cautiously. She waved at the man, as if she didn’t see her.

“She was packing her clothes,” I noted. “She is probably in the bedroom, waiting with the bag.”

Translating what I said in their language, he pointed for her to go in which she did slowly, walking in, looking around. Then four shots rang out and the woman staggered back, falling to the ground, blood all over her front, never once getting off a shot.

The man was shocked, and loosened his grip, and I spun around, away from his gun hand and with full force, drove my left fist into the back of his head. He stumbled, but tried to raise his gun hand, before I lunged at his arm, getting the gun pointed downward, and then bringing my left elbow up with full force under his jaw, the cracking sound of bone and teeth ear-shattering.

His body went limp, as I held him up and took his gun away, before letting his unconscious body slump to the ground. I grabbed my gun and stepped back.

Looking over at the woman, who appeared dead, I walked and with my foot, pushed the gun out of reach. "You are good, Emily," I yelled.

It took a minute before she walked out. "Is she dead?" she asked.

"I'd say so. Hard for someone to survive four gunshots."

She looked down, hardly appearing shocked at the events that had unfolded.

"Good!" was all she said with a coldness even I couldn't imagine her having.

Chapter 37

It wasn't long until the police arrived and locked down the scene. Emily wanted to up and leave, not wanting to wait for the detectives, but I told her no. We needed the cops on our side and not hunting us down. I called Manny, asking whatever pull he had, to help us. He did what he could, which wasn't much, but did drive down to lend assistance.

After fifteen hours of grilling, going over and over what happened, we were finally released, with warnings not to stray too far away. Exhausted, we made it back to my hotel room just short of noon the next day, Emily with her bag in hand, now minus her gun, which the police kept as evidence.

My attempt at getting her a room of her own failed, for she felt safer with me nearby and I couldn't talk her out of it. I was tired and angry I was involved in another mess with the woman I didn't trust or care for. I plopped down on the bed, hoping to close my eyes and have it all go away. My wish didn't come true.

"I'm taking a shower," said Emily gleefully. "Care to join me?" She said it with way too much spunk for someone with zero sleep.

I opened my eyes and sighed. "You've got to be kidding me."

"I never kid about such things. You washing my back…and my front…would make a bad day better."

"I'm not sure if you're a sex addict or just bat-shit crazy. But you know the answer is no!"

She shrugged. "Can't blame a girl for trying. I figured I could relieve the stress that is wrecking that beautiful body of yours. Your loss. The door will be unlocked if you change your mind." She walked away, stripping her clothes and tossing them on the floor, before entering with one last come hither look, showing lots of skin, before shutting the door.

"This day keeps getting better and better," I said sarcastically.

I closed my eyes again, trying to forget yesterday's events, but failed. My mind raced over what all had happened. The two people who were after Emily were Chinese, from what the police told me, a fact I couldn't overlook, even with over one billion Chinese on the planet. It might have been a coincidence, but I'd had a major run in with two powerful Chinese men last year, using an underage girl to try and frame me. They had been murdered while I had been tied up by The Butcher, the killers never found.

My thoughts had concluded my Russian associates had eliminated them. But when I called Aleksi several weeks later, he claimed it wasn't him, even though he'd threatened them. I wasn't sure if it was true or not, but I'd left it alone, hoping it wouldn't come back to haunt me. Now Chinese people were trying to take Emily, apparently to get to Brandon. I needed to get answers from him on what was going on. But he wouldn't return my calls, even after leaving another message early this morning about what happened.

My eyes remained closed, and I may have even fallen asleep for a few minutes, when I heard the bathroom door open. Emily stepped out, her hair wet, her naked body barely wrapped in the hardly large enough hotel towel. She walked over to the bed and sat on the edge, the towel coming loose and revealing her wet chest.

"Like what you see?" she purred, leaning forward towards my face.

"*No*," I said forcefully, once again, this time almost in a yell. "Get dressed and act like a normal person would act, for Christ's sake."

"I wanted to lay down and sleep some," she declared. "Or fuck, if I can get a rise out of you. Either way, I plan on staying naked for now."

In disgust, I hopped out of bed and went over to the sofa. "The bed is all yours."

"Come on, Jarvis. Don't you remember how great it was? You and I entwined in a heated passion, like wild animals. No one will know. I won't rat you out to your lady cop girlfriend."

I'd had enough of this. "Emily, this is the last time I'm telling you this. Stop now or I throw you out on the street, and you can deal with whatever dangers await you." I sat up on the sofa. "Don't you understand! I don't want to have *anything* to do with you. What happened between us is the worst mistake I've ever made, and I'm paying for it even today. Please close your mouth and your legs, and act like something other than a sex crazed maniac."

It could be I finally got through to her; she shrugged her shoulders and laid down on the top of the covers to sleep. I got up, steaming, grabbed clean clothes and went into the bathroom, making sure to lock the door, then took my own shower to wash away the day I had. Once I was done, I dried off, flipped down the toilet seat and made a call back to Denver. April answered on the third ring.

"Damn, it's good to hear your voice," I said.

"What is wrong?" she asked, sensing my frustration.

I told her the whole story, including all the details about the crazy woman sleeping on the bed.

"Wow. She really is a whack job. Are you flying her back to Denver?"

"I was hoping you could fly out and take her. I don't know if I can survive in a confined space thirty thousand feet off the ground. I might be tempted to open the door and jump out. Or maybe throw her out."

April laughed. "I wish I could, but I have Denver PD work the next two days. Can't you just put her on the plane by herself?"

"It crossed my mind, but I should make sure she makes it there in one piece. Besides, Brandon isn't calling me back and neither is Sue. Something is going on. I probably need to come back and search for answers."

"What about the Rocky case you're working?"

"It can wait for now, though I have news there as well. But best not to talk about over the phone. How are things going with the Hester family?"

"No issues at this point. Though T and Parker think someone has been watching and following them at times when they go out. Nothing for certain, but a possibility. They've been taking most of the duties this last week, as my bosses haven't been keen on me taking a lot of time off. I had to take extra shifts to cover manpower shortages."

"Good money to put away for that bike."

"I know. In time that salesman will cave. I have him on the ropes." She paused. "It will be good to see you, especially since you'll be all in one piece. If you survive the flight with Emily, that is."

"It will be good to see you too. I will hopefully get a flight out tomorrow. I will let you know once I have the reservations."

April and I exchanged goodbyes and then I spent the next hour booking airline seats. I found a first-class flight leaving tomorrow morning, which I immediately reserved. There was no way in hell I was going to sit in the tight seats of coach with Emily.

Once that was done I got dressed and quietly laid down on the sofa, closed my eyes and did my best to sleep. I had the gun nearby in case someone tried to break in or if Emily came after me with more of her sexual advances. I was always prepared for the worst.

Chapter 38

It was a quiet flight. I spent most of it listening to music and ignoring Emily, especially after her question over whether I was a member of the mile-high club. At this time, it seemed best to ignore her advances, for my verbal rejections didn't seem to faze her and possibly added fuel to the fire.

I noticed, on takeoff and landing, I wasn't even gripping the arms of the seats like I normally did. Apparently I was more afraid of her than the plane crashing.

When we hit the ground, we gathered our luggage and grabbed a cab, heading back to my place, my cold shoulder routine continuing. April was waiting for us in her police uniform and driving her squad car. Knowing from my text we would be there shortly, she'd sat there on her lunch break eating a sandwich, ready to lay her eyes on Emily. If there was any crap, April would handle it.

"An officer of the law waiting to meet us," commented Emily while getting out of the car. "Should I be honored or worried?"

After retrieving our bags from the trunk, I paid the cab driver with my credit card, gathering the receipt to add to my expenses. From there, I went over and hugged April.

"This must be the girlfriend," noted Emily, walking over with her hand out. "I'm Emily."

April looked her up and down and didn't put out her hand. "I'm aware who you are."

"Tough lady," replied Emily dryly, pulling her hand back.

"I am. Best you stay on my good side." April's look was cold and threatening.

I smiled cheerily at the two, while going to my Mustang and tossing Emily's bags in the trunk.

"What are you doing?" asked Emily. "I thought I'd be staying here."

I tried not to laugh and failed. "Never in a million years. My last experience with you in my place does not leave me with a warm and fuzzy feeling."

Emily had a surprised expression. "Oh come now, it wasn't all that bad!"

"You shot me in the ass!"

Emily gyrated her hips in a sexy manner. "It could have been much worse. As I recall, it could have been much better if you'd succumbed to my wishes."

"And I suppose if I hadn't, you wouldn't have shot me?"

Emily now smiled. "No, I would have. It would have been a more desirable moment before the pain."

"I think I made the correct choice. But you aren't staying here with me."

Emily crossed her arms. "Where then?"

"My first choice was with Brandon. But he isn't returning my calls. That leaves The Mission as my next option."

April looked surprised. "Sam is fine with this?"

I nodded and closed the trunk.

"What is The Mission?" asked Emily.

"A homeless shelter I've done work for. Pastor Sam has a room you can stay in."

Emily frowned. "I'm not going to stay with the unwashed of the world."

I glared at her. "They aren't unwashed, but down on their luck. And I really could care less about your opinion on this. It will be the safest place for you to stay."

"She really is a bitch, isn't she," declared April gleefully.

"What did you call me?" demanded Emily, trying to sound tough, staring at April with a cold glare.

April just smiled, without once blinking and crossed her arms. I knew she could have called her much worse and would have no issue decking her if necessary.

"Why can't I stay in a hotel?" Emily pleaded, now looking at me. She knew she was out of her league challenging April.

"Because I can't watch you there, and with people at the shelter I know I can trust, you'll be safe. And I'm *not* footing the bill for an expensive hotel until I hear from Brandon."

"We can use his credit card. It won't cost you anything."

I grabbed the purse from her and found her wallet. Despite her protest, I pulled out the card and broke it in two.

"What the fuck, Jarvis!"

"What a potty mouth," said April.

"I suppose you're all prim and proper, never uttering a foul word."

"Lady, if you want to get into a pissing war, I can fucking curse you under the damn table!"

I laughed. "You can't use the credit card anymore. It is too easy for someone to track you. For now, you pay cash for anything you need."

Emily looked angry. "I don't have much cash."

"Good. Because you shouldn't be out shopping until I get a better handle on what is going on."

"Then what the hell am I supposed to do?" Emily's face was contorted, as if she was in pain.

"There is plenty of work you can do at The Mission to keep you busy. About time you accomplished something decent in your life other than trying to seduce anyone with two legs."

"I will not lower myself..."

"Fine with me. Then you can live on the streets with the other unfortunate people with no money. Less for me to worry about."

She was fully pouting now, unsure what to say.

"You'll do your part to assist and try not to make passes at the help there, trying to get out of work. Now get in the car. April and I need to talk." I really was tired of all her crap.

I thought she might throw a temper tantrum, but she finally sat in the car defeated, slamming the door in the process.

"Wow. Not sure what you saw in her enough to jump in bed with," proclaimed April bluntly.

Neither did I—it wasn't one of my finest moments. "I was a weak man then, easily seduced by her feminine ways."

"Sounds like a brat to me."

"She puts on a good act. You should have seen the look on her face after shooting that woman in her condo. She was cold as ice. Then she was all 'let's have sex' just because it's what she wants and gives her control. One of the worst decisions of my life was giving in to her."

April smiled. "I'd love to talk about your failings all day, but before I have to get back out on the streets, I need to let you know what happened this morning with T."

I frowned, concerned that something bad had happened. "Doesn't sound good."

With my arm around her shoulder, April had my attention as we took a little stroll around the parking lot to keep Emily from eavesdropping.

"No. All had been going well. T had noticed the last couple of days, or at least from his words, *sensed* that someone was watching him. He was with the son at Park Meadows Mall, when one man distracted him for a minute, while another grabbed at the boy."

"Damn. How did he handle it?"

April smiled widely. "Quite well. From what he told me, he clocked the one distracting him when he knew what was going on. The boy started yelling, alerting T to what was happening. He then chased down the other man who was having a hard time getting away, since the boy was fighting him. T grabbed him around the neck in a sleeper hold, until the man passed out."

It was my turn to smile. I knew T could handle himself and it sounded like he did great.

"The mall security showed up and once T was able to explain what was going on, the police were called, and the two men were arrested."

"Any IDs on them?"

"Yes. I'm working now to get names through the Douglas County Sheriff's office. Hopefully I will have them by this afternoon. But it sounds like they lawyered up immediately."

I nodded. I wasn't surprised. "Likely someone Perry hired. Don't sound like pros though. Were they armed?"

"From what I understand, they only had knives, but no guns."

"Must have thought they could handle T. Not likely they'll make the same mistake again. I'll go have a talk with Perry once we can connect him to them."

"Perry isn't intelligent, is he?" asked April with a smirk.

"No he isn't. Each time he acts, he makes it worse."

"Well anyway, I thought you should know. When I get more, I'll pass it on. I need to get back to my shift. Try not to strangle Emily on the way to The Mission."

It was comforting April trusted me. She was handling this entire mess with Emily like a champ, which only made me love her all the more.

I stepped in to kiss her, followed by a long hug. "No guarantees," I whispered in her ear. "Are you stopping by tonight?"

“Do you think you can function after being verbally assaulted by her these last few days?”

“I need alone time with you to get her out of my head.”

April gave me a wicked smile. “Head it is then. But you need to reciprocate.”

All I could do was laugh. All was right, and balance to my world was in the process of being restored.

Chapter 39

The drive over to The Mission was quiet, which was fine by me. I thought once we arrived, I'd have to drag Emily from the car, as I went to open the door, she just sat there. Walking to the trunk, I grabbed her bag and then back, where after about five minutes, she finally stepped out, having resigned herself to her fate. We went inside, where I had her meet Sam.

There wasn't a lot of interaction, and she led us to the room where Emily could stay. It was an extra that Sam used when she needed to spend the night. Emily looked it over with disdain, which was no surprise.

I dropped her bags on the bed in the bedroom and quickly got out of there as Sam was giving her the list of rules she needed to follow, which I was certain would lead to an argument. But I was leaving it in Sam's hands, knowing she wouldn't take any crap from Emily, or she would be out on the street.

It was now mid-afternoon, and after a quick detour for a sandwich, I decided to stop by Barry's office. I had called ahead and learned he was in. I wanted to talk with him about the latest developments and what he wanted to do now. Someone trying to grab the ten-year-old son wasn't a good thing. It was Friday, but the boy was off school, as I'd learned it was a teacher training day. He needed new shoes, and Marilynn hadn't been feeling well enough to go with them. Wasn't sure if that was code for her being drunk or hungover. Maybe it was just as well, as she could have been a liability if she was there. T had handled it properly and once done with the police, returned the boy back to his house, a little shaken, but no worse for wear.

Once at Barry's office, I was in the door and waved to go on back by his secretary, who was chattering away on her headset while typing on the computer. I glanced at the screen and saw it was a shopping site. Nice to know she could multi-task, able to shop and gossip at the same time from what I could hear.

I walked through the door and sat down. Barry was reading papers from a file that sat in the middle of his desk. He looked tired, with bloodshot eyes, his dress shirt open, the tie hanging from his coatrack next to his jacket. I don't think I'd ever seen him dress in anything other than his work clothes. He tossed the papers back into the file, leaned in his chair and put his stocking feet on top of the desk.

"Tough week for you?" I inquired.

"Too much to do and not enough hours," he replied. "I may even go home and sleep tonight instead of scoring with one of my lady friends."

"Wow! You *are* tired." I snickered.

"April give you the skinny on what happened?" he stated, his eyes closed, his face pointing to the ceiling as he talked.

"I'm sure you were thrilled. More to use against Perry."

"I am, but I'm tired of it. We need to bring this whole thing to a close. I'm sick of him and his lawyer, with all the crap they're pulling. I'm worried one of the kids is going to get hurt. And I don't want that."

"Gee Barry, you almost sound civil. What the hell happened? You're normally such a shark about stuff like this."

"Don't you get tired of all of it? Things never seem to get better, no matter how hard you try."

I nodded, much the same emotions I'd experienced these last few months. It was hard to help people when it didn't appear they wanted helping.

I leaned back in the chair, which was devoid of cushion. "Sure, I feel that way sometimes, maybe more lately. It does wear on you. Though I always thought you were basically bulletproof."

"Don't get me wrong, I love putting it to creeps like Perry. But it seems like the creeps are everywhere and there is never any progress made. Even with a large payday, it sometimes…and I stress *sometimes*…doesn't seem worth it."

"Save your money and then you can retire. I'm thinking about trying to start my own bar. After Boone's closed, I need a place to go and unwind. Nothing in the area fits what I'm looking for. I'm been thinking—why don't I just open one myself. I'll be looking for investors. Take this money you'll earn and invest it with me. That is if I can find the time to get it off the ground."

His eyes opened in surprise. "You running a bar? Seems farfetched."

I nodded my head. "I've come to the conclusion I can't do sleuthing forever. One can only cheat death for so long."

"How long are you in town for?" wondered Barry, changing the subject.

"Not sure. I came back with Emily White. Two people tried to grab or kill her. Not sure which. And Brandon isn't returning my calls. I need to find out what is going on there. I'm figuring on being around for several days."

"Emily White? Is she staying at your place?" Barry said with a knowing smile, his eyes closed again.

"Hell no. I put her up at The Mission."

His eyes opened briefly and he smirked. "Oh boy, she'll love it there."

"Sam is dealing with her now. I told her to hand Emily a pair of old overalls and have her paint walls. Should be quite a battle. Emily doesn't have any money to speak of, and I destroyed her credit card Brandon paid for. She'll have to work for a living for now, until I can get him to handle her."

"Good. I want to set up a meeting with Perry and his lawyer. I plan on squeezing them about this latest incident. I know we don't have all the facts or the names of the two men, but as you well know, Perry is behind *all* of this. I plan on grabbing him by the balls and squeezing until he deals. Otherwise he'll understand if we make the connection between the two men and him, then he is going to jail."

"Now *that* is the Barry I know and love. What more do you need from me?"

He opened his eyes again, looking my way. "Once we have the names, if you can run down any connection. I'm sure they lawyered up and will be out on bail. Maybe you can visit one of them and with your natural charm, get them to rollover on Perry. Then we can use that and hopefully put an end to this crap."

"I certainly can. Did you ever learn who the other investor was who took over forty percent of his car dealership?"

Barry took his feet off his desk, leaning his chair forward, grabbing the file and paperwork and tossed it to me. Grabbing the sheets, I started reading, flipping past the first page, to the second. There was the name of a Private Equity firm, Revive Speculations. There was a long list of names of investors in the firm, three of which I knew. I shook my head and cursed out loud.

"I figured that would be your reaction," stated Barry.

I looked over the last page again, making sure I didn't read it wrong. Windsor Bowles, Christina Bowles and Simon Lions. Lions, who was now dead, was known as the original Front Range Butcher and the mastermind behind the reincarnation of The Butcher last year. Christina, who was his sister, was involved as well, now out on bail awaiting trial. And finally, Windsor, the husband of Christina, and a state senator, his bid for a US Congress seat now shelved while he awaited the fate of his wife. It would seem their involvement with this company was purely a coincidence, but it didn't thrill me to encounter this family once again, since they continued to invade my sleep.

"They were part of this investment group?" I asked.

"They were. Not lead members, but a place to shelter their oil money from the Lions' fortune. Obviously, Simon is no longer a member, now that he has passed on. His shares went to the sister. With her impending legal issues, the group could ask her to divest. For now, they continue to back her and the senator."

"Any thoughts on them buying into Perry's business?"

"Nothing seems to be shady about it. An oil company with a stake in a car dealership seems a natural connection. I'd image they got a bargain on the price since Perry was in debt. They have investments in many other businesses along the Front Range. Anything that they can get at a bargain and turn a profit in the long run. That is how most Private Equity firms work."

"Any other names on here that have checkered pasts?" I inquired.

"None of them are saints, if that is what you're asking. Rarely are successful business professionals not toeing the line when it comes to ethics. I could dig deep on all of them and find something fishy."

"Can I get a copy of this?"

Barry nodded and called in his secretary. She must have finished up her online shopping and chat. She stepped in to gather the paper and returned with a copy, which I thanked her for.

"I may check into these other names, with my own contacts," I mused. "And once April shares the names of the two assailants, I will look into them and pay one or both a visit. I will let you know if I come up with anything."

Barry said thanks, ready to call it a day. Walking out the door, I hopped into the Mustang, feeling tired. Deciding to head home, I navigated the city traffic, which was nearing a rush hour peak.

Once I arrived, I walked in and April was sitting on the sofa, reading another one of her J.D. Robb books she enjoyed. I reached out my hand to her, which she grabbed, and I pulled her up to stand. I stared deep in her eyes, swept her off her feet and carried her into the bedroom, where we carried on an explicit love making session to end the day on a high note.

Chapter 40

After a good night of sleep next to a woman I adored, we were up early, as she had the morning shift. Since I hadn't been home much lately, there wasn't much to eat, but I did have four slices of bread that we made into toast, which she took on the run after saying a quick goodbye.

After showering and enjoying my breakfast, along with swigging down a bottle of water, I sat at my computer and opened my email. I found a message from an odd email address, with an attachment of a password protected zip file. I checked my burner phone and found a text message with twenty odd letters, numbers and special characters, coming from the burner Rocky had.

I opened the attachment and typed in the gibberish, needing three tries before I got it right, and the zip file opened to reveal two pictures. They were of the men who'd tortured Rocky before he had freed himself. Neither of the faces were familiar, both white males with broad cheekbones, bushy eyebrows, close cropped blonde hair and noses that appeared to have been broken a time or two. If they weren't related, I'd be surprised.

I contacted Agent Catalina Alegre with the FBI, diligently working on a Saturday and tried my smooth talking to get her to agree to run the faces through their database in hopes of getting names.

"What's in it for me?" she asked, her resistance to my charm impressive.

"The thanks of a grateful citizen for the fine work you've done for our country," I responded, sounding as serious as I could.

A puff of air came though the speaker. "More bullshit from you. Does it ever end!"

I laughed. "Only when I'm dead and buried. Though what is carved into my tombstone may keep it going long after I'm gone. But I do appreciate your help. Agent Price won't take my calls anymore."

"I need to add you to my blocked list as well. This may take a few days, as I'd need to do this discreetly. What are you expecting to find out about these two?"

"I suspect they're hired killers. I'm hoping with their names we can trace it back to those who did the financing of the hit."

"Who're they trying to kill?"

"Tried and failed to kill an associate of mine. Could be part of a bigger scheme. I'm working on putting together all the pieces."

"From the pictures, they appear to be deceased."

"No comment."

Catalina's curiosity was piqued. "Is this related to the plate number you had me look up?"

"They appear to be connected," I acknowledged.

"I need details before checking. I don't run stuff like this just because you ask nicely. What do you have on this case?"

I gave her a few details, though I stressed I had no hard proof yet, just enough to continue to dig.

"If true that could be big. For my help I expect to be kept informed. Cracking open a potential conspiracy like this can make a career."

"Or be a career killer," I retorted.

Much like with The Butcher case, she was playing the angle on job advancement, which was important to her. She wanted to run the Bureau someday. Though in the current toxic political environment, I wasn't certain why.

"I will share when I know more. In the end, I likely will need the Bureau's power to shut down what is going on. Especially if those involved are tied to any of the other three-letter government agencies." I decided to push my luck and ask one more favor. "While you're at it, can you check on a name for me? Stetson Poole. Might be an alias used by this organization."

"You *must* be feeling brave," she said with a tinge of annoyance.

"I'm buoyed by the comradery we've built between us," I noted, trying not to laugh.

I could feel her smirking through the phone. "Comradery that for now is a one-way street. This better lead to something worthwhile. I'll call if the faces or the name lead to anything."

The call ended, so I turned back to the computer, my attention on the Hester case. I had the names and addresses of the two men who had tried to grab the boy from T. Both were locals, and according to what April had learned, both had records, though nothing major. One had an assault charge that had been plea bargained down—the other harassment. They had several other charges that had been dropped when witnesses had failed to follow through. I did a quick search on the internet to see if anything else came up about them.

The first name, Jason Furst, came up with nothing. When I checked social media, I found zilch there as well. No obvious digital fingerprint, which was unusual in the internet age. Stats provided by April showed he was thirty-four, over six foot and heavy set with short umber hair. He lived in Englewood and had a job at a Shell Food Mart nearby.

The other, Rambert Ikenberry didn't have anything on the web, but had a Twitter account where he posted from time to time. Mostly crass stuff about immigrants and people of color. To say he was a racist was kind. He didn't seem to like anyone or anybody that wasn't of the opinion that white people were becoming extinct and needed to rise up and take back their country.

Other details from April, said he was thirty-two years old, about 5'10" and 170 pounds, with buzz blonde haircut and one tattoo on each arm. He was unemployed, drawing payments from the government via welfare and food stamps. He'd been the one that had distracted T, likely using his hatred to draw his attention. For his racist words, he got decked. He would be a tough nut to crack. I decided to go track down Jason first and see what I could get out of him.

I then checked on the other investors in the Private Equity group, Revive Speculations. Of all the other names, only one showed a possible red flag. Rourke Welles was a hard-nosed businessman who lived in Texas and was also an oil man. He had close ties to the Lions family, at least to the father of Simon Lions senior. He'd lobbied hard to remove regulations and environmental restrictions on oil exploration, especially when it came to fracking, a controversial method of extracting oil and natural gas from deep underground. He'd backed many conservative causes including Windsor Bowles campaigns in Colorado. He had a home near Dallas, and another in Aspen. But what caught my eye were pictures of him with other men on his website.

One was Brandon Sparks, while the other was Tyrell Powers, whose organization I'd come up against a couple of times. Though the pictures didn't imply any type of partnership with either man, it didn't explicitly say they *didn't* have business dealings. Either way it was worth delving into deeper when the mood struck me.

With information in hand, it was time to go find Jason. The Shell Food Mart was on the corner of South Logan and Hampden, near Swedish Medical Center. I thought I'd stop there first, where I could top off my gas tank and see if he was working. The drive took about twenty minutes, as it was just after rush hour. The weather was rainy today, my wiper blades squeaking across the glass, a lingering chill of winter hanging on, though spring had officially arrived over a month ago.

I pulled in beside a pump and topped off the tank, requiring several gallons to fill my gas hungry muscle car. I stepped inside, spotting an older woman, with reading glasses hanging on her nose, behind the counter. The receipt machine at the pump didn't work, which was par for the course at most of the pre-paid pumps I'd used through the years.

"A receipt please," I uttered nicely. "Pump three." What I wanted to yell was 'why was there never a working receipt maker at these pumps?'

Without a word or a smile, she handed me the paper. She had been reading her *People* magazine and apparently I had made her lose her train of thought.

"Is Jason working today?" I asked. I had waited until she had started reading again on purpose. I enjoyed aggravating people.

"No," she answered without looking up.

"Do you know when he is working again?" I tried to smile, which often would stop a charging rhino, but she wasn't even giving me a glance.

"Probably never. Idiot called in sick again. I had to cover his shift. I expect he will get fired here soon by the boss. He hates paying overtime."

"Sorry he kept you from your celebrity fix. How is Brangelina these days?"

She finally looked up at me as if I was nuts. "They're divorced."

No surprise I didn't know this, for I didn't follow the tabloids closely.

"The Kardashians?"

"Either make a purchase or leave," she said, before going back to her reading.

I thought about telling her to have a nice day, but figured it was too late to save her. Why was it everyone in the world seemed grumpy these days?

I made it back to my car and headed north on Logan street. I travelled up a block and then turned left on East Girard Avenue.

Jason lived in a two-story white and beige structure that appeared to be a former office building turned into a multi-tenant home with several doors, only one of which was labelled with a house number. I parked out on Girard and knocked on the door. An older man answered, wearing a dirty t-shirt and shorts, a strong smell of cheap booze on his breath.

"Yes," he mumbled. He was holding a magazine in his hand. Maybe he was a relative of the lady at the Shell station.

"I'm looking for Jason," I said.

"Door is around back, through the gate and up the stairs."

"Thanks."

"And keep the fucking noise down."

I smiled and walked away. I wasn't sure what noise he was expecting to hear, but maybe Jason had a lot of parties. I found the gate and walked through, under an awning, across the weedy grass until I found the stairs. They were a bit rickety, and I walked gingerly, worried it would come crashing down. I pounded on the screen door several times before I got a response. The inside door opened a crack, with a sleepy-eyed face peering through.

"I don't want any," he growled, sounding tired or drunk. From what I could tell, he wasn't holding a magazine.

"Jason, we need to talk," I said, opening the screen door.

"Leave me alone."

He tried to push the door shut, but I had my foot wedged against it.

"Perry and Rambert called me in. They want me to talk with you about what happened. Why you failed at grabbing the kid. We need to figure out what to do next."

The two names and what I said seemed to wake him up, his eyes alert with fear filling them. "Ok. Let me put pants on and I'll be right back."

I let him close the door and waited, trying not to move too much. It was probably two minutes when the door opened, and I was allowed in. Looking around, the place was a mess; empty beer bottles and dirty paper plates on his coffee table, the brown carpet looking in need of a major cleaning, the place smelling musty, which was rare because of the dry Colorado environment.

Stepping towards Jason, I punched him right in the gut to prove I wasn't messing around and to get his attention. It was a good-sized gut, plenty of fat to keep him from too much damage. He doubled over and let out a loud gasp, before taking two steps back and plopping down on the badly worn yellow fabric sofa.

"*That* is for fucking up the mission," I yelled firmly, not worried about the old man below.

I was worried Jason might start crying, his face was a combination of pain, sadness and fear.

"I'm not totally to blame," he babbled desperately, once he'd gotten his breath back. "Rambert couldn't handle the big black guy. He was supposed to put him down, while I ran away with the kid."

"Even if you did, it sounded like you couldn't even keep a ten-year-old under control. He was making enough racket to bring the mall cops to you. Admit it, you *both* screwed the pooch."

His eyes couldn't look at me as he kept rubbing his stomach. He wasn't in shape, and clearly didn't have much going for him, by the looks of things. Walking over to the end table, I saw several pieces of mail, a couple stamped final notice. It would seem he was behind on his bills.

"Not going to get out of your debt screwing up," I declared. "Perry isn't going to pay off for mistakes like this. What were you supposed to do again to earn your money?"

He seemed afraid to say anything.

I walked over to him, staring down with my best tough guy glare. "You better talk about this before it gets worse."

"We were to watch them for a couple of days, waiting for the right moment. Rambert was supposed to distract and stop the black guy. Do what it took to put him down. I would then grab the kid and run away, carrying him to the car, where we would get away."

It sounded like they had a driver waiting. I needed to squeeze out of him who it was.

"Where were you to take the kid?"

"Once the kid saw his dad in the car, he wouldn't be scared

anymore, and we'd go back to Perry's place. That was when we'd get paid."

Jackpot! This confirmed Perry was involved.

"And since you failed, Perry drove away, likely when he saw the cops arrive."

He nodded, looking nauseous. "Do you mind? I need to go to the bathroom. Your punch upset my stomach."

I waved for him to leave, wondering what else I could learn from him. He was gone for about ten minutes, before returning, and taking his place on the sofa. The man was a mess and I suspected this mistake wasn't going to improve his life any. For that fact it could get worse, as Perry wasn't going to be thrilled with what happened and could send a body after Jason to punish him. It was difficult to feel sorry for someone trying to grab a kid, yet I was.

Trying to figure what to do next, my phone rang, from a number I didn't recognize. I excused myself, walking outside at the top of the steps and answered.

"Jarvis, are you alone," uttered the voice. It wasn't the clearest transmission, yet I recognized the articulation.

"Hold on a second," I replied. Then I spoke to Jason. "I need to take this call. Hang tight and think over what we should do next."

I went down the stairs and into the yard, away from eavesdroppers, doing my best to keep my phone dry from the light rain.

"I can talk now. Is this who I think it is?"

"It is. Sorry I haven't gotten back to you. I've been on the move and had to dump my phone. This is a burner."

"I think it's about time you told me what is going on." I said firmly. It wasn't often I was pushy with Brandon Sparks.

There was a long pause. "Did you get Emily back into Denver?"

"I did. But two people tried to grab her, and one was killed. We spent time with the police and for now they let us go. But they could come back at her eventually."

"Did you shoot the person?"

"No, she did." I left out the part of her apparent glee in killing someone.

"That weapons training paid off. Who tried to grab her?"

"A Chinese man and a woman. The woman was killed. I

subdued the man and he is in custody."

"If it's who I think it is, he won't be for long and will be flying back to China."

"This all speaks to my issues with the Chinese," I grumbled. "You need to give me more than what you've told me to this point. I need to know what I'm up against."

There was another long pause.

"Come on, Brandon. You owe me at least that much from all we've gone through these last few years."

Still silence.

"I've been trying to get a hold of Sue, but she isn't answering. Is she with you?"

"No. But I had people with her."

"Then why isn't she answering her phone?" The frustration in my voice was clear.

"She has never been a fan of yours. Maybe she doesn't want to talk with you."

"Though that is true, I doubt that is the reason. She always, at the very least, returns my calls. Especially if it's important, which I stressed in my voicemails. I have a feeling something isn't right."

Another pause before Brandon spoke. "Maybe you should check on her. Do you have her address?"

"No I don't, and I can, but you need to come clean on what the hell is happening. I'm being stretched thin here trying to cover everything for you."

"Reluctantly, yes you're correct. How much longer are you in town?"

"As long as I need to be."

"Let me check and I will get back to you."

"Soon!"

"Yes. No later than tomorrow. I will text you Sue's home address."

"Fair enough." I hung up, wandering the backyard in thought. I got a chime on my phone, with the address, which I promptly added to her contact info. After finishing, I turned and saw a man walking through the gate, mostly ignoring me and then up the stairs to Jason's place. From the description I had, it appeared to be Rambert in all his racist glory.

I could walk away and let the two of them hash it out, for my head was spinning from being pulled in too many directions. Making the decision, I began walking away, but I soon heard sounds of yelling coming from upstairs. Shaking my head, wishing I'd just leave it alone, but knowing I couldn't, I decided to make the trek back up the stairs and deal with the two of them.

As I climbed the rickety steps, I checked to make sure my gun was on my back hip, for the possibly of using it just ratchetted up a notch.

Chapter 41

The noise *had* been Rambert screaming at Jason, claiming their trouble with the law was his fault. Jason was cowering some, trying to defend himself, but Rambert was too forceful, threatening to hurt him, a large knife in his hands. I entered and Rambert turned around, surprised by my presence. His yelling now was directed at me.

"Who the fuck are you!" he said, the knife now pointed in my direction.

"He is the guy I told you about," said Jason. "Perry sent him."

"Does Perry not trust me to finish the job?" asserted Rambert, this time not in full yell mode.

"Obviously he doesn't after the mess you made grabbing the kid," I stated calmly. My hands were at my side, ready to grab my gun if necessary.

"If *Jason* had kept better control of the kid, we would have been fine. I mean how can you not be stronger than a ten-year-old? What I get for hiring on a wuss to help me."

"You said you'd take out the black man, but you didn't," countered Jason, his body shaking.

Rambert went on a raging, racist rant, including mentioning the N-word several times when talking about T.

"Say what you want," I said, once he was finished. "But it sounds as if he was a better man than you."

Rambert didn't like my comment and started coming towards me with his knife. I pulled my gun and pointed it at him, which got him to stop.

"I think my gun trumps your knife. Put it away before someone gets hurt. Right now, Perry has no issue with me shooting you since you made a mess of things."

"If you didn't have that gun," Rambert said bitterly.

"If you didn't have that knife. Believe me when I say this, you're out of your league. Now pocket that thing before I take it from you and have a seat."

He was a tough guy, but not tougher than a bullet. He folded it back up and put it in his pocket, walking to the sofa and sitting down.

"If you geniuses want to get paid," I said while lowering my gun to my side. "Then we need to go see Perry and see what can be done to salvage this mess. Otherwise I have a feeling he is going to want me to make you disappear."

Jason looked worried at the words. "What do you mean, 'disappear?'"

"What do you *think* he means," replied Rambert. "He is going to kill us."

I smiled. Fear was my leverage on them and I was going to use it to hopefully bring an end to this whole situation.

"There must be a way to fix this?" said Jason, his voice quaking in fear.

"Like I said, we need to go see Perry and work this through. Jason, call a cab and we'll drive down there."

"I have my own car," scoffed Rambert.

"Nope. We're all going together. And I'm not driving, and have you stick me in the back with your knife. Jason, make sure to ask them to send a mini-van or SUV with three rows of seating. I want to be able to keep my eye on both of you."

Jason hesitated, but I waved with my gun and he got up and made the call. It took about fifteen minutes for it to arrive, and I had them both out and down the stairs first, warning them that if they ran, I'd shoot them.

The Yellow Cab, a Chevy mini-van, was sitting at the curb. They both took the far back seat, while I sat in the second row, with one eye on both. I gave the driver the address and we were off.

Since I had followed Perry extensively during the initial part of the investigation, I knew his routine. Every Saturday he would go into his office, late in the morning since he was always hungover from a night of debauchery with one of his girlfriends, and would work for a few hours. While we were driving, I sent a text message to Barry, telling him I thought we could wrap up this whole case today and would he be available to finalize things with Perry's lawyer.

His reply came quickly and not with a happy tone, judging by his response in all caps and with several four-letter words. I let him know that I thought I had Perry by the balls now and would squeeze him to settle. Barry responded back that he would be ready, and if I screwed up the whole deal, he would have my balls for breakfast. I responded with a smiley face and put my phone away.

The ride over didn't take too long, and we arrived just after noon, the rain falling lightly. I paid the cab driver, got the receipt and led the way to Perry's office. We maneuvered around a couple of sales people, one a Hispanic lady that Rambert had distain for.

Perry's assistant wasn't working today, probably home resting up from her night of satisfying her boss. I waved Jason and Rambert to walk in first, while I trailed behind them, preventing Perry from seeing me. The look on his face was of surprise and then of anger.

"What the hell are you two doing here?" he growled, tossing down the pen he was holding.

"We were told you wanted to see us," divulged Rambert. "You wanted to work out what to do since we botched the grabbing of your son."

"Are you two idiots," Perry yelled. "Being seen with you after what happened could screw me. Now get out of here."

"But he said you wanted us here," explained Jason, pointing at me.

I moved into the room, where Perry could see me. His face turned beet red, which I enjoyed.

"What the fuck are you doing here, Jarvis!" he yelled again.

"Like they said, I'm here to work out how we're going to handle this whole mess you've gotten yourself into. I believe I have you red-handed and it's time to end this crap and settle."

Perry's head dropped to the table, knowing he was screwed. Neither Rambert or Jason understood what was going on, looking at each other is shock.

"I'm confused," uttered Jason.

"You idiots brought the PI here that has been making my life a living hell," growled Perry.

"He told us, he worked for you," protested Rambert.

I smiled. "Actually, I said Perry sent me."

"He was hired by my wife's lawyer." Perry's head remained on the table.

"Then the man who was guarding the kid worked for you?" asked Jason, connecting the dots.

I smiled and nodded my head.

Rambert went off again on one of his racist rants, calling me an N-word lover. I walked over to him and was in his face.

"Say that word once again and I will knock you on your ass."

"You think you're tough with that gun of yours." He snarled.

"My gun is put away. One punch and you'll forget who you are."

Rambert was trying to summon the courage, but knew he was no match for me. He backed down and stepped away, finding a chair to sit in, cowering in fear. I doubt his views would change any, but it was thrilling, and immensely satisfying to put him in his place.

"Perry, you have only one option and that is to settle and settle now," I said firmly. "If you don't, I'm calling the police and having you all arrested. They will drag you out in front of your employees and your business will be ruined. It's your move."

"If I do, it will leave me with nothing." He raised his head and stared at me, defeat in his eyes.

"Probably true. She'll own the final sixty percent, with the other forty being held by Revive Speculations. If you're lucky, they'll decide to keep you as the face of the company, since you're such a TV star. Pay you a salary, though not what you're used to making. It won't be much, but it's better than being in jail. Now get on the phone and call your lawyer, or I dial the police."

He was cornered with nothing more he could do. Beaten, he reached into his wallet and pulled out a business card and started dialing. Being a weekend, he got an answering service, but told them it was an emergency and that he needed his lawyer to call him right away.

Standing by the door, to make sure no one tried to run out, I texted Barry again, letting him know we were about to close the deal.

"Have a seat, Jason," I said, his nervous twitching bothering me. "We're going to be here a while, until the deal is done. Once all is finished, we'll get the charges dropped against you and Rambert. Though a little time in jail with a person of color being his cellmate, might enlighten Rambert on being a better human being."

I leaned against the door, surveying the room, knowing I was in control of the situation, anger and defeat on the various faces. Jason appeared to be mumbling to himself, Rambert giving me the stink eye from time to time, and Perry with his head in his hands trying to rub away the pain of his downfall. The phone rang, and he answered it, his lawyer on the line.

"We're going to settle this," he uttered dejectedly over the phone, the tone of a beaten man.

Those were magic words to my ears, as I gave him the number to conference in Barry, then let them hash out the legalese, while I was counting to myself the final fee I was about to collect with a large grin on my face.

Chapter 42

With a good feeling the end was nearing on the Hester case, the next day April and I took a drive to Sue's place on the west side of town. She lived in a nice two-story house, in a good neighborhood, with an attached two car garage. The grass in the front looked long and in need of trimming, an indication that no one had been home for a while, which was disconcerting.

We tried ringing the doorbell several times but got no answer. There was no pile of papers on the front porch and their mailbox was a community one, preventing us from seeing if there was lots of mail. All the curtains were closed, and after checking around in back, we couldn't find a way in.

We decided to knock on a neighbor's door and see if they knew anything. The one adjacent to them was answered by a white man wearing jean shorts, a tank top, with short blonde hair, nice tan and a hoop earring in each ear. He crossed his arms when answering, shifting his weight to his left leg.

"Can I help you?" he said, seeming a little put off we had interrupted him. We could hear a TV playing in the background that sounded like the ladies from The View arguing.

"I'm a Denver cop," disclosed April, who was in uniform, but off duty for now.

"And I'm a private detective," I added, showing him my license.

"Sweet. You make a cute couple. What can I help you with?"

"Do you know the lady next door?" inquired April, while pointing at Sue's house.

He glanced to the house and nodded. "Oh, yes we do. Nia and Sue are good friends. Me and the hubby have dinner with them occasionally."

"Have you seen them lately? We've been trying to get a hold of Sue and she hasn't called us back."

"Are you friends of theirs?" he queried.

April looked at me. "I know her from her job at Sparks Builders," I said. "Her boss, Brandon, asked me to check on her. She hasn't been to work for several days, which is unlike her."

He thought it over for a minute, his right hand on his chin, before answering. "Come to think of it, I've not seen either of them for several days either. Normally you'd see one of their cars in the driveway, but that hasn't been the case."

More evidence that something was wrong. I wanted to get inside and look around. I had searched for a hide-a-key, but didn't find one, which was probably good in the long run as burglars often looked for them. Unfortunately it didn't make our job any easier.

"Any chance you have a key to their place?" I asked.

The look on his face told me the answer, his eyes scanning down and then to the side, but he didn't say anything.

"It's really important we make sure they're okay," noted April. "You are welcome to go in with us if you're concerned about us stealing their stuff."

He thought it over a little longer, then nodded and walked away, leaving the door open. Once he returned, he walked out, bare foot and led us to her front door.

"When they're away, I often come by and water their plants," he explained, while putting the key in the lock. "They didn't say anything about leaving. I hope their spider plants, ficus and rubber figs are still alive."

The health of the plants was secondary to Sue's and her girlfriend's welfare, the threat on their lives what I was most concerned about. He opened the door and walked in, with April and I right behind. There was a smell coming from the main living area that wasn't pleasant, one that indicated we were going to find a body. The thought of it being Sue, a person I enjoyed conversing with, sent a shiver down my spine.

"Oh my, what is that smell?" he asked, choking while covering his mouth.

"Please step on out," said April hurriedly, her cop instincts instantly recognizing what we were going to find. "We need to secure the room."

He looked surprised but did as he was told. April had her gun out, as did I. We moved through the living area and into the kitchen where the smell was horrible, and we found the body. To my relief, it was neither of the ladies. Instead, the corpse was a man. It appeared he'd been shot twice in the chest, but no gun was found. From appearances—the body decomposing, the blood pool on the floor dry—he'd been there several days.

"I need to call this in," said April, sounding stoic, her police training kicking in.

I nodded. "Let's make sure there isn't anyone else first."

She looked at me and wasn't happy. "Fine, but don't touch anything."

It didn't need to be said, but I nodded anyway. We searched the rest of the first level, going room to room; a work study, bath and laundry area. Then went upstairs, checking the huge bathroom with shower and large two-person Jacuzzi, and second bedroom before looking in the master bedroom.

On the floor, in the master bedroom, was a second body, another male. No blood this time, but the man's neck clearly had been broken. His weapon was missing, his holster empty.

Searching further, we found the large walk-in closet was open and there were gaps where the clothes hung and on the shoe rack, indicating someone had grabbed what they could and left. From there, we went to the attached two car garage and found one bronze BMW and nothing else.

Opening the garage door, I found a small trail of blood that stopped suddenly, as if an injured party had gotten into another car. We made it back to the front door, where we found the neighbor standing there, chewing on his knuckles.

"Oh god, please tell me they're okay," he said in a high-pitched, shaky voice.

"There are two dead bodies, but it's not them," explained April, leaving out the part about the blood outside. "Neither of them is home. Right now, we don't know what happened to them. I'm going to call it in."

April pulled out her cell phone and made the call, while I stood there, thinking.

"There is a bronze BMW in the garage. Do you know whose car that is?"

"That is Sue's car. Nia drives a black Lexus. It matched well with the tone of her skin, she always told us." He stood there, his body shaking, arms crossed, the distress about his friends evident.

"Did she leave it outside most of the time?"

He thought for a minute. "At times, yes. Though I tried not to snoop too much on their comings and goings."

"And you didn't hear anything or see them leave?"

"No. What would I have heard?"

"Gunshots. The person in the kitchen was shot twice. Looks like he has been in there for several days."

"Oh my god!" he quivered. "How can this happen in this neighborhood?"

I knew the answer, knowing it had nothing to do with the neighborhood, but didn't tell him. Revealing the real reason wouldn't make him feel any better.

"What about the second body?" he wondered. "Were they shot too?"

"No. Looks like a broken neck."

"Is that what the horrible smell was?" His face contorted, remembering the odor.

I nodded.

"No I didn't hear anything. Though I do have the TV on at a higher volume than I should. Hubby gets mad at me about it. And when working in the yard, I have my wireless headphones on. I like music playing while I work."

"Can you call your husband and see if he heard anything?"

"Sure thing. I hope they're okay. They're the sweetest couple. When we're out together, everyone comments on us four and how perfect we are for each other. Though I think most people get the couple arrangement mixed up."

I smiled and thanked him. It wasn't long before the local police showed up, since we were in Lakewood. April had to explain she was off duty but was helping me off a concern I had about the residents living there. I wasn't sure they were thrilled, yet they couldn't argue about us helping them out in discovering the two murders. I used client privilege to ward off many of their inquiries, which didn't endure me to them.

It was a good two hours before we could leave, collecting another stern warning to be available for more questions. The local cops weren't sharing who the victim was, but I had taken pictures with my cell phone and sent it to Brandon.

We were driving back to Denver as April needed to start her shift soon, when he called.

"Who is in the pictures?" he asked.

"Two dead bodies at Sue's home," I said. "Do you know either of them?”

“Neither was my man inside,” he replied, his voice cold as ice.

“We found blood outside. From what we can tell, they may have left in Nia’s black Lexus. The police are looking into it.”

There was silence on the phone. Then, “I think it’s time we talked.”

I wanted to say, duh, but resisted. “I’ve been saying that all along. Where and when?”

“I will come to your office. Say four today.”

I agreed and hung up. Hopefully he would clear up what was going on. I was totally in the dark on his situation. Which seemed to be par for the course these days.

Chapter 43

April dropped me off and headed to work, having the evening shift tonight. Feeling exhausted, I walked in and, after grabbing a beer from the fridge, sat down on my sofa. I took a long drink, tasting the cool brew on the palate. I leaned back and closed my eyes, weary from the day and it was only early afternoon.

A nap sounded like a grand idea, but I desired to stay awake. I needed to be sharp to face Brandon. I wasn't going to accept any half-truths from him. No matter what it took, I wanted the whole story. I was tired of my clients leaving out key details that could help the case. It made the job and my life unnecessarily difficult.

My thoughts were interrupted by my cell ringing, caller ID showing it was Sam. I hoped it was good news.

"You're going to owe me big time," she said with spite in her voice. "This woman is a lazy, crazy, major pain in the ass. Not to mention a world-class flirt with anyone she can manipulate to get what she wants."

I hadn't filled Sam in on Emily's character when arranging her to stay, leading me to say…nothing.

"I'm about to slug and drop her out on the streets with the rest of the trash."

"I'm okay…with that," I said, nearly laughing as the words came out.

"You knew she would be a handful, didn't you," accused Sam with more spite.

"I plead the fifth." I was doing my best not to laugh, while taking another sip on my beer.

"Do you have another plan for her before I punch her?"

"Working on it. Hopefully I will have answers after a meeting I'm having at four."

"You have until tomorrow or I drop her off at your place. Are we clear?"

If Sam didn't slow down while pushing her out of the car, I was fine with that. But I decided to withhold the suggestion, for I wasn't certain I could finish the statement without laughing hysterically.

"I will call you in the morning. I promise."

"I'm not kidding, Jarvis," she threatened before hanging up.

I chuckled to myself, happy to learn I wasn't the only one who was easily driven mad by Emily. Sam had dealt with all kinds while working at The Mission, but Emily had a unique, to say the least, personality that would someday cost her. I hoped Brandon had a place for her, because there was no way she was staying here.

I slowly finished off my beer, killing time thinking about nothing at all, leaving only a blank mind while counting the bumps on the popcorn-coated ceiling. An effort at the moment to flush my brain of all that had happened.

A few minutes before four, I heard a car parking outside. Getting up, I placed the empty beer bottle in my recycle bin and opened the door.

The car outside was a large, newer silver Cadillac SUV, with a driver behind the steering wheel and another who stepped out from the passenger side, and then walked around and opened the door for Brandon, after scanning the area for any possible danger.

Down the stairs he walked, dressed more casually than normal, with plain stone-washed jeans, banana colored polo, New Balance tennis shoes, with plain black ball cap, wrap-around sunglasses and gun strapped to his belt. He was blending in, looking like any other man, excluding the fancy car, two guards and 9mm on his right hip.

Once inside, Brandon instructed the other man to keep an eye out, before closing the door. I offered him a beer, which he accepted, the first time I recalled him drinking anything other than whiskey, which I would have offered if I had any. I held the bottle while he walked the room, pulling out a device he turned on, lights and indicators giving him information he was gauging. He moved into the bedroom and bathroom before returning, putting it in his pocket.

"Can we turn your music on?" he requested, after I handed him the beer.

I nodded and walked over to my stereo, flipping it on to my favorite station, setting the volume until he agreed to the level. He took my chair, while I sat on the sofa, resting my right hand on the padded arm.

"I'm being cautious," he explained. "I was scanning the room for bugs. And I wanted the music on to protect from any laser eavesdropping devices."

"All clear on the bugs?" I wondered, hoping for a positive answer. I had enough issues and didn't need paranoia adding to them.

"Yes. I know you've had visitors over the last year. I needed to be sure they hadn't planted anything."

"I doubt April would have done anything," I protested, smiling.

"Not her. But your Chinese foes," Brandon pointed out.

I scoffed. "Are you talking about Guo and his man? They never got far enough in to plant a bug."

"But the woman did," answered Brandon while cradling his beer.

He was talking about Milani, used by Guo to try and blackmail me. I wasn't sure how Brandon knew all of this, since I'd never told him. But he was a powerful man with lots of resources. It was hard to be surprised.

"It should be safe to talk. Hopefully you'll share—finally—about what is going on. I'm getting a little tired of learning stuff the hard way."

Brandon shrugged as if he didn't care. Our business relationship was complicated, and often I felt he held over me the work I'd done that he knew about. One couldn't deny he'd been helpful when I needed him. I did owe him a debt, though I might not live long enough to clear it.

"I didn't care to share at first, I thought I'd be able to work my way out of this jam. But now the situation has become…dire. And it's time to fill you in, to figure a way out that works for us both."

"I could walk away now and not lose any sleep over what happens to you," I declared rather coldly.

Brandon didn't appear concerned. "I figured as much. But I know you do care about what happens to Sue and what happened to Rocky. You may be tough, but you aren't callous. I know you've lost sleep over those who die under your watch."

I shrugged this time, trying to match his apathy. "Not sure these deaths *are* under my watch. I'm uncertain what has happened to Sue. And when it came to Rocky, *you* asked me to look into this death." I had not revealed to him that Rocky was alive. I was holding that card in reserve.

"True. But I know you well enough, to figure your concern for a woman's life is enough to continue, especially Sue who, though you both act like you don't like each other, I know there is a respect there."

Though we had clashed a few times, he was right—I did like and respect Sue. Partly because of her work ethic and her devotion to her boss. But mostly because she had a spunky side I admired and enjoyed sparring against.

"If you don't tell me all that is going on, I'm prepared to walk away. I won't feel any remorse for what happens in the future. Yes I will feel bad if the worst happens, but it will be on you and not me."

He took a long draw on his beer. "Fair enough. Where should I begin?"

I left the question unanswered, as it seemed abundantly clear on where he should start.

"I have many business interests besides construction," Brandon began. "Without getting into the finer details of what they might be—I'll admit—they consist of a borderline nature."

"I'm totally shocked," I said sarcastically. I knew, as did most, that his dealings weren't always of the legal kind.

"I've grown to trust you in our time together. And I gather you won't reveal to the authorities all of the details."

I nodded. It wasn't my intention of giving away details about his business, unless it furthered a cause I was passionate about. And I could always hide behind client confidentiality.

"One of my dealings was related to activities going on in Southern California. Items brought in from overseas to be resold at a nice profit. Though these items were things the government frowned upon capitalists like me selling."

"What were those items?" I queried.

"I will get to that in due time." He stopped to take a sip of beer. "Those I was working with needed the extensive pull I had with customs. Getting them to approve those items on arrival, if they were inspected. Contacts I had built up over time, who had been properly compensated. Getting me materials and people to help strengthen my profit margin when building my construction projects. I was contacted many years ago, via parties I knew, bringing the two of us together to meet to see if we could work out a deal."

"Who was that person?" I inquired.

"Maximillian Conway."

I was surprised, though maybe I shouldn't have been, as the last time we talked he had revealed knowing Max better than he had led on previously.

"You said you didn't know him."

"Purposely omitted on my part."

"You lied."

Brandon shrugged. "At the time I didn't feel it was important to know."

I wanted to get mad at him but held it back. "Is that how you became connected to Rocky?"

"Not exactly. That happened after the fact. I knew of him, and knew he was an enforcer for Conway. But nothing more until later."

"Did you know about the attempt to kill Rocky and his family?"

"Absolutely not. I had no prior knowledge of it. It was like I said before, after he was injured, he reached out for my help, figuring he could trust me. I figured he'd be a good ally to have for work I may require in the future."

Brandon always had an underlying reason for helping, usually to further his own cause down the line. It was much how I'd become indebted to him.

"And you were able to keep this hidden from Max?"

"Yes. Because we weren't directly tied together in any way. After those initial meetings, my involvement was with other parties."

"Who were?"

Brandon stopped to sip more beer, a tinge of distaste showing on his palate. I wasn't sure he was impressed with my choice of brew.

"The Chinese government. Or at least a small segment running their own private business."

"Crap!" I yelled out, bitter this key fact had been hidden from me. "And these are the same men I've had run-ins with over the last couple of years?"

"Yes. But on a totally separate matter. They had several other business dealings that I'm not involved with. Only this venture in

Southern California was I a part of."

"And the Russians?"

"I have no ties to them in any way."

"What does all of this have to do with the trouble you're in?"

Brandon finished the beer and put the empty bottle on the table. He leaned forward, talking more softly. "I was trying to divest myself from the whole operation. The plan was to move onto more profitable and legitimate businesses. An effort to make my life less complicated. It would seem they weren't thrilled I was taking those measures to do so."

"They were applying pressure?" I put two and two together. The math wasn't hard.

"And threats, which I don't take kindly to. I had to take my own measures to stop them. Drastic measures."

I leaned forward now as well, a tense frown on my face. "What did you do?"

"After several of the threats against me and those I work with crossed the line, I had two of their agents who were in town last year killed."

I looked at him as if he was crazy. "You mean…."

He nodded his head. "Yes, those same two men that were harassing you."

I let out a long, multi-syllable curse word, as the revelation stunned me.

Chapter 44

I grabbed the empty beer bottle and dropped it in the recycle bin, and then began pacing the kitchen floor. Much of what happened last year was now running through my head. The confrontation with Guo in my apartment, the game that Milani played on me of being the woman in trouble and then trying to seduce me. The arrest for rape and then being cleared, but blackmailed to help find the Russian, Aleksi Platov, who helped get them off my back with a fake bomb. Then when the two Chinese men turned up dead, I was questioned, but didn't know anything since it happened while I was tied up by The Butcher.

I'd assumed Aleksi had been the one to take them out, even though he denied it, but now I learned it was Brandon. And for my trouble, I was now neck deep in another mess that threatened the lives of many, including myself. It was a game I had grown tired of, but deep down knew I couldn't just simply walk away from. I was angry, and it would show.

"Damn you, Brandon," I yelled, walking back into the living area. "Do you know what I've been through, thanks to you leaving out all of these pertinent details? I'd be within my right to grab you by the shirt and pound on you right now. At the very least, I should walk away from this mess and let you deal with it."

Brandon sat back in the chair, looking calm as ever, my threat not bothering him at all, which didn't douse my rage.

"I understand you're mad," he said with no emotion "But you should take a seat and calm down, and maybe together we can figure out what to do next. Whether you like it or not, you're involved."

"And all thanks to you!"

His calmness wasn't helping my anger. I needed to strike out. My fists clenched in rage. With a short, snapping motion, I punched Brandon in the left bicep.

"Do you feel better?" he said, rubbing at his arm, the only indication he had felt the contact.

"A little, though I'm still pissed! Honestly I should toss your ass out of here."

"I wouldn't advise that," he proclaimed with a stern look. "It would not end well for you. Now are you going to calm down and work through this with me?" He waved his hand towards the sofa.

A touch of rage had been released, the rest having to wait to vent another way. After a few more paces, I reluctantly sat down again.

"Thank you," Brandon stated. "I do believe we can come up with a solution, though it may take a collective effort. But you're a smart and tough guy. I know there is a way out of this."

"Short of dying, I'm not certain how." The tension in my body was subsiding…slowly.

Brandon shrugged. It would seem dying didn't bother him much.

"Give me all the facts on everything," I asserted. "And don't leave anything out or I will be inclined to come back and shoot you!"

There was little worry on Brandon's face. When it came to my threats he was Teflon.

"Guns and drugs," announced Brandon, matter-of-factly.

"That is what is being brought in?"

"Yes."

"It never bothered you the damage these items would cause?"

"If not me, then it would be others. I was simply brokering an arrangement to get the items through customs."

"Same old line used by most criminals. I'm sure the money paid to you was paramount."

He shrugged, not caring. "Philosophy is often lost on me and social ramifications don't sway my business decisions. And yes, money was and always will be a deciding factor."

"Then why stop now?"

Brandon leaned forward again, whispering. "Because the Feds are snooping too closely at my business. In the past I've been able to fend them off. But as I've grown older, I've determined it is time to clean up my act and stick with the legal side of my business dealings. I'd rather not spend my golden years behind bars."

"And maybe a last-ditch effort to get into heaven," I noted.

He shrugged, holding up his hand, with thumb and index finger a quarter inch apart, indicating a little of it was true.

"Might be too late to confess your sins and cleanse your soul."

He tugged at his pant legs as he crossed them, looking

unconcerned.

"If you were cleaning up your act, why kill the two Chinese men?"

"The only reason one would need, which was to kill them before they killed me."

"Is that true?"

"Yes. I had inside information they were coming to kill me, or at least inflict dire pain. It was imperative I act before they could."

I shook my head in disgust. "But that only made the situation worse?"

"It would seem. But at the time I had little choice."

"And now they're after you, and those who work for you and ones you care for."

"Yes. They came after Sue and Emily. Possibly Rocky too. Not sure if that was part of what got him killed or his quest to find the killers of his family."

"Sounds like the two items aren't too far apart. Especially since Max is involved with the illegal goods coming in, though he claims, reluctantly. Did Rocky know about them?" I was hoping to confirm what Max told was true.

"I'm uncertain. We never discussed it. But it could have had a hand in his wanting to leave Max. Even though he said they parted on good terms, one can never say for certain. Rocky was a complex person. He could kill someone without a thought if it served his needs. But he had a moral code, which was his family. When they were taken away, those morals were stripped from him."

What Brandon said lined up closely with what Max had said. I leaned back and thought over the words I was hearing. The plot to this story was a complicated one and I wished I could thumb to the final chapters to find out how it ended. But that wouldn't work here.

"What about Sue?" I asked. "Do you think they have her?"

"I don't think so," he said, sounding unconcerned for her wellbeing. "I believe she is in the wind with her girlfriend. I confirmed this when you sent the picture to me of the two dead man in their house. Neither was my man inside."

"What about the blood outside, I found?"

"It was from the man I had there. He was wounded, and they

dropped him at a hospital, then left without being seen. He died a couple days later."

I was mad again. "Another item you failed to mention."

"The item seemed inconsequential."

No shrug from him this time. Maybe his shoulders were getting tired. I knew the statement was bull but decided to leave it be.

"Then the two of them are on their own?"

Brandon nodded.

"Why haven't they contacted you? Or did they, and you feel that was inconsequential as well."

Brandon shook his head. "They haven't contacted me because she knows it's better to stay low for now."

"Sue? Is that smart?"

"Not Sue, but Nia. She is highly trained and is guarding Sue."

"Her girlfriend is her bodyguard?"

"Yes. I put them together. The relationship bloomed from there."

"Did Sue know about her?"

"Not at first but learned later when a drunk guy tried to accost her outside a bar. Nia broke the guy's arm and put an end to that. Sue wasn't happy with me for a while, but I told her the feelings Nia had for her were real and not part of the job."

I rubbed my temples, trying to calm the blood flow that was giving me a headache. "Then Sue is safe with her?"

"For now. I imagine they will try to contact me eventually. Since I dumped my phone, it will be more challenging. But we have other ways to get in touch with each other. But part of the plan was always for them to hide out for several weeks before trying. They had a go-bag with what they needed to protect themselves and plenty of cash. I'm certain they're holed up somewhere remote."

I was pleased to know that Sue was likely safe. It was one less item to worry about on a list that had become unwieldy to manage.

"What about Emily? I have her tucked away, but she is driving them nuts. I need to get her somewhere else before they toss her on the street."

Brandon closed his eyes, sighing at the thought of dealing with her. An emotion I shared.

"I can take her with me," he uttered reluctantly. "She is a little more civil when I'm around. It would seem time hasn't changed her much."

I shook my head aggressively. "Not at all. She spent most of her time with me, trying the seduction angle. But I know better now and flatly turned her down. The routine is getting old."

"She needs help, there is no doubt. But I promised her mother and can't let anything bad happen to her. I'm the only family she has left."

I stood up to pace, rubbing my head. "Will she listen to you?"

"Somewhat. More than with anyone else. If it serves her needs, she'll turn on me as well. At least she doesn't try to seduce me."

"Maybe she needs a woman bodyguard like Nia. Or at least a man she isn't attracted to."

Brandon seemed amused, a smirk on his face. "If it has two legs, she can work the seduction angle, again when it suits her needs. But I'll handle it. Where is she at right now?"

"The Mission of the Invisible Souls. Pastor Sam took her as a favor to me. But I'm going to owe her big time now. Maybe you can make a large donation to soothe her."

Brandon smiled, leaning back in my chair. "Once this is over and we're all still breathing, I might be inclined to write a check. I can always use more charity donations for tax write-offs. Why don't you call them, and we can swing by and get her out of their hair?"

I stood up to get my cell phone, but before I could reach it, it started ringing. The number was the Mission's and I figured it was Sam calling to say she had finally kicked Emily to the curb. But instead, it was one of the ladies that worked there.

"Sam asked me to call and see if you can come right over," voiced the woman, sounding out of breath.

"What is wrong?"

"There are two men here looking for the woman you left here. Sam is trying to delay them, but I believe they're here to take her forcefully. Please hurry as I think they're armed."

"I'll be there as fast as I can," I said, deep concern filling my mind about what might happen. "And contact the police!"

I hung up the call, then quickly grabbed my gun and motorcycle gear.

"Let's go, Emily's in trouble," I announced to Brandon, as I rushed to the door, hoping I’d get there in time before someone got hurt.

Chapter 45

The best thing about a motorcycle is that it can go places a car can't, and normally a lot faster. It's significantly more dangerous, but I didn't care at the moment. I took several back roads, running stop signs and weaving around cars, going faster than I should. I was determined to get there in time, hell or high water, mostly because I didn't want to see Sam or anyone else hurt because I'd left Emily in their care. Sam was a tough lady and I knew she could hold her own, but if they were armed, she wouldn't stand much of a chance, since she had a strict no guns allowed policy at The Mission, leaving her nothing to defend herself with.

It didn't take too long to get there, and I flipped down the side kickstand, removed my helmet and ran in the front door past several people running to get outside. Stopping one, I asked where the trouble was, and they pointed. I had my leather coat open and my gun out.

As I ran towards the commotion, I soon heard a gunshot. Several more people were running away from the scene and I ran through the hallway into the open eating area, with several rows of tables and chairs, food and utensils abandoned. Two men were standing, guns drawn, down one of the aisles between the tables, with what looked like Sam on the floor. One was yelling at her.

"Tell me where she is, or I'll shoot you in the other shoulder!"

I could see Sam bleeding from her left shoulder, grasping at the wound with her right hand, her face contorted in agony. I was pissed that my private eye world had again spilled into the life of someone I cared about, causing them pain. There was no way I was letting them shoot again, as I pulled out my gun.

"Go ahead," she finally said, yelling through the pain. "I have no idea who you're talking about or where she is."

He aimed the gun, but before he could shoot, I yelled out for him to stop. He turned, the gun now aiming my way and I fired my Berretta twice, hitting him with both bullets in the chest, knocking him backwards, before he fell to the floor. The other man saw what happened and turned, his gun at his side. My aim was now on him, and knowing he couldn't raise and shoot fast enough, he began to run, jumping the food counter and into the kitchen area.

I went to check on Sam, who, through gritted teeth, said she was fine and waved for me to get him. I quickly checked on the fallen man, but he was dead, though I kicked his gun away from the body just in case he came back to life. I then hopped the counter and headed towards the kitchen.

I heard the noise of items falling over, and I approached the kitchen carefully, hitting the doorjamb and peering around the corner at a low angle. A bullet came my way, but it was high, and I fired back in the general direction of where the shot came from, but I missed. I heard footsteps and a door opening and soon was after him. There was no chance he was getting away.

He went down a back hallway and out a fire escape exit into the alley. He was in full gallop, but I wasn't far behind. I shed my leather jacket at the door, knowing it would slow me down in a foot pursuit. It was a comfortable day, probably upper sixties, and I was in good shape, figuring I could outlast him in a long chase. The only question, was he in better shape than I was.

Out of the alleyway I went, my eyes remaining on him. He was fast, now pulling away some, running on the back streets behind The Mission, a mostly residential area. He went two blocks west then cut down suddenly south, hoping to lose me. I could see him and kept my pace steady, hoping he would wear down. I had my good running shoes on, while he was in boots which was a disadvantage for him.

I had a good rhythm going, arms and legs in perfect time, sweat starting to form, the gun strapped back into my shoulder holster. He was probably a block ahead of me, but I was closing the gap. He kept looking over his shoulder, hoping I had stopped, losing ground each time he did, his face growing red from the strain. His running style wasn't as clean and certainly not made for a long chase. There was little doubt he was in trouble.

He darted up a driveway and hopped a fence into a backyard, hoping to shake me. I was now a couple hundred feet behind, when I hopped the fence in pursuit. He tried to hop the back fence into the adjoining yard, but he caught his foot and fell over, landing on his side. I could hear the wind go out of him, and when he got up, he gingerly started limping, working back to a hobbled run. He turned to see me, and reached for his gun, but he'd lost it in the fall, it now lying on the ground.

He wanted to go back to it, but realized I was closing in and turned again. Hopping the fence, I cleared it and was now only fifty feet behind him, as his running had slowed. Coming to the gate of the other yard, he fumbled to get it open, not caring to jump it after what'd happened, and then I was on top of him, and with one quick motion, I tossed him to the ground.

Reaching into his boot, he pulled out a knife, but I had my gun out, my index finger waving, letting him know he had no chance against me. He dropped the knife, knowing he was beaten, his chest heaving in exhaustion and pain.

"Not used to the altitude, it would seem," I noted. "Stand up slowly and let's head back to The Mission."

We took the long walk back, where he slowly limped, while I was a step behind, gun ready if he tried anything. The police had arrived, one of the officers being April. She looked at me like it was a normal day, and cuffed the man, leading him into the building. Once inside, I handed her his gun and knife, which I had retrieved.

"How is Sam?" I asked.

"Go in and check," replied April. "But don't wander off, the detectives will want a statement."

"Who is here?"

"Cummings. Mallard is on vacation."

"Oh joy." Cummings and I had a history, with not an ounce of respect between us.

April laughed, and I walked in to check on Sam. They had brought in a stretcher, the paramedic working on her shoulder. When she saw me, I got a weak smile from her.

"Did you catch him?" she asked.

"Was there ever a doubt?" I bragged with a confident grin. "There was no way he was getting away. I don't think he is from here, he was having a pretty hard time with our mile-high air. How is the shoulder?"

"It hurts like hell. But I'll live. But damn, Jarvis, you're going to owe me big time!"

"To be expected. Brandon said he'd make a monetary donation. And I figure I owe several hours of community service."

"*Hours*, I was thinking more like *weeks* after this and dealing with that crazy woman you left here."

"Do I need to call Parker to cover things while you're on the mend?"

"I already called him. He is on his way. Besides I won't be in the hospital long. It will take more than a bullet in the shoulder to keep me from doing my work."

"I have no doubt. Call if you need anything."

I grabbed her blood-covered right hand and squeezed it. I felt bad for what happened, but happy it wasn't worse. Sam was as tough as they come and I was convinced she'd be fine.

I walked away to find Cummings, the frown on his face telling me his attitude towards me hadn't changed.

"Jarvis, do you ever plan to move out of Denver?" he asked in all seriousness. "Because if you do, I will be the first to help you pack."

"Nice to see you too, detective," I said, while crossing my arms in defiance.

"Hand over the gun."

I pulled out my Berretta, making sure the safety was on, and handed it to another officer standing next him to bag it.

"The man you shot is dead. I understand from Officer Rainn you ran down the other one."

"Yes I did. She has his gun and knife. I did my best not to get my prints on them."

"Good to hear. Tell me what happened."

I gave him the whole story, about the call and what I found when I arrived. I didn't give him all the details on why Emily was there or the threats on Brandon. If he inquired more deeply, I'd send him to my client.

"Did you know these two men?" questioned Cummings.

"No. Though I believe they're from out of town. Any ID on the dead one?"

Cummings waved over to the CSI tech and she brought over a bag of the contents of the dead man's pockets.

"Looks like a California license, from the San Diego area. Any clue of who they might work for?"

"I've been working a case in San Diego. There is a cop there who's been helping me. He might be able to shed a little light, if they're local thugs. Not sure if it's related to what I'm working on."

"Give me his name."

I gave him Manny's name and everything else I knew, or at least wanted to tell him at this time. He grew frustrated when I claimed I needed to talk with my client first before saying much more, but after a while he let me go, with a warning to be available for any further questions. I saluted, which pissed him off more, and walked away, trying to find out where Emily was. It took a few minutes to track her down. She was her normal bizarre self.

"Killed a guy, I hear," she said, her smile turning wicked. "All to save me. I should thank you in a special way, if you'll let me."

"Don't flatter yourself. Sam is the one that saved you by not giving you up. I saved Sam because she is ten times the person you are and doesn't go around wanting to fuck every guy she sees."

"Oh pooh, Jarvis. You're no fun. Besides I think Sam is into the ladies anyway. I swear I saw her staring at my ass a few times."

I about lost it. "The only thing about your ass she cared about, was getting it up and moving to help out around here. And then she was about to kick it when you did little or nothing. Don't get all hot and bothered. If anything, you owe her a debt for who knows what those men would have done to you once they had you."

I might have finally broken through that tough exterior and gotten to her, by the angry look on her face.

"All of this leads to one major question," I proclaimed. "How is it they found you? We took away your phone and credit card. Did you make any calls from here to anyone?"

"No," was all she said.

"What about buying anything?"

Her eyes shifted away from me, looking in the distance.

"What did you buy?"

"Nothing major. I just needed a few more clothes. It couldn't pack much to take with me."

"How? I took away your credit card."

"You're not brainy for someone who thinks they are. I have the credit number and security code memorized, which means I can order anything online I need."

"Damn you. I told you they would be able to find you if you used it. All for clothes you could have gone without. I'm going to tell Brandon to cancel that card."

"You wouldn't dare!" She was really mad now, but I didn't

care.

"Damn right, I will, and he will agree, knowing it's the smart thing to do. Now get your things and let's go. Brandon should be outside waiting to take you away."

"To where?" she asked with a sullen look. She was in full pout mode now.

"I really don't care. So long as it's far away from me."

Emily stormed off and, about fifteen minutes later, returned with her bag. I walked her out and Brandon drove off with her to who knows where, saying he'd contact me if he needed anything else.

Once I was released from the crime scene, I grabbed takeout, went home and ate. Then I hopped in the shower to wash off the horrible day, and crashed in my bed. I hoped to sleep but found it difficult until April snuck in at around midnight. As she curled up next to me with her naked body, I felt a supreme closeness most couples who shared a bed experienced, an intimacy without being physical that made me feel secure and loved, more so than at any time in my life, intertwined together where we slept until late into the next morning.

Chapter 46

April had the day off but would now have to take a shift watching the Hester kids in the afternoon since Parker would need to fill in for Sam until she was on her feet, as T couldn't cover the whole day.

The day started off better than yesterday ended, as April surprised me with morning passion, which I never turned down, and after getting hot and sweaty together, we showered and went out for a late high protein breakfast at a nearby restaurant. From there we split up, her heading to relieve T, while I headed to Denver Police Headquarters to get more details on the two assailants. At least I was hoping for more info, since Detective Cummings wasn't the sharing kind.

My first foray was with Bill Malone, my Denver cop friend, to see what he knew. He gave me a sour look when he saw me, a pile of paperwork before him, a half-eaten sandwich and bottle of water to the side.

"I heard you were the hero yesterday," declared Bill without looking up, his eyes on a page in his hands. "One less bad guy in the world we have to worry about."

I didn't feel heroic, just doing what I had to do to protect a friend. "Any name on the dead man?"

"You'll have to speak with Cummings. He gave me strict orders not to talk with you about this case."

"And you always follow orders," I said with a smirk.

"The detectives bellow and we jump. I could care less if he gets mad at me. But I'm too busy at the moment to look up anything for you. You'll have to plead your case with him." I could see a small grin on his face as he continued to look over the paper in his hand.

"You love it that I have to deal with him, don't you? Might be the happiest you'll be all day."

He waved me to walk on, the grin growing to a smile. I'm sure he'd love to sit outside Cummings' closed door, listening to him raking me over the coals. I wouldn't grovel, but getting a name was important and hopefully a connection that proved fruitful. Time to play nice to get what I needed.

I reached his office, but to my annoyance, he wasn't there. I waited at the door and couple minutes later he walked in, coffee and a cinnamon roll in his hand, a large bite already taken out of it. It looked good, but I resisted asking him for a taste, even though I knew it would piss him off.

I waited for him to sit and then wave for me to take a chair. I let him finish eating, watching him try his best not get crumbs and frosting on his shirt and tie.

"I'm guessing you're wanting the name of the dead man?" He brushed the crumbs off his white dress shirt and blue tie, having failed to keep them clean.

"If you're willing to share."

Cummings grunted. "Not in my nature, but I will try to be civil, even though we don't have much. The IDs on both men were fakes. We are checking fingerprints now, but no hits so far. The guy you ran down has lawyered up and apparently is missing his tongue, as he won't say a word. They're working on bail now."

"You know he'll skip town."

"I suspect as much. But I can't babysit them. If they do, then the city gets to keep their bail money."

A small victory, it would seem!

"Anyone claim the dead man?"

"Nope. Do you think anyone will?"

I shook my head. "I doubt it. I have a feeling these might be hired guns working for someone. Part of a case I'm working in California, as I mentioned yesterday."

Cummings looked interested, now putting down his coffee and leaning in his chair. "Anything else you care to share? Knowing you, I'm certain you didn't tell all."

"Not much else to say. All I know for certain is wherever I turn, I keep running into trouble."

He smirked. "Nothing new for you. Since I've known you, trouble seems to be your shadow everywhere. The lady who was shot, Sam, said there was a woman there they were after. Emily White. I remembered the name and checked our database and found out she is the one you shot a few years back. I believe you got involved with her sexually, and then she tried to use you to kill someone. Why were you helping her?"

"Client hired me to bring her back to Colorado since she was in danger."

"The client you won't name."

I smiled.

"Well it seems the danger followed her here. Where is she now?"

"I don't know. My client took her away. He has a means to protect her."

Cummings leaned forward in his chair and took a long sip on his coffee, which looked and smelled horrible to me. His face told me a lecture was coming.

"I can take a wild guess who the client is. And your client privilege only gives you a little leeway in my book. If more bodies turn up I'm going to lock you up. Mallard gives you a lot of leeway, but I'm not as kind."

"Gee Dan, I hadn't noticed," I said with my best snarky voice. "If the fingerprints lead to a name, will you share?"

"No. But I'm sure you can get your girlfriend or Bill to find it for you. Now get out of here. I'm sure you have more messes that I'll have to clean up before this is all over."

I strolled out without saying any of the words I wanted to spew out at him, saving them for another time. Cummings was a pain in my ass, but I had better things to burn calories on than going one on one with him. When I got into my car, my phone rang. It was Barry.

"Are you available to come to the Hester house?" he said. "I'm heading there now to try and wrap things up with the wife. She has decisions to make and I'd like you there."

"Anything to worry about?"

"No. But I received an intriguing offer and I'd like you there to hear it, along with Marilynn."

Barry wouldn't reveal over the phone what it was, so I told him I'd head to her house.

Once I'd passed through security, I drove to the front and parked, and Carlotta greeted me at the door, leading me to the main dining area. Barry was already sitting, along with Marilynn, with a glass in her hand of purple liquid, though I couldn't tell what it was. When I asked, I was told April was with the kids in another room.

I took a seat across from Barry, who had a folder, which he opened, sliding paperwork in front of her. Her eyes looked clear, which was good to see. Making legal decisions with a sober head was always best.

"How are you doing?" wondered Barry, looking her straight in the eye.

"I'm doing better."

"What are you drinking?"

She slid it forward for him to smell. "Grape Juice."

"You've been staying clear of the alcohol?"

"Yes. I came to the realization it wasn't helping me."

Barry smiled in agreement. "That *is* good to hear. We were concerned." He looked my way and I nodded my head.

"As were my kids," added Marilynn. "My daughter came up to me one day, wondering if she was going to lose me too. I'd had a little to drink and she was worried they were going to take her away as she'd seen how I wasn't in control. Honestly, it scared me. I really wouldn't know what to do without them."

"If you need further help, let me know," Barry proclaimed. "There are good programs that provide assistance. People you can talk with. Know that I'm there for support."

"As am I," I added.

There was a line of wetness running down her face that she wiped away. Hopefully she could overcome this. The love of your children was strong motivation.

"We have good news," declared Barry, opening the folder in front of him. "The end of this battle is near. They have agreed, after a vigorous negotiation, to settle, giving you a fifty-five percent share of Perry's business."

She smiled. "Finally!"

"But we've had an additional offer. A substantial one I think you should consider. A buyer, with cash to purchase that fifty-five percent."

Marilynn and I looked at Barry with surprise on our faces, the news shocking to hear.

"I know," replied Barry to our reactions. "It came out of the blue. But I'd strongly consider it, if I were you. Running a business is tough, which maybe you're not up for, right now. Plus, you do have debts, including the house, whose ownership will be passed onto you as part of the deal, which will include that debt. The offer is cash money that you can use to pay that debt, and if properly invested, will cover you for many years, as well as your children's college needs."

"What is the offer?" asked Marilynn.

Barry flipped a couple of pages and slid it towards her, pointing at a line on the page.

"Oh my," she said, holding her hand to her mouth. "Am I reading that correctly?"

Barry said the number out loud and it was big. A high seven-digit dollar amount that was impressive.

"This is minus my fees, as they're paying me outside this amount. This would provide you plenty of money to live on for many years, if you manage it properly, which I can assist you with."

"What would you do?" asked Marilynn of me.

I wasn't the best person to ask, since managing money wasn't always my strong suit. But an amount like that was hard to turn down.

"It is your decision," I replied. "But I'd strongly consider it. As Barry says, you would be set financially."

She looked at the number for several minutes, before taking a long drink of her grape juice before standing up.

"I need to call my parents. Please excuse me."

We both stood as she walked out of the room. Barry grabbed all the papers and neatly sorted them, back into the folder.

"Big news," I said to him. "Who did the offer come from?"

"The other owner who bought interest from Perry."

"The Private Equity firm?"

"Yep. Revive Speculations. It seems they're hot for owning most of his dealerships. Though Perry will have five percent and his salary for being their spokesman."

I stopped to think over why they would do this. "Hostile takeover, in a manner of speaking?"

"Possibly. Could be part of their plan. Maybe they brought the ladies in to seduce and blackmail him, hoping the wife wouldn't find out. But she did and that brought them in to buy the rest from her. Offer was a good one, though not full value. Cash money was not easy to pass up, especially since she had no skills to run the dealership."

There was little doubt about that. She was having a hard enough time raising her kids and keeping her own life together. The buyout would make it simpler to move on.

"Was that what you wanted me here for?" I asked.

Barry walked over and sat beside me, leaning in to whisper. "Yes, but there is more. I got a call from a lawyer asking me to get in contact with you. Someone you spoke with before. Torey Whitelaw?"

It was a name I knew, the lawyer for Simon Lions who had, in a roundabout way, threatened me. And then shortly after, three men showed up to try and convince me via a beating to stop my pursuit of him as a suspect in The Front Range Butcher case.

"What did he want?" I inquired with spite.

"He says Simon Lions Junior wants to talk with you."

Great, I thought. Just what I needed to go eye to eye with the serial killer.

"About?"

"He would give me no details. Just wanted me to contact you. Says he wants you at the prison where they're holding him at 10 a.m. tomorrow."

I wasn't sure what to say. I'd had enough of the man when I subdued him after he tortured Melissa and me. Those moments continued to come to life in my dreams and I didn't care to see him again, other than to testify at his trial, which was months away.

"Any thoughts on why he'd want to see me?" I wondered.

"I've been racking my brain since the call. I doubt he will be confessing his soul. Maybe he wants to face the man who beat him. Little doubt he is crazy. The question is, would it help you any facing him again? Knowing you, I'm certain the whole ordeal weighs on you."

I stood up and walked to the window, looking outside. It did weigh on me, there was little doubt. The question was, would it help my sanity to face him again or would it make it worse. I spent several minutes thinking it over before turning to Barry.

"Call him and let him know I'll be there," I declared, uncertain if it was the correct decision, but knowing that I'd regret it if I didn't try.

Chapter 47

Everything got settled, as Marilynn got feedback from her parents and decided to take the deal, walking away with the money. Barry said it would take a couple of weeks to finalize all of it, but the end was in sight. It was decided April and T would remain available to keep an eye on things, checking in from time to time, but with the agreement in place, the threat should be minimal, and Marilynn and her kids could live their lives normally without fear. All of this was good news.

I tried not to burn too many brain cells thinking about my meeting with The Butcher but failed. April did her best to take my mind off it through seduction, which worked for an hour. But, when it came time to sleep, it was a restless night. Once I found slumber, it wouldn't last long, horrible images arousing me each hour, until finally daylight filtered into the room.

I got out of bed, tired of staring at the clock, time moving at a snail's pace as I shook the exhaustion from my brain.

I let April sleep, leaving my place quietly. The weather crisp, but dry, I was dressed in full motorcycle gear, as I climbed on the Harley and began to ride, heading south, finding a quiet country road away from the city, hoping to clear my head. The freeing feeling the two wheels on the payment gave me was cathartic. An emotion only someone who rode a motorcycle ever felt, the joy of the unique journey it created. Taking backroads, seeing the landscape as it was meant to be seen. The day would come when I'd travel the western United States this way, one of those bucket list items I longed to accomplish.

I found an out of the way small diner and ate breakfast before taking the trek back to town. Finding the Englewood Federal Corrections Institution on West Quincy was no issue, as I'd been there before, talking to Darren Woodley who had been initially charged with being The Butcher. Little did I know at the time, he'd been framed, by the real Butcher. The facility was where Simon Junior was being held and awaiting his day in court, which likely was still months away, his sleazy lawyer doing his best to stall the proceedings.

I went through security without a hitch, and made it to a private meeting room, arranged by the lawyer, Whitelaw. I sat in the uncomfortable metal chair, a tad anxious at why I was here, until a guard brought in Simon, dressed in prison orange, shackled from wrist to ankle, placed in a chair across from me and bolted down for my protection, the guard leaving us alone.

The smile he wore was spooky, his face the same as I remembered. The brown hair longer, a touch of growth on his checks that looked like a poorly maintained grass yard, with patches of hair and spots of no growth. His chained hands were linked, the nails looking as if they had been chewed off, uneven and dirty. The eyes were deep with evil pools of brown, just like his father's.

I waited for him to speak first, for it was his show and I wondered what his motive was to see me. A confession of his sins would have been nice, but I didn't think his sociopathic mind would allow it.

"Good to see you, Jarvis," he said with a toothy grin.

Though I tried to be relaxed, I felt the rigid tension across my muscles. "I wish I could say the same."

"Last time we were together was thrilling." His grin grew larger and his fingers started to twitch.

"From your side maybe, but from where I was, not so much. At least until I busted your nose, broke your arm and cracked your skull. How is everything healing? Looks like your nose didn't heal well; it's a little crooked."

He tried to raise his hands to touch it but couldn't because of the chains. It actually looked fine, I just wanted to mess with him. I needed to tip the scales in my favor in advance for the coming onslaught of psychological games his family was good at playing.

"Funny. Trying to get me to admit guilt through my actions. We both know I did nothing wrong."

I felt disgusted at his words. "Short of kidnapping Melissa, drugging me, strapping me naked to a chair, while she was naked chained to a table as you started carving into her skin." I felt the location on my left arm prickle where he'd cut me as well. "And then you took a slice of my skin for good measure. Other than those little things, sure, you did nothing wrong. Give me a break, Junior, you know better."

His grin was a full-fledged smile now. "All I did was what I was trained to do."

"Trained by a nutcase. Your father, the original Butcher. Possibly even your aunt, Christina. You come from a long line of crazies."

His demeanor remained relaxed. Much like his father, it took a lot to rattle him.

"Our family had a different way of raising their kids. Of course, Dad is no longer with us to defend himself. I'm sure his death was at your hands."

I shook my head. "No it wasn't. Though I can't feel pity for his death, for his was more humane than any of his victims, or yours."

My words didn't seem to bother Junior any, his eyes glistening at the thought of what he'd done to those poor women.

"He told me a few times about your chats," he claimed. "The psychological battles and one-upmanship between you. How are you sleeping these days?" His joy was getting annoying.

"Like a baby," I said, though it was lie. "How about you? Had any visits yet from inmates looking to make you their boy toy!"

Junior growled. "Very mature, Jarvis. I suspected, when I asked for this meeting, you would try to get under my skin with your words. Dad warned me you would play mind games with him."

I now smirked. "From the man who never gave a straight response and often would answer a question with a question." I stood up from my chair. "Nevertheless, I'm about to walk out of here, since you're wasting my time. Tell me why you wanted to talk now or I'm heading home and having a beer."

Junior just looked at me with a toothy grin without saying anything. I shrugged and walked to the door, calling for the guard.

"Fine, you win. I will tell you if you sit down."

The door opened, and I turned to face him. "I've lost my patience. Tell me now or I'm gone. And the next time you'll see me is as a witness in your trial, which will lead to a conviction and your execution."

Junior waited, staring intently on me, biding his time to build the suspense.

"You should have let me finish the job and you'd both be together," he finally said.

I was surprised by the words. "What did you say?"

"You and Melissa would be together forever, hand and hand in the great beyond." He said it like he was a preacher doing a church sermon.

I waved for the guard to close the door, as Junior had my attention now. I walked towards him.

"Such a shame," he added. "Her being in Colorado Springs and you here in Denver. When you could have been together for eternity."

Anger was building, tension growing in my muscles. I imagined bashing his head on the table several times, face bruised and bleeding, skull crushed by the force, until his breathing stopped. The hatred I was feeling was scary, more so than I'd felt in a long time. But instead of pounding him, I slammed my fist on the table, the sound echoing off the walls.

Simon pulled back on his chains, startled by my reaction, the momentary tension quickly turning back into his morbid grin.

"How is her new job working out? I hear she went back to where she started all those years ago, working for the law firm Pendleton Brothers, though now as a full-fledged lawyer and not a legal assistant. That must be exhilarating for her."

"You son-of-a-bitch! If anything happens to her, there will be nowhere you'll be safe."

He continued smiling. "Don't worry, Jarvis. I have no intentions of hurting her…or having someone hurt her. I like Melissa. She seems like a wonderful person. And oh my…such lovely skin she has. I really enjoyed seeing and touching all of it." He paused for a minute, staring at me with total joy as my anger continued to seethe. He yelled, "guard, I'm ready to leave now."

The door opened, and the guard walked in, releasing the chains from the bolt on the floor and table. I stood there angry, still wanting to pound him until he couldn't speak another word. I knew he'd played me well, getting under my skin just like his father had. As he shuffled away, he turned for one final dig.

"Jarvis, what I just said holds true, for now. But know with a simple call that can all change. Keep that in mind for my reach, like my father's, is infinite…"

I stood there red faced, wondering if I'd ever be free from the Lions' family evil.

Chapter 48

As I stepped outside the corrections facility, my head spinning from my confrontation with Simon Junior, my cell phone starting ringing. Caller ID told me it was FBI agent, Catalina Alegre calling, leading me to answer.

"What are you doing talking with The Butcher?" she asked.

Maybe I should have been surprised but I wasn't. Everyone seemed to be nose deep into my business these days.

"Keeping tabs on me or on Junior?" I queried.

"Possibly a little of both. You didn't look thrilled when you walked outside."

Now I was surprised. "Am I being watched by the eye in the sky?" I proclaimed, while checking for cameras.

"No. I can see you. I'm parked next to your motorcycle."

I checked off into the distance and saw her, leaning on her red, modern Mustang as she put her cell phone away. Her chestnut hair was blowing in the wind, a little longer than I remembered it. Her black pantsuit fit the FBI wardrobe profile and her 5' 9" solid frame, her jacket open, revealing an off-white blouse buttoned professionally just below her brown-skinned neck. She stood up from her car when I approached, a tiny smile on her face, which was progress from her throwing me in a holding cell when we first met.

"I'm touched you drove all the way down here to say hello," I joked, while smiling.

"I was hungry, and I thought you'd buy me lunch and tell me great tales of your private eye world. I never get tired of hearing how you defeated The Front Range Butcher single handedly."

I laughed. "Nice to see you in a good mood. Anywhere in particular you'd like to eat?"

"Somewhere without plastic trays and utensils. The 49th Food & Spirits is just down the street on Kipling."

"Sounds like you know the area," I commented, while putting on my motorcycle jacket and gloves.

"Come down here occasionally to talk with inmates I've put away. Always best to know the local cuisine."

"Lead the way."

I had my helmet on and followed her out the parking lot, and as she said, the restaurant was close by. Once inside, we found a seat on the outdoor patio, under a large umbrella that protected us from the sun, which was warm today. We each ordered drinks from the friendly waitress, Catalina going with unsweetened tea, while I decided on ice water. Though the waitress suggested it, we decided on passing on the appetizer.

"Nice Mustang. Looks to be fairly new."

"A gift from my boyfriend. I believe he was hoping, after buying it, I'd move in with him."

This was the first time she had shared anything about her personal life.

"You declined?"

"Best for me to have my own place. My hours make it difficult for full-time cohabitation. I'm sure you understand that in your line of work."

"I do. April's hours and mine certainly don't make it easy for a personal life. We try to have sleepovers a couple times a week, though lately with my working in California, that isn't possible."

Our drinks arrived, the waitress requesting our orders. Catalina decided on a chicken pasta salad, while I went for the turkey sandwich with pub chips.

"Enough about our personal lives," Catalina said after a long drink of tea. "What was the meeting with Simon Junior about?"

I'd grown used to her nosy demeanor, which used to aggravate me. "I didn't hear a please in the request," I said with a smirk.

"How about a '*fucking* please tell me about your meeting.'" Her voice was loud and turned the heads of the couple in the table next to us.

"Better," I said, smiling ear to ear. "After jerking me around with small talk, he finally made sure I understood he could get to me, even when behind bars."

"He threatened you."

"In a roundabout way. Like his father, he never comes out and says exactly what he means. He told me he knew about Melissa moving to Colorado Springs and her new job."

Catalina enjoyed a long drink of her tea. "The woman you rescued from him. And your response?"

"My first reaction was to pound him senseless. But

unfortunately, the guard was nearby. I called him a S.O.B and said if he did anything to her, there was nowhere he could hide. He said she was safe for now but warned me as the guard took him away that his reach was infinite."

Catalina nodded, while finishing her tea, the waitress there with a refill before the glass hit the table. I was enjoying my water, finding it clear and cold, which was everything I hoped for in H2O. It was topped off as well.

"Are you taking his threat seriously?" she asked. "Since he is behind bars with little chance of getting out, I imagine he is fucking with you."

I agreed, to a point. But knowing his family influence and wealth, I couldn't discount it completely.

"You are correct. But Simon Senior did the same thing, playing mind games, but then backed up his threats by sending people after me. I'm not certain what resources the son has, but the same lawyer Senior had, arranged the meeting and may have organized the threats against me last year."

"Including Wolfe?" she questioned.

I nodded. "Though he came to see me after the case was over, saying I had nothing to fear from him anymore. And he may have been the person who ended Simon Senior's life. Though I have no proof of that."

"Interesting. How did he go from working for Simon and then against him?"

"I believe because he was lied to. Apparently, he doesn't like to be taken advantage of."

Catalina looked surprised. "A killer with a moral code, at least to some degree."

Our food arrived, my sandwich looking wonderful. I started taking it apart to add mustard when my phone rang. It was Detective Cummings. Surprised, I answered it, after letting Catalina know I needed to take it.

"We got a hit on the two men. Both are from out of the country, here on a work visa."

"Who sponsored them?" I asked, while piecing my sandwich back together.

"A company called Worldwide Toys Inc. Home base appears to be Southern California. Though no address, only a PO Box."

The news about who hired them wasn't a shock and confirmed a great deal. It was good information to learn and surprising that Cummings had shared it. Maybe he wasn't a complete jerk after all, despite our past encounters.

"Are they hired guns?"

"I'm not certain. My resources are limited. We sent it off to Interpol and the CIA, but they rarely answer us lowly city detectives."

"Fortunately, I'm sitting eating lunch with FBI agent Alegre. She might be able to dig up info if I pass on the names. Say hello to Denver Detective Cummings, Catalina." I held up the phone and she said, "Hi".

"A woman Fed. Nice. I will send the names to your phone. The one we arrested made bail and will likely skip town, as you mentioned earlier." He paused for a minute allowing me to grab a chip, which was saltier than I cared for. "And there was one other thing we found on the dead man's body. He had a business card for a Shark Tail Detective Agency. We tried calling them, but only get a recording. No luck with them calling me back."

"I doubt they will. Thanks for the info, Dan."

He didn't acknowledge my thanks and just hung up, which was standard operating procedure for him, reaffirming my earlier jerk notion about him.

I grabbed my sandwich and took a large bite, the mention of the business card ringing a bell. My thoughts turned to the faces of the two hired men, going back in time to California. *They now seemed familiar, from somewhere.* Then it hit me, though I had only got glimpses of them while sitting in a chair, looking through a window of the leasing office. I was now fairly certain the two men had been the same two who tried to find me after I'd broken into the Shark Tail Detective Agency office. I cursed myself that I'd not remembered them, a job skill I was normally proficient at. Too many faces and names to keep track of.

"Your mood seemed to change from happy to mad, quickly," noted Catalina, reading my face.

"I was internally chiding myself for missing a connection. A mistake a good detective shouldn't make."

"It happens to the best of us. Though I wouldn't go so far as to call you good," joked Catalina with a smirk.

Her humor aimed at me, flipped the switch back to happy. When the text came through with the names of the two men, I forwarded them onto Catalina, who had finished half her salad.

"Now I need to check on these two as well," she chided, after reading the text.

"It's worth dessert if you can," I bribed.

That seemed to persuade her. "I did get the names of the two men in the other photos you sent me. Before I share, I need to know a little more of what is going on."

"As I said, they tried to kill my client and nearly succeeded. They're dead now. I'm trying to figure out why they came after him and if someone hired them."

Catalina took two more bites and another long drink of tea. She looked around, making sure no one was listening, before leaning forward and talking in a lower voice.

"They were a brother hitman team out of Europe. Quite good from what I've read. Right up there with Wolfe. Big money to hire them. Probably twenty-five grand or more. Good at torturing their victims. It would seem like they enjoyed their work a little too much."

"Yes, they tortured him before he was able to get free of them. Killed one, dumping him overboard, while he tortured the other one before killing him and burning his boat, making everyone think it was him that had died, and allowing him to go back underground."

"Sounds like one tough man," stated Catalina.

I nodded, while taking more bites of the turkey, which was falling out, and a few more chips, even with the sodium. I wasn't sure why I was telling Catalina all of this, as I normally withheld info, for safety and to be a jerk. But even with our pretentious working relationship, I felt like I could trust her, even though I did withhold the entire story about Rocky, whom she didn't know. And the power of the FBI might come in handy when dealing with whomever was running this illegal operation.

"And what about the other name, Stetson Poole?" I inquired.

"Not a damn thing," answered Catalina. "Which is odd. But I will say after I checked, someone called my boss, asking why I was looking up that name in the system."

This had my attention. "Really. What did you tell him?"

"Only that I had a lead on a name a snitch gave me, but it didn't pan out since nothing came up."

I laughed. "I'm a snitch?"

"What was I going to tell him? That a two-bit PI asked me to look up a name as a favor? Talk about a career killer!"

"I charge more than two-bits for my services," I noted with a smile. "But I see your point. Did he say who called him?"

"No. But that is normal. Higher ups like him get the calls from those in power. Politicians, wealthy donors and those in other three-letter organizations. I try my best to stay out of that mess, especially with today's chaotic political climate."

I finished up my sandwich and chips, while she did the same with her pasta salad. She was fastidious in her neatness, constantly wiping her face, mouth and hands with her cloth napkin. For me, it was all I could do to keep the mustard off my shirt.

"You believe this organization is bringing in guns and drugs?" questioned Catalina, while folding her napkin neatly and placing it on the table.

"I do. Though for now, I have no proof. But I'm hoping to get it."

"We could call the ATF and the DEA and let them deal with it."

"I doubt my client will go for that. He wants blood for the death of his wife and child. Until we know who was behind the bombing, he will want to handle on his own, with my help."

Catalina frowned. "Sounds like you'll be getting into deep shit on this one. Might be best to walk away."

"If it was possible, then I would, but I owe him a debt. He has gone to bat for me on several occasions."

"Even if it gets you killed?"

I didn't relish the thought. "I will do my best to prevent that."

"A private eye with a moral code. Not sure in this case that will get you much."

I smiled. "It allows me to sleep at night, most of the time."

Catalina cracked a grin, which was surprising, as she often didn't laugh even at my A-plus material.

"Nightmares or not, I will take you up on your offer of dessert. I know the Mount Blackburn Brownie they serve can cure all that ails you."

I laughed and ordered two, hoping the high calorie dessert

superseded The Butcher's frightening words.

Chapter 49

The suspension on my bike felt the lunch in my stomach, sagging when I climbed on, but managed to glide down the road, though riding a little bit lower. I stopped by The Mission to find all was going well, with Parker handling things. Sam was out of the hospital back to work, her arm in a sling, but there making sure all was running smoothly, albeit from her chair and on pain meds.

As I left their parking lot, I sensed a car following me. At a red light, I checked my mirrors, seeing the expensive black Mercedes-Benz, with no front plate and darkly tinted windows that made it hard to see who was driving. From what I could tell, it was one person, though I couldn't make out a face. My plan had been to head back to my place, but instead, I decided to take a drive and see if they continued following me.

Travelling north on South Broadway, I turned right on Evans Avenue, driving at a nice smooth leisurely pace, checking my mirrors, seeing the car behind me. When I approached South Emerson Street, I turned right, keeping my twenty-five mile per hour speed, until I came to the eastern edge of Harvard Gulch West Park. I found an opening on the side of the road, and pulled over, stopping by the curb, sitting there waiting for the car to pass me and park several spots down. I took off my helmet and motorcycle jacket, placing them on the seat, while making sure my .38 was handy, pulling and holding it up on my chest, my left arm hiding it as I walked forward.

Approaching the car on the passenger side, I was out in the grass by several feet looking at the rear of the car, my eyes watching for any sign of movement. The car was running, and the passenger window went down, and I was ready, with my gun extended, feet stopping, eyes trained for aggressive action. The door opened, but no one was in the seat, though I could vaguely hear a deep voice speaking words. I couldn't make out what they were.

"Turn off the car, I can't hear you," I shouted forcefully. "Any sudden moves and I will shoot."

The engine turned off. "Jarvis, I'm here to talk," said the voice, one I now could hear and recognize.

I kept my gun out. “What about?” I queried.

“A threat on your life.”

“By you?”

“Yes, if I decide to accept the job.”

I walked over to get a better view and saw him sitting in the seat. Wolfe filled the car with his scary but well-dressed presence. His expensive wraparound sunglasses covered his eyes, his short stubbled ebony hair darker than the dark chocolate skin gracing his head. His fingerless-glove-covered hands stayed on the steering wheel, showing no aggression. I walked a little closer, lowering my gun to my side.

“I’m not armed,” said Wolfe. “I came to talk only.”

“You could have called, but instead you followed me, making me cautious. What is going on?”

“Calls have a way of being monitored. Best you step into the car, away from prying ears. I will not harm you.”

I hesitated, wondering what this was about. I wasn’t sure I liked the idea of sitting in a confined space with him. Even if he wasn’t armed, which I doubted was true, he was dangerous enough with his hands.

“You can keep your gun out, if you feel you’ll be safer.”

Deciding to obey, I walked over and climbed into the car, pulling the door shut, but not completely. I rested the gun on my lap still held in my hand, my body turned to see him clearly, my eyes scanning for anyone else coming.

“There is no one else around,” Wolfe proclaimed noticing my concern. “I work alone.”

“I’m a naturally heedful person these days. Not certain who I can trust.”

“You fear me that much?” Wolfe said, his hands remaining on the steering wheel.

“You’re a dangerous man. You made that clear to me last year when you approached me about my working on The Butcher case.”

“I’m dangerous when I *want* to be. Now isn’t one of those times.”

I nodded, but remained vigilant, with the gun at the ready. The inside of the car was luxurious, with all tan leather interior, plush carpeting and all the tech money in a car of this price can buy. The darkly tinted windows were filtering the sun, but the car temperature was rising. Wolfe had on a coal colored jacket, open to show a tan cotton shirt. He had to be getting warm but showed no perspiration. I know I was sweating, even though I was wearing a sleeveless t-shirt with Sturgis design. Though my sweat may have been caused by more than the heat.

"Shall I turn on the car and start the air conditioning?" voiced Wolfe, noticing my sweat.

"You may. But don't put it in gear."

He nodded and turned the key, then put the air on high, then returned his hands to the wheel.

"How long have you been following me?" I asked.

"Since the correctional facility. A little birdy told me you would be there."

I took a shot at guessing who that was. "The lawyer, Torey Whitelaw?"

He nodded. "We had a chat a few days ago. He wanted to hire me to put the fear of god in you. Mostly to intimidate, for now."

"And your answer was?" I was hoping for a no, for I didn't need any more complications in my life.

"I asked when and where, which is when he mentioned he was setting up a meeting with you and his client for today. I told him I'd think about it, but that I had other things on my plate more important than spooking a local private eye."

He was looking right at me, with little emotion on this face. But for whatever reason, I believed what he said. Even when he had threatened me in the past, he'd been straightforward and truthful.

"Then you haven't given him a definitive answer of no?"

"As of yet, that is correct. I felt I should talk with you first."

"I appreciate that. Facing off with you isn't on my bucket list."

He nodded. "I don't desire pursuing a job that leads me to come up against you as well. There are more deserving fish in the ocean for me to spear. Especially when the lawyer of a serial killer is the one asking. I may be a hired gun, but I do have limits on the jobs I'll accept."

"Then why are you here?"

He put his hands up, and I motioned he could put them down. He turned to face me, a stern look on his intimidating mug.

"Only to warn you. There are enough evil people in the world, we don't need to have less who play for the other side."

"And which side are you on?"

He grinned, his teeth as shiny as his diamond studded earrings. "Normally the one that pays the most."

"Would you be willing to take out Junior as you did Senior? It would make my life less complicated." I was only half-heartedly saying it, though in reality I wouldn't have shed a tear over his demise.

"Murdering people for pay is against the law." He said it as if he thought someone might be listening.

"Then I can step out without fearing you coming after me."

"Yes. But there are many more out there willing for the price. And the price is steep for what would be a simple job."

"Many have tried, and all have failed. It may not be as simple as you think." I sounded cocky, but the statement was based in fact.

"Confidence is good to have but won't stop a bullet," warned Wolfe, while pointing his index finger at me. "There are men out there nearly as good as I am who won't hesitate. And they will use any means necessary to put you down, including using those you love against you to draw you out."

There was little doubt about this, I'd already experienced this with both April and Melissa. The only way they'd be truly safe was for me to get out of my line of business. But I needed to finish the job at hand first.

"Whitelaw has those types of connections?" I queried.

"Indeed," replied Wolfe, nodding his head. "A rolodex full of numbers, many itching for an easy payday."

"I'll do my best not to make it too easy," I replied with a grim look. "I appreciate the heads up. Are you in town long? Do you plan on stopping by and seeing Sam?"

"It had occurred to me. Though I understand she was shot recently. Are you pursuing the culprit?"

He'd known about the shooting at The Mission. *Why was I not surprised?*

"I am. Heading to California in the next couple of days. The man who shot her is dead, but his partner is out on bail. I plan on finding and paying him a visit to learn who paid them."

"May I reach into my coat pocket," he asked.

I nodded, my hand ready on the gun. He pulled out a card and handed it to me. Looking at it, all that was on it was a ten digit phone number.

"If you need help, you may call that number and leave a message. Leave your name only and a time to call, and the system will reach out to me. I can normally be anywhere in the US within twenty-four hours."

I nodded while climbing out of the car, placing the gun back into my holster and the card in my back pocket.

"Can I afford you?" I asked.

"No, but there are always low interest payment plans," he said with a smile.

I closed the door and he drove off. There was little doubt he was a lethal man. But so had been Rocky, and he'd been a reliable ally when I needed him. Having another as a resource was nice to have, though it seemed most of the ones I was using were playing in the deep end of the pool. An end I've been trying to stay out of and not get swallowed up by.

Chapter 50

After a better night of sleep than I expected to have, thanks to a vigorous workout at the gym and in my bed with April, I flew out the next morning to California ready to hopefully wrap up this case. I had sent the info on the two men who have been hired to kill Rocky to him, saying I was ready for the next step in the case. My plan was a simple one for now and that was to try and draw out the man who I had chased down after the shooting at The Mission. And there was one way I knew of doing this.

I picked a different hotel again, this time one just north of the San Diego airport. Once checked in, I trekked to downtown San Diego, locating a parking spot two blocks from the Shark Tail Detective Agency office. With lock picks in my gloved hands, I broke into the office, finding it the same as before. I paraded around in front of the camera for several minutes, then dragged a chair over, climbed up and disconnected the cables from it.

I sat and waited for nearly thirty minutes, using my phone to check out the sports scores, seeing the Rockies in the hunt in the early going of the Major League Baseball season, a west coast trip on their agenda as well. Catching a game at Dodger Stadium might be a welcome distraction from what lied ahead of me. I looked over the cost of tickets for when Colorado played them in three days, wondering if I could work it in the expense report.

Finally, I heard someone fiddling with the lock. I leaned back in the chair behind the desk, pointing my Beretta which I had retrieved from Detective Saiz. When the door opened, I saw the man who I had run down, stepping in, looking up to see me, reaching for his gun.

"I wouldn't do that, Stefan," I said, my sight on the center of his chest, using the name I had learned from Cummings. "Close the door, pull the gun out with two fingers, place it on the floor and slide it over here."

He hesitated, so I pulled back the hammer on my gun. That was convincing enough, and he did what he was told, the large 9mm Sig Sauer now sitting on the desk before me.

"You're breaking and entering," he said with a slight accent that sounded European.

"It is hard to break and enter at a company that doesn't exist and is merely a front to scare off those who get close to the real operation."

"You're the punk detective in Denver who shot my partner," he said, with a tinge of anger.

I sneered at him. "I believe your partner shot my friend first, then aimed at me before I killed him. I didn't have much choice. And then this punk ran your ass down. Too bad they couldn't keep you locked up long enough for me to talk with you. Well, here I am and we're going to talk."

He crossed his arms. "I won't say a thing."

"I think you will, because it will be the only thing to save your ass from a first class beating."

He laughed. "By you? I doubt it very much. In a few minutes you'll be begging for your life as we will be cutting you up piece by piece."

I shrugged. "You mentioned we. Could you mean your new partner? I have a feeling he is out cold right about now."

Stefan looked confused by my words. I pulled out the burner flip phone and made a call, putting it on speakerphone.

"Do you have him?" I asked the person on the other end.

"Yes," said the female voice. "He is out cold, tied up and in the trunk. Shouldn't double-park on the street. It makes us other drivers with road rage a little tough to deal with. Their car will be towed away here shortly."

Kit had done her job as planned, walking up to the other man and then with her charm taking him out.

"Thanks," I replied before hanging up. "A tempting face makes it easy to fall prey to a strong woman. Your partner never saw it coming. Now move away from the door."

Stefan took a couple of steps to the side, not knowing what to do. He was in a tight spot, and it would only get more difficult for him once he saw what I had planned.

"We need to speak to your boss, Edwin Ware," I said, standing up, my gun pointed.

"I have no idea who that is." Even if he was in a tough spot, Stefan didn't look nervous.

"Sure you do. Hell, that probably isn't even his name. Much like the ID you had in Denver which was fake. Tell me where he is and how to get a hold of him and you get to keep your teeth."

Stefan was a good-sized guy, probably 6'1" and around one ninety-five in solid shape. Though not in good running shape, as I'd discovered, he did seem tough, at least on the outside.

"You don't scare me. And I doubt you'll shoot me, it will make too much noise."

"As will your screaming in pain, but I'm not worried because it's late in the day and a weekend. No one is in the offices next door. And besides, it's not me you should be scared of."

On cue, after I opened the door, in walked Rocky. He'd taken up station outside, making sure there wasn't a third person lingering around. His blonde hair was cut shorter, though had grown back to nearly reach his shoulders. Kit had told me he'd lost weight but he'd gained much of it back, a good thirty pounds of pure muscle larger than me, rehabbing these last couple of months from the torture he'd endured. His skin was tanned, his arms huge and his hands covered with gloves one would use for punching. It was good to see him up and moving, ready to strike back at those who had ruined his life.

He nodded at me, stepped into Stefan and hit him with a jarring right that sent him back against the wall. A second punch to the stomach doubled him over and he was down on the hardwood floor.

"I may not scare you, but I bet *he* does," I stated, while leaning against the wall, my gun now holstered. "And he has a lot of pent up anger since someone, maybe your boss, sent two men to kill him and failed. Now either tell us what we need, and live to see the day through clear eyes, or he starts breaking bones."

Stefan shook his head, continuing to refuse to speak. He did his best to stand and tried to take a swing at Rocky, who dodged it with little effort and then did a one two combo Ali would have been proud of, knocking Stefan flat on his back. Rocky then picked him up and flipped him face first into the wall, pulling his left arm behind his back and then started to push upward by his wrist. Stefan started to yell, but Rocky covered his mouth.

"I'd talk before that wrist or shoulder bone gives out," I announced, as if doing play by play.

I waited until I heard a pop, the wrist giving out first, bone sticking out of the skin. Rocky released him, and he slid down to the ground in pain. I wasn't thrilled about doing this, but people had come after him and me, with no mercy. We were just paying them back with their same type of treatment. To win this battle meant we would be going beyond the rules to get results.

"Have you had enough yet," I said. "This man can go all day. These people killed his wife and young son. He has nothing to lose and we'll find Edwin Ware one way or another."

Stefan was crying, the pain unbearable. "My phone…" he said, though his sobs. "There is…a number…I call."

Rocky searched him, pulling out the Android phone. It was password protected, but Stefan's fingerprint unlocked the screen, which he happily provided from his functional right hand. I searched through his history, finding several numbers.

"Which one do you call?" I inquired.

"EW," he replied, the sobs continuing.

"Will he answer?"

Stefan looked like he was losing consciousness, his eyes fluttered and his head lolled. I kneeled and slapped his face.

"Hang in there, Stefan. Will he answer or is it an answering service?"

"He answers."

I pressed the phone icon to dial the number. A voice answered, which I recognized as Edwin's from our previous encounter.

"Time for a meeting," I said curtly. "Private eye to private eye, if you really are one."

"Who is this?"

"Jarvis Mann. We met once, along with a San Diego detective."

"Yes, the asshole who threw my keys on the roof. Cost me a fortune to get someone out to retrieve them. What do you want?"

"Right now, I want to discuss your business, Worldwide Toys and how we can get involved in that lucrative endeavor."

"I have no idea what you're talking about."

"Sure you do. Adorable little stuffed animals filled with drugs. Or maybe plastic toy guns that aren't toys. We've seen your operation and want in on it, or we go to the cops."

"Not going to happen."

"Then I show you we mean business. We'll be in contact. And Stefan here is going to need a doctor to straighten out his arm."

I added the number to my phone, then pulled out the battery and

SIM card from Stefan's phone, breaking it in two. Rocky and I walked out the door, down to the street where Kit was waiting in an SUV. She drove me to my car, where we would head off in different directions for now and plan our next move. One that would likely be a risky one.

Chapter 51

I headed back to my hotel after picking up fast food takeout, while Rocky and Kit headed back to wherever they were staying. I laid on my bed and rested, a baseball game on the TV that I half watched, the sound turned down low while I ate. I fell asleep with a full stomach, my gun handy and woke up the next morning having slept poorly, numerous images jumbled together into a collage of evil affecting my slumber.

After a shower and breakfast at the hotel, I checked out, returning my rental car to the airport. I then booked a flight for Denver that I had no intention of taking, then grabbed a cab, paying cash after being dropped off at a designated location.

Fashion Valley Mall was the venue given to me by Kit where I should wait. It was a large open-aired upscale mall in the Mission Valley district of San Diego. It stretched across several blocks and was the largest mall in the city. A great place to spend your riches or go into credit card debt. But today I was using it as a stopover, getting lost in the throng of shoppers carrying stuffed plastic bags, waiting for Kit to come and pick me up, once we knew it was safe.

I found an open table with an umbrella on the second level food court area and took a seat, pulling my tablet out of my travel bag and connecting to the free mall Wi-Fi. I checked on the news, finding it depressing, the world of politics in our great country a mess, no matter whose allegiance you pledged to. All the talk about Russia and China made me think back to my previous cases and how they were involved in internet theft and hacking on a grand scale thanks to their association with a US tech company. Were these same people involved on the potential election scandals that dominated the headlines as well? The solution for now was getting a cheese covered pretzel to overturn my anger and hunger.

I strolled around looking at the shops, very few of which I'd ever purchase products from, let alone walk into. My window shopping was a cover, to spy for anyone trailing me. At this point, unless I was being followed around by sun drenched teenagers and mothers with strollers and spoiled kids wanting everything they could get their hands on, I was safe.

Wiping the cheese and salt from my mouth, I returned to the

food court, having finished my pretzel with a smile, and sent a text message from the burner flip phone, wishing it had a full keyboard to type on.

While waiting for a response, I double-checked my personal smartphone, making sure it was off, the SIM removed. With the people I was up against, I didn't want them tracking me. The booking for the flight to Denver, a diversion in case they were watching my purchases, which was likely. Using the credit card for anything else going forward was out of the question. I had brought enough cash from Denver to get me by. I didn't want an electronic trail left for them to discover. Only my burner phone would be used for communication and only when necessary. If the number was discovered, it would be tossed away. I felt I was on a black-ops mission. I wondered if Jason Bourne enjoyed pretzels covered in melted cheese.

I received a text back that Kit was nearby, pulling into the lot near Bloomingdales. I walked out, watching for the nineties white Jeep Grand Cherokee, which I found pulling up to me. I hopped in after tossing my bag in the backseat. We drove quickly out of the lot, Kit watching the mirrors closely.

"I wasn't followed," I said, reacting to her glances.

"Have to be certain. If they find out where we are, we lose the element of surprise. And we're likely dead!"

I couldn't argue about being cautious, especially if those we were going up against had the resources we suspected they had.

Kit drove around in circles for a while, before finally heading east through Granite Hills, into a more mountainous area, where the housing was more spaced out and certainly more expensive. We travelled on a nicely paved two-lane road, La Cresta, passing a couple people on horseback, before turning onto a driveway, leading up a moderately steep hill to a rectangular beige house, with pitched shingled roof with a flat top.

The structure was on a crest, surrounded by a few green bushes and yucca plants, the ground mostly dirt, sagebrush and rocks, from small to larger boulders. If I were to guess, the location and size of the house and land would value at around a million, which for this area, probably wasn't a high dollar amount.

Along the half-mile driveway, we passed a shirtless man, sweating while jogging, his longish blonde hair flowing behind him, his movements fluid with each stride of his Nike Swoosh running shoes. I could see scarring on his muscular back and chest, likely from the torture he'd endured recently. But they could have been past wounds, since I'd never seen Rocky with his shirt off.

We passed him, pulling up to the side of the house, and then inside the two-car garage once the door had opened, parking next to another SUV, this one a blue Toyota Four Runner maybe a couple of years newer.

I grabbed my bag and walked through the garage door opening as Rocky met us, sweat glistening, but his breathing under control. He led the way up a twisting set of flagstone steps to a deck on the backside of the house and then through a sliding glass door into a sparkling kitchen of shimmering white walls, stainless steel appliances, marble tiled floors and granite countertops.

Rocky grabbed a bottle of water, drinking the twenty ounces completely down, before offering us both one, which we accepted, as I tossed my bag on a spare padded oak chair.

"Thanks for coming," said Rocky while wiping down his body with a towel. "I've been thinking over our next move and wondered what your thoughts are?"

I could see his healed wounds, the scars tracking across his skin, once deep in nature and certainly painful. How he'd survived the torture was hard to fathom. I wanted to ask him what they had done but decided now wasn't the time. Since our confrontation yesterday to attempt to bring Edwin Ware out into the open had failed, we decided to meet up to plan what to try next.

"I have a couple of ideas," I announced. "But I'm hoping you can give me more background on what you think we're up against, to see if it lines up with what I've learned."

Rocky nodded, grabbing a green t-shirt from the back of a chair, putting it on to cover his scars, before taking a seat across from me, Kit now sitting to my left, drinking her water.

"Tell me what you know already, and I'll try to fill in the blanks," stated Rocky.

"Where to begin," I answered, knowing all that had happened would take time to detail. "It started with Brandon hiring me to look into your death," I said. With the help of a couple sips of water, from there I gave him the highlights of each step, from when I flew out to California, the connections to the people I tracked down, my battle with Luciano Duarte and my suspicions with what is going on with Worldwide Toys and what I'd seen while following their trucks. It was a lot to cover and took fifteen minutes to go through it all, up to where we were after yesterday. "Quite lot has happened, with a lot of moving parts, though I'm not certain what all the pieces mean."

Rocky listened intently to every word I said. He was a sharp man, and one who verbally kept things sparse. I hoped that wouldn't be the case now.

"I will give you a little background," decided Rocky. "At least the facts you don't know. When I worked for Maximillian Conway, I oversaw security, in a manner of speaking. Protection for him in his business dealings. A couple of which weren't always of a legal nature. He was a bull when it came to property, and occasionally he would use...*influence*...to put it kindly, to finalize the deal."

"Would 'coercion' be a more accurate term?" I asked, even though I was certain of the answer.

"Yes. I might even say *threats*, where he dearly wanted the deal to happen. Especially when it aligned with other deals he had or was making. He was never satisfied with the riches he'd obtained and always wanted more."

"Part of what made him successful." I noted.

Rocky gave a slight nod. "He was a bull when he made his first million, and every million afterwards, which was in the hundreds. My job was to make a difficult deal a reality. If he thought my presence was enough to sway someone, that was all I'd do. My physical stature often intimidated. Those who were tougher required me to take a more direct approach. One that at times required threats and even violence."

I knew Rocky was capable of violence. I'd seen it many times when he was helping me, and especially last year when he beat, shot and then burned alive in the trunk of his car, Vicente Duarte. He had a cold killer's mentality, when necessary. And was one of the toughest men I'd ever seen.

"That was the job you then wanted to walk away from?" I asked.

"Yes. It was time to move on, and with a family, I needed to find an occupation that didn't put them in harm's way. A quieter world living away from the violent life I had led. In the end I was wrong about that line of thinking, as I suspect my old life came back to haunt me."

Rocky was a man who rarely showed emotion. But I was seeing it now, as I saw it when he avenged his wife and son's murder. It was a cross between sadness and rage. He stood up abruptly and went to grab a banana. Peeling it, he took a one-third bite out of it.

"It wasn't your fault," said Kit quietly, reaching out her hand to put it on his massive shoulder after he sat back down. "It was the bastards who killed my sister and your sweet son. We'll get them in the end."

"In my conversations with Max," I said, "he vehemently pled he had no issue with you leaving. Was that true?"

Rocky looked up from the banana. "At first he was a little put off and concerned about all I knew about him and his company. But we came to an understanding. After much debate, I convinced him I'd never speak of the work I did for him, or what I knew about his business."

"And yet someone hired Vicente to kill you and your family. Vicente told you it was someone inside Conway's company. After you left to come back to San Diego, what did you learn?"

"Nothing immediately. When I first flew to California, I took time to think over my next move. Everyone out here, from what I knew, figured I was dead and buried all these years. I didn't want to expose to them I was alive immediately. I purchased a boat on the Oceanside Harbor to live in, mulling over my options. I was mad, but didn't want to act stupid, at least right away." There was a slight twinkle in Rocky's eye, as he took another bite of the banana, leaving only a third left.

"You must have been poking around a little, it sounds like they found you?"

"I started asking around. Putting out feelers. Seeing who all worked for Max. The man who replaced me, Justin Lowry, was still in charge of security."

"Did you have suspicions about him being involved?"

"I did. We didn't always get along. Justin was someone looking to move up the ladder quickly, no matter who he stepped on. He wasn't my first choice to replace me, which I made clear to Max."

"It would seem like resentment wouldn't be enough to want to murder your family? There had to be more to the story."

Rocky finished off the banana and threw away the peel in the trash barrel nearby. I had grown hungry, wondering if there was an apple or an orange handy. But I remained silent, pondering if the growl in my stomach would trigger an offer.

"I agree. But he was first on my list. And after what happened on the boat with those two maniac brothers, my suspicions became more valid."

I nodded, waiting for him to continue, my hunger growing. I knew I had a granola bar in my bag but resisted grabbing it for now.

"When the two brothers got the drop on me and started torturing me in ways I really would prefer to not get into, they kept asking me about my connection to the government and what I was telling them about Max's business dealings. It would seem they thought I was about to flip or had already. They talked quietly on the deck of the boat thinking I couldn't hear them, but I heard them say Lowry's name."

"I'm to assume they were mistaken about you flipping?" I said after a long drink of water, to calm my growling stomach.

"Hell yes," Rocky said, his muscles swelling at the accusation. "I'd never make a deal with the Feds to save my ass!"

"Was that all they wanted from you?"

"No. They wanted me to tell them everything I knew about Stetson Poole."

"What did you say?"

"Nothing. I've never heard of him."

I was surprised by the statement, since Max had told me otherwise.

"Then Stetson Poole isn't name you warned Max to be on the lookout for?"

"Hell no. Where did you get that information from?"

I looked Rocky right in the eye and he read my mind before cursing up a storm at the man he thought was an ally.

Chapter 52

When men are angry, they either want to punch a wall or drink. Rocky chose the latter and went to the fridge, pulling out three beers, sitting one in front of Kit and myself, then popped the top and took a long swallow. An upgrade from the filtered water, he was never one to go with a common beer. The Blue Moon Belgian White bottle was frosty, with a hint of orange flavor to it which I enjoyed. It didn't solve our problems but helped us forget them for a couple of minutes.

"You're certain that was what Max said?" asked Rocky, after I had given him verbatim what he'd told me when I mentioned the name Stetson Poole.

"Word for word. Said you warned him to be wary when the name came up in relation to the operation he was in."

"What operation?"

"The one I mentioned run by the CIA, NSA or another government agency through Happy Child Imports, now apparently known as Worldwide Toys. An operation funneling in guns and drugs illegally for money. He wanted out, but they wouldn't let him out. He said you killed people who tried to persuade him to change his mind, which then was enough to get him out of the operation, for the time being."

"I did a lot of nasty work for him, but I don't recall anything related to guns and drugs."

"Then nothing related to his son and his drug issue?" I inquired, a sinking feeling growing I'd been lied too.

"From what I know, his son is a successful lawyer in Northern California. They weren't on speaking terms last I knew, though I didn't care to delve into his private life. If it was related to his son, I wasn't involved."

I cursed myself for not investigating what I was told and being sloppy. If I had dug into it deeper, I probably would have learned the truth.

"Max likely told me all of this to put me off the trail. I was never completely certain he was telling the whole truth, and I should have investigated into it further. Of course, in my line of business, everyone seems to be lying or hiding information, the truth rarely spoken. But it really doesn't matter as the name has important meaning. The question is, what?"

I took a sip of the beer, a pleasant aftertaste filling my mouth. A step up from my usual brew, since cost was often an issue. For now, the name Stetson Poole needed to go on the back burner, the mystery to remain. An answer had to be found, but we had other things to consider.

"Then you didn't know anything about the smuggling operation?" I asked.

"Not a thing. Being the snoop you are, it sounds like you've dug up a few things. What can we do with what you've learned?"

"A couple key facts come to mind. One more conservative, while the other is a little more out there." I took another sip of beer before continuing. "The conservative option is, I know where their CPA, Carlton Gilpin, works. Or at least one of their accountants. If we can get a hold of him, we might be able to glean valuable information. If he hasn't gone into hiding, that is."

"Why would he do that?" asked Kit, who was enjoying her beer.

"I paid him a visit. Put the fear of God in him. I doubt he would say anything from his reaction, as he said they'd kill him. But easy enough to watch his work and see if he shows. Then we grab and hold him."

"Kidnapping," stated Kit, a sour look on her face. "I'm not sure I'd be thrilled with committing a federal offense."

I smiled. "Only if we take him across state lines. And even if we did, we'd be holding him as a material witness."

"I doubt he would see it that way," replied Kit. "If he can be convinced to testify, then we might be able to pull it off. But it could be risky."

"I can be persuasive," added Rocky, the muscles in his chest swelling to demonstrate his strength.

"He is quite timid," I noted. "One stare from you and he would likely pass out. Though he may be just as afraid of who he is working for. Still, it would be worth a shot."

"Can't we just break into his office and steal his records?" wondered Kit.

"He claimed everything is electronic. No literal paper trail to find. Short of hacking into his cloud storage, which isn't one of my strengths, I don't know that we'd find much."

"Kit has skills in that department," claimed Rocky.

"I do, but I suspect he has serious security in place to protect what he has. High level encryption with master password and key that could be extremely difficult to crack. He would have to give it up or it would take months to break into."

Rocky smiled this time. "As I said, I can be persuasive."

Hunger was taking over me, leading me to ask about food options. There were red crisp apples and Rocky tossed one to me. I took a big bite, while he started on another banana. Maybe that was the key to his recovery. Potassium and beer building strong muscles and bone. There had to be worse diets out there.

"What other ideas do you have?" asked Kit. "If that was the conservative one, I'm interested in hearing the crazy one."

I swallowed down the juicy fruit, satisfying my hunger for now. "I followed them around, containers from the shipping yard going to a warehouse in Santa Clarita. From there they off loaded into a smaller transport truck, which then went to a small airport in Agua Dulce. We need to get inside somewhere along the line and find out what cargo is in there."

Kit rolled her eyes, while drinking her beer, then got up and grabbed an apple for herself, taking a large chunk. I had eaten half of mine. Rocky was half-way through his banana, listening intently, back to showing little emotion. I'd have hated playing poker with him.

"How heavily guarded is the warehouse?" he questioned.

"As you would imagine, they have people and guns everywhere. The warehouse is inside a ten-foot-high wire fence that might be electrified. I didn't get close enough to say for certain."

"And the cargo in the shipping yard?"

"Guarded as well. The San Diego cop I was working with and I approached, and we were immediately confronted by two armed men. Not to mention the shipyard itself has its own security. Getting inside would be challenging."

Rocky finished off his banana, followed by the beer, tossing both away, before grabbing a second beer. He twisted off the top and took a quick swallow, while pacing the tiled kitchen floor, then stopping to look out a window that sat over the sink.

"Are the vehicles in transit guarded?" he asked, continuing to stare out the window.

"Armed men in the cab of the semi and in the smaller trucks. Driver and one other from what I could tell. I didn't see a trailing vehicle when we were following but doesn't mean they don't use them at times. I'm sure there'll be GPS on the trucks, allowing them to track their movements."

"Sounds like the weakest link is when the cargo is in transit," declared Rocky after another sip of beer. "Seems like we could take one from them and use it as a bargaining chip."

"Possibly. But we would need more recon to find out for certain. And with only three of us, that might be stretching it."

Rocky turned around, leaning on the kitchen counter. "We will need more bodies, one of which should be female. Kit and another lovely dangerous lady would be a good distraction for the men with guns." He looked at Kit, who smiled.

"What did you have in mind?" Kit queried.

"Clothing which leaves little to the imagination. It's California. Women in bikini tops are seen all over. I'm sure it will be enough to pull their attention."

"What do you think, Jarvis?" asked Kit.

"It worked on me, to a point."

"Until you tossed me on the bed and pulled your gun." She pointed out with a laugh.

I shrugged. "I'm cynical because of previous encounters with other females. I doubt these men will have my past history."

"We need another pretty face to make sure the odds are stacked. What about April?" asked Rocky.

I thought about it, but didn't think she could get the time off, since she'd used her paid days working the Hester case. And it was hard to say how long this would last. Sam would have been another good choice, but she was laid up with the gunshot wound. I pondered another that might work, though I'd need to make a call.

"No. But I may have someone who could work. They likely will want to be paid. Is money an issue?"

Rocky shook his head. "I have plenty to work with. Offer them five thousand. I'm sure that is enough for several days work."

Finishing up the apple, I tossed the core into the trash, holding onto the first beer, savoring each sip. With five thousand to tender chances were good I could get her.

"I'll need to make a call. But I will do it from a pay phone away from here. I'll need a car."

Rocky tossed a set of keys to me. "You can take the Four Runner. Don't let anyone follow you back."

"No worries. I'm thinking we need at least one other to help and possibly two. Any ideas? They need to be skilled in this line of work."

"I do have one in mind," said Rocky. "Though you may not like it."

"It's your operation. You make the call."

"He is brutal and tough, though I only know him by reputation. But you've gone up against him. I'm not certain how to contact him, but you might."

I looked back at Rocky, wondering who he had in mind, and then it dawned on me.

"You don't mean…"

"Yes I do. Wolfe would be a dangerous man to have on our side. And for the right money he can be hired."

I knew he was right. I reached into my bag, going through a few pockets, until I found the card Wolfe had given me, with the private phone number on it. It seemed I was always teetering on the line of good and evil. I grabbed the keys and headed out the door uncertain any amount of penance would save me. Yet I was willing to see this through to the end, come hell or high water, which I was certainly wading in.

Chapter 53

As I opened the door to the truck, Kit came gliding into the garage in her running shoes.

"Do you have any idea where you're going?" she asked pointedly.

I thought for a moment. I had lived off the GPS on my smartphone, but I couldn't use it and Google Maps wasn't an option on the burner flip phone. And pay phones were harder to find these days, since everyone has a cell phone to make calls on.

"I was going to try and head west along the same path you took here and hope to find the mall again. I saw a couple of payphones there. Otherwise, no, I wasn't exactly sure where to go."

"You need me to drive," said Kit confidently. "I've lived in this area all my life and know every street, every shop, on every corner."

Kit had her brownish blonde hair tied back, her tank top holding her modest and braless chest in place. Her tanned skin had a nice glow to it, not a hint of makeup could be seen. Her jeans were faded blue and fit her lower form well, but not so tight as to leave little to the imagination. With her charms and looks, I had little doubt she could charm any man into doing what she wanted.

I nodded my head and tossed her the keys, then moved to the passenger side and soon we were on the road. I pulled out my smart phone, turning it on without the SIM card and in airplane mode, finding my address book and looking for phone numbers. There were several choices I mulled over and decided on using them all. I programmed each into the flip phone, cursing as I missed the full on-screen numeric keyboard, having to type with just a numeric keypad.

"How is Rocky doing?" I asked, once I'd finished. "He appears to have bounced back, looking tough as always. But seeing those scars tells me he went through hell."

Kit kept her eyes on the road, answering when we hit a traffic light.

"It is always hard to say with him. He is one tough S.O.B, but he was really hurting when he called me. Keeps most of his internal pain hidden inside. When he unleashes the rage, it can be brutal."

"I've seen it a couple of times. I'd hate to be on his bad side. Do you think he will ever talk about what they did to him?"

Kit let out a low whistle. "He told me shortly after I picked him up, but nothing since. When he called me, he could barely stand. I got him into my car, which was no small feat and took him to a doctor I knew personally. He fixed him up off the books as favor to me. It was a month before he could walk without assistance."

"Is the house you're in now where you've been staying the whole time?"

"Not at first. The doctor, who was a former lover of mine, let us use a couple of rooms he had at his place, which was huge. Once Rocky was coherent enough, we worked on finding a place to live and rented the house. It wasn't cheap, but money isn't an issue for him. And it was far enough outside of the city that we aren't seen all that much and away from prying eyes that might find out he was alive."

Kit continued to drive, finding a gas station that had an outside payphone. I got out and made my calls, leaving messages for several people to call me on my burner phone. I wasn't picky, knowing I needed good help, no matter where it came from. Once that was done, I hopped back into the Four Runner as we headed back to the house.

"You looked surprised when Rocky mentioned Wolfe's name," noted Kit.

"I was. The two of us have a complicated history. He was hired to scare me off a case and if I didn't do as he said, then he was going to kill me."

"I'm guessing you stopped investigating, since you're alive," joked Kit.

"You would think that was the case, but I didn't. He gave me a lead on who the killer was, and they were arrested, though it turned out that was false. After I started up again, Wolfe came after me, but I convinced him the person who hired him lied. Once I proved to him that my words were correct, he then took out his anger on his client."

"Who I'd assume now is dead, knowing his reputation," added Kit.

"You've heard of him?" I asked.

Kit laughed. "Anyone in our profession knows of Wolfe. He is a killer extraordinaire. When he is hired, the life expectancy of his target is null and void. If he was paid to kill you and you survived, it is a testament to you."

I shook my head, not feeling all that fortunate. For at the time, I feared I *wasn't* going to survive. Yes there was skill involved, but a touch of luck as well. Now to look to hire him for this mission seemed like a risk, especially after our last conversation in Denver. But his ability might be a tipping point against our foe.

Once we were back at the house, after Kit drove around to make sure we weren't followed, I got a tour of the inside. There were two floors; the upper level where the kitchen, living place, three bedrooms and two full bathrooms resided. Most of the flooring was red mahogany hardwood, other than the tiled kitchen and bathrooms, with no carpeting in sight. Each room was painted a different color, to set different moods–the kitchen white, the living area a sky blue, the master bedroom fuchsia, the two other bedrooms, one green and the other yellow.

The lower level had two more smaller bedrooms, one bathroom, an entertainment area and an impressive gym, where Rocky was working out while watching a movie on a big screen TV, a group of superheroes saving the world. I was wondering if this was inspiration for the group we were about to put together. If only I had a shield made of vibranium.

Once we were through the lower level, we went back upstairs, where Kit said I could take the third bedroom, the one in yellow. Walking in, I tossed my bag on the queen-sized bed, sitting on it finding the pillow-top mattress softer than what I had in all the hotel rooms I'd stayed in on this trip.

"I'm in the green room," stated Kit with a smile. "We will be sharing a bathroom. I'll try not to walk in on you while you're showering. One other note; I don't lock the door when I'm bathing."

With a wicked grin, she displayed in full force, she spun and walked out of the room, where I wondered if she had handled the sleeping arrangements. I took a minute to clear my mind of thoughts of her and I in an impure way. A complication I didn't need distracting me and one a good workout required to completely shake.

Once changed and in my workout clothes, I went downstairs to the gym and surveyed my options. An elliptical, treadmill, Bowflex machine, free-weights, barbell and bench, and finally a heavy bag and free-standing martial arts bag to hone your punching and kicking skills.

After a light stretching, I started with the treadmill for twenty minutes, then the elliptical for another twenty, then used the Bowflex for all kinds of arm and leg work. Though my arms and legs were weary, I wrapped my hands before putting on a pair of light padded boxing gloves and began hitting the heavy bag with various jabs and hooks, with visions of The Butcher's face as motivation, until I was exhausted. Breathing hard, I found a mini-fridge and grabbed a bottle of water, drinking half of it, while walking around to keep my limbs loose.

"Not too bad," said Kit, who had been watching me. "We will have to work out together. Hell, we can even spar a little on the mat. I could use the competition, as Rocky's boxing skills don't match mine."

Rocky turned while slowly walking on the treadmill. "I take it easy on you since you're my sister-in-law. Besides, I don't normally need to box, my foe is often already dead from my loaded Glock."

I laughed. "Any time, Kit. Just don't make me look bad in front of Rocky. He might have to waste one of his 9mm shells to put me out of my misery."

Laughter filled the room which was good to hear. I grabbed a towel and dried off, finishing the water before grabbing another, when my cell phone rang. I answered it and began the afternoon arranging to bring in more help for our operation, to fill out our magnificent team of six we had decided on.

Chapter 54

The next day, we began the recon work, with Rocky watching the CPA in the Four Runner while Kit and I were watching the truck transports from Port Hueneme to the warehouse in the Grand Cherokee. While parked outside the port entryway, we waited for a while, not spotting anything. Since I didn't have Manny's badge to get us in, we stared from a distance with binoculars, though it was difficult to see much. I watched for the leasing company name on the trucks that they had used before, but no semis with that name passed us. We decided to move onto the warehouse location instead.

Our drive was quiet, Kit listening to traffic and news radio behind the wheel, while I gazed out across the road, amazed by the extreme volume of vehicles of all makes, models and conditions, occupying the pavement. If it had four wheels, was street legal and made in the last fifty years it appeared to be in motion in Southern California and contributing to the worst smog in the country. Hardly a fact the Chamber of Commerce bragged about.

When we arrived, we took up station a distance away, and saw no trucks as of yet. Several men were patrolling the secured area, each carrying weapons, though doing their best to conceal them. After several hours, we picked up lunch from the golden arches, returning to find the location quiet. We called it a day, figuring no shipments had arrived. This happened for two more days before we saw activity, this time in the form of three semis hauling containers to the warehouse early in the morning at around 8 a.m.

Though there were quiet stretches while we waited, Kit was a bit chattier than Rocky would have been. She told me what her life was like, where she was from, the places she'd been, and the work she did, which she claimed was thrilling, though I thought sounded dangerous. She talked of how she met Rocky and her idea of setting him up with her sister, which he resisted at first, until he met her.

It appeared it was love at first sight, and within six months they were married. Kit was happy she had found a soulmate for the sister she cared for deeply, but sad about the dark life he'd left behind coming back to kill her and their beautiful son. Kit had made a promise to Rocky she'd help bring the people to justice, though I'm certain their justice would be brought about by a bullet.

With three days and much time to kill, I gave her a rundown on my life, in bits and pieces. My upbringing, how I had gone off the rails and how my father used drastic measures to get me back on the right side of things. The evolution of my business as a private eye, and the dangers I'd faced. Those dangers that led me to meet Rocky, where we had partnered up on other cases. I even shared about my personal life and the horrors I was experiencing from my battle with The Butcher, a fact I often didn't reveal so openly. It was somewhat therapeutic, though more of a way to pass the time, as talking about the weather would only fill a few minutes.

The routine at the warehouse appeared the same as the last time, with the trucks arriving, being unloaded and then leaving empty. Smaller trucks then were loaded, soon heading out to the same airfield out west as before. We saw no extra security for any of the transports, but the driver and passenger of each truck were definitely armed with large handguns and carrying communication devices on their belts. Each of the men looked large and formidable. From what we saw, the routine didn't vary any from each delivery. A sign they had no worries about getting caught. This we could take advantage of.

When nearing the end of the third day, we spotted a change in the routine. Two men with guns were hustling to a truck and drove out the gate, appearing to be coming our way.

"Crap," I said, sitting behind the wheel of the Grand Cherokee. "What do you want to do?"

Kit turned and immediately started kissing me. I was caught off-guard and it took me a minute to understand but I started kissing back, just as a man came knocking on my window. I pulled away and looked at him, as he waved for us to get out. I rolled down the window, smiling and looking nervous, as if we'd been naughty teenagers caught in the act.

"Is there something wrong?" I asked, showing a flushed face of someone embarrassed, which I sort of was after Kit's passionate kiss.

"We need to know what you're doing here?" the man said with a raspy voice of a heavy smoker.

"Getting alone time with my lady, is all," I replied, while

keeping an arm around Kit, holding her close. "I have to make sure her burly boyfriend doesn't catch us." I looked Kit in the eye. "Isn't that right, sweetie?"

Kit smirked. "Yes, that would be bad for both us if we get caught. He is quite jealous."

Either he wasn't buying it or didn't care. "You were here yesterday and the day before. I must insist you step out."

"Absolutely, we were here," I said, sheepishly. "I can't go a day without being with her."

"I'm not going to ask you again," he demanded, patting his gun in the holster to show he was in charge.

I looked at Kit and she shrugged. I slid out my side, while she did the same on hers, since the bucket seats didn't allow us going out the same door. The second man was on her side checking her out, her smile seeming to warm him up some. I concluded my smile wouldn't help me with my guy any. It was best to play innocent and dumb.

"I don't understand the problem," I stated. "This is a public street and we were just smooching, which I don't think is against the law."

"Let me see your ID!" He sounded grumpy.

"Why?"

"Because I said so. Please don't make me use force."

I looked the man over. He was an inch or two taller than I was, and thicker in the neck and chest. He had a buzzed blonde haircut, tanned skin, an earpiece with coiled wire wrapped around his ear and what looked like a 9mm under his shoulder. His tough look probably scared many, but I wasn't like most people he'd confronted.

"How are you doing, sweetie?" I called over my shoulder to Kit.

"Just fine."

"This man wants to see our ID. What should I do?"

"I'd give it to him," Kit said joyfully.

"OK. I'll do that right now."

I reached for my back pocket and then kicked the man between the legs. Unless he was lacking testicles, this works a hundred percent of the time. He grabbed for his groin and then slumped over, dropping to his knees a nauseated flush expression on his face. I grabbed the gun from his shoulder holster and pistol whipped him on the back of the head. I carefully checked him, and he was out cold. I turned to render assistance to Kit, but she had her man on the ground, holding him around the neck until he passed out.

"Grab his gun, any other weapons, walkie-talkie and any phone he might have and let's get out of here."

I gathered everything, we hopped back in the Cherokee and we drove off. I handed her the gun, brass knuckles, mace, baton, phone and walkie-talkie. She promptly removed the battery and SIM from both phones, effectively disabling them.

"Sloppy," I said. "They made us which isn't good."

"Probably have our plate number now. We'll need to lose this SUV and find different wheels."

"Call Rocky and see if he can pick us up somewhere. I'll find a place to dump this once we're certain we aren't being followed."

Kit kept an eye on our backside, while calling Rocky and arranging a meeting place. We drove for a while, but no one was behind us. With Kit directing me, I found a lot with an open parking spot, left the vehicle, while walking away with all the items in a bag she was carrying. We had to go about four blocks to meet up with Rocky, baking in the afternoon sun as I was sweating from the heat. Both our heads were on a swivel, careful to make sure no one had made us. It looked like we had gotten away cleanly.

"That was an awesome kiss," admired Kit. "When I grabbed you, I wasn't sure you understood at first. It took you a few seconds to respond."

"I'm little slow sometimes, but I understood the gist of it."

"I gathered. You kissed me back, with tongue added. The facial hair tickled a little bit, but I have to say I didn't mind it."

I frowned. "Don't get any ideas. It was all for show and it worked, which is most important. Looks like you didn't have any trouble with your man."

"He was smitten with my first smile and when I told him I enjoyed fooling around where people could see me, his eyes glazed over. He let me get too close to him and I was able to wrap him in a sleeper hold."

"Good to know you can handle yourself."

"Was there ever any doubt?"

I laughed as we came to the rendezvous point. The Four Runner pulled up and we hopped in, Kit in the front and me in the back. I continued to keep an eye on our rear, but all looked clear with nobody following.

"What happened?" asked Rocky, sounding a bit peeved.

"They made us," stated Kit. "Jarvis and I made out like a couple of teenagers to throw them off. Then got the best of them."

Rocky turned his head and looked at us both.

"Made out like a couple of teenagers?" he asked, a confused expression lining his face.

"Don't ask!" I replied.

Kit laughed. "Jarvis is a great kisser when the pressure is on. But nevertheless, we subdued them while getting their weapons, radios and phones. Don't worry, the cells are off, the batteries and SIMs removed too."

Kit showed him the bag. The guns were large 9mm, both Browning's. We had grabbed their extra clips as well. It never hurt to have backup firepower when you were about to face a strong adversary.

"What do we do now?" asked Rocky, driving us back to home base.

"I'm not certain," I said. "We can get back to the house and talk over where we're at. We may need to reassess things. They might toughen their procedures now that they think someone is on to them. What about the CPA?"

"From what I can tell, nothing different going on. He goes into this office each day and doesn't appear to be watched or even with anyone else. We might want to grab him while we can. They could draw ranks around him if they come to the conclusion we know about him."

"We have help coming in tomorrow," I declared. "If we do take him, where do we keep him stashed?"

"We can probably keep him comfortable in one of the downstairs bedrooms. But someone will need to stay with him."

I nodded. It was a good thing I had three people coming into town. I just hoped it was enough.

Chapter 55

When we got back to the house, we determined it was too late today to grab the CPA. The plan was to get him first thing in the morning, just as his office opened at 9 a.m. which was where the three of us were right now.

Rocky and Kit sat in the Four Runner, while I waited outside the locked office door on the second floor, stomach full of a bacon, ham and sausage omelet from Tom's Place across the street, when Carlton Gilpin walked up. It didn't appear he recognized me, my sunglasses and Rockies ball cap working as a disguise, as he smiled while unlocking his door, offering me coffee after he strolled in.

"No thank you," I stated. "We need to talk."

He turned around and I removed my glasses, allowing to see my face. It took a minute, but he soon remembered and started backing up out of the waiting area in fear, into his office. I followed him, to make sure he didn't do something stupid. He moved, reaching for his desk phone. I stopped him by pulling it from his shaking hand and unplugged it from the base. He was looking around the room, trying to decide what to do. But he was put on this planet to crunch numbers and not for courage.

"What do you want?" he said, sweat now covering his forehead.

"You need to come with me. It's time we talked."

"Why? I have nothing to tell you."

"I think you do. You're helping Worldwide Toy's launder money from their illegal operation. You're going to help us bring them down or at least turn over information we need."

"I told you before, they will kill me." His whole body was shaking.

"We can protect you."

He didn't seem convinced. "Who are you? For all I know you're just a guy with nothing to offer. I know what they offer. I've seen it and it scares the hell out of me."

"I'm here with a team of people to figure out who murdered a woman and a three-year-old boy. Both were murdered by people inside Worldwide Toys. You're going to be leverage to get us answers."

I stopped talking and he started looking at the door as if he was waiting for someone. I glanced around but didn't see any camera like I saw at the Shark Tail Detective office. But that didn't mean they couldn't be listening in.

"What are you expecting?" I asked, reaching for my gun.

His eyes looked down. "No one."

"Shit." I pulled a radio out of my pocket. "Be on the lookout, we may have company coming. Pull up to the back exit and I will bring him out."

I grabbed him by the arm. "Where is your cell phone?"

He hesitated. I squeezed his bicep until he winced. He found it in his inside jacket pocket and handed to me. I took the battery and SIM out and put all the pieces in my back pocket. I looked around and didn't see a computer.

"And your computer?"

He waited again, and I squeezed even harder, his face contorting in pain.

"In my bag," he yelled.

I released my death grip and found the bag on the floor, checking it in case he had a weapon. Inside was a computer, power supply, wireless mouse, pens and paper, but no gun. I tossed him the bag then grabbed him by the arm, leading him out of his office.

"Say a word or try to run and you're dead," I stated, with my gun in his ribs.

He nodded, as we made it down the stairs to the back exit. The Four Runner was waiting, and I shoved him in the backseat. I was about to get in, when I heard the sound of squealing tires, as a white Ford SUV came rolling into the parking lot.

A pair of armed men jumped out, seeing us and taking aim. I fired five shots in their direction, the two men hitting the ground for cover. But it wasn't them I was aiming for, instead I hit the front grille of the Ford, the target being the radiator, the steam of the hot liquid spewing in the air letting me know I'd hit my mark. I hopped in the Four Runner yelling for Rocky to punch it, barely getting the door closed as we roared away. A shot took out the back window, as I pushed Carlton down, but we were out on the street, making our escape.

"I told you they would kill me!" screamed Carlton, his face down on the vinyl seat.

"How did they know we were there?" I yelled.

He didn't want to talk. Pressing the gun barrel to his leg got his attention.

"It would only be a flesh wound, but it would hurt like hell," I explained convincingly.

"Alright! They found out about your earlier visit because my office was bugged."

"Why didn't they send somebody after me?"

"At the time they didn't know who you were, since you claimed to be Edwin Ware at first. They thought you might be a Federal agent. They didn't want to jump too quickly until they had a better idea of who you were. They warned me they would continue listening, and if you returned, I was supposed to stall, then they would get men there quickly to handle you."

Rocky had us going fast out onto North Lakeview Avenue and up and over the Santa Ana River. Checking out the busted back window, I didn't see anyone following us, as their SUV likely wouldn't go very far because of the wounded radiator. But that didn't mean they wouldn't call in reinforcements looking for us.

"What is your plan?" I asked of Rocky.

"We'll get on the Riverside Freeway and try to put distance between us and them."

"What if we hit traffic?" I said, knowing that was more than likely.

"There is an Express Toll Road we can take," said Kit. "Normally it's clear because of the cost."

"You need to make sure they aren't tracking him," stated Rocky. "Or they will find us anywhere we go eventually."

"I took care of his phone. How about your notebook, Carlton? Does it have LTE?"

He didn't answer, which probably meant yes. I pulled out the sleek Lenovo unit, found the SIM tray and removed the card.

"What about his clothing?" asked Kit.

Carlton continued to cower. I grabbed him by his work coat and pulled him up, my gun now pointed at his shoulder. He nodded his head after I pulled back the hammer on my Beretta.

"Strip," I said. "All of it and hurry."

He was slow moving at first, but I waved the gun at him and he finally peeled off his clothes more quickly. As he got down to his t-shirt, socks and underwear, he stopped.

"All of it. And don't worry I won't get any jollies out of seeing you naked."

Carlton pulled the rest of it off, his eyes staring down, his cheeks red with embarrassment and I handed him a blanket that was sitting in the back, to cover up. I then gathered all the clothes and rolled down the window, tossing them straight onto the side of the road as we entered the Freeway.

Traffic bogged down as we suspected. We jumped on the toll road and were back up to full speed. Rocky was being smart and not speeding, to avoid the attention from the highway cops looking to pad their ticket quota. Their reaction to a naked Carlton in the backseat if pulled over, wouldn't bode well either. We then turned and headed south on highway 241 past Anaheim Hills, into a mountainous area and past Santiago Canyon, through Orchard Hills and into Foothill Ranch. Not completely certain where we were headed, I had been watching the signs as well as for a tail, on the whole drive. But Rocky and Kit knew the area extensively. I trusted them to get us back safely.

"Where are we headed?" I wondered.

"To the house, eventually. It will take time, but we'll get there. I'll then take Carlton in while you and Kit track down new wheels. We'll have to dump this one now as well. But Kit has connections and can get us two others to work with."

"And what is your plan for Carlton?" I queried, his stocky frame shaking under the blanket.

Rocky laughed. "He and I are going to chat about his life expectancy. He will live a long and fruitful life. All he needs to do is give us what we want."

Carlton slumped down in his seat, a white look of terror on his mustached mug. I placed a hand on his shoulder.

"I think what he is trying to say, is we can be just as scary as Worldwide Toys. Time to pick your poison!"

The chuckling from the front seat didn't seem to bring the color back into his face.

Chapter 56

Rocky tried dragging Carlton into the house, but he started to yell, which was a mistake. Rocky popped him one in the jaw, knocking him out, picked him up and threw him over his shoulder and up the stairs. Kit took over driving, while I moved up front and we went to her contact, making a deal for two older cars in exchange for this one and the one we left behind which we gave him the location to. She pulled out a big wad of cash, paying for everything off the books. From there, she took the cherry red 2000 Nissan Xterra back to the house, while I drove a gray late nineties Dodge Durango to pick up the three people we were expecting at the rendezvous point.

When I thought about the point where we would all meet, I figured Starbucks would be the easiest. Picking one was difficult, as there are numerous options near the San Diego Airport. I decided on one on El Cajon Blvd a few blocks off I-805. Each of the three people were coming in today at varying times, though all in the afternoon. I was supposed to meet them at 4 p.m. giving them time to land, get a cab and get to the location. The three didn't know about each other, and none of them had ever met before.

It would be interesting bringing them in on what we had in mind. Mostly though money was the deciding factor, as Rocky had promised them five thousand each for the work, which should only last a week or so. Substantial wages that were hard to turn down, no matter the danger involved.

With written directions from Kit, I made my way across the city and found the Starbucks. Walking inside, I saw two of the faces I was expecting, the third apparently not there yet. I walked up to Gisella Altsmann, a strong, beautiful Russian woman who worked for the Russian gangster, Aleksi Platov. I needed another woman to help with our plan, and she seemed like a good option if available.

We had met on a limo ride in Northern California where she had taken me to Aleksi to talk. Though I hadn't seen her in action, Aleksi had bragged about how formidable she was. He left it up to her if she wanted the work and called me back agreeing after I told her the price.

As I approached her, she stood up, nearly matching my height, lean with good muscle tone exposed by the sleeveless tan blouse she was wearing. She put out her hand, which I shook, finding it firm and soft, her nails painted blue and grown long enough to scratch with. I motioned her to walk over to the other table, where T was sitting. He stood and shook her hand as I introduced them.

"What does T stand for?" wondered Gisella.

"Tewodros," he replied. "It is African, specifically Ethiopian. My mother named me after an Emperor. Most people get the pronunciation wrong, so T stuck over time, especially when I was in the military."

"Kind of like Mister T," noted Gisella.

T laughed. "Sort of. Minus the gold chains, fame and wealth. But I do pity the fool who gets in my way."

Gisella smiled and sat down across from T, while I took a seat next to him. I had met T as a homeless veteran on the streets and he helped me to track down why other homeless people in the area were being moved out and why his friend, Parker, had been stabbed. Now he was a working man, no longer homeless, in his spare time a volunteer at The Mission of the Invisible Souls, helping however he could.

I wasn't sure he could get away, after Sam got shot, but she was back working again, even with her arm in a sling, and gave her blessing for T to help me if he wanted. He was a big man, though mostly quiet, a gentle giant who hardly came across as intimidating but was tough when it mattered.

"What is the job at hand?" asked T, while stirring his coffee to keep the cream and sugar from settling.

"We will discuss once we get back to the house. I'm waiting for another person to arrive. He should be here by now, but maybe his plane was late arriving. If either of you need additional refreshments, help yourself, and I will pay."

"Nothing here I care to eat or drink," commented Gisella. "Hopefully we'll have real food where we're headed."

"The house is completely stocked with plenty of food choices. And the man in charge of this operation is a darn good cook."

I debated on getting hot chocolate, but before I could stand, I sensed a change in the room. I turned around and walking in the door was Wolfe. Everyone in the place had eyes on him, the nearly shaved black head, glistening diamond earrings, expensive brown suit over a silver silk shirt. Behind him he pulled a twenty-inch carryon luggage. He strolled to the table, a tower of strength, acknowledged everyone and pointed to the door.

"I'm ready to go," he said in his baritone voice.

I nodded and led the way to the Durango, each of them putting their luggage in the far back. We headed off back to the house, as I took the same route, continuing to watch for any sign of a tail. It took around forty-five minutes to get back, the traffic in full rush hour mode.

After pulling into the garage, I led the way up the flagstone steps into the kitchen. Kit was sitting at the table enjoying a beer, munching on salted crackers. I introduced her to everyone, her eyes not wanting to leave Wolfe, his form difficult for her ignore. It was possible she had found someone else to covet. Which might mean she'd stop coming on to me, which was good.

"Where is Rocky?" I asked.

"In the first bedroom on the lower level," replied Kit. "That is where he put Carlton. I believe he is trying to persuade him to turn over his digital files."

I excused myself and headed downstairs. I imagined Rocky working over the portly man, finding him battered, bruised and bleeding. When I got to the bedroom, the door was closed. I listened for a minute, not hearing much, then I knocked before walking in.

Carlton was strapped via his hands and feet with plastic ties to a chair, naked as before, with only a towel over his lap. The only marks on him were from the initial punch before he was carried in, only sweat on his exposed skin, and a nervous twitch to his body. Rocky was sitting on the edge of the bed, just staring at him, not saying a word.

"Would you tell him to stop looking at me like that?" shouted Carlton.

"I think he is attempting to mind meld with you," I replied dryly.

"It is spooky. Hell, if he'd at least speak or yell at me, it would be better than this."

"Tell him what he wants to know, and he'll stop."

"But he hasn't said anything!" Carlton claimed in a panic.

"I told you before what he wants. To catch the killers of his wife and son. And information on Worldwide Toys will help him with that. Especially money information."

"Honestly I can't. You don't know what they'll do to me." Stark terror filled his eyes and face as he whined.

I walked over and looked him square in the eye. "Most certainly more than stare at you. But it won't matter if you tell us anything, because now that they know we have you, they will assume you've talked, even if you keep your mouth shut. And we won't hurt you if you do tell us and might even be able to get you protection from those in the government."

"But they *are* the government. The CIA with long arms. What protection they provide won't last."

"The agency is tough, but there are other US agencies as well. And I have contacts chomping at the bit to bring down this operation, if we can provide proof. And you're the first piece."

"And what is the second piece?" inquired Carlton.

"That is what our team is working on and why I'm here. Is he safe to leave here?"

Rocky nodded, finally speaking. "Yes. He is strapped down tightly, and the room can be locked from the outside. He can sit while we go upstairs to talk and think about what to do next. If he thought my *stare* was spooky, he'll be begging for the stare to return once I start phase two of my interrogation."

Rocky walked over and lightly slapped Carlton on the cheek, his body tensing up at the contact. We left the room, bolting and locking the door, heading upstairs to discuss phase two. It was going to be a doozy of a mission to pull off.

Chapter 57

Our power sextet was meeting out on the deck, relishing the cool evening air as the sun went down. We had enjoyed a meal prepared by Rocky and Kit of New York Strip steak, baked potatoes, corn on the cob and salad; with a bottle of expensive red wine to wash it all down with. A high protein meal to fuel us for what lay ahead. Hopefully it wasn't a last meal.

The outside deck was made of natural redwood that looked like it had held up through the years, the sharp red color showing little signs of fading, the wood showing no give when it was walked upon. There were several padded outdoor chairs, and two chaise loungers, that both Kit and Giselle stretched out on. I was sitting in one of the chairs with a nice view of the orange sun setting on the horizon. The nearest neighbor was off in the distance, well out of hearing range, a wall of tall yucca and cactus plants up and down the hill providing further insolation from any snooping.

"Who is going to explain why we're here?" questioned Giselle, her head back on the chaise, soaking in the remaining sunlight.

Kit and I looked at Rocky as he sat in a wide wrought iron chair that fit his form well. It was his show, so we let him talk.

"Several years ago, my wife, Claire, and son, Madden, were killed in a car bomb. I was badly injured, and through help from several associates, I played dead, starting my life over with the name, Rocky. After a long quest, I'm finally nearing who it was who ordered the hit on me and my family."

In all the years I'd known Rocky now, he'd never mentioned a last name, always going by the single moniker. It seemed unimportant in the grand scheme of things and possibly was all he cared to be known by, since it was a tribute to his son.

"Through the help of Kit and Jarvis," continued Rocky, "we have come to the conclusion that someone in an organization labelled 'Worldwide Toys' was involved. We have a name, Stetson Poole, who ordered the hit. But we can't find any history of this name and who it belongs to. But it's from good sources that the connection between Worldwide Toys and Stetson is real, as is the connection to an Edwin Ware who runs what appears to be a phony detective agency in San Diego."

"How do you know it's phony?" asked T.

"Jarvis…" Rocky waved at me to explain.

I nodded. "I've met the man and been in his office, which is an empty space other than a table, chairs and a phone. When I broke in, I discovered a camera, and soon after, they sent two men to get me. I was able to elude them, but they left a threatening message on my car window to leave the case alone or I'd be dead."

"Knowing your nature, you didn't take heed to the warning," stated Wolfe, his wine glass gracing his hand, his diamond ring sparkling in the waning light.

"Correct. Though I did become much more cautious."

"Being the pest he is," said Rocky, with a wink. "Jarvis continued to dig, finding the connection between all the parties, and learning who their CPA was. Carlton Gilpin is someone we have tied up in the downstairs bedroom, and we're attempting to get him to give up his clients, who he has been laundering money for. That was part one of our plan to flush them out."

"And what is part two?" queried Giselle.

"The name 'Worldwide Toys' we believe, is a front, for smuggling in illegal guns and drugs into the US, to be distributed to various illegal organizations; gangs, mobsters and other groups who promote violence. All in the name of profit."

"Do you know who is running this operation?" inquired T.

"We don't know specifically," answered Rocky. "Though we do know a former boss of mine, Maximillian Conway, is involved, as well as the Chinese Government and people who work within the CIA or another US agency or agencies."

"Are these the same Chinese Government folks who were meddling in your life last year, Jarvis?" asked Giselle.

"Yes they are," I replied.

"What we plan on doing in phase two," continued Rocky, "is to steal one of their transport trucks that are hauling the guns and drugs. And then use it as leverage."

"Sounds risky," stated T.

"We've been watching them," I explained. "The trucks are mostly unguarded during transport, other than the driver and one passenger, both of which are armed. But we believe we have a way to draw them out. Done properly, we take them without bloodshed."

“That is where you two ladies come in,” added Rocky.

“I believe Giselle and I have the goods to do the job,” noted Kit. “Tight tube top or a bikini, showing enough skin to get any red-blooded American boy’s attention.”

“Not sure I brought anything like that to wear,” noted Giselle. “I was expecting to be working and not seducing.”

“We can go shopping for clothing to turn their heads before we bust them open.” Kit smiled at her words, and Giselle soon followed, nodding in approval.

“That sounds more like what I enjoy,” replied Giselle.

“And you won’t be alone,” added Rocky. “Jarvis and I will be nearby to render additional assistance if necessary.”

“Where do you plan to keep these trucks?” asked Wolfe. “Downstairs in your garage?”

“That part we’re contemplating on how to handle,” answered Rocky. “We’ll need a secure place to keep them. Preferably a large location. If anyone has any ideas, I’m open to hear them.”

One idea came quickly to mind, one which should work for what we needed.

“I have a possibility,” I said. “I will need to run with it on my own and see if it will work. If they agree, security wouldn’t be a problem. I can do this tomorrow.”

“Keep me informed. If anyone has any other options let me know. If we can’t come up with a suitable idea, we’ll improvise.”

“The trucks they’re using will likely have GPS for tracking,” claimed Giselle, her eyes closed and looking relaxed. “It will have to be disabled after you take them.”

“Yes, we have thought of that. Kit is a closet nerd, who can handle getting them offline.”

“Good, I’m no good with computers,” said Giselle. “Other than when they piss me off, then I just shoot them.”

“We will use that as plan B,” replied Rocky with a grin. “We’ve got the truck models they’re using when we were watching them. Kit wrote it all down. But we have no internet here, because I didn’t want any type of connection to the outside world that could be traced. She’ll have to do her research offsite somewhere.”

“I can probably find somewhere when we go shopping,” added Kit.

“And what will Wolfe and I be doing?” wondered T. “I’m

starting to feel left out, and I look lousy in a tube top."

"I have different tasks for both of you. Though it's not exciting, T, you'll be babysitting our guest, Mister Gilpin. It's not a fun assignment, but an important one. You'll be sleeping in that room as well. We'll work out how and when he'll sleep. Sleep deprivation will be our ally in breaking him."

T smiled, though he didn't look thrilled. But he couldn't argue about the pay. "I only need three to four hours' sleep a day. Got that way from my days on the street."

"Good. We'll give you breaks from watching him from time to time. I'm hoping to break him soon and get the information we need. We have his notebook, but it's locked out and he won't give us the password yet. But we'll have it in time and then maybe Kit can comb through the files and find what we're looking for."

Rocky got out of his chair to go grab a beer, asking if anyone else wanted one. I was thrilled to get more of his high-end brew. I might have to make room in my beer budget to keep a six-pack in the fridge back home. After he returned, he looked at Wolfe, sizing up the large man, who was enjoying his wine, swirling the liquid in the crystal tumbler.

"You're probably wondering why I asked Jarvis to bring you on?" stated Rocky.

"Yes I had."

Wolfe took a long drink of his wine, before standing up, to face Rocky. He had removed his jacket and silk shirt, now wearing a tight black Pittsburg Steelers t-shirt, his chest and arms straining at the cotton fabric. The fading sunlight reflected on his nearly bald head, as if a spotlight was shining on him, drawing you to notice his overwhelming, and dare I say, cool presence. He stood there looking directly at Rocky, waiting to hear what he had to say, his perfectly manicured index finger lightly tapping on the wine glass in his hand.

"I wanted your skill set for a couple of items. The first I will divulge now, the other at a later date. A man like you with your reputation, is what I was looking for. I want you to go and threaten Maximillian Conway and his wife. I want him off guard and looking over his shoulder. I'd do it myself, but I want him to keep believing I'm dead, at least for now."

"Threaten him how?"

“Anyway you want. Drop him a line. Pay his wife a visit. Follow him wherever he goes and make sure he sees you. Whatever works to spook him. A subtle threat would be best.”

“And if he sends someone after me?”

“Deal with it…however you want. I can tell you all about his head of security, Justin Lowery. And believe me he is no match for you. You might even put him out of commission as a warning. Injure him only for now. A broken bone would be good enough if he tries to make a move on you.”

His glass now empty, Wolfe went to pour himself more wine from the bottle on the table. If he had any feelings about his mission, he didn’t display them.

“When should I start?”

“Tomorrow is fine if you’re ready.”

“And when will I learn of the other task you have for me?”

“When we’re ready to grab those transport trucks, I will fill you in.”

“What about weapons?” asked Giselle.

“I have a locked room downstairs, with plenty of options to choose from. If we need anything else, we can get it.”

“I already got what I needed,” proclaimed Wolfe. “It was why I was late getting to Starbucks.”

Rocky nodded. “Kit has the sleeping arrangements. You’ll find cash money in your room as payment for your services, as well as a burner cell phone to use, programmed with everyone else’s number. As was explained before, don’t use your personal cells. Leave them off, with SIMs removed. These folks have a lot of connections. And we don’t want them tracking us down until we’re good and ready. Questions?”

I looked around, and no one seemed to have anything for now.

“I have one,” I said, breaking the silence. “Are you planning on cooking big meals like that for us every night? The gym downstairs is going to stay busy.”

Rocky looked at Kit, before answering. “Kit will work you hard and help you burn plenty of calories. All you have to do is ask.”

I looked over at her smile, which stretched from ear to ear. Hopefully he was talking about sparring as she had suggested. For if not I might be in trouble.

Chapter 58

I made it through the night unscathed, with sleep coming easily on the queen pillow-top bed. I was up and moving as the sun was rising, dressed in my running clothes, outside ready for a jog. In the fresh air, I saw Wolfe stretching, ready to go on a run of his own. He wore a tight, black, sleeveless water-wicking top and matching compression leggings that ran to the bottom of his calves, the material forming to his muscular tone as if it was painted on. Strapped to his right arm was a cell phone, with wireless headset in his ears, playing his workout playlist, his head and shoulders slightly swaying to the tunes. He finished stretching and took off running down the driveway. I decided after a quick warm-up to follow him, as he jogged on the road outside the house, a steady uphill climb ahead of us.

The sun was slowly rising over the mountains to the east, the air crisp but comfortable, perfect for a morning run. My playlist was playing as well, giving me rock tunes I enjoyed exercising to, the sound low enough to hear any traffic coming on the road. Starting slowly, I built up my speed, staying behind Wolfe, but matching his pace, though with more effort on my part, as he moved with grace and showing little strain.

It felt odd being on the same side of a man who only last year was hired to kill me, and was offered the job again, within the last few weeks no less. Our initial face-off had scared me like I hadn't been scared before, his presence and confidence difficult for me to match. But I had won the battle of wills, even convincing him the man that hired him; Simon Lions Senior was a lying, manipulative psycho serial killer. Though we didn't end up on the same side, we at least weren't at odds against each other, which was good for me, because he was the one man I wasn't sure I could defeat.

We were working together, which was good for our cause. He appeared to be a man of his word and did what he said he would do. Though at a high dollar cost, which didn't bother me, as Rocky was the one paying. A cost he didn't appear to have trouble bearing.

Sweat was forming, my pulse rate was steady, and I was starting to feel the climb in my calves at around the one-mile mark. I had no idea where this road led to, other than further up into the hills. I started to slow down, coming to a stop, knowing I'd reached my limit and would now turn around and start the slow descent.

Wolfe seemed to sense my stopping and did the same, turning around and passing me on the way back down, with little change in his exertion level.

"That was all you could take?" he said incredulously, while passing me.

I smiled, for I'd been challenged. Like all red-blooded males, I had to rise up and meet it, even if it killed me. I picked up the pace and headed downhill, catching up, and then jogging alongside of him, hoping my legs held up. On his left bi-cep I noticed a tattoo of Martin Luther King Junior with an inscription saying *Free At Last*. Fitting words on this powerful, proud man I was running next to.

"Damn, you're in shape," I said, impressed. "You and Rocky should go running. He is a machine when he gets going."

"Good to know *someone* might give me a run for my money. I thought you could hold your own."

"Been a tough year. I haven't kept up like I have in the past. Things on my mind have been distracting me." I wasn't certain why I was telling him this.

"It's those things that will get you killed in our line of work."

I couldn't argue with those words. There was a lot I needed to think over once this case was finished. These last few years had taken their toll on my body and mind, which was soon to reach forty in a few months. And this 'about to be forty-year-old' on his worse days felt much older, like the burning in my legs which never happened when I was twenty-five, no matter how far I jogged. I slowed down, hands moving to my hips, deciding to walk the last half-mile left to the house.

Wolfe slowed down as well, deciding to walk the last part with me. It didn't appear he sweated much, as his skin and clothing were dry. Mine was soaked, as was my hair, which I combed backwards with my fingers. The burn in my legs was subsiding, my heartrate slowly ebbing, breathing now under control. I wiggled my legs as we walked, hoping to keep the muscles loose.

"It appears you decided not to take the contract on me?" I inquired, once I found my breath.

"Still deciding," replied Wolfe calmly. "If an unnamed pain in the ass PI continues to cause grief, I might take the job. Especially if they up the price."

"I'll keep that in mind the next time I feel like being a pain the ass."

Wolfe nodded slightly "How is Sam doing after being shot?" His tone showing concern.

"Hanging in there. She is tough as nails and was back to work within a day or two. Not much short of death will keep her from the work she does."

"Did you track down the other man involved?"

"I did. Rocky broke his wrist when we tried to get information out of him. Not quite the same as a bullet wound, but close on the pain level meter."

He gritted his teeth in anger. "Good. I would have broken both wrists and possibly his ankles, before making him eat a bullet. I have a special hatred for men who hurt women. It is the one thing I won't do in my line of work." The bitterness in which he spoke showed a side I'd not seen before.

"Glad to see you have morals."

"A few," Wolfe replied, his voice calm again. "I probably can count them on one hand though. I'm hardly a saint."

No surprise there. Many times, I wasn't either, but I had my moments.

"I came to that conclusion last year. And if the outcome had been different, I'm guessing we wouldn't be talking right now."

He turned his head, staring with a professional coldness I'd seen before. "No, we wouldn't. Because you would be dead."

"I'd have done my best to prevent that from happening," I countered, though not convincingly.

"You would have failed." There was no expression of remorse of that possibility in his voice, leaving me with a frosty feeling, even though I was sweating.

"And here I thought we were bonding." I stated with a sigh.

"We're on the same side for this case, but in my business, it makes no sense to bond with people. For there is nothing to prevent it from being different the next time. Whether it be the contract from Whitelaw or someone else. You could again be the one in my crosshairs."

"You could simply decline the job, like you considered doing with Whitelaw."

"On what grounds?"

"That even though I'm a pain in the ass, I have a good heart and a fun sense of humor," I said with a gleeful smile.

Wolfe didn't smile back. "An attitude like that will get you killed."

"It may, but if I can't find happiness in life itself, then it isn't living, and I might as well be dead."

"You may get your wish. If I happen to be the one, then I have enough respect for you to make it quick and painless."

I lost my smile with that comment.

"What a nice gesture on your part," I said sarcastically. "I can't add a chicken scratch on the moral scoreboard for you with that proclamation."

Wolfe didn't respond, his cold, professional demeanor on full display, as we went up the driveway, then up the steps, in total silence. As we entered the kitchen, Kit and Giselle were making what appeared to be protein shakes in a blender with a motor that sounded like it could power a jet engine. Wolfe kept on walking while I grabbed an apple, thinking over what to have for breakfast.

Once the blender had finished, Kit poured out equal amounts into a glass and handed one to Giselle. After a sip, Kit turned and looked at me.

"Did you two have a good run?" she asked after wiping the shake from her upper lip with a napkin.

"Good workout, though not the best company," I replied after taking a bite of the apple.

"Not really a surprise from what I heard about him. Best to stay on his good side."

"He doesn't appear to have a good side. He was hired to kill me once in the past, but I convinced him otherwise. He says next time he wouldn't hesitate but would make it quick and painless."

Both Giselle and Kit smiled, though I wasn't certain why.

"Don't take it personal," declared Giselle. "I'm sure it's just business. If I was hired by someone, I wouldn't hesitate either. But I'm not certain about the quick and painless part."

I didn't feel much like smiling, for it was hard not to take it personal. Others had tried to kill me in the past, an action I'd been able to prevent to date, but had grown tired of confronting. I finished up the apple, tossing it in the trash, not thrilled at the likelihood I might have to look over my shoulder the rest of my life.

Chapter 59

After making two slices of toast and having an orange, I changed into jeans and a long t-shirt before taking the Durango, while Kit and Giselle took the Xterra for clothes shopping, with Wolfe in the back. He'd asked to be dropped off further in town where he'd get his own transportation for his intimidation task against Max.

I stopped off at a convenience store with a pay phone and called Manny. It was Sunday, and I assumed he was off working out or sleeping in after bedding one of his lady friends. Instead, to my surprise, he was at work when he answered.

"Where are you?" he inquired, not sounding pleased.

"I'm in town, but won't say where," I replied cryptically.

"You need to come into the station. There have been allegations made against you."

Great, just what I needed to add to my stress level. *Why couldn't someone call and invite me to a friendly dinner or out for drinks for once!*

"By whom?"

"That private eye, Edwin Ware. He filed a complaint against you for breaking into his office and injuring one of his associates. You and another man snapped his wrist bone, from what they're saying. They couldn't identify him though, only you."

I thought it over, wondering why they called the cops. My only conclusion is they were trying to bring me out in the open.

"I think it's best I stay away. This might be a ploy to track me down."

Manny sighed. "I hate to do this, but it's not a request. I'm in hot water here as well. Ware mentioned about the time we both pulled him over and rousted him. Claimed harassment and brought up the part about you tossing his keys on the roof. My boss wasn't pleased I was helping you. He was threatening to suspend me if I don't bring you in."

There had to be a way to get this to work out for me, my mind going over various options, but I couldn't see it yet. Me driving in and giving myself up wasn't ideal, especially if I was arrested. I didn't want to get Manny in deep trouble, since he'd been helpful, and I was hoping to ask him for more assistance today.

"I'll come in on one condition," I proclaimed. "I want to be able to meet my accuser at the station. I'm positive that is all he wants anyway, but I need to be sure. Can you call and tell him I'm coming in and that he needs to come down to identify me?"

Manny agreed to call Edwin Ware immediately after I hung up. He called me back in about ten minutes, saying Ware had agreed and would be there shortly.

I killed time driving around, not wanting to beat Ware to the station, happy not to be in a rush, before I headed to police headquarters. Hearing my stomach growl, I decided I might have lunch later at the Pit Stop Diner if I wasn't locked up for the day. *I wonder if they deliver to a jail cell!*

When I arrived, I stashed my gun under the seat and walked into the station, my eyes open for an ambush that didn't happen. Once I got to Manny's desk, he was sitting there, his eyes pointing to the other side of the room, where Edwin Ware was lounging, reading a newspaper. I took a chair across from Manny, smiling, though I wasn't sure why.

"I was beginning to think you weren't going to show," remarked Manny.

"I nearly stopped at the diner, since I was hungry," I uttered with a grin. "I wanted to make sure he got here first. Hopefully this won't take long, and I can chow down afterwards."

"Let's hope it ends like you expect… quickly. It will be great to get my ass out of a sling. If we weren't already shorthanded, my boss said he would have already shut me down from field work."

I felt bad that Manny had been reprimanded. Needing him as an ally would come in handy for what we had planned. I hoped this situation didn't screw that up.

Manny stood up and walked over to Edwin Ware where they began talking. After a couple of minutes, both came over to the desk as I stood to face my accuser.

"Mister Ware is now saying that it's all a misunderstanding and that he is willing to drop the charges," informed Manny.

"But on one condition," added Edwin. "That you and I have a private conversation."

This didn't surprise me in the least bit. It was what I expected. An attempt to draw me out in the open. Now I needed to know why.

"Really," I responded, feigning surprise. "And where would you like to talk?"

"Outside would be best," replied Edwin. "I'd prefer not to talk in here. Too many chances for people to eavesdrop. It will be perfectly safe."

He didn't show much emotion with his words, and his comment about being safe was a tad ominous. I had to pretend to believe standing in front of a police station would be a relatively secure area to talk, so I agreed.

Manny had him sign paperwork, and once finished, we stood outside on the sidewalk, finding a shady place to converse. He turned to face me once we were out of earshot of anyone around.

"That wasn't nice, what your friend did to Stefan's wrist," observed Edwin. "Going to be several weeks before he'll be able to do his job properly."

"A shame. It wouldn't have happened if he'd told us where you were," I replied. "It would seem your people are loyal to you."

"Indeed. They know what will happen to them. But I'm here now. Tell me what you want to talk about?"

I was ready for the question, an answer already formed. "Since you appeared unwilling to let us in on your operation, I wanted to mention that we're watching you and it won't be long before we know what you're up to."

Edwin let out a puff of air, appearing unconcerned. "Really. What do you expect to find?"

"Illegal activity perpetrated by people you work for. I won't go into details, but we're gathering essential data. And your little detective agency scam isn't scaring us away."

Edwin seemed to get a chuckle out of what I said.

"Nothing to find, as there is nothing illegal going on. But if there was, I'd have a message for you from someone who doesn't like nosy private eyes messing in their business."

I didn't say anything, just waited for the coming threat.

He glanced around before speaking. "There are powerful people involved, those that can make a mess of your life. And who can get to those you love with little effort." He paused, giving his best intimidating stare. "My advice is to walk away now before you or that attractive cop girlfriend of yours get hurt. And believe when I say it won't be pleasant. After which we come and end your life in a similar manner."

I mulled over what Edwin said, with the thought of slugging him in the jaw being a strong temptation, if it wasn't for where I was standing. I decided to counter his threat with one of my own.

"Funny you should say that, as recently I had a conversation with maybe the scariest man I've ever met, and you're nowhere in his league when it comes to intimidating someone. Maybe your boss is more frightening than you are, but I'll wait to see when we meet face to face, which I suspect will be soon." I took a step forward and pointed my finger at him. "But know this, that if anything happens to my attractive cop friend, no matter whose fault it is, there is nowhere on this planet you can hide from me and I will bring the force of many powerful suns down on you, which is another way of saying I will kill you!"

Edwin took a couple steps back at my words, possibly thinking I was going to punch him, a glimmer of fear on his face. Instead, I turned around and headed back into the police building, hearing him yelling at me to stop, though whatever he was saying came out in a stutter. But I didn't care one bit what else he had to say, happy to get in the final word. It had been a long year and I was tired of people trying to intimidate and scare me. Even if I didn't put the fear of God in him, I was happy to think I might have given him more to think about.

Back inside, I signed in, went to Manny's desk and asked him if he wanted lunch. He was enthusiastic about a free meal, and we walked over to the Pit Stop Diner, where I paid for burgers, fries and shakes, knowing I needed one more favor. We found a seat with a clear view of the parking lot as I wanted to keep an eye on the Durango to make sure no one messed with it. After a few bites, I made the request, the look on his face priceless.

"You need me to do what?" he said, nearly spitting out his soda.

"We need a place to stash a truck or two, preferably inside, for maybe a week or so. I'm wondering if you know anyone with a storage place or warehouse we can use?"

"What is going to be in the trucks?" he uttered after another bite of his burger.

"Best you don't know. But it's important to this case I'm working on. Remember the containers at the port we wanted to get a look inside? It's related to that."

Manny shook his head. "Man, oh man. I get out of one mess and you want to drag me into another."

"I don't need to bring you into it. You can play ignorant if asked. Just a name, if you have someone and I will handle the rest. We're hoping to keep it off the books for now."

"How big are the trucks going to be?" wondered Manny with a sigh.

"Probably box freight type, maybe twenty feet in length."

"I have a friend who runs a storage facility. I'm not sure if they have anything inside that large, but they do have space for larger vehicles for storing. If you're worried about it being seen, you can get one of those large canvas covers that go over trucks and RVs. He might sell them or if not, would know where to get a set."

"Where is it located?"

Manny gave me the name and looked it up on his phone, showing me the location. It was in Sabre Springs in the northeastern section of San Diego. I'd have to run it past Rocky, but it might work for what we had in mind.

"Can I drop your name?" I queried.

"I'll call and let him know you'll be contacting him. He owes me a couple of favors. But promise me when this is all over, we can go out for a night of heavy drinking and you can give me the whole scoop on what all of this is."

"Deal," I said, while holding up my paper cup with chocolate shake, happy he was helping me. "After we're done here, I may need one more favor." I added, pressing my luck.

Manny shook his head. "I'm reaching my limit for what I can do without getting myself in more trouble."

"I know. But I need you to delay Edwin. I have a feeling he is waiting outside, hoping to tail me. I can't have him find where I'm staying at. I need a clean getaway."

"If you want me to shoot him, you're out of luck."

I smiled. "No. Just stall him. It's a busy parking lot but once I leave, I'm sure he'll reveal himself. Then if you can pull him over and run him through the system, that should be good enough."

Manny thought it over for a minute, while finishing his fries. "Oh what the hell. I'm sure I can find reason to detain him. If he complains I'll tell the Captain he didn't finish filling out the forms before he left."

I nodded my head and thanked him, putting out my hand which he shook. After leaving I did a once over on the Durango, checking for anything suspicious, satisfied there wasn't a tracking device or worse, a bomb. Glancing over my shoulder while in the driver's seat, I got a good laugh at the sight of Edwin getting pulled over and yelling at Manny as I drove away, free of him trying to follow.

Chapter 60

It took a little prodding, but I was able to arrange space at the Oversized Storage Facility, thanks to Manny's friend, though it did cost most of the extra cash I had to keep it off the books. Once I was back, I let Rocky know all that had happened, including my run in with Edwin Ware and about the location to store the trucks. He didn't appear worried about Ware but knew we would have to keep any eye out for him, for he was a key player. And he seemed in agreement the storage unit would work, if we were able to pull off the theft and get the cargo trucks there without getting caught.

Rocky had spent the day working on Carlton, finally getting him to give up his password on his notebook. When I arrived, Kit had the notebook and was searching through the files. She ran into an entire folder of password protected files which had a different code than the one logging into the machine. Rocky went back to Carlton, and after twenty minutes, returned with that password, aggravated he wasn't given it in the first place, which I'm certain Carlton paid for physically.

"Silly games he is playing," tutted Rocky with a stern expression. "I don't have time for it and it cost him a few broken fingers." He handed Kit a piece of paper with several passwords. "Different password for different months of data. He said there are sub-folders named via the months and years."

Kit started working her way through the files, opening several of them. It was a lot of information and certainly material we wouldn't completely understand. Someone with a knack for financial documents and spreadsheets would have to define what it all meant. But it certainly was important.

"We should copy all of these files and preferably get them stored to a cloud server somewhere," decided Kit.

Rocky handed her a flash drive that was 256GB in size, one of three he had, two remaining in the package.

"We have no internet here at the house," said Rocky. "It was your idea to keep us off the grid here, in case they tried to track us down. A lot of digital fingerprints left behind when you browse the web."

"I wasn't lying," replied Kit. "We can make multiple copies on these flash drives, but they can be easily erased with a strong magnet, stolen or lost. Always best to have them in a secure cloud location as a backup to give us leverage. The information then can be shared from there with whomever you wish."

"How do you suggest getting the file uploaded to the cloud?" I queried.

"We can find an internet café we can hook up to and upload them. Though it will take a while depending on how many gigabytes of data there is, as they often don't have the most robust speeds. If we split up at different locations, it will be faster."

"You and Giselle start working on that now," declared Rocky. "Then tomorrow we head out to watch their movements. Once we feel good about our plan, we can decide when to act. I'd like to get this done this week if the timing is right."

Once the files were copied onto the three drives, Kit and Giselle left with two of them, the third locked away by Rocky for safe keeping.

Sitting on the deck, relaxing on a lounger, I twisted open a beer, taking a long drink. I thought about a text I had quickly sent to April from my main phone, turning it back off before returning to the house, warning her about the threat to her and others I cared for. I didn't worry about her, knowing she could protect herself. Still this dangerous life of mine was getting far too complicated. And visions of retiring from this profession returned, with starry-eyed thoughts of starting the bar and grill floating through my mind once again. A pipe dream but one I was seriously thinking of pursuing.

Out on the deck stepped T, with a beer in hand. He sat on the chair next to me. I was certain the job of watching Carlton was boring him, and it was good he got a break from him from time to time. He was looking good, an air of confidence in his stride, as life had improved for him from his days on the streets. We had talked a time or two about his military service and the toll the Iraq war he had participated in had taken on him. He'd found help once we'd gotten him connected to the VA.

Once he had navigated through the mountain of government red tape, he found the proper help that guided him through the pain, the friends he'd lost, and the injuries he'd endured. He was a big strong man, but even the strongest can be brought to their knees by the ravages of war.

"How is Carlton doing?" I asked.

"Once we straightened out his fingers, he was doing a tad better," replied T with a smile. "And at least he has clothing on now and not just a towel covering his lap. I wasn't thrilled having a half-naked man in the room with me."

I chuckled. It would have made me uncomfortable too.

"Thanks for setting me up on these last two jobs," commented T. "It is nice getting paid well above minimum wage."

"Glad to help. You did a great job on the Hester case protecting the son. What is it like being in the action again? Not quite the same as Iraq, but it can be tense."

T nodded. "Not the same, but it brings back memories of those days. Therapy has helped me face the problems instead of burying them. To this day, I continue to see most of those horrible moments of death and destruction in my dreams, but not as often. My therapist says they will never leave me completely."

"Ghosts and horrors of our past will forever haunt us," I added knowingly. "I have many as well."

"What do you do to face them?" inquired T.

I held up my beer. "And I work a lot and try to have sex whenever possible. Unfortunately, April is back in Denver right now, leaving my nights open for the ghosts to invade my thoughts."

T laughed. "Good you have a sense of humor about it. Often best to laugh instead of cry."

I couldn't agree more, and we continued to chat about various things, until exhaustion overtook me, and I fell asleep in the lounge. My dreams were all over the map, including April and a pair of unknown male faces trying to get to her; toys, guns and drugs littered in the background. I tried to warn her, but couldn't speak, doing my best to save her, as she was in danger. Then I saw the faces of Simon Senior and Junior both laughing, scalpels in their hands ready to carve into skin of an unknown, faceless victim. I reached out to try and stop them, then suddenly rose up from the chaise, a bellow coming from my throat, the feeling of a soft hand on my arm. My eyes opened to see it was Kit staring down at me, a look of concern on her face.

"Are you OK?" she asked. "That appeared to be one hell of a

nightmare."

I shook my head to clear it, not sure where I was at first. I felt sweaty, with the cold shakes, even though it was quite warm in the later afternoon heat.

"I'm fine," I replied eventually, though not believing my own words. "A stressful, realistic vision I was having. What time is it?"

"Nearing 5 p.m. Giselle and I are back and we're going to work out and then spar. I thought I'd see if you wanted to join us. Your chance to show us how good you are in hand to hand combat."

It sounded like a good idea, a way to shake those horrible visions. I nodded, before going to my room and changing into my workout clothes. When I joined them, they each had on gloves, and were alternating, holding punching pads while the other boxed into them with a series of jabs and hooks. They both looked skilled, with quick reflexes, good snap, with power behind each punch. I grabbed another set of gloves after stretching, preparing to join them. Kit turned to me with the punching pads, and I snapped off a few good shots that felt invigorating.

"You know what you're doing," observed Giselle.

"I trained with a county sheriff in my hometown when I was younger," I remarked while continuing to work the pads. "His way to get me back on the straight and narrow. I was a bit of a troublemaker growing up."

"Weren't we all," replied Giselle.

After I was done, Kit grabbed a full-length padded strike shield, and handed it to me. I faced her and she began with punches, followed by a series of kicks. Front, side, semi-circular and roundhouse, a couple of which nearly knocked me off balance. Her movements were fluid and powerful, her technique flawless.

"Not bad," I said with admiration, as she backed away smiling, her breathing heavy.

"My turn," announced Giselle.

I repositioned myself to face her, and soon felt myself backing up with the force of each punch and kick. She was stronger, though her technique not quite as good. They both were powerful and formidable warriors who could handle themselves. Not to be outclassed, I handed the pad to Kit.

"Let's see what you've got, big boy," said Kit, throwing out a challenge.

I worked the bag over with a series of punches and then did a spinning kick, though I wasn't as good on the kicking side as they were. Kit held her ground well, though a couple of my punches pushed her back. I finished with a flurry, and then backed up, my arms weary from the intense exercise; heart racing, sweat covering my body, a satisfied sensation I could compete physically with the other professionals in this group.

"Not too bad," said Kit as she walked towards me. "Kind of exciting, seeing you all hot and sweaty."

She was within a few inches of me, a wicked smile on her face, having tossed the pad to the side. Then suddenly she jumped me, wrapping her legs around my waist, twisting and flipping me to the padded floor, where she was sitting on top of my chest, lightly tapping my face with her gloves.

"Never let your guard down with a desirable, dangerous woman," she said with a joyous smile on her face. "That is how we get you. And now we're even for what you did back at the hotel room."

Her move had surprised me, a lesson learned, as I lay there catching my breath from the thud my body took when hitting the pad. I heard Giselle clapping, thrilled at what her female counterpart had done. Kit stood up, extending a hand, pulling me to my feet, a tired grin on my face. I probably should have retaliated but decided against it and wasn't sure I had the energy or the skill to match her, even if I chose to.

T walked into the room with an announcement. "Rocky is planning on starting dinner soon," he said. "Time to wrap up your workout, though I think I might like to join in next time, if I can break away from CPA sitting."

I stripped off my gloves, announcing I was going to take a shower, heading upstairs to my room. I stripped down, and stepped through the glass door, enjoying the hot water from the rain showerhead above, the comforting liquid rolling down my sweaty skin.

Grabbing the soap, I began to suds up starting on my face and working my way down, when I heard the door open and someone stepped in, their warm female body now rubbing up against my backside, her hands caressing my firm abdomen and working their way down, bringing excitement to my tired body. I let the water rinse the soap out of my eyes and turned to see Kit standing there smiling.

"Hello," I said, trying to remain cool.

Kit's hands continued to work my lower regions, now grabbing my butt cheeks, her naked, exciting form caressing against my front.

"I enjoyed our workout," she purred. "I thought we could work off our stress in another more strenuous and pleasurable way."

Even with all the moisture in the shower, my mouth had gone dry. I worked up enough saliva, to speak.

"I'm not sure that is a good idea," I stammered, trying to keep calm.

"I can feel one part of your body that disagrees," she cooed, while grabbing onto me with a light stroke that further engorged me.

"Difficult for that part of my body not to be aroused, with a beautiful naked woman in the shower giving me a hand job." I noted.

"I'm sure I can up the pleasure orally."

Kit started to slide down my body, kissing my chest, but I grabbed her arms, pulling her back up.

"No matter how much my body wants to, I must say no," I said begrudgingly. "A few years ago, I'd pick you up and take you without a second thought. But my mind is in charge these days, and I must remain faithful to the woman I'm with."

"She doesn't have to know, because I won't tell," claimed Kit, who then kissed me hard on the mouth.

It felt good, but again I pushed her mouth away, then hugged her, whispering in her ear.

"You're a wonderful, sexy woman, any man would give his left nut to make love to. But I'm not that guy anymore. I'm sorry."

There was a pouting look on her face as she realized she had lost. "I have to say I'm disappointed, but I will respect your wishes."

"Good. Now can I continue getting cleaned up? I'd like to eat because I'm famished."

"Sure. But only if I can watch. Then leave me alone to finish what I started on my own. It appears the handheld showerhead will have to suffice."

I laughed and finished cleaning up, finally stepping out and drying off. Walking out of the bathroom, I tried to ignore the moans of pleasure I was hearing, the lower half of me protesting and wishing I'd been a part of.

Chapter 61

We began our new round of surveillance the next day, this time rotating those of us who were watching, and the vehicles we were using, in shifts. Rocky paid to add an eighties black Jeep Wrangler and a 250cc blue Ninja crotch rocket motorcycle, which I rode.

On Monday, there were no trailers coming in all day, only men walking the grounds outside for security. On Tuesday, it was much the same, only it rained most of the day, the guards remaining inside, while I got soaked sitting outside with the bike, my raingear doing a poor job of keeping me dry.

As we hit midday Wednesday, the rain had cleared up, but no deliveries, which was making Rocky anxious. He was worried we had scared them away when Kit and I got caught, and when we'd grabbed Carlton. He started talking about getting inside the warehouse to see what we could find, which would have been a risky endeavor, when finally, after lunch time, two tractor trailers showed up with a shipment. Now it was a matter of waiting to see if any of the onsite box cargo trucks were loaded and left with a shipment.

Both Kit and Giselle had taken up station a distance away from the warehouse, sitting in the Jeep working on their tans, the soft top off today, since the sun was in full bake mode. I waited on the motorcycle at a different location, keeping eyes on the facility. Rocky was in the Durango with T, having chained down Carlton and knocking him out with enough sedatives that he didn't need to be guarded. Wolfe hadn't returned from his mission, with Rocky saying he was already preparing for his next task, though what that task was he didn't detail.

It took about an hour to unload the two trailers into the warehouse, and once they pulled out, two box cargo trucks took their place, and were loaded in about thirty minutes. Another fifteen minutes passed, and then two men got into each cab, both armed from what we could tell. They pulled out one right after the other. A third Ford F250 then followed out after them, with two more armed men inside.

They had changed up the routine, and added more security, probably in response to us. Rocky quickly called me on the walkie-talkie we were using to keep us all connected, the communication device built into the full-faced helmet I was wearing.

"Jarvis, can you follow them and get a lead on where they're going?" he ordered. "We will stay here for now and see if any more trucks arrive."

I agreed, putting on the leather jacket and gloves, and took off after them, keeping my distance. The nice thing about a motorcycle is you can lag behind, but quickly catch up. And with the lane splitting laws in California, one can maneuver through heavy traffic easily, though at additional risk. The route we started on was different than the one they had used the last time I had pursued them. They tracked back to Newhall Ranch Road but headed west this time to I-5 and then south on the multi-lane interstate, where they cruised in the middle lane unconcerned about the heavy traffic, the three vehicles lined up one after the other.

I remained several cars back, in the stop and go traffic, with clear sight on any changes in their route. We drove through a mountain canyon into the San Fernando Valley where the Transverse Range circled this region north of the Los Angeles Basin.

It was maybe twenty minutes later when they moved to the far-right lane, soon exiting on Highway 118, known as Ronald Reagan Freeway, then heading west for a short time before exiting on San Fernando Road, a sign showing we were headed to Whiteman Airport.

After a couple more turns, we entered on the north side onto Airpark Way, where the winding road took them to a series of long buildings where they parked, near a medium sized turboprop cargo plane. I continued past to the south side of the airport, finding a blind corner for cover.

I removed my motorcycle gear and maneuvered the maze of buildings until I could get an eye on them with my binoculars. They were loading the boxes onto the plane, small enough to fit inside, but big enough that it took two people to carry them. Feeling exposed, I worked my way back to the bike, when a security vehicle for the airport pulled up, rolling down his window.

"Can I ask what you're doing here?" said the Hispanic man, dressed in light blue shirt, with badge and label with the security company name on it.

Without Kit there I couldn't use the 'we were making out' excuse. I remained calm, my mind quickly coming up with a response when I looked over towards the runway, pointing at a plane taking off.

"I love seeing the planes coming in and out," I said, with my friendly, non-dangerous smile on full wattage. "These smaller single and dual prop aircraft glide through the air with such grace."

"You really shouldn't be here," he sternly remarked, his left arm extended, pointing at me. "Please exit the facility or I'll have to call the police. And don't come back or you'll be arrested."

I smiled, putting on my gear and slowly drove out, as he followed me. I headed back the way I came, stopping in the nearby AutoZone parking lot, where I made a call to Rocky.

"Where did they end up?" he asked.

"They went to Whiteman Airport this time. As before, they were loading on a cargo plane, but I was chased away by security before I saw them leave. I'm assuming as before they're headed with the goods elsewhere for further distribution."

"Head back this way and we'll meet at Rustic Eatery. Get off at Magic Mountain Parkway exit and head west. It's on the right in the same building as a Starbucks."

I made my way back, taking about twenty-five minutes, with no issues finding the place. I walked in and the four of them were sitting at a small table eating sandwiches. I went to the counter and ordered a chicken breast sandwich with cheese, fries and ice water to drink. Once I had my food, I pulled up a chair on the side, taking a small corner of the table, enjoying a large bite of my meal—I was hungry.

"It would appear they have changed up their routine," remarked Kit, speaking in low tones since the restaurant was busy.

"And added more security," noted Rocky. "Probably because of them catching you and Jarvis making out."

Giselle looked at Kit with a questioning eyebrow raised, bumping her shoulder. "Way to go, girl!"

"It was all an act to throw them off when they spotted us. Jarvis isn't even that good a kisser!" Kit smiled at her jab.

"Ouch!" I said, my pride hurt. "My lady back home would tell you otherwise. Our lip lock was a reflex reaction and not passionate. But nevertheless, we need to figure out if we can pull this off with the resources we have."

Rocky was looking out into space, chewing on his beef sandwich. There was little doubt he was fully invested in getting this operation to work, and to find out who was the person behind the death of his wife and son. Closure was important to have, allowing one to move on. I needed the same with my brother Flynn's death. Rocky had risked it all to get where he was and wasn't about to stop now.

"Yes we can, with the proper planning and execution," he declared confidently. "We may need one more day of observation to plot out how it will go. When we get back to the house, we can go over the routes they used and look for locations that will work best for us. Then tomorrow we can give it a go, depending on if they have more shipments coming in."

"If there are two cargo trucks, are we going to grab them both?" asked T.

Rocky nodded. "The more we have to bargain with, the better."

"That would be six guns we need to take out," I added. "A lot of firepower to go up against. It would be good if we had Wolfe helping as well."

"He is off on another task and isn't available," said Rocky dismissively. "It is up to the five of us to handle it."

"Risky," I claimed.

Rocky looked at me with a serious but confident glare. "It always is with what we're doing. And it's never stopped us before."

I shrugged, he was correct. To me though, this seemed like the longest odds yet we'd gone up against.

"Don't worry, Jarvis," said Kit, putting her hand on mine. "You've never had a secret weapon like Giselle and I. We can neutralize several of them with the proper attire showing the right amount of tits and ass. They'll never know what hit them."

Having seen and felt Kit's in the warm, wet shower the day before, it was hard to argue with her confidence.

Chapter 62

We worked out our plan, everyone contributing to what they felt would work best. We ironed it out and went over it several times, using paper road maps of the area to plot out the locations where everyone would be waiting. We talked and plotted up until midnight, then we called it a night, Kit whispering in my ear one more time that she was up for adult pleasure as I headed to my room.

I whispered thanks, but no thanks and shut my door, wondering if I should have a gun on the nightstand for protection. Or better yet an adult toy to give her as an alternative. It appeared operations like this heightened her libido.

It seemed as if the sex gods were testing me, trying to get me to give into the passion of these women. First Emily and now Kit. Though Emily's tricks of seduction always had an ulterior motive, where Kit appeared to be in it for the release of pleasure only. Emily, I could ignore with no problem, but Kit had been the ultimate challenge of my will. I was proud I had passed, though wished those sex gods would quit teasing me and move onto someone else. I didn't need the distraction, my mind and energies best spent on this case.

The next morning, I was up early getting in a quick run, this time on the treadmill, then moving to the weights, working the upper body building strength and confidence at what lay ahead. Rocky and Kit joined me, and we spent time sparring, Kit and I giving Rocky a few pointers, his boxing skills not up to ours. After a big breakfast and shower, I joined the rest of the team, wondering if this would be the day that we made our move to commandeer the trucks.

Today Rocky and T drove a black Ford F250 he'd picked up with Kit's help to closely match the security truck. How they continued to get these various vehicles, I didn't care to know. I wondered if we were using hot cars with phony plates. Driving the Jeep with the top off, the ladies were decked out in tube tops and short shorts as part of their distraction plan, while I was again on the Ninja.

Rocky, T and myself alternated watching the warehouse,

making sure not to be seen, while the ladies waited at a location that allowed them to go in several directions, once Rocky gave the go ahead. I was feeling confident we could pull this off without a hitch but knew there was a good chance that something would go wrong and we'd have to improvise.

We had prepared for several possible contingencies that might arise. But minimizing bloodshed was important, otherwise it could bring us larger problems with the police that we didn't want. And with the weapons our opponents had, bloodshed would be difficult to avoid.

If they continued to use the trailing security vehicle, we knew it had to be neutralized first. Getting familiar with the area had contributed to how we would attack it. It would have to be taken out without drawing attention and before they had entered either the interstate or the highway. They had used only one route out of the warehouse, up Rye Canyon Road. When they reached Newhall Ranch Road, they would go left or right.

The first set of trucks went left as I followed them on the bike for a while, figuring their destination was Whiteman Airport, the same as yesterday. I followed until they got on I-5 and then headed back, satisfied in my assumption. It was now a waiting game to see if there was a second set of trucks today.

It was several hours when the two cargo trucks returned. Now it was a matter of if they had a second plane to meet on their agenda.

The sitting, watching and waiting was always the hardest and most boring part of surveillance work. The weather was comfortable, the sun warm, but not a baking heat, with a nice breeze, a few clouds or possibly smog providing filtering of the rays. Keeping alert to everything going on around you without zoning out was challenging. I listened to music in one ear, always odd with stereo music, as you often only heard half of the instruments and vocals, while the other ear remained alert, waiting for a call from Rocky on the communication earpieces we were using. I needed to be ready quickly when he gave the word. I was anxious to get this operation going, confident in the skills of those I was working with. Hopefully the skills of our opponents weren't up to ours.

From a distance, it appeared the two trucks were being loaded. It was about ninety minutes later when they pulled away from the dock, the drivers and passengers preparing to leave. Rocky told us to quickly get into position, and I jumped on the bike and headed to my spot, parking, gun in hand but concealed. I stood on the side of the road, waiting. If everything didn't line up properly, we would call it and wait for another opportunity.

Rocky and T showed up, T walking to the side of the road near me, while Rocky positioned himself. He had a tough job, taking out the rear tire of the trailing Ford security truck. Not an easy task in motion, though if he was lucky, it might slow down or stop if they hit the light at the intersection where we were expecting them.

He'd added a silencer to his Glock, concealing himself as best he could. Traffic wasn't heavy, as we could see them coming up Avenue Stanford, the cargo trucks in the lead, the Ford following. They weren't going too fast, the speed limit only thirty here, and as they approached on the two-lane road the intersection with Avenue Scott, Rocky kneeled down using a tree as cover, ready to shoot. The light was green and the cargo trucks rolled through, as the Ford started to slow down right before the light, its rear tire hissing from losing air, hit by Rocky's expert aim, the pop of his gun barely audible.

The passenger stepped out to see what had happened, and on cue, I ran out in front of the now stationary Ford, taking the driver's side, while T took the passenger. I opened the door, putting my gun into the ribs of the driver, who looked at me in surprise.

"Move and you're dead," I declared. "Don't be a hero. Turn off the ignition and hand me the keys. Nod that you understand."

He looked over at his partner, who was in the sleeper hold grip of T, struggling, but soon out cold. He looked down at the gun next to him, but I pushed the barrel deeper into his side. He got the message and nodded, while turning off the truck. I took the keys and put them in my pocket.

"What is going on?" came a voice over his handheld radio.

"Tell them nothing is wrong," I demanded. "You just hit the light. They should continue, and you'll catch up. Say one wrong word and this bullet will go right through you."

He nodded, saying word for word what I had told him. They seemed satisfied, and when the conversation was done, I pulled a taser out of my pocket and zapped him in the neck, knocking him out cold. I then grabbed his handheld radio, while T muscled the other man back into the cab. He then grabbed the man's gun and placed it on the dash for all to see. Rocky then pulled up next to the F250 with his Ford, and T jumped in as I tossed him their radio.

"We'll call it in," said Rocky. "And we'll let the ladies know they're on their way. Looks as if they're headed to Aqua Dulce. You know what to do."

I nodded and ran back to the bike, hopping on and back on the road. The call Rocky mentioned was to the police, to let them know two armed men had been seen in a truck, passed out. This would keep them tied up indefinitely, trying to explain what had happened and why they had guns.

With the truck Rocky had, he could catch up to the cargo trucks, appearing to be their security guards. With the bike, I could eventually catch up, ready for my part when the ladies did their thing.

The cargo trucks had turned right on Newhall Ranch Road, the eight-lane thruway, becoming six lanes, with lots of stop and go, going through several districts for many miles, before winding down south where it became Golden Valley Road. This was the same route I had followed them on initially, which worked well for our plan.

The ladies in their Jeep had sped on past us, moving to get into stationary position on the side at a bus stop section. As we neared the area, I moved past everyone, using the bike's speed, then getting in front of the first cargo truck. I then braked, putting on my turn signal, forcing them to slow down. I saw the Jeep and turned in behind them as they pulled out, timing it right and crashing into the side of the truck enough that it had to stop. The Jeep took the brunt of the force, the ladies shaken by the impact but unhurt, the damage to the cargo truck small. I dismounted and stood there, ready to act when I needed to.

"Motherfucker," I could hear Kit, who was behind the wheel of the Wrangler, yell. "Look what you did to my Jeep."

Giselle stepped out from the passenger side, in tight jean shorts and tube top. She walked over to the passenger's side of the truck, holding her hand to her mouth, as if in shock. The door opened and out climbed the passenger, a large, pale white man, in faded jeans, tan jacket and black boots. If he was armed, he was hiding it under his jacket or had left it in the cab. Giselle walked up to him and put her hand on his arm.

"Are you both OK?" she said. "Oh my, that could have been horrible. Sweetie, are you alright?" She was talking to Kit.

"I think so," answered Kit, her body shaking as she walked over, leaning into Giselle. "Daddy is going to be pissed at us. I don't think the Jeep is drivable. Look at the damage." She put her hand to her mouth, a look of concern. "He is going to dock my allowance and that will seriously cut into my beach and party time."

I could see the top button of Kit's shorts were open, revealing her swim trunks, or possibly, knowing her, a section of her *naked* lower half. The man was staring, a grin forming on his face. He waved for the driver to join him, which he soon did, another large Caucasian, dressed nearly the same.

"I guess we need to exchange names and numbers," said Giselle sadly. "She isn't kidding about her dad being pissed. Maybe we can work out an arrangement. Reporting this would ruin our exciting day. Do you guys like to party?" As she said it, she hip-bumped the driver, whose eyes lit up as if it were Christmas."

"Hell yes!" said the driver. "But it will have to be after this delivery. Once that is done we can party all night if you'd like."

"Oh my…that sounds great," cooed Kit her hands on his chest. "Forget this accident and buy us a few beers, and my friend and I can provide you enjoyment you'll remember for a long time. We like to team up, if you know what I mean."

They were both so mesmerized that they had no idea the two men in the other truck had already been disabled and dragged out onto the side of the road. I walked over, looking at Kit and Giselle and gave them the signal, while tossing the taser to Kit.

"Sweat dreams, boys," said Kit, her tone cold.

She took the taser and zapped the passenger in the side, and he slumped down, then hit him again in the neck until he was out cold. Giselle kicked the driver in the groin, karate chopped him on side of his head, then grabbed the taser from Kit and zapped him. I walked over and started dragging the bodies to the roadside.

"Good job, ladies," I said. "Let's get that GPS offline."

Giselle had found the keys on the driver, tossing them to Kit, who climbed into the driver's seat. They had a third-party GPS system, which she found right away, and pulled all the wires out, disabling it. She then fired up the engine, as Giselle climbed into the passenger side.

I waved at them, and they headed down the road, while T drove the other truck, its GPS disabled too. Rocky had the Ford, while I drove the bike, leaving the damaged Jeep behind. We were off to the storage unit, which was a lengthy drive. But it looked as if we had accomplished our mission and had obtained two big bargaining chips.

Chapter 63

When we arrived at the storage facility, Manny's friend led us to the location where the two trucks would be parked, and provided us huge canvas covers for the trucks to further shield them. Once backed in place, with a set of bolt cutters, Rocky removed the lock from the back gate of one truck and climbed up inside. I was on edge in anticipation of what we would find. We would look silly if there was nothing in the back other than toys.

He opened the first cardboard box, dug around inside tossing out various toys which had me nervous, before finally finding what he was searching for. He stood up, holding in his hands a fully automatic rifle, of which I was unfamiliar.

"This is a Chinese QBZ-95 automatic rifle," he noted, admiring the weapon. "Used by their military. It has a thirty round magazine and uses 42mm ammunition, made in China. I imagine there are boxes of ammo in here as well."

"Then the Chinese are involved?" I asked, figuring it was proof of their involvement.

"Likely. Let me see if I can find any drugs."

Rocky opened two other boxes, before he found wrapped up packaging under a pile of large, stuffed bears. He pulled out a bowie knife and cut into the package.

"Probably opium," he said. "Heroin or crystal meth another possibility."

We went to the second truck, cutting open the lock, finding it was loaded with much the same cargo, though with different types of illegal guns and drugs.

"Then we have what we need to proceed?" I remarked, thrilled this phase had completed smoothly.

"Yes. Let's lock this back up and cover the trucks. I'm sure they have a replacement padlock in their store."

Once that was done, we returned to the house, happy with what we had accomplished. Now it was up to Rocky on where we were going from here. But everyone was starving, prompting him to grill up chicken, and fry potatoes, while Kit put together a salad.

Once we finished off the meal, we sat on the deck, each of us with a beer or glass of wine in hand.

"What now?" asked T, enjoying his second beer of the evening. It was an obvious and direct question.

"We let them stew for a few days," replied Rocky. "Mindful that it's always possible they could find us. It's a big area for them to cover, but we suspect they have a lot of resources."

"And then what?" queried Giselle.

"We let them find us, or more to the point, Jarvis," said Rocky with a smile.

This wasn't a surprise to me, Rocky and I had already discussed what to do if we made it this far.

"I will jump back on the grid and when they show up, I will then offer them a deal."

"Wouldn't they just kill you?" remarked T.

"Not with them wanting their merchandise back."

"You mean the trucks?" inquired Giselle.

"And Carlton," added Rocky.

T looked surprised as he drank his beer. "You're going to turn him over to them?"

"No. But they will think we are, once we show them we have the files. We have other plans for Carlton if he agrees."

"And if he doesn't?" wondered Giselle.

"He won't have a choice," I replied. "He knows they will likely kill him. He will make a deal with the Feds to get protection."

"When will that happen?" inquired T.

"Tomorrow. We want him off our hands before starting the next phase of this operation."

"Do you still need us?" wondered Giselle, pointing to herself and T.

I looked at Rocky, who shook his head.

"If you want to head back to wherever you came, I'm fine with that. Jarvis, Kit and myself should be able to handle it from here."

"I don't know," said T. "I'm really enjoying babysitting Carlton. He is such a pleasure to converse with."

After the laughter subsided, I went and got another beer. It would be my second and final one for the night. I needed to remain clear headed, in case Kit tried her seduction routine one more time. I didn't need a repeat of the Roni incident from my past.

"Once I get things arranged for Carlton to be picked up, you can head out, T," I said. "You can even fly back on the same flight if you'd like to spend those last couple of hours with the stimulating CPA."

T laughed, finishing off his beer and tossing it into the recycle container. He walked over to the rail and stared out into the distance, darkness starting to set in, a cool, damp breeze coming from the west.

"Giselle, you can take off at any time," added Rocky. "I'm assuming if anyone asks, you've never met me, or Kit."

"My memory is always erased after any job like this," replied Giselle. "You've nothing to worry about. If you ever need anything else and the pay is the same or better, you can always track me down. Jarvis has a good number to reach me at. I'm going to retire for the night. It's been a pleasure."

Giselle stood up, giving fist bumps to everyone, while Kit stood and hugged her, whispering in her ear, which brought on a smile, before she left us for her room.

"I think I'm going to retire as well," said T, while turning from the railing. "It's been a long day."

"If you can hang in a while longer," Rocky said. "You can help me inform Carlton of where he is going next. If he doesn't like it, you can pop those fingers of his out of place once more."

T smiled and waved for Rocky to lead the way, leaving Kit and I alone together. I finished up my beer, wondering what pass she was going to make at me this time.

"We're alone," said Kit. "And I see a goofy smile on your face."

She wasn't lying. "I'm just waiting to see what indecent proposal you toss at me this time."

Kit frowned. "I'm leaving my dirty thoughts to myself. I've learned my lesson. My bad luck the good-looking guy in the group is a choirboy."

"Hardly. I'm working on being faithful, something that has been hard for me in the past. It's good practice, you're certainly a smoking temptress."

"Not to worry. I've found that showerhead has a setting that provides extreme ecstasy, without having to worry about someone else's pleasure." Kit ran her hands down her body, as if in ecstasy.

I smiled. "Then I don't need to worry about locking my bedroom door tonight!"

"No but I'll leave mine open in case you change your mind. I'm sure you have a couple of tricks in you to trump the showerhead."

I laughed, being flattered by the offer. But I'd sleep alone, dreaming about the one I was passionate about, April.

"Thanks for helping find my sister's killer," said Kit seriously, switching to a quieter tone.

Even with her temptations and the danger I'd faced, and would still face, I was happy to make a difference.

"We haven't found them yet, but I think we're getting close. Let's hope no one else gets killed in our pursuit."

As we sat contemplating, Rocky walked back on the deck, a look of satisfaction on his face.

"He is a go for turning himself in," he said.

"What did it take to convince him?" asked Kit.

"My charming personality and the will of my soul."

"I suspect it was a little more than that," I remarked, interlacing my fingers and cracking my knuckles.

"True. But he bent to my wishes before I bent his fingers again. I believe the memory of the pain was enough to make him understand. Now you just need to arrange things with your FBI friends, and get him out of here alive."

"I'm going to retire as well," announced Kit as she went to hug Rocky before leaving the room.

Rocky and I were alone, one of the few moments lately we had time to talk. I looked at him, the powerful man I knew, nearing the end of the mission he'd spent years in pursuing. He stared up into space looking at the clear black night sky, a waxing crescent moon, with stars sprinkled all around it.

"How are you doing?" I asked of him, knowing all he had been through, hoping he'd share the pain.

"Good," he replied, looking back my way.

"It's been a long road for you. All you've endured to get to this point. Are you ready for what is coming?"

"You know the answer to that. You've been there yourself. I'm ready to close the loop one way or another."

"It took its toll on me. I'm sure you're no different. Losing those you love leaves permanent scars that never heal."

Rocky nodded, a stern expression on his face, the muscles in his arms and shoulders tensing up.

"Maybe not completely, but once I avenge their murders, I know I will have honored their lives, by taking the lives of those involved."

I thought of the name on his boat, labelled as a reminder of what he needed to do.

"Is that where the name on your boat came from?"

"Revenge is all I have left…I will see it through to the bitter end."

The air grew chilly with his words. I stood up, understanding his fierce emotions. I placed a hand on his shoulder, then walked away, wishing and hoping this prideful man found the peace he was desperately searching for amongst the violence he was about to commit and face.

Chapter 64

Catalina was receptive when I called, not a single curse word to be heard after I explained on the payphone what we had for her. She even conferenced in Desmond Price to get his take on what to do. They quickly made arrangements for a private charter jet, which arrived late afternoon on Friday at Van Nuys Airport.

I drove Carlton and T to the airport, as they'd agreed to fly T back to Denver, dropping them off at a closed section where the two men got on board with no hassle. I handed Catalina a flash drive and told her about Carlton's notebook, which he was carrying. They flew off back to the Front Range, eager to dive into the financial details of what was going on. I left out the part about what our next plans were and drove back to San Diego, making a quick stop at a location to survey, before dumping the Durango in a parking lot, and taking a cab to a hotel in Torrey Pines, near the famous golf course that hugged the Pacific, where I enjoyed a quiet evening of rest and relaxation.

The next morning, I brought my phone back online for good, anticipating they would track me via my digital fingerprint, which was fine, for I was prepared. A quick text was sent to April letting her know I was doing well, that T was returning to town, the case nearing a conclusion and I loved her. She responded all was good with her and that she loved me too and couldn't wait to jump my bones when I returned. A sentiment I shared wholeheartedly.

After breakfast, I took the hotel shuttle to the airport and rented a car; a modern Ford Mustang that I wanted for speed. Driving the newest version of the classic car had good and bad merits. It had many nice conveniences, but I missed the basics of my Boss 302. Though I would have liked the heated leather seats for the cold days of Denver winters.

My destination today was to visit Maximillian Conway. It was a Saturday which led me to believe he was either home, playing tennis or golfing. Since Wolfe had been tasked with putting the fear of God in him, I decided to try his home first, which was in La Jolla.

I parked in his driveway and stepped out of the car. A man was outside smoking a cigarette, a large handgun under his armpit.

Extra security at the house was a good sign. Wolfe had obviously made an impression.

"What can I help you with?" remarked the man after seeing me, dropping and crushing his cigarette, a hand on his gun barrel.

"I'm here to see Maximillian Conway," I said confidently.

"He isn't taking visitors right now. You'll have to leave."

"Tell him it's Jarvis Mann. I'm here about the threat on his life. I have information that will shed light on who is involved."

He stepped in closer, the gun now down at his side. "I said leave."

"If you say so."

I turned as if to leave and then punched him right above the sternum and below his Adam's apple. It caught him completely off guard, and he gagged to breathe, his frame slouching. I grabbed the gun arm and twisted the Browning free from his hand, before pushing him back into the arch on the front entrance. I looked at the gun and the safety remained on. I popped out the clip and ejected the bullet in the chamber, tossing everything into the bushes. I then grabbed him by the shirt and dragged him through the front door.

"If you can talk, call for Mister Conway," I ordered calmly.

It took him a minute to find his voice, then he finally called out. Max walked in, dressed casually in black jeans, a long-sleeved white dress shirt, sleeves rolled up to his elbow, his bare feet in black leather loafers. As he saw who I was, he let out a long sigh. My popularity in southern California was starting to match that of what I had in Denver, which I took great pride in.

"You need to improve your protection," I declared. "Someone a whole lot better at killing than I am is after you. The guard, your wife and you would be dead if it had been the killer I know is on the job."

"What do you want?" inquired Max.

"We need to talk…in private. I have important information you need to hear."

I released his sentry, and Max told him to go back outside. He then waved, taking us down a hallway and then into his office. It was huge, with a massive oak desk, expensive leather chair, large screen TV, a fully stocked bar and a gigantic plate-glass window with a wonderful view of the ocean. Max walked to the bar, asking me if I wanted anything to drink, which I declined. He poured himself a glass of dark liquor with a couple cubes of ice in a tumbler, before sitting down in his high-back chair.

"I'm listening," he said, after a sip.

"There is a contact on your life," I said, while standing near the window, enjoying the view.

"I'm aware. A man payed a visit here at the house and scared my wife, before coming to see me."

"You know who this man is?" I asked.

"I do. A well-known killer named Wolfe."

Several birds were circling above the water, enjoying the breeze.

"Then you know his reputation."

"Yes. He is extremely expensive, with a nearly perfect resume."

"What did he say to you?" I asked, playing dumb about his predicament.

"That I had seven days to divest myself from all my business ventures, or my wife and I would be dead." Max took another sip from the tumbler, his hand a little shaky. "Or I could buy him off by doubling what he was being paid."

"Which was?"

"Twenty-five thousand."

I whistled at the dollar amount, even though I already knew it.

"And what are you planning on doing?"

"I haven't decided yet. Divesting would take a great deal of time and cost me a lot of money. Not only in getting a low-ball value for what I own, but the massive taxes I'd have to pay on the Capital Gains."

"Then fifty thousand sounds like a bargain." For a man like him, it was petty cash.

"Possibly. But I don't like being threatened or squeezed for money." He took another sip, then swirled the glass, the ice making a clinking sound. "You said you had information."

I turned from the window. "I know who hired Wolfe and why."

Max turned his chair to face me, his eyes wide in anticipation.

"It's someone after you for the death of his wife and child. The trail is leading back to you."

Max leaned forward and stood up, sitting his glass on the desk.

"It couldn't be!" Max said, full of anguish.

I nodded.

"You can't mean Garrett!" Max moaned, a shocked look on his face.

I nodded again, letting his reaction play out.

"But I thought…he was dead. At least for good this time."

I shook my head, his emotions immediate. Max grabbed the tumbler and downed the rest of the drink, and then went over, filling it up, his hand shaking while holding the scotch bottle.

"You have to believe me," Max said after drinking half the glass. "I had nothing to do with their death. I'd never hurt a woman and a child…a baby even."

I walked over and sat in his chair. It was soft, comfortable and probably cost over a thousand dollars. Oh the life of luxury; one I'd never live, but enjoyed tasting from time to time.

"He believes you did," I insisted forcefully. "And even if you didn't, you probably know who did. That is why he is coming after you, to clear the ledger…to even the score, if that is even possible."

He drank the rest of the glass and poured again, adding more ice. I wasn't sure of his tolerance to the scotch, but it wouldn't take long before soberness would slip away. Loosening his tongue to reveal all was good, but I didn't need him passing out before I'd gotten what I'd came for.

"I don't know what to do," he said, standing there, his hand continuing to quiver. "I'm in a bind either way. If I find out who killed them, they will kill me."

"Then you *know* who it is that ordered the hit?" I rocked back in his chair, the leather as soft as I'd ever felt.

His head lowered, thinking over an answer, before speaking. "A hunch…maybe."

"What about your head of security, Justin Lowery? I hope that wasn't him I encountered outside, as you would be in big trouble. Could he be involved in ordering the hit?"

"No that wasn't him. Justin is too busy with other tasks besides protecting me. He has his own…*agenda*." Max walked over to the window, now looking out upon the blue water, the waves washing over the sandy shore. "It's possible he may have played a part. I turned a blind eye to all of it, knowing it was business, no matter how uncomfortable I felt about it. I really did want to walk away, but they wouldn't let me."

"Who is pulling the strings on all of this?" I asked, my feet now resting on his tabletop, thoroughly enjoying the position I was in.

"I'm not really certain. They have this detective agency that does their dirty work. Edwin Ware is their main security man. He is a mercenary with military skills, and a readily available vicious team to squash any resistance."

I scoffed. "I've run into his men and I've beaten them. But I know there are more out there looking for me. I expect to be visited by them any day now."

Max downed more of his drink, as he leaned against the wall. I got out of his chair walking to the other side of the room, looking over shelves of trophies, diplomas and accolades. Tennis, golf, degrees from expensive colleges, and several businessman of the year awards. All on display showing a successful man who was strong and powerful, who I was witnessing falling apart before my very eyes, mostly from fear.

"Stetson Poole," I said, after turning around to see he'd retaken his chair.

He delayed again answering, looking at the remaining liquor in the tumbler, as if it would provide the answer.

"A code name for someone important in this organization."

I frowned, not that he could see, for he couldn't face me.

"You told me it was one of Garrett's aliases."

"I'm sorry. A ruse I used to throw you off. It's an alias to the man running this operation."

"Guns and drugs?"

He nodded half-heartedly, now leaning back in his chair. At least he hadn't got more to drink. He was feeling his limit.

"Is Stetson the man who ordered the hit?"

He shrugged. "Possibly. Though I have no idea who he is. We've never met."

"And he has ties to the Shark Tail Detective agency and Edwin Ware?"

"Yes."

I headed for the door, looking back at him, his eyes closed, a trickle of tears running down his cheek, the look of a beaten man.

"If you have any recourse to him, let him know we will be meeting here real soon. Both Rocky and I."

Max looked up, unsure who I was talking about.

"You heard me, tell them Rocky is coming after them and nothing is going to stop him."

I walked out of the house, the guard still searching the bushes for his gun. I strolled away, happily knowing I'd left an impression that would trigger what we were hoping for.

Chapter 65

I picked up the tail I'd been watching for in my rearview mirror a few blocks from the Conway house, which is what we wanted. I had rented the Mustang to give me a power car to elude them, even paying for the rental insurance which I never did, in case it got damaged. In the end, we *wanted* them to catch me, but not too easily that they'd get suspicious.

I drove down the road like normal, stopping at a McDonalds' drive-thru to get a drink and snack. They laid back watching me, sitting in their newer Chevy Camaro, then following me as I left. It was their muscle car against mine and I planned on using that muscle out on the roadway.

I worked my way to La Jolla Village Drive, using the onboard GPS, which I'd also paid for, having it direct me to I-5. The sweet voice told me when to turn, going north, where I merged into the late Saturday morning traffic, which wasn't overly crowded, the multi-lane interstate showing me room to work with. I merged to the far left and slowly pushed the gas pedal, the engine roaring to life, and was soon going the speed limit of sixty-five miles an hour, the road clear in front of me.

Checking the rearview mirror, I saw them a couple of cars back, weaving around slower vehicles, to catch up. Soon they were matching my speed. I increased to seventy, passing Torrey Pines, then Del Mar Heights, North City, Solana Beach and San Elijo Lagoon. I planned to use as much of the free mileage I was allowed on the Mustang driving up the coast, taking my followers for a joyride while keeping to the speed limit as not to attract any police car's running radar.

The new Mustang was performing beautifully. The ride was smooth, the powerful V8 engine roaring down the road effortlessly. As I watched the coming exits judging the room I had, I now was going to test its handling.

I was nearing the Poinsettia Lane exit in Carlsbad, and did a sudden lane change across five lanes, right before the turn off, causing a lot of horns to honk, but thankfully not an accident. I roared down the exit faster than I should, hoping to hit a green light, but failed. I had to slam on my brakes and go to the shoulder of the road, around three stopped cars.

I took the right turn, after a momentary stop, again with horns-a-blaring and roared down the road, zooming through a couple of green lights, before turning right on Batiquitos Drive. I followed it before it started to wind and took a left into a housing community. I drove around coming to a cul-de-sac, where I parked and waited, enjoying my McDonalds vanilla shake and salt-free fries. The shake was thick and the fries cold, having sat in my car all this time. I had watched my rearview mirror on the entire drive, knowing I'd lost the Camaro, as they couldn't make the lane change as quickly as I did. I gave it twenty minutes and took a different route back to my hotel, thankful for the bevy of multi-lane road options here in California.

When I pulled into the parking lot and stepped out, two men came up to me. When I reached for my gun, one of the men showed his, warning me to stop. I nodded, as the other came over and took my weapon, waving me to go to their car. I climbed into the back seat of the dark blue Cadillac XTS, where Stefan was sitting, his left arm in an air cast. I smiled, and he punched me with his good hand in the jaw, a good shot, though not jarring. I played my part perfectly so far, internally pleased to be where I was.

"Feel better?" I said, rubbing my cheek.

"I will when I get even with your large friend for breaking my wrist."

I snickered. "I warned you if you didn't talk that is what he would do. You're lucky he didn't snap your arm completely off at the shoulder. And I will warn you again. It would be a mistake to go up against him. Next time he'll likely kill you."

Stefan didn't seem convinced, the macho blood running through his veins making him fearless. He shrugged as if he didn't care, which was fine with me. A man's ego can often lead to his demise.

"Were those your men in the Camaro following me earlier?" I inquired.

"You thought you'd gotten away from us, didn't you?" he proclaimed with a beaming smirk.

I shrugged. "They ate my dust, after I lost them. I should have deduced they would have backup. My bad for not being more diligent." I was convincing with my lie.

"We have long arms that reach everywhere. You won't slip free from us for long."

"We've done well up to this point," I said with a grin, while pointing to his injured arm. "Would you like me to sign your cast as a memento?"

"If you do anything stupid, Garth up front will shoot you," Stefan said in a grumble, not finding my humor funny.

I looked over the seat to see one of the two men pointing his Sig Sauer at me. They must have gotten a volume discount on the German made weapon.

"Loved your songs, Garth," I said, jokingly. "But I was sorry to see you sold out and went to Vegas."

Garth looked confused by my humor and frowned. "Shut up!" was his only response.

Stefan told the driver to go, and we were off, back on I-5 where I had lost his other men.

"No blindfold?" I commented. "I'm guessing you aren't worried about where you're taking me."

"No. We're going to take a walk on the beach and have a conversation."

"Darn, I wished you'd told me that. I didn't bring my sunscreen."

"Sunburn is the least of your problems."

He was probably right but walking on the beach couldn't be all bad, short of the sand getting in my shoes. They likely wouldn't kill me in such a public area; at least I hoped not.

The car headed south on I-5 past Mission Bay and then exited onto I-8 heading west. We entered the Ocean Beach district, once I-8 ended, and then took several roads until we hit the Voltaire Street parking lot, near the Ocean Beach Dog Beach. I sat and waited patiently until the door opened and I was led out to the public area where there were many dogs running, leash free, enjoying the sand and water with wild abandon.

The two men that had sat in the front of the car followed Stefan and me as we approached Edwin Ware, who was throwing a tennis ball for his black and brown German Shepard to retrieve, each time getting a little more sand on his mouth and snout, not that the canine cared.

Edwin looked at me when I walked up, a sour expression filling his face, before tossing the ball once again. He was in beige shorts, an orange tank top, his feet bare as he carried his shoes. His skin was tan, as was many in this state, the warm sun a year-round bronzing treat.

"Let's go for a walk," he said.

I nodded, walking beside him, admiring his beautiful dog running in full stride, gleefully enjoying the exercise. Checking out the other breeds present, Labrador Retrievers seemed to be the most common; black, chocolate, yellow and golden, and other canines from small to large, all enjoying the day among themselves and their owners.

"I believe we have things to work out amongst us," remarked Edwin. "Right now, you're costing us merchandise and money, meaning our customers are unhappy not getting what they were expecting. We need to come to an arrangement to get this resolved. I'm here appealing to you to return our goods before we have to get nasty."

"I believe you've already gotten nasty," I replied, tutting. "Attempts to kill myself and people I know, and threats against those I care for."

"Does it matter if I tell you it can get much worse?" Edwin pointed out.

"I'm sure it can, but it doesn't matter because you don't scare me, and I can give as good as I get, as you've seen."

"I could turn you over to Stefan and he will make you rue the day you stole from us."

I did my best not to laugh. "Not going to happen, because I have answers you and your boss want. Answers about who is behind this and where your merchandise is."

"I'm certain we can beat that out of you." He said it as if he was talking about the weather, calm and cool.

"No need for violence, as I will freely say who is involved. But I don't know where the merchandise is. For it was moved before I came back out into the open."

Edwin grabbed the ball from his dog, who didn't want to give it up. He pulled a treat out of his pocket before feeding it to him and then tossing the ball as far as he could. I thought about telling Edwin he threw like a girl to aggravate him but held that to myself.

"Ok then. Tell who is behind the theft of our trucks?"

"I'm surprised you haven't already figured it out. You tried to kill him twice, both times failing, though the first time you successfully killed his wife and son. He is out to get the men responsible. He already has killed at least one who was involved. But he wants the rest, including the money man."

Edwin nodded, keeping his emotions hidden. His dog ran off with the ball this time, laying down in the sand, tired of playing. I understood his emotion, I was tired of playing our crazy game as well.

"It would appear Garrett Owens is difficult to put down. The question is what do we do to put an end to this?"

"Simple…he wants to meet, with *all* the major parties embroiled in this endeavor. We know Maximillian Conway is caught in the operation, reluctantly. As is a woman high up in the Chinese Government. And we know someone in the CIA, or with ties to them, is involved. He wants to meet them all and has a proposal that he believes will be beneficial to all implicated."

Edwin sighed. "I will need more than that to take up the chain of command."

"That is all you get. He has the trucks and your CPA, Carlton Gilpin, with all his files. If you don't agree, then he takes it to the FBI and brings you all down."

"How do we know you have Gilpin?"

I pulled from my pocket and handed him a flash drive.

"Files from his notebook. Detailed ledgers of the money he was laundering for you. Oh…and this is not the only copy."

He held the drive in his hand, a frown on his face, before putting it in his pocket.

"And if we kill you?"

"He goes to the feds immediately. If I don't call him back this evening by 5 p.m. then the deal is off. I have two promotion hungry contacts at the FBI, both of which you don't want to go up against. They're tough and ruthless. With the information we have, your operation will be taken down in time. At the very least it will mess it up to the point where you'll have to move it or shut down, losing a whole of money and leaving you with numerous pissed off clients."

Edwin shook his head, not happy with what he was hearing.

"I'm sure a few of those clients might take their anger out on all of you," I added. "Honestly, I'd deal with us. You might be surprised at the results."

We had walked up to where his dog was, and Edwin crouched down to pet him on his stomach, as he rolled in the sand. I heard him use the name, Zeus, which seemed like a proper name for such a strong dog. Maybe someday I'd be home enough or live somewhere large enough to enjoy the company of man's best friend.

"None of this is pleasing to hear," said Edwin, standing, Zeus now on his harness and leash. "I will have to contact my people to see if they agree. If they do, what is next?"

"We set up a meeting place, at Garrett's choosing. But there is a time limit. You have until tomorrow at midnight to call or the deal is off. And if all the parties are not at the meeting location, the deal is off as well. Is that clear?"

"I will take this up with my superiors. How do we get a hold of you?"

I pulled a piece of paper out of my pocket and handed it to him. "Here is a number. It is only for this use. It goes dead at midnight tomorrow." I stopped, pointing my finger at Edwin. "And a word of warning…I wouldn't waste time trying to find him, for Garrett is a ghost…a living breathing and *deadly* ghost."

"I will let them know. Anything else you want to add?" asked Edwin.

"Make sure your boys, especially Stefan, stay away from me and my girlfriend in Denver. If she or I sniff them being anywhere near either of us, the deal is off as well. And I don't think your bosses will be pleased."

"Fine. We will be in contact," uttered Edwin, walking away.

"I'm guessing I'm on my own to get back to my hotel?" I queried.

"Yes, you are. I wouldn't want you to think my men are anywhere near you and screw up this deal. I'm sure you can find a suitable ride back to your hotel."

Edwin walked back to his car, Zeus jumping in the back seat, his driver waiting to drive them away. I made it back to the Cadillac as Stefan started to get into the back seat.

"Can I have my gun back?" I asked of Garth, his Sig Sauer at his side.

Stefan nodded, and I got it back, tucking it away into my holster which was covered by a light jacket.

“This isn’t over,” warned Stefan. “I will get even in time.”

They all got in, pulling out and driving away, leaving me behind to deal with the sand in my shoes, hoping that was the worst annoyance I had to encounter for the rest of the day.

Chapter 66

I relaxed that evening in my hotel room, enjoying a room service dinner that cost an arm and a leg, found a funny movie with Tina Fey, who always made me laugh, and fell asleep with the door bolted, my 9mm on the nightstand within easy reach. *Boy, was I living the life.*

The next day, I hung around the hotel, enjoying their fancy restaurant grill, then walking the beautiful grounds while admiring the lush green of the golf course. I worked out in their opulent gym, swam for about an hour in their Olympic sized pool, and sat at the bar, enjoying a cold beer on tap while shooting the breeze with a couple travelling from the Midwest for a weekend away from their kids. All the while I waited for a call from Edwin Ware, or whomever, on another burner phone I'd bought just for this initial contact.

Once I heard, or didn't hear, it would be tossed away never to be seen again, on the electronic garbage heap of technology obsolescence our wonderful country built up higher every day. It was a relaxing day, one I'd not experienced much of lately. No one threatening my life or shooting at me. No car chases or gang members beating on me. No woman trying to seduce me at the pool or in the shower. It was the calm before the storm, but I didn't care and was enjoying every second of it.

After a light meal at the bar, I headed back to my room, feeling relaxed and a tad alone, wishing April was here to curl up with.

As I stretched out on the bed, the burner phone finally rang, the voice on the other end when I answered, was unfamiliar.

"We've agreed to your terms. Where and at what time do we meet?"

"Are all the parties we discussed going to be there?" I asked. "Because if they aren't, we'll not show up and turn over everything to the authorities."

It got quiet, as it appeared he'd muted the phone, probably for someone else listening in on the speakerphone to answer my question.

"Yes, all parties will be there. We will need an extra day for one to arrive. Tuesday will be the earliest we can meet."

This worked out well for our timeframe.

"Wednesday morning 7 a.m. at Triton Track and Field Stadium via the main entrance only. Don't be early or late. And don't call back on this number as it will be out of service. If you decide to back out and not show, then everything goes to the FBI. We will see you then."

I hung up the phone and removed the SIM card, breaking it in two. I grabbed the other burner phone and called Rocky.

"We're a go on Wednesday morning at seven," I said. "Are you ready on your end?"

"Do you really need to ask?" replied Rocky. "I've never been readier."

"Silly question on my part. I've already checked out the stadium after dropping off T and Carlton with the feds and I feel familiar with its layout and the area around it. It will be good to finally have this all wrapped up."

Rocky agreed and hung up. With the plan already mapped out several days ago, there was no further communication planned until we met up early that morning. We knew all wouldn't go according to how we schemed it, but it didn't matter. It was time to put a close to this once and for all. For Rocky's peace of mind, as well as my own sanity.

I sent a text to April to see if she was available to talk. Instead of answering back, she called me, though this time on my tablet via Skype. When the picture synced up, I saw a fetching face I had missed, her hair held back by bobby pins, her face tanned with full wattage radiant smile. I smiled back, thrilled to see her.

"This *is* a pleasant surprise," I said. "I don't recall us ever Skyping before."

"I thought it would be a nice change of pace, getting to see your smiling, attractive face. How have you been?"

"Hanging in by the skin of my teeth. Hopefully this will be all wrapped up on Wednesday and I can fly back home."

"That would be great. I've been chomping at the bit to get you alone."

I smiled my devilish grin. I had been longing for passion as well, especially after the temptations from Kit, which I decided was best to not bring up.

"I'm assuming no attempts to grab you by the bad guys I

warned you about?" I queried.

"Nothing yet. I've been working nearly non-stop since you left, padding my bank account for that Harley. But if they try anything, they're in for a world of hurt."

"I have no doubt you can handle them. I've seen you in action and you have the scars to prove how tough you are. Besides, I warned them if they tried anything, I'd bring the hammer down on them."

April snickered. "And I've seen your hammer in action, so I know how hard it can be."

I laughed. Oh how I missed our repartee. It was quite fun to banter back and forth.

"How are things going back in Denver?" I asked.

"Good. I stopped by The Mission to see how Sam was doing. Her arm will remain in a sling for another week, then physical therapy. But it hasn't slowed her down any, which is no surprise. That woman is driven by her mission, if you pardon the pun." April's face beamed at her humor. "I saw T there as well and he told me of your adventures. I wish I could have joined you."

"Why, do you like being a temptress?"

"These days only with you, but I'd have enjoyed tasering those idiots. Roasting their nuts with a thousand volts would have been fun."

I laughed out loud as I got up to get bottled water out of the mini-fridge.

"I can't tell you what we have going on next, but I will explain in great detail when I get back to Denver."

"Let's hope you survive to recount the story," said April, with a slight look of concern. "Do you truly think it will be over after Wednesday?"

"One way or another, as I'm getting homesick. Though I don't mind the weather here compared to winter and early spring in Denver, the amount of people and traffic here is off the charts compared to the Front Range. I'll never complain again about the crowded streets of home."

"Sure you will. It's what we do to pass the time stuck in traffic."

She was probably right. We like to complain, just to complain. Even when life was good, we find items to bitch about. It was part of the American spirit.

"I hope that isn't the only thing, or person, you're homesick for," declared April, giving a wink into the camera.

"I can't wait to get home and wrap my arms around you. Yes, I miss you like crazy."

"We could play and tease each other a little, being on camera," suggested April with the wicked tone, I'd enjoyed often. "A little virtual foreplay to tide us over."

"We certainly could. Though I need to make sure I don't over stress my hands, in case I need them for gun play in a couple of days." I feigned seriousness.

April laughed. "You'll need to do the proper finger stretches to limber up. I may as well, though I do have devices to assist in the pleasure department to prevent injury."

"Ah yes, the nightstand drawer of battery-operated devices. I wonder if there are others who use Skype for such joyful endeavors."

"There is little doubt of that," remarked April, sliding her chair back, removing her top. "Why else would Microsoft have paid 8.5 billion dollars for Skype? Their executives knew the value of virtual sex would pay them back in the long run."

"Let the games begin," I said, while removing my shirt, hoping the hotel Wi-Fi could hold up to the digital heat we were about to create.

Chapter 67

I slept in the next day, tired from my Skype encounter with April, but so relaxed that I slept for ten hours without waking. Monday and Tuesday went by slowly, time killed working out in the hotel gym to remain limber. I was ready to get on with what we had planned. I crashed early Tuesday night, and was up while it was still dark the next day, driving to the stadium where we would set up.

I drove the Mustang on North Point Lane, going one way, where it looped around and back the other way, parking on the side I needed for a quick escape. I strolled across the street to the entrance to Alex G. Spanos Athletic Performance Center and Training Facility, and how you entered Triton Track and Field stadium. This time of day, at around 5:30 a.m. the facility was closed. But Rocky had a key—where he got it from, I had no idea. He was there waiting with Kit and we were inside and soon out down the bleachers and on field level.

Triton Track and Field Stadium was part of UC San Diego, a modern facility known as one of the top track and field venues in the country. The nine-lane track surface circled the hundred plus yard grass field, surrounded on three sides by eucalyptus trees in full bloom outside the six-foot fencing that enclosed the stadium. The area remained dark, daylight many minutes away.

Rocky walked over to a locked gate and opened it, hopping into the cab of one of the vans and then pulling it onto the grass next to the broad jump lanes, while Kit closed the gate, locking it. We walked the area, watching for any signs of trouble and nothing presented itself, so then we headed over to the bleachers and sat down, waiting for time to crawl on.

"How have you two been?" I said with levity, trying to lighten the mood. "It's been ages since we've talked."

Rocky didn't seem to hear me, appearing to be 'in the zone,' as athletes would say.

"I think he is ready," replied Kit. "I've seen that look before and he won't come out of it until this is over."

I'd seen it too, though this appeared even more intense than I remembered. But the stakes were at their highest point in his mind.

"What is that other entrance down by the scoreboard?" I asked.

"It goes under the road and out to the soccer fields on the other side," explained Kit, while pointing. "The gate is locked, but we have the key if needed. You told them to come in via the main entrance by the sports facility?"

"I did. With all the tree cover surrounding three quarters of the field, it's hard to imagine them arriving in any other way. Unless they breach the fence area where Rocky pulled the van in."

"If they do, we'll see them coming and react," replied Kit, patting her 9mm that sat on a hip holster.

Everything went quiet again, and being stir crazy, I stood up, walking the track area, running through the plan one more time. I had my gun under my left shoulder, loaded, with four extra clips handy. I hoped I wouldn't need to use it, but nothing in explosive situations like this ever goes smoothly. I was concerned Rocky might go off and start killing everyone, vengeance consuming him, much as it did when he locked the wounded Vicente Duarte in the trunk of his car and set it on fire. But sitting down and having a heart to heart with him wasn't going to do any good. I'd need to keep sharp and watch all around me for danger. I was eager to get back to Denver to touch April's skin in person, preferring not to arrive in a body bag.

The sun was now rising, the warmth starting to build on this cloudless day. School was out for the summer, meaning there weren't as many people around the area as there would be during the school year. It was getting close to 7 a.m. I took double-steps up the bleachers to the entrance watching for their arrival.

Then as it crept closer to our deadline, four vehicles of various kinds pulled up, bodies exiting, a couple I recognized and others I didn't. I went back down the bleachers announcing they had arrived.

The three of us moved out onto the grass field, spreading out. I unclipped my gun, making sure it was handy. Rocky and Kit both did the same as bodies started walking down the steps of the bleachers.

Leading the way was Stefan, his arm no longer in a sling, the cast protecting his left wrist, in white slacks, aqua cotton shirt, gun holster strapped over top for everyone to see. Behind him was Edwin Ware, dressed in beige slacks, yellow silk shirt and beige jacket, which flapped in the wind revealing the gun under his armpit. Then it was Maximillian Conway, followed by another man I didn't know, which I assumed was Justin Lowry, his head of security. Both were dressed in dark slacks and cotton shirts, with no jacket, a holster on Justin, but no sign of one for Max.

Behind them were two other people, both who looked Chinese. One a woman probably in her early fifties, in a full-length gold silk dress, with a see-through black mesh top that looked like mosquito netting, and was open, flapping in the wind. Behind her, a large man in black jacket and slacks, with frog buttons, a red neck collar, with no apparent gun that I could see.

At the top of the bleachers sat another man, large in size, dressed in gray slacks and red polo who I didn't know. It was quite a group to keep track of as they approached, fanning out before us—Edwin, Max, and the Chinese woman in the middle.

"We're here," said Edwin. "Who is doing the talking?"

"I am," answered Rocky.

"We're listening."

"We have your two trucks full of your merchandise," stated Rocky. "And we have Carlton Gilpin, plus his files, which we proved to you via the drive Jarvis provided you. We're here to make a trade."

"What for?" asked Edwin, though I had already told him the answer when on the dog beach.

"The person who ordered the hit on me, my wife and child."

"And what happens to them?"

Rocky twisted his head to the side. "After we discuss on why they ordered the killing, they die."

Edwin nodded. "I only see one cargo truck and no sign of Gilpin."

"They're close by. Insurance in case you decide on acting rash."

Edwin turned to the Chinese woman. She was tall, nearly six foot, slender with small hips and chest, long black hair parted to the side and tied up in back with a shiny barrette that might have been garnished with diamonds. Her face was smooth and powder white, with dark eye liner and narrow manicured eye brows. She took a step forward, in front of Rocky.

"I have lost a husband and a brother," she said, her English a little broken, but understandable. "Are you the one responsible for their deaths?"

"No," replied Rocky, looking her square in the eye. "I've killed no one of Chinese nationality. Who are you?"

"Ting Feng," she replied.

"The party boss from China," I said, knowing the name from my encounter last year.

She glanced at me, walking over, looking me up and down.

"And who are you?" she asked.

"Jarvis Mann."

She nodded. "Yes, the detective, from what I gather. You're the one responsible for their deaths."

I shook my head. "No I wasn't. I battled Lok in a martial arts duel and won, but he was alive when we finished. A different man killed him, which I believe you're aware of. Your husband, Guo, threatened me, and I threatened back, but I did not kill him."

"You knew the parties who did?"

"One case yes, which I told Guo. But his death I wasn't involved in."

"You realize why I want the men responsible," said Ting, little emotion in her voice. "Much like this man here wanting those who killed his family."

"Their deaths wouldn't have happened if they hadn't threatened to kill me. I'm sorry for your loss but can't say I'm sorry they're gone. Hardly the same as the killing of his innocent family, who threatened no one." I pointed to Rocky.

Ting stood there, glaring into my eyes, a stare I matched, until she backed off and went back to Rocky.

"You understand my grief, don't you," she revealed to him.

Rocky looked at her for a minute and nodded. "I do, which is why I have a peace offering, a trade to mitigate our grief."

"It would need to provide extreme value for me to listen."

"It does. I have the man who killed your husband."

I was shocked by the words, not knowing this was part of the plan. Rocky waved towards where the scoreboard was, and three people walked up from the tunnel, the gate now open, one male and the other two, female. It was a slow trod, taking several minutes to see who it was. The first I noticed was Brandon Sparks, in his usual western attire; blue cotton shirt, black jeans and highly polished black cowboy boots.

Next was the woman to the left, and I recognized her as Sue, Brandon's assistant, dressed in white slacks, pink satin shirt, her face covered in sunglasses. To the right was a black woman, dressed in running shoes, loose blue jeans, white cotton shirt with three buttons open to show adequate cleavage, her short black afro unaffected by the wind, and a gun holster strapped to her right hip. I'd seen her a couple of times in the past, and knew it was Nia, Sue's girlfriend and bodyguard.

As they continued to walk, I saw Brandon's hands behind his back, and soon learned they were being held there by plastic strapping that bound his wrists together. It appeared he was being held against his will, his face sullen at his predicament, a prisoner at the hands of Sue and Nia, a fact that threw me for a loop.

"What is going on here?" I said to Rocky, not knowing what he was doing.

"I'm trading Brandon for the killer of my wife and son," replied Rocky, not looking at me when he answered.

"You can't do this…" I started walking towards him, but Kit grabbed me by the arm and chopped me on the back of the neck with a force that buckled my knees. I went for my gun, but it was gone, now in Kit's hand. I was seeing stars, as I kneeled there in the grass.

"Sorry about that, Jarvis," said Kit as she took two steps back. "But it has to be this way."

The sense of betrayal hit me like a wave, even harder than Kit's blow. The people who I trusted had taken a path I didn't understand or want to travel down. I feared where this was all headed.

"Rocky, you can't do this," I repeated, while rubbing where Kit had hit me.

"Stay out of this, Jarvis, and you won't get hurt further. This is between me and the person who killed Claire and Madden."

My eyes were clearing slowly, but I had no idea what to do. I was truly in the crossfire of all these powerful people with no one, it would appear, on my side.

"Did you order the hit on me and my family?" asked Rocky of Ting.

"No, I did not."

"Then who among you did?" queried Rocky. "I said they were

to be here. Was it you, Max? Or maybe Justin—he never liked me much. How about Edwin? Are you the mastermind behind all of this? I'm willing to trade the life of Brandon to be face to face with the man or woman responsible."

Rocky waved his hand towards the three to his left. Nia pulled a knife out of a pouch on her ankle and stabbed Brandon in the right kidney area. He screamed, dropping down to his knees and then over on his side. He moaned on the ground, barely moving, blood now covering the grass. Nia took the knife, wiping it on Brandon's shirt and then put it back in the pouch. I looked at Sue, and she stood there emotionless, without even looking at her dying boss on the green and red stained field. The surreal scene playing out before my unbelieving eyes.

"What the hell are you doing," I yelled. "Sue, you can't be a part of this?"

She looked over at me. "I'm taking over his business, with Nia by my side." Her words were cold, with no emotion.

Nothing made sense of what was going on. I put my head on the grass cursing where this was leading to.

"She is a strong woman," proclaimed Nia. "It was time for new blood at Sparks. She is in control now and will continue his business, including this deal he was trying to back out of. We're in all the way and are willing to invest more to make the operation even larger and more profitable."

Rocky walked over to where Brandon lay, his moaning clearly audible, life slowly leaving him. Rocky glanced down, kneeling to check on his status.

"He is slowly dying," he announced without feeling. "A fit end to his reign, which these two ladies will inherit." He stood back up and walked over to Ting. "Does that show you how serious I am? I've taken care of the man who killed your husband. Watch as his life slowly ebbs away. Now it's time for you to give me the killer of my family."

Ting nodded, convinced of Rocky's intentions, turned and walked back to her bodyguard, where she uttered, "I'm satisfied." I looked over the horrifying scene in a trance, wondering what would happen next, when everyone in front of us turned to the man sitting in the bleachers, now standing, clapping his hands, and slowly walking down.

“Wonderful performance,” he expressed gleefully, as he got closer. “My, oh my, Garrett, you’re truly a sight for sore eyes. You make a teacher dammed proud of his student.”

I glared over at Rocky, seeing a faint smile as the man walked to join us, and then embraced Rocky as if they were old friends. I had no idea what the hell was going on, but it couldn’t have been good.

Chapter 68

The embrace lasted for a couple of minutes, the man pushing Rocky away, looking at him, with a beaming sense of pride. His stature was like Rocky's; muscular build, large arms and legs, tanned skin and long, even blonde hair past his shoulders, much like Rocky used to have. Though he was probably fifteen years older, I could be looking at twins in many ways. It was eerie to see, and I needed answers.

"Who is this man, Rocky?" I asked, now slowly getting to my feet, an eye on Kit who I kept to my right to make sure she didn't karate chop me again.

"It's Rocky now?" said the man. "I like it. It fits you—for you're a rock of a man."

"He took the name from his son," I explained. "Who was killed brutally along with his wife."

"Isn't that beautiful to hear," he replied, unfazed by the news of their death. "You seem to be a friend of Garrett's. Who are you again?"

"Jarvis Mann—private detective. And friend is too strong a word. We were work associates, and on the same side, until today."

The man came over to size me up, walking around, staring me up and down. I rubbed at my sore neck, stretching it out, trying to look larger, though he had me by two inches and thirty plus pounds.

"So you're the one who's been a pain in our ass," he remarked. "You don't seem all that formidable."

"I have a tendency to surprise people with my skills," I replied.

"Maybe we should see it in action…"

He stepped in, taking a punch with his left hand. I stepped back and blocked it with both hands up. He came back with a right which I ducked, while throwing a body punch with my left, hitting him in the stomach which was hard as a rock. I don't think he even so much as felt it, as a smile filled his face.

I danced back, expecting an onslaught, which I got, as he used his body weight to drive into me. A left right combo came fast and furious, which I blocked before another left got through, hitting me in the cheek, which I absorbed but fazed me. I jabbed back catching his shoulder and a glancing blow to the chin, but then a right hook caught me square on the cheek, the hammering punch weakening my knees and dropped me to the ground. He stood over me, counting, reaching ten, before he stepped back.

My eyes cleared, though slowly, and I glanced at him, a brimming smile and not a bead of sweat showing on his face. He put out a hand, which I grabbed, as he helped me up.

"Not bad," he commented. "You let me in too close and I used my body weight advantage against you. But you do know how to box. How are you with a gun?"

I looked over at Kit. "If I get it back, I can show you!"

He laughed while pointing at me. "I love the attitude. We could use a man like you on our side. You appear fearless, or maybe dumb. Sometimes they're closely aligned."

I was shaking and rubbing my head, clearing the cobwebs. It seemed like an odd time to be offering me a job. I decided to ignore it, figuring there were important questions to get answers too.

"Again, I must ask, who you are and how do you know each other?" I probed hoping for a clear response.

"Shall I tell him, Garrett, or do you want to. Or should I call you, *Rocky*?"

Rocky looked over at me, a perplexed expression on his face. It would seem he might be in a little bit of shock about what was happening as well.

"You can tell the story," uttered Rocky, no emotion in his tone.

"Firstly, my name is Haywood Montgomery." He started pacing while he was talking. "I've been in the espionage business for years. That name is the one Garrett knows me by, it's the one I used when I found him many years ago. He was living on the street, using what I saw as a unique skill set to survive. I took him in and made him my 'ward,' as others would call it. Trained him to be everything I was; smart, tough, ruthless and a stone-cold killer when necessary. It wasn't long before he became the younger version of me. A person I was proud of and was grooming him to be my successor in my long line of businesses."

This was quite a revelation, Rocky being an apprentice to this man. But there were a lot of things about his life I didn't know.

"Is this true, Rocky?" I asked.

"Yes. He pulled me out of the streets and built me up."

"I was a proud teacher, molding his talent," added Haywood. "It took a few years of training, but before long, he was nearly my match. That is when I sent him out on his own to prove himself."

"Is that when you started working for Max?" I inquired of Rocky.

"Not at first. I worked freelance for a while and was making a robust living at it. Then Haywood called me up about an opportunity to work with Max. His business had grown and needed better security. It was my foot in the door to his organization. A link Haywood wanted to leverage, using his contacts for an operation he was working on. I'd worked for about a year before he approached Max with the idea. I told Max he could trust him."

"Did you know Rocky and Haywood were connected?" I asked of Max.

"Not in the manner he is describing here," replied Max, who seemed legitimately surprised by what he was hearing as well.

Haywood walked over to Max and patted him on the shoulder. "It wasn't important you knew. It was important you be sold on the idea, which you were. And made a whole lot of money, not to mention give you an avenue to launder your other ill-gotten gains."

"And now I'm caught up in this mess, with someone out there trying to kill me." Max looked sullen as he spoke the words.

"It's the price you pay, Max," asserted Haywood, his arm around his shoulder. "Didn't you know that someday we would be taking over your business empire? The hit on you makes it neat and tidy. At least once you divest it all to me, then I can take it over."

"*You* ordered the hit?" asked Max.

"No. That was Garrett…I mean *Rocky*. I liked his idea and plan to profit from it. Max, you'll sell to me or your wife will die, all with one phone call. I have people there waiting. Hell, you'll make money enough to live well. Though I want your assets at ten cents on the dollar, which would still be a huge chunk of change for you to retire on."

"You and Rocky have been working together all this time?" I asked of Haywood, my confusion on what was happening evident.

"No. I wasn't even certain he was alive until I saw him today. I knew about the hit, thanks to Justin feeding me information. Max's life is an open book to us, including your visit to him a few days ago."

Max looked like he was going to be sick, as Haywood continued to pat him on the back. He glared at his security guard, Justin, but he didn't react, just stood there and smiled, proud of his accomplishment.

"I should have known you were involved," said Max to Justin.

"An offer was made, and I accepted. Hard to turn down those types of dollars. If I were you, I'd make the deal and live longer."

Haywood gave Max one more pat and walked over to Rocky. "Now we need to resolve our business. We need the other truck and our nerdy CPA, Carlton, back. What do you say, Rocky?"

Rocky looked him square in the eye. "I mentioned my terms. I took care of Brandon for Ting, and now I want the person who killed Claire and Madden. Until that happens…no deal."

Haywood chuckled. "Oh come now, we're a team. We can put the band back together again. I'm giving you the opportunity of a lifetime to run this operation, while I sit on a beach drinking Mai Tais."

"Dealing guns and drugs?" spat Rocky, with spite in his voice.

Haywood frowned. "What…are you too good for this type of work now?" He came up to Rocky, nearly nose to nose. "I *know* the shit you've done in your life, son. Rousting drunks on the street, stealing food from stores, robbing old folks of their retirement money. Then I found you, and you moved onto a higher level of crime. Collecting protection money, beating up people who didn't pay their debts, and even killing those who challenged us. I hardly think selling guns and drugs on the street is any worse than anything else you've done in your life."

Haywood stepped back, the look on Rocky's face one of conflict and hesitation, one I'd never seen before. He seemed intimidated by this man. Much as I had been intimidated by Wolfe, though maybe for another reason. It could have been fear, like I experienced, or maybe it was respect for the man who gave him a life when he had nothing. It was hard to see him cower, especially when I knew how strong a man he was in a fight.

"What is the purpose of flooding the streets with more guns and drugs?" I protested to Haywood. "Besides the money, which I'm sure you love like a sexual partner. Don't we have enough of both in our country? People, many of them kids, dying every day from a hail of bullets or poison in their veins from your greed."

Haywood walked over to me now. If he put his arm on my shoulder and acted like we were pals, I was going to slug him. But he kept his hands to himself.

"Jarvis, do I sense a liberal bleeding heart inside that tough exterior? Don't you understand this is all part of the plan to keep the poor masses at bay in our great country? Give them guns and drugs and let them fight it out among themselves. The black, Mexican and Chinese gangs. The white militia looking to stand up and overthrow. All of them dragged down into the gutter, sticking needles in their veins, killing each other over turf. We even have the painkilling opioids, coke and meth for those in the middle class to mask their agony. Keep everybody bickering and brawling among themselves while we clean up with more money than we know what to do with."

"Then do the Russians or Chinese swoop in and take over the country?" I wondered aloud, looking straight at Ting.

"They can," boasted Haywood. "We don't really care. Whatever makes the most profit. Chaos is a money maker for us."

Much of what he was saying was burned into the headlines every day. People at each other's throats, either being in power or wanting to be in power. Whether it was at a national or local level, discord seemed to be the rule of our once mighty nation. I hated it but didn't know what I could do personally about it, other than to fight for what I thought was right. And right at this moment, on the turf I was standing on, was the need to fight for Rocky. He had fought for me in the past and now I would return the favor, whether he wanted it or not.

"Rocky, we've stood side by side and fought many a battle. You were there to save me from those two horrible men who were about to kill Melissa, Bill and his family. And we stopped them together."

"It won't do any good, Jarvis," mocked Haywood.

I ignored his words. "And then you helped me protect my sister-in-law and my niece, while I found who had killed my brother. And you were there when the brutal mobster was put down, a fist bump for his wife, who stood up to him for the sake of her son."

"Stop, before I deck you," said Haywood in anger, getting closer to me.

Continuing to ignore him, I moved to look Rocky in the eye.

"And last year, I helped you track down Vicente, the man who was paid to kill your lovely wife Claire and your beautiful baby boy, Madden. And together we stopped him too. We got those guns and drugs off the streets, the cops shutting down what was left of his operation."

Haywood grabbed me by the shoulder and threw me to the ground, as I tumbled in the grass. I felt the fall along my sore neck and shoulders, pushing myself to stand, refusing to let the pain ground me. I staggered back to Rocky, getting in his face.

"You and I took them all down, and even though it was in a violent manner, we won a victory over evil. And we can win again if we stand up to this man." I put my hands on his shoulders. "I know he meant something to you at one time, but you've evolved and become more of a man than he will ever be."

Haywood sucker punched me in the kidney, and I crumpled down. I tried to roll, but he kicked me in the stomach, knocking the wind out of me. I moved to regain my balance, when I saw him pull a switchblade out and come towards me. I did my best to stand, but I didn't have much to defend myself with.

"Enough," yelled Rocky, who grabbed Haywood and pulled him back away from me. "Who the fuck ordered the hit on my family!"

Haywood pulled free from his grip, closing the blade and putting the knife away.

"Haven't you figured it out yet," said Haywood.

"What I learned was a man named Stetson Poole was behind the killing," I gasped, talking through my pain.

Haywood looked surprised, or maybe impressed. I couldn't tell for certain.

"Where did you hear that name?" he asked while standing over me.

"A gang member. A relative of Vicente Durante. The man who was hired for the killing."

"Impressive. It would seem you're skilled at your job, Jarvis Mann."

With the pain in my side, I didn't feel all that good, no matter the compliment. I rose up to my feet, working through the agony.

"I'm good," I said, with a tense grin. "A royal pain in the ass good, I've been told."

"Who the fuck is Stetson Poole?" yelled Rocky.

Haywood smiled, it directed right at Rocky. "*I am*. One of my aliases. I was the one who ordered the hit on your family."

Rocky looked shocked and confused, the man before him a mentor, who had now admitted ordering the killing of those he loved. The conflicted emotions running through him like a freight train, his back now turned, hands to his head, body shaking like I'd never seen before. It was several minutes before he gathered himself, face remaining red from the internal torture, before finally speaking.

"Why?"

Haywood laughed, even though it wasn't funny. "To bring you back to who you were. That woman and child made you soft. You were no longer the man I knew, trying to exit the game I had constructed for you. You couldn't leave, because I made you what you are. I *own* you. And I wasn't going to let a little pussy turn you into a wimp of a man."

I scanned the parties around me, the words upsetting to hear. Kit's face was contorted in anguish hearing the facts about her sister, her hand still holding my gun at her side, body tense as if she wanted to strike. The red in Rocky's face was subsiding, though his muscles swelled with stress. Everyone else remained motionless, letting the scene play out before them, while I continued to press for answers, even though I knew each one would create a larger spark that would eventually ignite the powder keg before me.

"Then why kill Garrett?" I asked. I was trying to stroke Rocky's anger using his real name.

"He wasn't supposed to die. Those idiots screwed up. They were there, using a remote detonator. They were to set it off with the wife and kid inside the SUV, and with Garrett nearby to watch. But he was too close and was killed, or so I thought."

"Garrett wasn't the target?" I bellowed in shock.

"Absolutely not. Why would I kill my best student and asset? I was pissed at the time and smashed the foot of the idiot who screwed up as an example. He had to have a titanium rod put in to stabilize his shattered fibula and tibia. I probably should have killed him, but it would have put too much suspicion on things. Besides, pain like that is a better lesson than death."

He must have been talking about Eugene Washburn. No wonder he walked with a limp.

"You wanted him alive, yet you tried to kill him again on his boat with the two brothers," I proclaimed.

He shook his head. "*That* hit wasn't my doing. Justin arranged it without my knowledge, or Max's, once he had learned Garrett was alive. He didn't want him back in the picture, thinking his stature in the business would be lessened. He wanted to continue his rise in the organization. Isn't that right, Justin?"

Haywood walked over, looking at him, the fear clearly showing in his eyes. Haywood grabbed his left hand and held it up for all to see. He was missing the last two fingers.

"I was a little kinder to him than the idiot on the bomb trigger," declared Hayward. "My sharp knife lopped them off quickly. It only hurt him for a couple of minutes, isn't that right, Justin?"

Justin didn't say anything, only nodded. It would seem everyone paid a heavy price when Haywood was displeased.

"If I'd known Garrett was alive, I'd have done like I'm doing now and talked some sense into him. Making him see my way is the only way his life should be lived."

Rocky's fists were balled up, veins bulging from his arms, his face growing red again with anger. He was the powder keg about to blow and who knows what was going to happen. I looked at Kit, her frame remaining tense, hoping she'd give me back my gun if all hell broke loose.

"Don't do it, Garrett," declared Haywood, sensing his anger. "I have a man upstairs with a laser scope ready to shoot you. Now it's time to tell us where the other truck is and give us Carlton. Then we can all walk out of here alive and start our new business together."

I looked up to the top of the bleachers but couldn't see anything. But then as I scanned up to the roof of the athletic center, I thought I saw a gun, but couldn't be sure. In my heart I didn't think it would matter, Rocky wanted revenge.

Ignoring the warning, Rocky started walking towards Haywood.

"Stop or else," said Haywood, taking a couple of steps back, those around him moving out of the way.

He continued to move forward, his pace slow but steady.

"I'm warning you!" Haywood had his arm up.

Rocky raised his fists, ready to fight.

"Last chance," announced Haywood, before he rapidly pulled his arm down.

If there was a shot, I didn't hear it. Haywood looked back, but nothing happened. He turned and Rocky hit him with a haymaker straight into his face that I even felt. He staggered back, his nose bleeding and crushed. Haywood went for his knife, but Rocky grabbed his wrist, twisting it sideways before he could remove it and punched him again in the jaw, dropping Haywood to the ground.

At that moment I heard a shot, wondering if this was the end, but Edwin Ware, a gun in his hand he was about to use, dropped to the ground with a hole in his chest that signaled his end.

Kit tossed me my Beretta, the safety off and I pointed it at Stefan, shaking my head for him to drop his gun. He didn't heed my warning, looking to fire instead, the thirst for revenge clearly on his face. I shot him center mass, his body falling backward, dead before he hit the grass. Kit, her gun drawn, yelled for everyone else to drop their weapons, which they did promptly. I scanned to check on Sue and Nia, but neither of them had moved, Nia's gun on the ground as ordered. Brandon remained on the grass, motionless, likely dead. The two ladies didn't appear to be a threat to either of us, but I kept an eye on them just in case.

"Lie face down on the ground or you're *all* dead," I threatened. "Sue and Nia, don't do anything stupid and just stand there."

Everyone did as they were told, while Kit gathered up the guns, putting them in a pile at her feet. Then we both stood back and watched the fight.

Haywood had worked his way back up to his feet, while Rocky had shed his gun holster. He planned on finishing the man who'd killed his loved ones, by hand.

"We don't have to do this," bargained Haywood. "We were a team once and we can be again."

"Not anymore. You killed everything I loved in this world. And I won't be able to live in peace until you're sent to the hell you deserve to be in."

"Love has made you weak, son," observed Haywood.

Rocky looked over his shoulder at Kit and I, then back at Haywood.

"You're wrong. Love gave me the strength to live a better life. And now love is going to kick your ass."

Haywood smiled again. "Then bring it on, because I'm better than you."

Rocky pulled off his shirt and tossed it to the side, and I could see his scars glistening from the sweat and sun. He moved in, fists raised ready to do battle. Haywood shed his shirt, wiping blood from his broken nose on it before tossing it away. His muscle tone for a man in his early fifties, was impressive; bulging veins, bi-ceps, tri-ceps and pecks to match any professional body builder. He was bouncing on his toes, his hands down, waving for Rocky to come and get him.

Rocky was steady, moving forward, looking for an opening. He did a left right combo, both of which missed, but kept coming forward. Haywood continued to bounce, twisting his body, as if he was Muhammad Ali, while Rocky looked like Mike Tyson. I hoped the comparison was wrong, for Rocky would be in trouble. Maybe I should hope he was Rocky Balboa instead. Though he'd lost many a fight as well.

The two men moved further out into the grass, giving themselves room. Haywood stopped his bouncing for a second and attacked, driving two body shots into Rocky which he blocked, before hitting him with a combo to the face which he couldn't completely deflect. He shook his head to clear the ringing and made his move with two left jabs, one that landed to the side of Haywood's neck, but he just grinned.

"Is *that* your best?" mocked Haywood. "I guess I should have spent more time with you in the gym."

"I didn't learn *everything* from you," Rocky replied. "I had associates give me a few pointers leading up to this."

Kit and I looked at each other, hoping the sparring work we'd done with Rocky at the house would help. His strength and power was unmatched, but he wasn't a natural boxer. Hopefully we had given him tips he could use to sharpen his pugilist skills.

Haywood continued to dance in an attempt to wear Rocky down. I knew Rocky was in excellent shape but he had been through a long recovery from the torture he'd endured on his boat. My own recovery from my beating was painful enough and he'd endured far worse. He remained one of the toughest men I knew, and was younger, which could be an advantage. Though Haywood may have had more experience to fall back on, I didn't really know his capabilities.

Haywood got cocky, shuffling his feet too much, as Rocky charged him in a bear hug, driving him to the ground, his arms punching the air to no avail. Rocky's full weight landed on top of Haywood, and you could hear a pained gasp of air escape his lungs.

While on top, Rocky started pounding with his fists, first on the chest and then in the face, Haywood failing to block most of the punches. Haywood twisted his hips and tried to fling Rocky off him, though he wasn't completely successful, he did free himself enough to knee Rocky in the hip and was able to slip free and get back up, kicking at Rocky, hitting him weakly in the jaw.

"That was a cheap move," panted Haywood, blood coming from his mouth now, as well as his bent nose.

"All is fair in love and war," replied Rocky, once on his feet, blood trickling down his chin from his mouth.

"It's not too late. We can call it a draw and walk away. Bros before hoes."

"You're wrong. It *is* too late. Bro is going to die today for calling my wife a hoe."

Rocky came at him with a flurry of punches, first to the body and kidneys, then to the chest and finally the head. The flurry was lightning fast, the sweat and blood flying. There was a loud crack and down went Haywood, Rocky standing over the bloody body, his foot now resting on his chest.

"I twink u brok me juw," I could hear Haywood attempt to say.

"Good," asserted Rocky, as he began to apply pressure with his foot. "Time for you to die."

I looked away, waiting for the sound of more bones breaking, when in a flash, I heard Rocky scream. Haywood had pulled out his knife and stabbed him in the leg, the blade protruding from his calf. He fell, grabbing at the knife, trying to pull it out. Haywood slowly rose, pulling another knife out from a sheath on his other leg.

As it raised up, a series of shots rang out, hitting Haywood in the chest, one right after another. He fought to stay upright, grasping for his bloody chest, a stunned expression on his battered face. Kit walked up to him with rage in her stance.

"My sister was much more to Garrett than pussy," she spat bitterly. "And my nephew will always live on in his father, who'll forever be known as Rocky!"

With a steady aim, she slowly pulled the trigger, putting one last bullet in Haywood's head, his body dropping lifeless to the ground, ending the fight along with his life.

She let the gun hang down at her side, studying the carnage at her feet, a blank expression on her face, before walking over to check on Rocky. The nightmare was over. Peace should now come more easily for them both. Vengeance for the death of their loved ones had been fulfilled.

Chapter 68

I walked over to Ting and helped her stand up.

"It is time for you to leave the country," I said, pointing to the carnage around us. "And never come back. There has been enough death, don't you agree."

She glared at the scene before us, the morbid bloody bodies lifeless, mulling over her options, sensing she could be next and nodded.

"Agreed. Though I'm not thrilled with the outcome, I'm willing to walk away to live another day."

"Living is a *good* thing," I replied. "Let's hope our paths never cross again. I suggest you stay in China, otherwise the FBI may be paying you a visit."

She waved for her guard to stand up and they both walked away, after she gave me a look that made me think that might not be the case. When they disappeared from sight, I heard a familiar voice.

"It's about time," uttered Brandon Sparks, who rolled over from his dead position, and stood up, blood all over his shirt, his hands free from the plastic restraints. "I was getting bored lying there moaning, trying not to move during all the commotion."

"You son of a bitch," I said bitterly, at the thought of being played. "I should have known better than to think Sue would have been involved in your demise."

"Did you like our performance?" said Sue sweetly.

My displeasure turned to a grin. "Award winning. When did you cook this up?"

"It was Rocky's idea. Felt it would give the Chinese lady closure to think Brandon was dead. We flew out a couple days ago and worked out the details."

I wasn't sure if there was closure for her, but it was a start and it beat more deaths.

"She is going to find out sooner or later you're alive and running the business," I pointed out.

"I'm retiring," announced Brandon. "Sue is going to take over, that much is true. Maybe get us on a more straight and narrow path. Though not too straight. We need to remain profitable and keep the shareholders happy."

"Especially the *majority* shareholder," added Sue knowingly, looking at Brandon.

"Why wasn't I informed of this devious plan?" I asked, a tad disappointed I couldn't be trusted.

"I told them to keep it a secret from you," announced Rocky. He was up on his feet, limping, his shirt now wrapped tightly around his bloody wound, the knife removed. "That way your reaction was genuine."

"And oh my, your reaction was precious," added Kit.

"Especially when you karate chopped me. I'm man enough to say that hurt." I put on an injured tone.

"A love tap. I *pulled* my chop. It could have been *much* worse." Kit started laughing.

I should have been angry the wool had been pulled over my eyes, but their plan was successful. All I could do was nod and say, "nice work."

"I hate to break up this party," announced Nia. "But what do we do with these guys on the ground?"

"We should kill them," said Rocky in anger, before he showed compassion. "But as Jarvis said, there has been enough death for today. They can walk away, if they want. But I don't want to ever see any of you again."

They all stood up, brushing the grass from their clothes.

"What about the hit you put out on me?" asked Max.

Rocky limped over to him and gave him a cold stare. "You can live, but as far as you're concerned, I'm still dead. Is that understood?"

He nodded, fear in his eyes. He'd seen what would happen if he didn't.

"If I find out otherwise, I know where to find you. Maybe it's a good time for you to divest and retire." Rocky limped over to Justin. "As for you, Justin, it's time for you to retire as well."

Rocky had one last punch in him and he landed a doozy to Justin's jaw, knocking him to the ground. He then grabbed the gun from Kit and pointed it.

"Your life is over," Rocky said with a long pause, firing the gun, the bullet lightly grazing the cowering Justin's cheek before embedding into the ground. "If you *ever* send men after me or anyone I care about, you'll lose more than two fingers. You'll lose your life exactly like the dead bodies you see now in the grass. Do you understand?"

Justin wiped at his cheek with his shaking hand, feeling the blood, and then nodded.

"Get out of here before I change my mind."

They all left, looking beaten, leaving us standing there. I hoped it was the last of the confrontation, but hard men who were beaten, often would feel their manhood had been emasculated and would try to recapture their vigor. For now, I didn't care. I was ready to end this case and go home.

"Time for us to leave," said Brandon, putting out his hand. "It's been a pleasure doing business with you all. And Jarvis? Be sure to send us that expense report. It can be one of Sue's first jobs as new CEO."

"What about that bonus?" I asked with a toothy grin.

Brandon looked at Sue. "She's in charge now. You'll have to negotiate with her."

"Oh crap," I replied. Knowing her, it wouldn't be easy pleading my case.

Sue walked up to me and put a hand on my swollen cheek, patting it lightly.

"Time to suck up to me, buddy boy. Give me ten solid bullet points in a PowerPoint on why you should get a bonus and I'll consider it."

All I could do was laugh as the three of them walked away, back towards the tunnel, Sue and Nia arm in arm. It would be a change with Sue running the Sparks empire, but I was certain she'd be great at it, for she'd been working under the master for years preparing.

"Time for us to go," said Kit. "We'll drive the van back to the storage place. We'll leave it there for you to do with as you please, Jarvis. If you want to turn them over to the FBI that is fine with us."

"Don't you need a doctor to look at that wound?" I asked.

"He's been through worse," dismissed Kit. "That doctor friend of mine will patch him up, like before."

"Like always, my physical wounds will heal," added Rocky.

"And the scars we can't see?" I asked sincerely.

Rocky looked at Kit and back at me. "As you mentioned before, they never heal completely. But I've honored their lives by avenging their deaths. Now I look forward to living in peace and remembering all the love they provided me."

It was good to hear. Living in peace was a righteous goal to have for all of us.

"If I don't see you again, take care."

I put out my hand and Rocky shook it, squeezing it like a vice, even though he was wounded and tired. Kit walked up to me and kissed me hard on the mouth. I had to say I didn't mind it one bit. It certainly was more enjoyable than being chopped on the neck by her.

"Take care, Mister Mann,' she said, wiping my lips after she was done. "If that little lady ever gets tired of you, I'm always available to spar."

She spun around, both she and Rocky walking to the cargo truck. I was all alone now, except for three dead bodies, and I needed to put distance between me and them.

I started walking away, reaching the top of the bleachers when I called Manny to let him know there was a crime scene at the stadium and he should have someone come out before an innocent person saw the three bodies. I hung up the phone as he cursed at me, and went towards the exit, when I saw a large black man standing there, leather case in his hands, dressed as if he was about to go out for dinner.

"*Four* bodies," noted Wolfe, who walked beside me, all dressed in black. "Their shooter on the roof is dead as well."

"I'm guessing this was your other mission."

"It was. Now it's time for me to disappear."

"As I recall, you do that well. That, along with killing."

"I'm exceptional at killing. Be sure to keep that in mind the next time you enrage someone who might employee me."

"I will." I looked at him, dressed in clothes that likely cost a fortune. "In this sun, don't you get hot all dressed in black?"

Wolfe turned to start walking away. "Black is always cool, Mister Mann. Don't you ever forget that."

Yes it was, I said to myself as he quickly disappeared into the eucalyptus trees. Yes it was…

Chapter 69

It took a couple of days, but I was finally back home, sleeping in my own bed, making love to April with the fervor of a stereotypical Latin lover, though I was hardly Latin. I relished in staying in bed, enjoying her company and pleasure. It was all we did for nearly two straight days, only going out to eat, but then returning to start up again when the mood struck us, which was often. Facing death often was an aphrodisiac for the soul, wanting to get the most pleasure out of life one could get. Thankfully I had a skilled lover who felt the same.

The pleasure had to end eventually. After April went back to work, I emailed Sue my expenses, with a congratulations on her big promotion, telling her I would work on the bullet points for that bonus, though the thought of opening PowerPoint didn't thrill me. For a faint moment, I considered asking about what happened to Emily, but then thought better of it. If I never saw her manipulative face again, it would be too soon.

From there, I'd contacted Catalina and Dezmond, telling them where the cargo trucks holding drugs and guns were parked, while giving them the location of the warehouse, though it might have been shut down and moved by now.

"We should have been given this information sooner," complained Dezmond, with Catalina on the conference call.

"I did what I could," I replied. "A few issues needed resolving first. From now on, I'm out of it and it's up to you to piece together what was going on."

"What can you tell us about this Haywood Montgomery?" asked Catalina.

"Not much, other than I believe he was working or did work for the CIA at one time. And that he is now—dead. You have the detective's name I called who should have been on the scene dealing with the bodies. He's a good guy and I'm sure he'll share what he knows. If you ask nicely!"

"Leaving us to clean up the mess again," whined Dezmond with spite in his voice, recalling our previous encounters.

"You had nothing without what I've told you. I'm sure you'll get to the bottom of it in time. But like I said, I'm done with it."

Hanging up the phone, I wasn't thrilled with their tone, but I was thrilled the guns and drugs we'd confiscated wouldn't get on the streets. I knew both were bulldogs and would do all they could to stop the influx. I knew it would start up again, with different players, in different locations. There was always a supply of both items, and it would seem always a demand from a section of the population to obtain them but any haul is a good haul. I was pleased to have a part in stopping the flow but knew I could never end it all until society demanded it. In the current political climate, I knew that was an impossibility which left me feeling sad.

Life was moving along at a swift pace, with a couple of new cases presented to me. But I needed to step away and find peace for a while. Whether it be in the mountains, or even a trip back home to Des Moines, leaving it all behind was in my thoughts. As was the dream of opening my own bar. It was out there, waiting for me to make it happen. But financing it was the biggest obstacle. I'd deal with that issue once I was done enjoying my time away. As I worked out the details with April, I truly hoped she would join me on the getaway.

While I was looking over options and reservation possibilities, my phone rang. It was Barry, no doubt checking to see if I was alive and breathing.

"It would appear you survived?" he asked.

"I did, plus I'm richer for it."

"In spirit or in dinero?"

"Both for now. Are you calling to bleed off my spirit?"

Barry snickered. "Not on purpose. But I got a call from your favorite lawyer not named Barry."

I swore under my breath. "Oh my, not Torey Whitelaw."

"Yes. He was bragging about a plea deal he was finalizing for Simon Junior."

I wasn't happy to hear those words. "What type of deal?"

"Avoiding a death sentence. Life without parole."

I cursed several times, this time out loud, into the phone at the thought of a prosecutor working a deal with that maniac and his shyster lawyer. The wheels of justice at times made no sense.

"My thoughts exactly," agreed Barry.

"Why would the D.A. do that? We have him cold on the murders."

"Saves money for the state and having to go through a media circus if it went to trial. And it clears the case off the docket of an overcrowded and overworked D.A. Smart lawyers can work that angle for their clients, especially a no win one like The Butcher."

I wasn't a huge fan of the death penalty, but there were cases, especially for serial killers, that I had no issue with it. Simon was an evil person, there was little doubt. And he needed to be put down. I'd have to wait for justice to be applied another way, and hope for retribution inside the walls of maximum security, which is where he would be heading.

"Whitelaw commented Simon wanted to speak with you again. Today if possible."

I shook my head. "No way in hell am I talking with him again. I'm through with the mind games. I'm to the point where I'm finally getting my life back in order. I'm not letting him inside my head anymore."

"You're sure?"

"One hundred percent. I've got a trip planned and I'm going to enjoy it."

"Are you taking April?"

"If all goes to plan, which it often doesn't for me. But I'm going, hell or high water."

"Good for you both," commended Barry, who then changed the subject. "Everything with the Hester case is going forward, with the transfer of assets moving along. I should have final checks for everyone who worked the case here in the next week. You did a good work on this, Jarvis. I really do appreciate you busting Perry's chops. I think it's a win win for all involved."

Barry wasn't often forthcoming with expressing his happiness with my work. It was good to hear.

"Except for Perry," I said.

"Yes. I'd say he is ruined, which doesn't break my heart."

"Few things do, Barry. That's what makes you a good lawyer."

"Beyonce broke my heart, when she married Jay Z."

I smiled, not that he could see. "Like you had a shot with her!"

"I've bedded hotter woman than her. When I work my magic, they can't get enough of the Barry love machine!"

"At least until they wake up the next morning when the booze wears off," I joked.

"Ouch, Jarvis, that hurts," said Barry laughing.

"You're bulletproof, Barry. I know there isn't much that hurts you. Can you give me an idea of how large the check is you're sending? This way I have idea what my budget will be for this trip?"

He told me a number. Added with the pay I'd already received from Rocky and the expense check from Sue, I might have cash to spare for once, even after paying for a much-needed sabbatical.

"Wow. The sky is the limit for this vacation. I can widen my search parameters."

"Take time to rest and get laid, my friend. Crime never sleeps, and I may have work when you get back."

I hung up the phone and started my search again, looking for a place that I'd never been laid in. The possibilities were endless.

Chapter 70

With idle time on my hands while I waited for April to get time off for our trip, I decided I was going to do a little snooping on Torey Whitelaw. From what Wolfe had told me, Simon Junior wanted to hire someone to threaten and possibly put me down. All of this being handled by Whitelaw, much as he handled the threats on me from Simon Senior. I wasn't sure exactly what I was going to do, but I planned to make my presence felt and heard. More therapy to shake the ghosts of these men from my conscience.

Whitelaw's office was on the west side of town, in Lakewood on South Wadsworth Blvd. I knew his car, an expensive silver Mercedes, from a meeting we had last year, and sat in the parking lot watching it from my Mustang. His practice appeared successful, with quite a few people coming and going from his first-floor location.

On the first day of my stakeout, he wandered outside at around lunch time with a young woman dressed in black and white business attire, appearing to be about twenty years younger. He opened the door to the passenger side of his car and kept a hand on her back as she got in. They then drove away, with me following. About two blocks away, they pulled into a restaurant parking lot and walked in together, again a hand low on her back. I wasn't sure who she was but didn't figure it was his wife. I then returned to his office, walking in stopping at the receptionist desk, looking angry when I approached.

"I'm looking for a young lady who I believe works here," I demanded, my hands shaking. "I'm peeved at her, as she keeps parking next to my car and banging her door into mine. I just went outside and the dent…oh my, it's ridiculous how big it's gotten."

The receptionist frowned. "I'm sorry to hear that, sir. How do you know she works here?"

"I saw her this morning. She was dressed in a black and white pant suit, has dark shoulder-length hair, probably early twenties. I saw her leaving a moment ago in a silver Mercedes with another man. I tried to get downstairs to confront her but failed. Do you know who she is?"

"I'm sorry, sir, but I can't give out information about people who work here."

"Then she *is* an employee of this firm? If that is the case I'll have my lawyer call her. He is a bulldog and she'll wish she'd left a note once he is done with her."

The receptionist looked flustered. "I'm sorry, sir, about the problem. If you want to leave a name and number I can talk with her and see what she says."

"Probably the daughter of a bigwig who works here and you're trying to protect her." I was working her with my angry tone.

"Sir…please…that isn't true," she uttered. Then her voice lowered. "She is just a young grad student working as an intern. I'm certain it was just an accident."

"Fine. May I have paper to write on?"

She handed me a notepad and I wrote out a fake name with random phone number, then handed it back to her.

"I'll be waiting for her call," I declared, while storming out the door, pleased at what I learned.

I was back in my car waiting, and an hour passed when the two returned from lunch. It was hard to say what Torey was up to, but I planned to find out. The day wore on, as I left and came back a couple of times from bathroom breaks and food, when the intern walked out alone and left.

About twenty minutes later, Torey came out and I followed him. He made a quick stop at a King Soopers to pick up food, then hit a liquor store for alcohol, before driving out to Willowbrook in Morrison to what must have been his home, a large two-story house with circular driveway on a quarter acre lot.

I drove past and found a place to park, pulling out my phone. I hit the speed dial for Barry's cell phone.

"Do you know much about Torey Whitelaw's personal life?" I asked.

"Maybe. Why are you wanting to know?"

"I've been surveilling him today. I'm now at his house. He took a young twenty-something woman at his office out to lunch. I learned it was a college grad intern."

There was a pause before Barry spoke. "From what I know, and this is all hearsay, Torey has been known to harass the new help. There have been a few complaints filed with the Colorado Bar Association."

"Has anything come of the complaints?"

Barry paused again, this time for a full minute. "How can I put this, trying not to sound crass." There was another pause. "The Bar Association likes to keep all of this quiet. Working to find a solution to the problem to prevent it from going public. Let's just say Torey normally settles the dispute quietly and the complaint is dropped."

"And he is married?"

"Oh yes. I believe he has five kids, from college age to grade school."

This was great information to know. He sounded like an older man in a position of power at his work, preying on a younger woman. This gave me options to work with.

"Then he is a hound, like you?"

"Hey!" Barry didn't like the comparison. "Don't lump me in with him. I don't manipulate women who work for me to have sex. Those women I bed, I meet either in a bar or at events I attend, and they disrobe for me of their own free will. He uses his status at work to coerce these young interns into sleeping with him, and he'll advance their careers. If they don't give in to his advances, then they don't last long working for him. It's sleazy harassment, pure and simple."

"Thanks for the info."

"What are you planning on doing?"

"I'm going to do a little coercion on my own. Best you don't know the details."

Barry snickered into the phone. "Yes, you're probably right. I wouldn't want to test my ethics and have to lie for you in court for what you're about to do."

Barry hung up, his continued snickering the last thing I heard.

With a plan in mind, I returned the next day, this time on my motorcycle, watching and waiting. Nothing happened that I could work with until the following day, this time driving April's car so as not to arouse suspicion. I saw the two of them leaving around lunchtime, heading to a different bar and grill a little further away from work, with a hotel across the street. It might have been a coincidence, but I didn't think so.

I went into the bar and found a stool at the counter, with a good view of where they were sitting. It was in a U-shaped booth, with

Torey getting as close to the woman as he could, hard liquor ordered likely whiskey, as it was happy hour, two being brought for both of them. He pushed the glasses towards her, trying to get her to drink. From the look on her face, she seemed uncomfortable with what he was doing and saying, grabbing the glass, smelling the booze, but not taking a sip. She was shaking her head at his words and when he tried to put his hand on hers, she pulled away.

I could read Torey's lips, the words, "you know you want to" rolling out of his mouth like the slime ball he was. From her look she wasn't happy, maybe even scared. I finished my beer, paid and walked over to their table. At first Torey didn't recognize me, but then his eyes opened wide.

"Hello Torey," I said, standing there my arms crossed. "It would seem you're harassing this young lady."

"What the hell do you mean, Jarvis?" replied Torey in protest. "We were having a quiet lunch, her and I."

"I doubt that. You're attempting to get her drunk with the two for one drinks. I think you're trying to persuade her into an act she isn't comfortable with."

"She is here because she *wants* to be, isn't that right, Karrie." She didn't respond to his question. "Besides, what business is it of yours? I could have you thrown out of here for harassing me."

I looked around the place and saw no one there that would cause me any trouble.

"I doubt that, Torey. And you certainly don't have what it takes to make me leave. I'm going to politely ask the nice lady here what you were trying to make her do."

"Don't say anything, Karrie." Torey gave her an intimidating stare.

"Sounds like a threat to me, Karrie. Are you here because you want to be, or is he trying to manipulate you?"

Karrie looked at me, appearing innocent and nervous at what was going on. I tried to convey strength to her to speak up. She looked down at her hands in her lap and then slid away from Torey to the edge of the booth seat.

"He was trying to get me to go to bed with him," she accused. "Said he could fast track my career if I was *nice* to him. If I didn't, then he would have to find another willing intern to work with."

"I'm sure he mentioned a couple of drinks would loosen you up, maybe even put you in the mood."

She looked surprised and then disgusted. "Yes, that is nearly word for word what he stated. I was afraid to drink it, since you never know what might have been added to loosen me up."

"Smart lady. Especially with scum like him. You don't need this job that badly, do you?"

"No. I was just scared he wouldn't let me walk out of here. The pressure he's been applying, both here and at work has made me…uncomfortable."

It was my turn to glare, staring straight at Torey, my intimidation stronger than his.

"I'll make sure that doesn't happen. Torey, let's go talk somewhere *privately*."

I grabbed him by the arm and pulled him out of the booth. He tried to resist, but he was no match for my strength. The bartender saw what was going on and came over.

"Is there a problem?" he asked of me.

"Yes. This man was harassing this woman and might have laced her drink with a tranquillizer." I pulled out my ID and showed him. "We're going outside to talk about the proper way to treat a woman."

The bartender looked at Karrie, who nodded to let him know what I said was correct.

"Good. We don't want slime balls like him as customers. But first he has a bill to pay, and then I don't want to see him around here anymore. Please take it outside and off our property."

I squeezed Torey's arm persuasively. "Give him your credit card. You can come back in and get it once we're done outside."

He did as he was told, and I led him forcefully out into the sunshine, pushing him off to the side and away from the front door.

"You made a big mistake," hissed Torey, mustering up what courage he had.

I crossed my arms, unafraid of his menacing declaration. "I've heard threats matching yours numerous times in my career. But here is the thing—I will ruin you if you ever harass an employee of yours again. I'll stop by your house, talk with your wife, telling her a story about your sleezy actions, and make a trip to the Colorado Bar Association to tell them how you continue to sexually harass young woman who come to work for you. I will make it my sole business to get your license to practice law revoked. Is that clear?"

"You don't scare me," he said, half-heartedly.

I stepped in and put my nose in his face. "Yes I do, because you know it's true. I'll go to the bar association and tell them all about you trying to hire someone to kill me on behalf of your client, Simon Junior. I believe both of those items would get you suspended indefinitely and certainly put a dampener on the plea deal you're working for him."

Torey stepped back, stunned I knew about his attempt to hire Wolfe. "I don't know what you're talking about."

"Yes you do. My information is solid. And know this, if you come after me with one of your hired guns, or dare come after anyone I care about, I *will* come and string you up by your small dick and balls, with all the women you've harassed watching and laughing. Is that understood?"

From behind me, I heard a giggle, and it was Karrie standing there having heard what I said. Torey's face flushed beet red in embarrassment, turning and walking back to his car, driving away, forgetting all about his credit card. I walked over to Karrie and smiled.

"Sorry you had to go through that," I said. "Many men don't respect woman and see them only as objects to provide for their pleasure. You don't want to work for a place like that, run by a pig like him."

"You're right," Karrie replied. "If I'd known up front I'd have never taken the job. Now I'm out of work."

I pulled out my wallet and handed her a card. It was for Barry.

"Here is my lawyer's number. Barry Anders is a pain in the ass lawyer, but he respects a woman and will treat you right. Tell him Jarvis Mann sent you. After cursing my name, he will help you find work, either for him or with someone else he knows and trusts."

"Thank you. How can I repay you for your help?"

"Don't ever let a bozo like that try to talk you into anything you don't want to do. And if he won't take no for answer, mace the S.O.B and kick them in the nuts."

She smiled wide. "There was *no way* I was going to have sex with him."

"Good. Now let's get you back to the office to pick up your

things."

"And what if he is there?"

"I doubt he will be, likely hiding from the shame. But if he is, you can practice the nut kicking while I hold him. I imagine the ladies in his office will get joy out of it."

We both started laughing as we walked to the car.

Chapter 71

Today was our last evening of vacation, returning to Denver late morning from seven days in South Padre Island. We spent the week staying in a nice hotel, soaking in the sand, sun and warmth together, a much-needed break for both of us.

April and I were coming out of the Denver movie theater, arm in arm, her head on my shoulder, after enjoying a two-and-a-half-hour superhero movie that made me wish I had super powers. Even in failure, with their strength, magical powers or weapons, they were able to save the planet in the end. It was a nice fantasy world to slip into and forget all that had happened over the last year or so. If only I had one of those high-tech suits to slip on and fend off the never-ending villains.

I felt tired, beat-up and worn down to the point of needing a lot of time off to build up my strength, both mentally and physically again, which we had accomplished together. But sadly, it all had to come to an end.

"What did you think of the movie?" asked April. I could feel the warmth of her body against me, which was comforting.

"Good escapist entertainment," I replied. "If I only had that type of power to save everyone."

"Not everyone was saved, even by them. Casualties will always be the reality."

"It seems those in the background who perished are easily forgotten in the movies. Same can be said about those that died on my watch. Over time it seems their memories fade from existence."

"I know for a fact you remember them all," stated April, squeezing my arm lovingly. "I've heard you recite their names, even as the list has grown longer. Some, though it sounds cruel to say out loud, deserved their fates."

I planted a kiss on the top of her head, knowing she was right. Even with the time off, I knew all that I had been through had taken its toll. I needed a better life and a better way to live and make a living. I had begun the search for the right spot to open that bar and was working on convincing investors. I even had Nick, the man who had filled many a mug for me at Boone's, committed to be my bartender, if I could put it all together. It was a pipe dream in many ways, but one I was determined to make happen. Even if I had to sell my soul to the devil, once again, to find the financial backing.

We reached my 69' Mustang, that still remained running faithfully after all these years, and I opened the door for April, as she slipped into the passenger seat after a long embrace, passionate kiss and a few bawdy words in my ear that stirred me, as they always did. She was fabulous, beautiful and the perfect woman to keep me on the right path, preventing me from slipping too far into a hole that I might not climb out of. Someday I'd come to the realization she was the right one for me, but for now that ultimate step would wait, as we both knew deep down our professional lives were too dangerous to commit fully.

As I walked around the back of the Mustang and reached for the driver's door, I heard a voice, calling my name behind me. When I turned around, I saw him standing there about five feet away, hair a mess and in need of a shave, a revolver in his shaky hand, pointed at me center mass.

"You've ruined me!" yelled Perry Hester, the tenor of his voice sounding of desperation.

"I think you ruined yourself," I replied, my eyes shifting between his eyes and his hand on the gun, nervous at what to do to defend myself, since I wasn't armed.

"I'm broke, thanks to you. My kids won't talk to me thanks to the poisoning words of their bitch mother."

"What did you expect, Perry, after sleeping around with two other women? You *had* to know it was going to come back and bite you in the ass. Believe me, I know what I'm talking about. I've been down that road myself and there was no one to blame but me."

His hand began shaking even more. "And those two bitches were conning me as well. Trying to shake me down for money. And now that the well has run dry, they could care less. I have *nothing* left..."

I heard the passenger door open and April got out. I glanced her way, waving for her to stay put. Perry looked like he was going to lose it completely and I didn't want her to get caught in the crossfire, as had happened once before.

Of all the threats I've faced these last few years, of all the people I expected would be coming after me, I honestly didn't expect Perry to be the one I'd have to fend off. But here he was, gun aimed at me, a crazy conviction in his eye, his plan to settle a score. My only hope to talk him off the violent, desperate ledge he'd crawled out on.

"Perry, put the gun down and let's talk about this. No need to do anything stupid and make things worse."

His whole body was tensing up and I wasn't sure I'd have much time to react if he fired. There appeared to be tears in his eyes, and his gun lowered slightly. I inched forward some, hoping to get close enough to grab the revolver. He saw me move and raised it back up, pulling back the hammer.

"I can't live with myself anymore," he cried out through the tears. "But I can't let you live either…"

"Perry, don't be…"

I lunged but wasn't quick enough, my hand a split second too late getting to his gun, as it went off, the bullet striking me in the lower chest. The pain was immediate, and I fell forward, my hand pushing the gun downward, when it went off again, striking me in the right knee. Crumpling to the ground, I twisted backwards landing on my back, the pain overcoming me in a flash of fury like I'd never experienced before.

I wanted to scream out but could only whisper "oh god" several times before I heard April yell. Another shot went off, but this time through my blurry vision, it was Perry taking his own life, shooting himself through the mouth, his body falling backward like a dead marionette. The only thought that remained on my mind—was that I was about to join him in the great beyond, meeting our maker to face the reading of our sins.

I felt pressure on my chest and could smell April's perfume, as she struggled to stop the bleeding, calling for assistance from anyone nearby in the movie theater parking lot.

"Hold on, Jarvis," she pleaded in a panic. "You've got to fight. I can't lose you now."

I wish I could have answered, as the fog grew thicker and I couldn't see anything, but I had no control over any part of my body. The pain was subsiding, but deep down I could feel myself slipping away, and there was nothing I could do about it.

Everything went dark and time seemed to stand still.

I felt nothing, and as if dreaming, began to sense things. A time and space different than what I'd ever experienced before. There were silhouettes there, outlines and shapes that somehow seemed familiar. They all remained foggy for a period of time, a slow focus building after who knows how long. Seeing a face unchanged from when I last saw her, right before she died on the ground, a woman who had no life, being a sex slave for a maniac. Dona Wiggins was there, looking at me but not saying anything. A face from the past, which soon faded away to who knows where.

Other faces paraded by in much the same way. Those who had died at my hands, or at the hands of someone I'd hired. Many deserved their fates. I saw them all, their expressions showing no emotion, eyes seeming empty but leering my way. Evil people like Roland Langer, Dirk Bailey, Merrick Jones, Marques Melott, Leather, The Bull, Simon Lions, Bronwen Pearson. They flashed by, one by one, and then back again, a parade of faces I'd tried to forget, but couldn't shake. They were in my nightmares and now it would appear, they were there in my death march.

There was no way to know how long or how many times I saw their faces, but soon they were gone, replaced by those I'd known and cared for. My mother and father, both looking younger than I last remembered them, no longer crippled by their cancer. Their faces looked happy, seeming to be peaceful, unlike their final days on Earth. I wanted to reach out, say hello but couldn't. I was paralyzed it would seem, with no ability to move or speak, leaving me confused.

Then I saw Flynn. The brother who I had lost to a brutal mobster. There was no smile, but he didn't seem upset or angry, his arm around a faceless body, which appeared to be female. Could it be he was still a skirt chaser in the great beyond? I wouldn't put it past him.

He whispered into the ear of the faceless one, words I couldn't comprehend, pointing in my direction. If only I could speak to him, tell him I was sorry for what happened, and let him know I made sure his family was safe from the evil man who had tortured him to death. But I couldn't unburden myself. I was caught in a static place, as if I was on the outside looking in. I wanted answers, but none were forthcoming, for I had no one to communicate with.

The various faces continued to pass by. Over time, though I couldn't gauge how much, events in my life played back to me. A young boy who worshipped his parents, to an older teenager who got into trouble and didn't care. To one who had to face what his destiny would be like, placed in a jail cell by his father to teach him a lesson. To the young adult who couldn't find love, and only cared for lust, sleeping around with whomever he wanted, not caring who it hurt. Days as a security guard, then working cases for another agency, to going out on my own, thanks to the money provided me by my father. The Bubble Gum Card that brought me new perspective. The client who was being stalked, or claimed to be, leading me to make a terrible decision. A college football player with concussion issues, making bad choices, and being blackmailed.

Case after case, no matter how simple, no matter how complex, flashed by in no particular order. I was reliving my life, but I didn't know why. If this was death, it played back to me in a revolving maze I'd relive again and again.

Though with all I was sensing, it would seem my eyes were open, but they weren't. I heard sounds, machine-like noises—beeps, chirps and air pump sounds. I didn't know where it was coming from but then the images suddenly stopped. I felt my body stir, my eyes heavy trying to open. I couldn't talk because of the tape on my mouth, a plastic tube between my lips. The restrictive sensation in my throat was startling.

I twitched and shook my head, lids feeling gunky as they finally raised, the light in the room so shocking to my iris that I had to close and again slowly open them, letting the light trickle in.

I had no idea where I was, or why I was there. I felt a hand on my shoulder and it was a nurse, trying to calm me, saying words I wasn't quite understanding. Many of my senses were awaking all at once, and I could feel needles and tubes seemingly everywhere, feeding me, providing medicine and controlling all my functions.

It was a scary feeling, though I tried to remain calm, but weakness overtook me, and I drifted off again, to a new set of dreams, this time images of places I've been and of those who remained Earthly bound. It would seem I was among the living world again, but at what cost?

Chapter 72

My eyes would open and close again, several times, though who knew how much time had passed. Each time they would remain open a little longer, gauging the activity around me. Faces of nurses and doctors talking to me, waiting for responses, with questions requiring yes or no answers, supplied with the motion of my head. I felt weak from the injuries and drugs trying to manage my pain.

Once my breathing had settled, they removed the tube, leaving a bad taste and soreness in my throat. It was days before I could successfully talk, then only in a weak whisper of one or two words at a time.

April had been by my side through most of the ordeal, sleeping in a fold out chair, talking to me even when I wasn't completely aware, yet somehow able absorb her words. Visitors had stopped by; Bill, Barry, Kate and even Melissa had made the trek up from Colorado Springs to spend time, speaking to me with words of encouragement that time would heal me, making me whole again. Words I needed to hear but wasn't certain I believed.

The days since the shooting added up, ten days lost in unconsciousness. Nearly three more weeks before I could begin physical therapy, having been moved to a therapy facility. Another ten days there before I'd made enough progress to leave and head home, wheelchair bound, with minimal strength to begin relearning to walk again, a brace covering my right leg from hip to ankle.

The chest wound was healing, the leg as well, the kneecap shattered and put back together again, tendon and ligament tears having been repaired, screws holding those parts together. It would take months to be physically whole again, and only with a lot of work. I was ready to face it, but had to wonder, what if I'd walked away from this violent world a little sooner? What if I'd cracked one less joke at the expense of a foe? Maybe I wouldn't have felt broken, both physically and mentally.

Home for now would have to be April's apartment, for the stairs down to my place provided too many issues for me. Her place was on the first floor, making access for now simple. Work was done to add handicap rails in the bathroom to allow me to use the toilet and the shower. I remained dependent on her assistance for many things, which I appreciated, but didn't enjoy. I liked being my own man, free to do anything I wanted without help and not be a burden.

I craved to have my total independence back, but it would take time. Though she was happy I was home, the stress had taken its toll on her too, but she did her best to hide it. She had been through it herself, having been shot. But having that experience didn't make it any easier.

After two weeks at home and a couple of secretive calls, she walked in on me reading in her extra room with a look of determination.

"Time we get out of the apartment," she announced, with forcefulness to her voice.

I closed the Ian Fleming novel I'd not read in years, the bookmark in place, doing my best to smile. I wasn't certain about leaving, venturing out into the world for all to see, the weakened man that I was. But April's will and powerful glare wouldn't allow me to remain stationary.

"What did you have in mind?" I responded, knowing she wouldn't take no for an answer.

"Hop in your wheelchair and I'll show you."

I'd built up my strength enough that I could move using a walker, make it to the wheelchair, and get situated. I got my leg propped up and unlocked the wheels, spinning to face the door, hoping to be free one day of the device that was uncomfortable to sit in. April always watched, but never interfered unless I needed help, and I wheeled out into the living area, where she opened the door and we made it outside.

After a little effort, I was situated in the passenger seat of her car, the wheelchair folded up nicely in the trunk, and we were motoring down the road. Soon we were in my old neighborhood, her place not far, and cruising down Evans, heading east. One right turn into a parking lot brought us to a closed building that once appeared to be a movie rental store, killed by internet streaming of Hollywood entertainment. There were several other cars parked in the lot, a couple I thought I'd recognized. I wasn't sure what was going on, but soon was in the wheelchair being pushed through a front door, a few uncomfortable bumps over the threshold.

A light was on and the inside had been torn out. It appeared as though the interior was going through a remodel. The center area was covered with a large white cloth, though I couldn't tell what it was concealing. April parked me next to it and locked the wheels.

"What am I looking at?" I asked, still confused.

"Hopefully your future," replied April cryptically.

From out of the back room stepped several familiar faces. Bill, Rachael, Monica, Ray, Barry, Melissa, Kate, Sue, Nia, Brandon, and several of my clients from the past. Even Helen and Jolene were there, my sister-in-law and niece making the trek from Iowa.

No one said a word, until Nick, who had been a hard-working bartender at Boone's before it closed, walked in and, with all his strength and a flourish, pulled the sheet off, revealing a U-shaped counter that looked a lot like a bar. I was stunned, confused by what I was seeing, though a nagging thought of what it might be trickled through my brain.

"A work in progress," explained Nick. "But we're getting there. With any luck we should be open in about a month."

"Open?" I asked, still confused.

"Your new bar," explained April, leaning down, placing her face next to mine. "I believe you wanted to call it 'The Private Eye Tavern.'

Emotions hit me like a wave, stunned by the reveal. I glared at all the faces in the room, smiles and a few tears flowed. It was an overwhelming feeling they had gathered there to surprise me.

"How?"

"Investors," said Nick simply. "Everyone in this room and a few others who couldn't make it."

I turned my head to look at April. "Even you?" I asked.

"Yes. I can wait on the motorcycle. Besides I can ride yours for now, for it will be a while before you'll be riding again."

I kissed her on the cheek, moved by what she'd done.

"And you better work hard to get back on your feet," added Bill. "You're going to be running the place and you need to earn your pay."

I looked at each of the faces, and nearly lost it. It was a wonderful gift, and motivation to be whole again. It would be hard work, but I knew I could do it. And even if it failed, it would be given everything I could give it.

"What do you think?" asked April.

"There aren't words. You all are the best." I wiped the water from my cheeks.

"Everyone wanted to thank you for all you've done for us through the years," said my landlord, Kate.

"And being investors, we expect cheap booze," added Barry.

The room filled with laughter, and the warmth of what I was experiencing from those around me felt supreme. I got the grand tour, hearing the plans for the inside layout, the design of the logo for the outside sign, and even threw out a couple of ideas that might be worth adding to the blueprint.

I was ready to start my new business life, being a simple entrepreneur hoping to leave my dangerous past behind, at least for now. The day to day of running a business, balancing the books, keeping an inventory, and hopefully making a reliable profit I could live off. A struggle it would most certainly be, but no more than when I began my own private detective agency all those years ago.

But hell, I couldn't leave behind Jarvis Mann PI completely. If the need arose and someone came a-calling, danger threatening them, who knows, I might put on the fedora once again. But only if the inspiration and desire were driving me and my small circle of fans demanded it.

One could never put a final "The End" on the last chapter without ending it with a question mark!

Thanks for reading ***Mann in the Crossfire***. I hope you enjoyed it and would love if you would leave a review on Amazon to help an Indie Author.

And be sure to check out my website for all the information about me and my books. You can also sign-up for my newsletter and I will send you a free eBook of the first novel, Tracking A Shadow.

https://rweir.net

Please check out the rest of the Jarvis Mann Detective series and follow the evolution of my hard-boiled detective. I hope you enjoy all of his adventures!

Enjoy the short story ***The Case of the Missing Bubble Gum Card***, where Jarvis Mann helps a young man find a valuable missing Ernie Banks trading card. Now PERMAFREE on Amazon:

http://www.amazon.com/dp/B00JGEZNSU

Tracking A Shadow where Jarvis Mann is hired to track down the stalker of his sultry female client and is pulled into a web of lies and deceit.

http://www.amazon.com/dp/B00MQHVKJA

Twice As Fatal where he works two cases that draw him into a seedy underworld, complicating his professional and personal life.

http://www.amazon.com/dp/B00XTNTHWW

Blood Brothers, where Jarvis is summoned back to his hometown of Des Moines, Iowa, to help his brother out of a life-threatening situation.

http://www.amazon.com/dp/B019S6AQXW

Dead Man Code, as Jarvis digs into a murder case of a computer software engineer and soon is confronted by Russian Mobsters and Chinese government goons, as all try to stop him from uncovering a crooked tech company.

https://www.amazon.com/dp/B01LY8JZND

The Case of the Invisible Souls, where he helps a homeless man find out why many of his brethren in the homeless community are disappearing, never to be seen again.

https://www.amazon.com/dp/B071SJPFTZ

The Front Range Butcher, Jarvis Mann faces a serial killer in a psychological battle of wills. Can he outwit such a mastermind, or has he met his match!

https://www.amazon.com/dp/B079MDS1K9

If you want to reach out please email me at:

rweir720@gmail.com

Follow R Weir and Jarvis Mann on these social sites as I appreciate hearing from those who've read my books:

https://www.facebook.com/randy.weir.524

https://www.facebook.com/JarvisMannPI

https://twitter.com/RWeir720